A.N. P

Hellfire
and
Honey

Eternal Alliances
Book One

HELLFIRE AND HONEY

A.N. PAYTON

CITY OWL
PRESS

HELLFIRE AND HONEY
Eternal Alliances, Book 1

CITY OWL PRESS
www.cityowlpress.com

Cover Design by MiblArt. All stock photos licensed appropriately.

Edited by Heather McCorkle.

For information on subsidiary rights, please contact the publisher at info@cityowlpress.com.

Print Edition ISBN: 978-1-64898-153-1

Digital Edition ISBN: 978-1-64898-154-8

Printed in the United States of America

To the ones who spent the most time believing in me.
You know who you are.

Chapter One

THE BATTLE HAMMER CUT THROUGH THE AIR IN FRONT OF ME. I spun away and an unpleasant breeze brushed my face in its wake. I waited for the sharp whip of fear, but exhaustion left only static in my head and an ache in my hands.

My opponent's muscles bulged as he lifted his hammer. I moved again, and the weapon plunged into the dirt. Perhaps he didn't recognize me in the darkness, or surely his strikes would be more accurate.

The vampire swung the hammer as though it were weightless. He was fast—too fast. Sweat soaked through my dress and cooled my skin. My lungs cried, but there was no time to catch my breath.

I dodged another swing. He was rested, fresh. I was not. He swung. I moved. Again. Again.

A swatch of silver moonlight escaped its cloudy prison. A beam of light illuminated our battleground, revealing the flicker of recognition in his eyes.

"Princess Salvatore." His growl of my name carried a distinct promise. New motivation bled the vampire's eyes from black to silver. He wanted to feel the life leave my body and carry news of my defeat to his king.

Armed with fresh resolve, his strikes quickened. Inhuman speed blurred his hammer and I narrowly avoided the attacks. The metallic edge of blood pooled in the back of my throat. He didn't give me an opening to slice with my sword and exhaustion threatened to drag me down. A few more swings and my head would be crushed against his hammer like meat on a butcher's block. The war would be over – my people defeated.

The last of my magic churned in my chest. I hoped I wouldn't need it for this fight, but the raining of cold iron around my head argued otherwise. I poured power onto the battlefield and my magic hunted for its prey.

The sneaking tendrils found the vampire. They wound around his legs, licking his skin and savoring the taste. The magic was savage, hungry, but I forced it to slow. If I worked the power too fast, he would feel it and flee. Too slow and his strikes would finally find me.

He swung the iron block and I sidestepped too late. His hammer crashed onto my sword. The force jarred my arms, and a cascade of glass splinters flowed down my shoulders. The hit emptied my lungs and locked me in place.

Leisurely, and with a faint smile, the vampire lifted the hammer again and aimed at my head.

The pattern of battle narrowed the world to a pinprick, this moment, the trajectory of the weapon toward my undefended face.

His hammer arched overhead, death in his eyes.

I pulled on my magic and pain stabbed me as power rushed from the depths of my soul. The twisted strands locked around the vampire's legs, arms, neck, and head. With a final heave that tugged the last wisps of power from my body, I hardened the magic coils to chain and drove them into the ground. The vampire's face twisted and he fought me, but his ability to block magic was weak. I dug the chains deeper and deeper into the dirt. His arms froze above his head and his knees locked. He shook with the struggle against my power and the weight of the hammer he couldn't drop.

"You have not won." The words came out flat as he struggled to shape his lips. "Our King will soon wear your blood."

"That sounds uncomfortable," I said.

My sword hung heavy in my aching hands, but the bite of victory was sharp. I heaved my weapon from the ground and stepped close. The vampire tried to burn me with his gaze, but my magic held him immobile. The sword slipped through his stomach and under his ribs. I found his heart and for a moment, we stared at each other with an unfortunate understanding. He had tried to kill me, but I killed him instead.

I cut through his heart and the silver bled from his eyes. My magic slipped away and the body fell to the ground.

With a ragged breath, I lifted the sword and sliced off his head. Some vampires could heal heart wounds.

The rush of battle faded. I staggered to my feet, one hand clenching my stomach, and spat bile and blood into the grass. My magic was almost gone, exhausted from a full night of fighting. It had already started to recharge, but would take hours to reach maximum strength.

"Took you long enough."

I jumped.

The old man stepped from a tree's shadow, cast by the moon overhead. His sword rested on one shoulder and his armor sported dents and divots, hits taken from hammers, swords, and axes. Zavier's body, though aged, remained toned and athletic. He smiled, but I knew he was not amused.

"I'm sorry," I said. "Did you expect my fifth kill to look as effortless as my first?"

"For a moment I thought he had bested you," Zavier said. So had I, but admitting that would make Zavier march me straight back to the castle. "Five tonight? You must be exhausted."

"I don't feel great." Knots nestled in my shoulders and aches in my fingers suggested a fracture or two. The sharp taste of vomit lingered in my throat.

"Did you heal?"

"Is that a joke?" Zavier knew my magic didn't possess healing capabilities.

"Maybe."

"I didn't think you knew what those were."

"Always such wonderful compliments from my Princess."

"I live to serve. What's the battle report?"

Zavier's smile slipped away.

"Our scout team engaged a force of two hundred vampires.

Reinforcements from our kingdom arrived within twenty minutes. We lost thirty-five soldiers and estimate the enemy lost about the same."

His words formed a noose around my heart. Thirty-five soldiers gone in the blink of an eye. Sons and daughters, mothers and fathers, who would not return home. Thirty-five funeral pyres I would watch from my castle windows and could only cry when no one was looking. Not that the Kingdom of Ededen cared if I mourned their losses. I barely held any of their favor, and only in part to my parents' disappearance.

The vampires had lost a similar number. Tonight's battle was unexpected, but we did well.

Thirty-five dead.

Zavier snapped me from my brooding. "I went to your room to notify you of the battle. Imagine my surprise when you weren't there."

I grimaced.

"Imagine your guards' surprise when you weren't there. Imagine the chaos that ensued as half of your staff searched the castle until we found the stableboy, who informed your Royal Guard and First Seneschal that you had left with the scouts hours ago."

"That's a lot to imagine."

"Sal, I need an explanation."

I sighed. I couldn't explain the failure I'd felt since my parents had disappeared, or the deep-rooted fear that they may have found the cursed Fields of Death and damned us all. Every decision I made carried my kingdom closer to the inevitable. I couldn't explain the restlessness, the call of the battlefield, how much my magic wanted to fight. I certainly couldn't explain the moments of hesitation wondering if my death was the right answer.

"I don't have one, Zavier. I needed out. The scouts hadn't seen anything all day and it should have been safe to go with them. I didn't expect to find two hundred soldiers on movement to their camp."

"We are at war. What made you think any scout mission would be safe?"

"Relatively safe."

"Sal."

I wanted to shrug off his criticism, but duty and responsibility reeled me back. I wrestled away from youthful urges of defiance. Zavier served as my First Seneschal, my closest advisor and second-in-command. He deserved an apology, as much as I could muster.

"I'm sorry, Zavier. I'm sorry that I disappeared and worried you."

He tipped his head. "Thank you, Princess."

Zavier held out his hand and I placed my sword hilt onto his palm. He fished a cloth from under his armor and ran it over the blade.

"You need a healer." He continued his systematic brushes across the metal. The motions betrayed a quiver though. His knuckles paled as he gripped the rag too tight. His lips pressed into a thin line.

There was more, something he wasn't telling me.

"Say it."

He remained silent.

"Zavier, what happened?"

My First Seneschal didn't look up from the sword.

"Three thousand more soldiers were reported joining the camp," he said.

"Our scouts didn't see them?"

"Not in time to gather our forces. The spies said they came from a back valley pass."

Thirty-five soldiers had given their lives in a well-fought battle. For nothing.

"These two hundred were a diversion. They kept us busy over here and snuck through a different way," I said.

"Yes."

"And we fell for it." I clenched my aching, broken fingers into a fist. The pain fed the coiling snake of anger inside me. Stupid, stupid. My father would have seen this coming. The serpent of rage stretched higher, ready to strike. Where could he be that was more important than here, with our people? "They waved a red flag at us, and we ran straight into it, like an angry bull."

"Yes, Princess. We did."

I clenched my teeth.

"There's more," Zavier said.

Of course there is.

"King Kadence was seen marching with his men into camp."

Great. The elusive King Kadence Hendrick of Vari Kolum hadn't been spotted since his parents died almost two decades ago, leaving their eight-year-old king of the vampires. His presence was an announcement of the vampires' assured victory.

The ground looked comfortable, inviting, and I wanted to sink into it and fall asleep. I didn't want to hear what Zavier would say next. I catalogued my injuries to prolong the inevitable. My fingers throbbed in a numb way that meant I had ignored the pain for too long. My arms were heavy, my back sore.

"Princess, I'm afraid our options are limited," Zavier said. "Do you remember what we talked about weeks ago? When it was obvious the vampires were establishing a siege camp and instead of the usual raids and battles?"

We had talked about a lot of things. Strategy, movement, statistics, personnel, and supply numbers. Everything had changed since then.

But I knew what he meant. I remembered the conversation as clearly as I had felt my blade plunge through the vampire's heart.

"Yes."

"I think it's time to utilize that strategy."

"How do you know?"

He handed me my sword, hilt first.

"First we find a medic, then I'll show you," he said.

Chapter Two

DREAD HAD STOLEN A PHYSICAL FORM AND TAKEN RESIDENCE in my valley. Perched on the highest vantage point outside Ededen's walls, Zavier and I observed the enemies below.

Beyond our grassy knoll, a nightmare spread. Campfires pulsed as soldiers pumped through the military encampment, the lifeblood of forces about to claim victory in a two-hundred-year war. Tents popped in neat rows, little pieces in a wartime puzzle. In the far distance, dozens of catapults peeked over the false horizon. Horses' cries drove up the valley slope and I half expected a stampede to swarm us at any moment. Other sounds drifted in the crisp air, honeybee hums of human voices, rich and pleasant. Music chimed, a fast-dancing rhythm that mingled with the pounding in my head.

"What are the statistics?" Looking over the massive camp as it chewed through the space between the mountains, I already knew, but I had to hear.

"The vampire army has doubled our forces. They have three thousand horses, twenty catapults and supplies on hand to last over three months. Their supply routes are well guarded, and they could acquire more at a moment's notice," Zavier said. "Even if we put a weapon in the hand of every capable witch in our kingdom, we would fall before sunrise."

Our forces would be equal with the vampires if my parents hadn't run away with half our army. But then, Zavier and I wouldn't be shivering on an exposed hillside, tired and injured from battle, counting vampires by the thousands.

"How long can we hold for a siege?"

Zavier stroked his beard. "The catapults would break our walls in a matter of hours. We would evacuate to the castle, where the smaller space could be defended better with magic. They would have to hold as a true siege."

"How many can fit in the castle?"

"Two hundred, on a good day."

That left thousands of people to die outside my doors.

"The siege would be awful," Zavier continued. "We have plenty of supplies, but our sewage and water system won't handle the stress. People would get sick, die, and the morgue would be overrun. Bodies would rot and disease would be rampant. We could survive two weeks."

Hope fled. We were done. My kingdom and my people would be crushed, and I would lead them to it. The enemy stared up from the valley and pierced my soul, but a shred of relief escaped the wound. Anxiety and fear loosened their grip on me for the first time since my parents ran away six months ago. I had tried everything, had fought and bled for my country, and still failed.

Only one option remained. Crystalline coldness rippled down my spine.

Zavier studied my face.

"You don't have to do it tonight, Sal." The gentle caress of his voice almost disintegrated in the wind. "They won't attack until tomorrow evening."

I ached for my father's advice. In the council room, he used to listen to his marshals, one hand scratching the salt-and-pepper hairs on his chin as he peered at maps and charts. I would give anything to hear his thoughts one more time. He always knew what to do.

"My advice isn't as good as King Tolen's would have been," Zavier said, "But I will support whatever decision you make."

The breeze bustled over our hidden ridge, and I lifted my face into it.

Cool air quenched my skin and calmed my racing pulse. The scent of clean, fresh grass swirled around us, twinged with the promise of fall.

"It's over. Let's finish it tonight." The words echoed in the hollowness where my heart used to be.

"They're watching this hilltop, Princess," Zavier said. "They'll see you as soon as you stand."

My arms shook as I heaved myself from the rugged terrain. Zavier grabbed my bloodstained hand before I made the final push.

"Sal," he said, "don't let this loss be your defeat. You are stronger than these circumstances."

I turned away to hide my quivering lips.

The grass strands recoiled when I stood, as though they had never been crushed. I raised my arms to the sky and stretched, turning my body into a beacon to our enemies.

Here I am, come get me.

I made quick work undoing the metal clasp at my waist and my sword dropped to the ground with a thunk, disappearing into dense grass. The knives from my boots and at my back followed. Unarmed and exposed within view of the enemy, goosebumps budded and I restrained the urge to rub my arms.

Grass crunched next to me. Zavier stood and shed his weapons as well.

"I'm not asking you to come with me," I told the old man. "I probably won't be coming back."

"I know." His sword made a much louder thud and he pulled out so many knives that I lost count.

"You have a family. Your wife and children need you," I said.

"My children are grown. Lily has told me many times how difficult I am. Perhaps she'd appreciate the break."

My laughter caught me off guard, a welcome, temporary, respite.

"Do you have a plan?" Zavier asked.

"Yes."

"No, you don't."

"I'm planning to walk toward their camp and not be killed immediately." Scouts from the towers would have seen us already. The decision was made. No turning back.

"You're going to hope that nobody shoots an arrow at us the moment we're in range?" He raised his brow.

"I'm going to hope nobody shoots an arrow at me. At this point, I may ask them to shoot you."

Zavier's lips exposed rows of perfect white teeth and his forehead creased into a million laugh lines. I had to grin with him, hiding fear behind a smile.

We started down the hill, Zavier first, and I followed. I imagined the vampires in their tall, rugged towers peering through telescopes as they tried to decipher what these crazy witches were doing. After centuries of war, I hoped an arrow-happy archer didn't cut us down in this field.

The grass ended at the crest of the hill and rock and patches of determined weeds poked through on the other side. The dim light created a treacherous descent. Streaks of moonlight served as a lantern for our journey, but the black-and-white filter played tricks on my mind. Each step was careful, the trail slow.

I expected the stagnant pool of fear in my stomach, but not the groggy indifference. My head had been emptied out and filled with water, sloshing with every step. I killed five vampires in battle tonight and now I was frolicking to their front door to ask them not to destroy my kingdom. What could I give in return? Almost nothing.

The expectation of our survival dwindled with every step.

The terrain flattened as the massive camp loomed closer. The scent of fires strengthened and singing grew louder. Between the crunch of dried weeds and gravel under our feet, individual voices belted into the night.

With a mechanical whirl, the gates slipped open. Glowing fire spilled between the cracks and a cluster of lights broke away. They moved at a brisk pace, bouncing up and down, toward us.

"They're on horses," Zavier said.

"I count five torches."

"They've decided to accept your invitation."

"Or to kill us from a closer range."

"Yes, or that."

We waited in the dark to see which would prove correct.

Horse hooves thundered closer and closer, matching the frantic beat of my pulse. The torch lights disappeared for a few moments, then five men appeared over a small slope. The horses neighed and struck the ground, urged on by their riders. The group formed a rough circle around us, blocking any escape.

I relaxed my shoulders and kept my palms open and loose. Enemy soldiers surrounding us in the darkness, eager to smash our heads or bleed us dry? *Excuse me while I stifle a yawn.*

Zavier looked bored, but tension tightened his hands as if they longed for a weapon. My own hands felt the same.

One man dismounted. He rivaled the width of a wagon and probably weighed close to one. His clothes were black, as was his armor. The moonlight caught the dark metal, illuminating enchanted symbols etched into the protective plates. The tip of a bow pointed over his shoulder, and a battle axe hung from the belt at his waist. The weapon dwarfed any other axe I'd seen, and he walked as though he didn't notice the weight. Red dreadlocks spilled from his scalp to his mid-back, adorned with golden beads.

"Look what we have here, boys." Sharp fangs shone through a wide smile. "Two lone witches out on a little walk. Seems an odd place for such a thing."

We didn't speak.

"Maybe these witches are looking for a bit of trouble. I would say they found it. What do you think boys? Should we kill them?" He pulled the massive axe from the sheath. "Or eat them?"

Blood rushed from my head. My instincts screamed. Flight or fight warred inside me, except running would prove futile. The slowest vampire could outrun the fastest witch. My magic pooled, barely recharged.

The vampire stalked to Zavier. I was a hundred pounds lighter than the old man and night hid the bloodstains on my dress. They had deemed him the greater threat.

"Actually," I broke the silence, "I'm in charge, so you should come stand menacingly in front of me."

My mother would have smacked the back of my head for speaking those words, but the battlefield had taught me that soldiers don't appreciate prim and proper. They liked grit, humor, and to laugh about death finding them in the night.

The giant shifted his gaze to me and his grin fell.

"All right, little lady. You're the one looking for trouble then?" He looked me up and down. "I don't think there's enough of you to go around."

The men laughed.

"I'm looking for your king."

"Why do you want him when I'm right here?" He stepped to me, filling my vision. Heat poured from his body, despite the two feet of space between us.

I held my ground. "That's a great question." I purred and blinked at him from under my eyelashes. The man's brows pinched. "Maybe you're exactly what I'm looking for. Come a little closer and find out." I stepped in his direction, a sly smile painted on my lips.

The giant staggered back, stumbled over his own feet, and teetered toward the ground. He clutched at his horse's reins to maintain his balance.

This man wasn't in charge of the unit. His bulk and intimidation were supposed to keep us in line. He wouldn't have a problem hammering through our skulls, but a little pushback and he crumpled.

"Any more theatrics you need to get out of your systems?" I spun in a slow circle and surveyed the crowd.

Zavier shot me a disapproving glance and I shrugged. Our chances of survival were already slim. I couldn't make things much worse.

Someone chucked behind us.

Another man slipped off his horse. His arms bulged through his shirt and layers of black armor covered his chest and stomach, which were thinner than the giant man's, more athletic and less, 'I will smash you with my giant axe.' Most vampires preferred battle axes or hammers—crushing a witch's head was a sure way to stop our magic and prevent us from healing—but a worn silver sword hung on this vampire's belt.

"Good job, Rayhan. They're quaking in their boots." The new man's grin was as dark as his hair. His jaw held a square line, his nose too symmetrical. He was striking, not traditionally handsome. Large and round, his dark eyes promised violence, despite the amused tone in his voice. Unlike Rayhan the giant, who would enjoy turning us to pulp, this man would kill us one slice at a time without breaking his smile.

"I tried."

The second man walked toward us, tense as though anticipating a fight he was prepared to end quickly and efficiently. As he neared, the icy prowl of his power spilled over me, revealing he was very strong, very fast, and probably resistant to some magic.

"What business do you have with the king of Vari Kolum?" The intensity of his attention burned into my soul and swirled around like a glass of strong whiskey.

"I will inform the king of that when we meet him," I said, my voice stronger than the fear twisting in my gut.

"*If* you meet him." He stopped inches away. A very short dagger could have pierced his heart.

"Are you armed?" The dark-eyed man asked.

"No."

He wasn't touching me, but I could feel him. He leaned close, his lips teasing near my ear.

"I have to search you," he said.

"If it would make you feel better."

"It would make me feel a lot better." A suggestive growl tinted his words.

He gestured to Rayhan. "Search him." Rayhan moved toward Zavier.

The vampire's palms touched the tops of my shoulders. Strength tightened his hands, but his touch remained gentle. Despite the half-smile across his lips, those black eyes stayed serious. He expected to find a weapon.

"Arms out."

I raised my arms. He wrapped both hands around my bicep and ran them down to my wrist. He did the same to the other side, but caught the edge of silk at the end of my sleeve.

He ran the fabric between two fingers.

"This is expensive."

"Yes, it is."

"There's blood on it."

"War doesn't care if you wear expensive things into battle."

He held my wrist captive in his hand and studied me. I couldn't read his expression. He leaned in and the smell of smoke, leather, and something sweet drifted around us. His scent consumed me and I recognized the predator craving my blood. My heart claimed my throat, a wild bird searching for escape.

His hands fluttered around the collar of my dress and circled the edge of the neckline. His fingers brushed my collarbone and heat trailed across my skin, a raging wildfire.

I jumped when his hands reached my hair. When had I closed my eyes? He loosened the tie and my dark hair tumbled over my shoulders.

"Do you expect to find something there?" I ignored the tingles as his hands moved through the knots in my hair.

"You'd be surprised how many times beautiful women have something hidden up here."

Satisfied my hair was unarmed, he ran the backs of his hands down my chest and stomach. He maintained a professional and thorough composure. He knelt and felt my legs, taking particular attention at each boot. Finally, he sat on his heels and looked up at me.

"This guy's clean," Rayhan said.

The second man frowned.

"Are you disappointed?" I asked.

"I am. It would have been more convenient to kill you right away."

He stood, a fluid motion between one breath and the next. I caught a flash of silver in his eyes before he turned.

The two vampires whispered, too quiet to be overheard. That was fine. I didn't want to hear if they were planning our executions.

"All right." Rayhan stomped to us and laid a heavy hand on Zavier's shoulder. The second man mounted his horse. Tension caught his shoulders and he clenched the reins too hard. He was struggling to keep control. "I guess you guys get to go see the king."

The cluster of five riders assembled around us. Rayhan led the way, and the dark eyed man trailed at the rear.

Night begun to fade. The moon lingered as the sun rose, an eerie mix of too dark, but not dark enough. Fresh dew covered the grass and my boots shone with moisture. It was colder in the dawn. I longed for a thick blanket and a hearty meal.

As we walked, the massive stretch of the vampire camp looked smaller than it had from the top of the hill. The little rows of tents appeared more manageable, less intimidating.

Did I make the wrong choice? Could we have survived an invasion?

No, that was the exhaustion talking. Being up all night, combined with the hike and expending so much magic during the battle had taken its toll. Dried sweat stiffened my dress and gore speckled the rich emerald fabric. I forced my feet to move. I didn't want to come closer to this place, to barter my life with the king.

I was tempted to pause, to simply stop walking. Maybe the vampires would kill me, maybe they would take me as a prisoner. They could try to ransom me, but my country didn't want me anyway.

I sighed.

"Are you tired?" Zavier asked.

"I am very tired."

"We're almost there." He wasn't talking about distance. We were almost done with this task, with my duty. When this was over, I could rest, either six feet in the ground, or at home with a clear conscience. Tears pricked my eyes, but I would not let them fall when our enemies watched every move.

Zavier grabbed my hand and I wrapped my fingers around his.

We approached the haphazard exterior wall constructed from a combination of wood and scrap metal sheets. Watchtowers stretched between one-hundred-stride intervals, composed of wooden planks, rough metal bolts, and nails. They swayed at the top, where archers aimed down at us. One tower stood on either side of the main gate, which was nothing more than two wooden slabs with hinges.

The gates creaked open and revealed a small crowd. Humans intermingled between vampires, watching and whispering. Most wore black, but there were occasional grey and white garments. Towels were thrown over shoulders, colored medical kits around some waists. The people held hammers, axes, or swords.

Rayhan raised his hand and the crowd dispersed.

The camp was tidy for its size. Tents clustered by unit, a fire with a rotating spit burned in the center of each section. The smell of roasting meat made my mouth water. My stomach twisted in knots. I hadn't eaten since yesterday.

The row of tents spilled into a makeshift courtyard. Even more fires burned in the open space. Tables and carts filled with food peppered the area. Men and women hustled, their arms overflowing with steaming meats and vegetables. Garlic, ginger, and less familiar spices cast around us.

A child ran to an older man and tugged on the white apron around his waist. The man plucked an apple from a bowl and passed it down. The kid skipped away, juice running down his chin.

"There's children here?" I had never seen a child in a war camp.

"Some of our soldiers are couples." The dark-eyed man studied me with his head tilted. In the rising sun, his eyes resembled two black holes claiming the rich rays of new light. "If they have children, there's nobody at home to watch them."

We had never sent our entire army to lay siege in a faraway land. If we did, I wasn't sure we would bring the children.

We passed the medical tent. The smell of blood and bodily fluids slipped between the flaps. Moans and grunts faded in the distance. Stables stretched to the back of the defensive perimeter, farther than I could see. Horses trotted in and out of rough stalls and some meandered in the grassy fields.

The deeper we trekked into camp, the less likely we'd ever make it out. It was a poor strategy to show the enemy the interior of a war camp and then send them home. These men assumed we'd never leave this place.

A lone tent perched before the stables. It spanned the size of four or five of the normal tents we passed. The rich red fabric created a blinding target among the sea of white. Darkness peeked through the open flaps and I expected teeth in the gaping mouth waiting to swallow us whole.

The men dismounted. Stablemen appeared and grabbed the horses' reins. They whispered softly to the animals and led them away with offers of apple slices and sugar cubes.

The second man shouldered by us, Rayhan at his heels. They disappeared into the maw of the tent, leaving us outside with the three other men. Noises filtered out.

Thunk.

Bang.

They were likely rearranging things inside, hiding strategies and sensitive information.

Rayhan stepped out. The sun cresting the horizon gave me a clearer view of the man. The symbols in his armor were engravings of ancient spellwork. I studied many languages to read some of the books in my father's study, although I wasn't fluent in any of them. The etched swirls and lines composed protective enchantments and spells to generate good luck. A very powerful and trained witch had carved them, which meant the vampires harbored one of our traitors.

Rayhan gestured to the flaps with one hand.

"Your demise awaits." He wiggled his eyebrows.

Zavier released my hand and numbness tingled my fingertips. I smoothed the green dress and wished I hadn't come from battle covered in blood and guts. If I had taken time to prepare, I could have made a better impression.

But this meeting wasn't about formalities. I needed to be real, authentic, personable. I needed King Kadence to see a desperate princess and find pity in his heart. If he didn't, I was sure to find a sword in mine.

I stepped into the darkness. Zavier followed.

The sun did not penetrate the tent's thick fabric, casting deep darkness inside. Lanterns lit the space, but I still had to squint. Woven tapestries dangled from the metal poles of the structure, illustrating massive battles and victorious heroes. One particularly muscular man held the bleeding head of an enemy in one hand and the rest of the body in the other. Pieces of papers peeked behind the tapestries, probably maps and documents they had hidden from us.

A long table stretched down the middle of the tent. Rich brown wood reflected the dancing flames of the lanterns. Simple black chairs sat around the table. Crates and boxes stacked at the edges of the room. Labels spelled *Food, Swords, Knives* in blocky handwriting on the front of each box.

At the head of the table, perched in the chair farthest from the door like powerful warrior ready to strike, was the dark-eyed man. He smiled and stretched both arms out.

"Welcome, Princess. The king of Vari Kolum has decided to grant you an audience. Please sit."

Chapter Three

My face grew hot. I should have listened to Zavier when he glared at me for my sharp tongue outside the gates. It was too late for standard pleasantries and manners. The king had seen one side of me and switching to a formal tone would make me appear indecisive and dishonest. Zavier couldn't step in for negotiations, or I would lose the little rapport I had built. I had dug a very large, deep hole, and now I had to lie in it. Fear tightened around my heart, choking me a little more. I was on my own.

I pulled out my chair and sunk onto it. I settled my legs under the table and crossed my ankles, rubbing my hands on the glossy tabletop. Years of etiquette and protocol lessons wasted. I wandered in uncharted territory.

Zavier took the chair at my side. Rayhan stomped to stand behind King Kadence.

I smiled. The king's grin slipped.

"Are you surprised?" he asked me. He had lit a fire under my feet and expected me to dance. Instead I just stood on the coals. He didn't know I was willing to do so much more for my kingdom.

"I am no longer surprised at any level the vampires will stoop to in this war." The words felt sharp on my tongue. Instant regret flooded me. Insults were not the best way to begin this conversation.

The king bared his teeth.

"And the witches have made only civil decisions. I've never seen a body wrapped so thick with magic that the vampire's eyes bulged and their muscles were lacerated through the skin."

"And the vampires have never bled any of our soldiers dry and left their withered corpses dangling from trees like crusted fruit we had to pick to bring home."

King Kadence pushed his fists on the table and stood. His chair screeched as it slid across the ground. I stood too, arching my neck to look the vampire in the eyes.

"Your people—"

Rayhan put his hand on the king's shoulder.

"We get it." The man's voice cut us off. "We've all done horrible things during this war. Now you both sit down and talk about it. Or, Kadence, we can kill them right now."

My hands itched for a sword to slice across the king's neck. Magic bloomed around me, looking for something to strike. I sat back down. The king and I eyed each other across the table.

The magic, though, I kept out. I let it drift through the room like a slow gas, silent and invisible.

The king spoke again, control steadying his voice.

"When my scouts reported two figures walking from the witch kingdom, I expected human defectors. We've had a few." I knew that. The scouts reported everything they saw. We had some humans come from the vampire kingdom as well, although not recently. "Imagine my surprise when it was the Princess and her oldest advisor walking toward our camp as though we weren't planning their deaths. I thought we'd have to drag you from the castle, kicking and screaming."

He angled toward Zavier.

"Zavier Croft. My father met you on the battlefield once. He said he barely escaped with his life."

Zavier bowed his head. "I won't speak ill of the dead and I don't have to. Your father was a great warrior."

King Kadence put his hands on the table, palms up. His armor molded to a body honed to perfection. He looked magnificent, with enough flaws to prevent him from becoming a marble statue. His eyebrows lacked symmetry, his jawline too sharp. He opened his arms, an angel offering us salvation, and he would look just like that if he ran us through with his sword.

My magic slid through the room, a winding river of power. I wrapped it around each lantern, tight but gentle, similar to setting a trigger in a game snare. If the trigger was too tight, the slightest breeze would collapse the trap. Too loose and the prey would never spring it. My magic became a whisper through the room, feeling up the boxes and crates, brushing across rows of paper.

"Why are you here, Princess Salvatore?"

King Kadence held a hand up before I could answer. Rayhan gave him a piece of paper.

"We have enough soldiers to fight two-to-one," the king said, "Those odds don't stack up well for you. Your people do better in small battles, with ample time to recharge magic between fights. One massive assault and your soldiers would be spent."

He met my eyes over the top of his page, then flicked them down and kept reading.

"If you locked yourself in the castle and trapped everyone outside, we estimate you could survive for two months. We also don't think you would do that. You would stuff people into the castle until it threatened to burst and then reluctantly shut the doors. I'm sure you have plenty of provisions inside, but sewage and wastewater would overflow within a week. People would die by the dozens and you'd, what, eat the bodies? No, you'd stack the dead in the basement until rats and disease amassed. You'd all die around the same time we'd catapult the front door to a million pieces."

He looked at me again and I settled a stoic expression across my face. "Your supply routes are surprisingly strong, but your army has been cut in half and your people's loyalty changes every day." He put the paper on the table with a smug smile. "You cannot win this war. We will crush you until there's nothing to put back together. I will ask again. Why are you here?"

I set my hands on the table to hide the tremble. "I am here to surrender."

The words fell from my lips. I thought saying them out loud would be difficult, dredging upstream in high water, but it felt like a lead weight dropping off my shoulders. I could breathe again.

"Zavier."

He didn't need a paper. He recited the words from memory.

"We are five thousand soldiers down. Half of our army marched out and never returned. Our trading partners value money more than loyalty and as long as we pay, we will have supplies. Decades of effort prove that our routes cannot be blocked, as many of our people have transportation magic. Your option then, is to fight us directly."

As Zavier talked, I shaped the magic. The lazy coils of power sharpened, tightened, into rows and rows of invisible strings. I scattered the strings across the room and they wrapped around boxes, papers, lanterns. They swallowed crates of food, maps, tapestries, enveloped them tight in the power, insects trapped in a spider's web.

The other end of the magic fed into me. I sorted the strings, tapping each one as it clung to something in the room. They twisted and turned at my will. I sent more power, and they thickened, strengthened to wire instead of web.

"If we armed every witch and loyal human that can hold a weapon, your armies will still crush us," Zavier continued, "There wouldn't be anybody left standing. If we harbor for a siege, thousands of our people would die outside the castle walls. It is imperative to our country's survival that we do not engage in direct combat with your amassed forces."

"You see where our hands are tied," I said.

"Yes," King Kadence said, "I do not see how it benefits me to accept your surrender. It sounds like we can, quite literally, swallow all of you."

In my mind, I gathered the magical wires together in a cluster. I imagined an arched wooden frame, waiting for the delicate strings in my hands. The strings pulsed with power as I drew them into their new spaces, settling one after another into the hollow place etched for each strand. The rolled jumble of wires uncoiled one at a time, by my direction, until they transformed into a beautiful harp. Soft but strong, powerful and graceful, the instrument waited for me. My fingers buzzed, eager to pluck the notes.

The magic connections tied to every lantern in the tent wound together into one string, vertical across the instrument. I plucked it. The magic sang me a rich note and the lanterns flickered out. The tent plunged into darkness.

I strung the cords, pushing power into each string of my invisible harp. One ran through the boxes of food and weapons. Another note carried magic to the pages hidden beneath tapestries. I ran my fingers across the strings and pushed the last of my power into them. The papers, supplies, glass, and wood in the room that my magic touched illuminated with a soft, blue glow. It swirled and danced with the pulse of the music, setting the room in a beautiful and eerie shadow, like being deep underwater and unsure if there was enough air to swim to the surface.

Both vampires had stood in the seconds of darkness. Rayhan gripped his giant axe and the king's eyes were deathly silver. I kept my palms flat on the table. Zavier sat loose in his seat, as though expecting tea to be served at any moment.

"A little jumpy, Your Majesty?" I asked.

"What is this?" The king strained to look at the pulsing blue lights as they shimmered across the room. About half of the boxes and crates were illuminated and almost all the stacks of paper. Exposed corners of maps peeked behind tapestries, dancing with my power.

"How familiar are you with magic?" I asked.

He didn't answer.

"To avoid forcing you to admit you know little about your enemy's greatest asset, I will explain some of the basics." My magic dwindled. At full strength, I could keep these items lit for hours. Tonight, exhausted from battle, without any sleep, and as my stomach tried to fold in on itself, I had precious minutes. It would undermine everything I said if the magic collapsed early.

Hurry.

"When magic touches an object, it leaves a residue. A kind of magical fingerprint. Some witches can identify this residue. I used a simple spell to illuminate the objects in this room that were made with the aid of magic."

"And you had to extinguish the lanterns?" the king asked.

"Yes, for dramatic effect."

"You're saying everything that's glowing was created by magic?"

"It was at some point in the supply chain, made, or handled by witches, yes."

He looked around, taking a mental inventory.

"As you can see," I said, "there are a substantial number of your supplies that involve my people. If you destroy us, if you crush our kingdom as you promise to do, the resources and labor to produce these supplies will halt. I am not naive. You would be able to recover these losses. But at what cost and how quickly? If boxes of food are suddenly missing from your haul, how many of your people will starve? Vampires don't eat much, so the humans would die first. Then your supply of blood would slowly diminish."

I gestured to other boxes.

"Fuel and oil would become an invaluable resource. People would fight for it, kill each other in the streets. How many more decades of loss do you want to face after declaring victory in this war? Is that your definition of victory, Your Majesty? To watch your children starve because pride consumed your country's essential supplies?"

I burned. Magic ate away at my nerves as it pulled reserve power from my body. My dress itched like sandpaper on my skin. Muscles twisted. I relaxed my hands on the table, my face calm, while my power consumed me from the inside out.

"How many have the ability to identify the residue, as you called it?" the king asked.

"Not many. It's rare."

Please stop asking questions.

King Kadence sat down. He tilted his head, a slight tip, a predator deciding if its prey was worth the effort. I struggled not to wiggle in my seat. The look on his face said he was imagining a thousand ways to kill me.

Rayhan kept his axe in his hand. He shifted from the glowing objects, as though he didn't want the magic to touch him, yet he didn't have trouble wearing the spell-engraved armor.

"You can stop now, Princess," King Kadence said softly. "You've made your point."

"Maybe a few lanterns could be lit first, so the darkness doesn't startle you again," I said. *I'm not burning away. Please, take your time.*

Rayhan lit the lanterns and once the yellow flames deepened to orange, I gathered the magical strings. One at a time, I untied the knots from my mental harp, pulled them away, and let the magic go. I did it theatrically slow, the glow fading from one object at a time.

Sweat trickled down my back. The magic was gone, depleted.

"It is tempting to kill you now, Princess," the king said. "There is a chance your people would follow me peacefully. Our spies say you're not exactly popular."

It was difficult to be popular when my family ran away and left a half-trained replacement to run the country.

"I am not here to beg for my life," I said. "I am here to negotiate terms of surrender that allow my people to survive, integrate with your kingdom, and eventually thrive. If my death is a condition of those terms, then so be it."

The king raised his eyebrows.

"You're telling the truth?"

With the entirety of my being, I was telling the truth. Once I stepped down that hill, I had no intention of returning home.

"Yes."

He leaned back in his chair and studied me. I returned the stare, my face blank. If he asked me to grovel, I would kneel. If he asked for my head on a platter, I would ask if he wanted a silver or gold one. After my parents abandoned our kingdom, I owed it to the people of Ededen.

Please, please.

"Bring in two scribes. Let's see if we can agree on the terms."

Relief flooded me. Zavier's shoulders sagged. My shaking hands longed to wrap the old man in a hug, but I didn't dare. Our country might have a chance to survive, grow, and prosper. They would hate me, but they would be alive.

Two people came in, a man and a woman, carrying ink, quills, and blank scrolls. They perched on each side of the table, between me and the king. In unison, they dipped the quills tips into the black ink and sat poised to write.

"Since you made the journey all this way, what is your first term, Princess?" the king asked.

"My first term is that all soldiers are released from duty and allowed to return to their homes as civilians without punishment for serving in our armies. Prisoners of War on both sides will also be released unharmed." The first few terms were obvious, but needed to be in writing.

"Done," the king said. "Tell me where your parents are."

My parents. Their absence was a constant thorn in my back, reminding me that they valued themselves more than their country, more than me. Every day, the thorn cut a little deeper.

"I don't know where they are. They disappeared six months ago, took half of our army, and we haven't seen them since. Our scouts are watching for them, but there has been no sign."

King Kadence pressed his lips together. He didn't like my answer.

"We've heard rumors they're searching for the Fields of Death."

The information jolted me. Surely the vampires didn't know more than our own scouts, who still couldn't locate my parents. If my parents somehow found the mystical Fields, they would ruin us all. I recalled the terrible stories every child eavesdropped on when they were supposed to be tucked in bed while the adults talked. The tales of demons and blood and death.

"For both our sakes, I hope that is not true."

He nodded, but a flicker of emotion I didn't catch ran over his face.

"My first term is that your coronation as queen will be completed immediately. I refuse to accept a surrender that will be overturned if your parents suddenly show up."

It was an easy term to accept. Tradition dictated waiting one year when a ruler went missing before crowning a successor, even if the individual was presumed dead. Half the coronation was already planned. Pushing it forward would be simple.

"Yes, done," I said.

The scribes scratched away on their scrolls, feathers dancing in the same rhythm.

"The surrender will be announced at the coronation and I will be presented as the reigning king," he continued.

"Yes, that's fine." Better to get it out of the way.

"Next?"

"Blood will not be unwillingly taken from any of my people," I said.

"That is contradictory to my benefit. We don't have enough human donors here to sustain our numbers indefinitely. Eventually our soldiers will go home, but we must eat until then," the king said.

"I propose setting a weekly or monthly quota for blood donation. If the quota is not fulfilled by volunteers, then we would implement a fair draft. It is not beneficial for either of us if witches are swiped off the streets and found half-drained in a back alley."

"I can agree to a quota system. I, or whomever I delegate, will be in charge of setting the limits."

"As long as it is realistic."

"Done."

"Done. Next?" I asked.

"The title of queen will be stripped of its authority and will be a title only. You will complete tasks that are delegated to you. I want you to sit on your throne, dressed up and pretty, and do what I tell you to."

I bit the inside of my lip. His words did not surprise me. Surrendering meant submitting to his authority. I couldn't do that and hold the majority of power over my people, but it hurt like skin torn from a fresh wound.

"Done," I said, my voice quiet.

"I expect you to submit to me in all things, immediately, without questions. You will not marry without my permission. You will not finance a project without my permission. I will own you, your ideas, and your decisions. Is that a term you can accept?"

"That needs to be clarified," Zavier started. I held up my hand and he stopped.

I didn't need clarification. The vampires couldn't burn down our villages, plunder our homes, or kill us in the streets. The king needed something to replace those. The war had to have a loser to bear the punishment and that would be me.

"Yes, I accept."

"Are you already betrothed?"

"I am," I said. Images of Reuben's face ran through my mind. I pushed them away, but the knowledge that I was about to cause him pain lingered in my heart. "It will be canceled tonight."

Rayhan whispered in the king's ear.

"I will have control of your personal staff and will add or remove employees as I see fit." King Kadence wanted spies in my rooms. I would have requested the same in his position. Refusing the term would give him an opportunity to propose something worse.

"Fine." I tried not to grind my teeth. "The vampires will share resources with the witches and will not force them to leave their homes."

"Done. Housing, land, crops, and livestock will be available for any vampires that wish to settle long term in the area."

"Done. Vampires will have to integrate into the community and work for their income the same way our people do."

"Done."

We had both leaned forward while we talked. I pushed back against the seat. King Kadence frowned. He was getting everything he wanted, but he wasn't happy about it.

"Those are all the terms I have. What else do you want?" Exhaustion tore me down. My eyelids weighed a hundred pounds. My dry mouth felt full of sawdust. I needed food and sleep.

"There's some schematics that our councils will have to figure out." Food, distribution of supplies, building barracks to house an influx of people. These were important, but they didn't belong in the terms of our surrender.

My surrender.

"There is one more thing," the king said.

What else? This night had taken so much from me, there wasn't much left.

The king held up his hand again. Rayhan patted down his armor and produced a small wooden box. He placed it on the king's palm. King Kadence opened the box, turned it toward me, and pushed it across the table.

A simple silver bracelet nestled in a cushion of black velvet. Composed of smooth, untarnished matte metal, the bracelet looked harmless, ornate, and pretty.

I reached for it.

"Don't touch that!" Zavier jumped from his seat and tried to snatch the box from under my fingers.

Too late.

Half of my soul severed, sudden and complete. Pain tore through me, worse than when I broke my ankle in my first sparring match. The part of me that was magic disappeared, a light thrust into a bucket of water, as though it had never existed. My magic snapped, pulling the air from my lungs. I couldn't move, couldn't breathe.

Warm hands peeled mine off the cold metal. I drew a ragged gasp and stood. There wasn't enough room in the tent. I needed to go outside, where I could see the sky and the sun and remember how it felt to be whole.

Zavier held me, which was wonderful, but he blocked my escape. My breathing was ragged. I reached for my magic. Faint, weak, but still there.

"It is my final condition that after the coronation fulfills the surrender, the princess will wear this indefinitely," the king said.

"No," Zavier said hard. "You're a fool if you expect anyone to wear that cursed thing."

I don't know how Zavier knew what the bracelet did before I touched it, but I agreed it was cursed. Its smooth surface lacked spellwork, implying the band held an enchantment. Few witches had that capability and my family employed the ones that did. The vampires had access to a very powerful rogue witch. The thought unsettled my stomach.

"Allowing the Princess to run rampant with powerful magic would be foolish." King Kadence's dark eyes played over me and I wondered if my pale face and gasping breath made me look like a powerful witch. "This band is enchanted silver. Instead of slowing magic like regular sliver, it halts the access completely."

Zavier's gaze narrowed. "What is your definition of indefinite, Your Majesty?" He stiffened the end of the last word, sending a sarcastic message in the form of a careful title.

The king crossed his arms, but he looked at me instead of Zavier.

"I can remove the bracelet, but only when I trust that you are not a threat to my rule. I cannot be coerced or forced to remove it early. Any trickery or threats and the band will remain sealed."

Zavier's lip rose. "She will not agree to this." His voice barely contained any trace of formality. He shook around me, his body vibrating with anger.

Zavier was wrong. I would wear the bracelet. Binding my magic eliminated it as a threat. As a ruler, I understood the need for King Kadence to require it. Dread stiffened my spine at the thought of the band touching my skin again. I locked my jaw and pulled Zavier's hands from my arms. Leaving his embrace was abandoning my only shelter. I expected to die when I came out here. If only half of me—my magic—died instead, I would accept that.

"Yes." The word burned my throat. "Yes, after the ceremony, I will wear the bracelet."

"Then we have an agreement, Princess." King Kadence walked to the scribes and collected the papers, quills, and ink. He sat next to me and passed me a scroll. The slanted handwriting was neat and legible. The terms were listed as we had discussed, almost verbatim.

Zavier took the document and looked it over. He set it back on the table.

"It's correct."

The king dipped a quill into the thick ink and signed both copies in a fluid motion. He handed me the still warm quill. I dipped it in ink as black as the king's eyes and signed my country, my freedom, and my life away.

"This is your copy." The king handed Zavier the scroll and he cradled it softly. "Get these two a horse. They have a coronation to attend."

We sat in a moment of silence as someone brought the horse up. Nausea replaced my hunger. An unusual combination of relief and sickness spread through me. Despite my exhaustion, I doubted I would find sleep soon. A whirlpool of thoughts and emotions turned in my head.

A stableboy peeked into the tent. The horse was ready. Zavier pulled out my chair and helped me stand. He bowed and disappeared through the tent flap.

King Kadence and I were alone.

"Successful negotiating, Princess. I'm eager to see how this goes."

"Thank you. I am as well."

As I turned, the king snatched my hand. He pressed it to his lips and his dark eyes locked on mine. I expected amusement or arrogance or triumph.

King Kadence's eyes drowned me in rolling seas of rage, hot and wild and bloodthirsty. Buried in the depths, tongues of hellfire roared and crackled, and I could tell he yearned to push me into the flames.

I jerked my hand from his and stumbled away. My magic flared, but it was weak. It fluttered and died. I reached for my sword and palmed open air instead.

The vampire smiled.

"Princess, are you ready?" Zavier stepped inside.

"Y-yes."

I didn't dare turn my back on the vampire, but I had a role to play. There were rules to royal games. I bowed, small and polite. Zavier led me out of the tent and I watched from the corner of my eye, but the king did not follow.

The sun blinded me and I blinked until my vision cleared. A small, chestnut mare stood nearby, saddled and wearing packs of food and water. It was less than a day's ride home. We must have looked desperate.

Zavier helped me onto the horse and took the reins in his hands while he walked beside the animal. Guards escorted us through camp, past the rows and rows of tents, around the medical tent, and to the haphazard, wide open gate. They stopped at the edge and we walked through unmolested.

The rocky hills and waist high grasses resembled freedom.

The gates creaked shut. Only the archers with their trained arrows watched us walk back the way we had come.

We paused at the crest of the hill to collect our abandoned weapons. On the other side, Zavier got in the saddle and I sat bareback behind him. I wrapped my arms around him and rested my head on his solid back. I needed to close my eyes for a minute.

"Princess?" Zavier's chest vibrated when he spoke.

"Yes?"

"There's no such thing as magical residue."

"I know," I whispered.

Our mare cracked over rocks and breathed softly.

"We're almost home, Princess," Zavier reassured me. "Then you can sleep."

My eyes burned, my stomach twisted into a thousand knots, and the headache building behind my eyes worsened.

"No, I can't." I groaned. "I have to talk to Reuben."

The man I'd been expected to marry for my entire life didn't deserve to have his heart broken, but each of the mare's soft steps drew me closer to the inevitable. Reuben was not going to be happy about any of this and neither would the rest of my people.

Chapter Four

THE FAMILIARITY OF MY ROOM EMBRACED ME. RUGGED GREY stone composed the towering walls. Slabs of smooth quarts covered the floors, polished to a shine. Thick rugs blanketed high traffic areas, so the cold rock didn't chill my feet. A white rug nestled under the quaint couch and coffee table that faced the grand fireplace. Another supported the four-poster bed that reached toward the elevated, arched ceiling. A sky-blue comforter spread across the mattress and tempted me with its fluffy bulk.

Tapestries and paintings hung on hooks pressed into the mortar between stones. My family's faces stared at me, preserved in canvas or thread, and silently condemned my failure as a ruler. They were all dead now, fallen in the centuries long war with the vampires, or missing.

Restlessness made me pace. I had changed into a clean, red dress and washed my skin with a warm cloth. There wasn't time for a bath. I needed to talk to Reuben and finish planning the coronation. If the ceremony didn't happen tomorrow, my careful negotiation with the vampire king would be meaningless.

The memory of King Kadence's eyes stopped my rapid pacing. Anger was too light to describe the look. A demon of rage and hostility peeked through, and it was eager for my blood, not to kill, but to hurt. I shivered, despite the roaring fire.

I read the coronation schedule while I paced. Much was already planned. The cooks were preparing food for the feast. Invitations had been hastily written on scrolls and messengers were delivering them tonight. When was the best time to announce surrendering after two hundred years of war? Before or after dessert?

The papers felt heavy. I dragged my feet across the white rug. Words and numbers blurred on the page. Maybe I could sit down for a moment.

"Miss?" Saffa peeked her blond head through the double doors and smiled. She had been on my staff since I was thirteen and we had grown up together. King Kadence controlled my staff now. Would he take her away? My heart ached.

I forced a smile. "Yes?"

"Mister Emerson is ready for you in the reception suite, as you requested."

"Thank you, Saffa."

She shut the door.

I straightened my red dress and ran a hand over my hair. The chestnut locks were twisted into a simple, proper bun. As long as Reuben didn't look closely, he wouldn't notice the grit of dried sweat and speckles of liquid that were likely blood. Rouge pinkened my cheeks and lips. It was irrelevant that I hadn't slept and had signed my life away to an enemy king. I needed to look royal.

I shuffled the thick pages. Everything was here.

My bedroom and adjacent reception room composed the smallest suites in the royal hall. The reception room was a glorified living room, a private place to meet important guests. My parents' rooms sat at the far end of the hall. After the coronation, I would take my mother's suites and these ones would wait for a new heir, if the king ever deemed it proper to give me a husband. A chill ran down my spine at the thought of the suitor the vampire may pick.

I ventured into the hall and opened the neighboring door.

The reception room stretched twice the size of my room. An intricate mosaic of black and red rugs hid the stone floor. Gold and red velvet couches gathered around the fireplace, which sparkled with semiprecious gemstones and painted gold flakes. At the far end of the room stood a long wooden table, simple but sound, surrounded with red velvet chairs. Paintings of landscapes and foliage lined the walls. Three great windows stretched proud above the gardens, which had started to drop their blooms.

Reuben turned from the window and smiled.

Reuben Emerson was very handsome—over six feet tall, blond, and athletic. His slim physique lacked the defined muscles of a trained fighter. His squared jaw sported a short, golden beard, and the perfect shape of his eyebrows suggested they were regularly maintained. He wore a white long-sleeved shirt and white breeches, trimmed with gold lace, and brown boots that had never touched dirt. He smiled, a ray of splendid sunshine. For a moment all of that perfect attention landed on me and the world held still.

"Princess." Reuben bowed and held out his hand. I wanted to smile back, but the weight of the papers and the news I was about to deliver dragged my lips down.

I gave him my hand. The strength in his grip surprised me and he lifted it to his lips, reminiscent of King Kadence, but Reuben's eyes were mild, happy.

I built iron bars around my heart. This was going to hurt both of us.

"Reuben, thank you for seeing me," I said. "Please, sit."

We sat on the plush red couch, turned to face each other. Dread cut me from the inside out. I kept my expression flat.

"These are copies of the engagement conditions our parents made twelve years ago." I set the pages on the low wooden table in front of us and kept one copy in my hand. "I've underlined page three, paragraph two, where it dictates terms and stipulations that necessitate a termination of the agreement."

He lifted the papers and shuffled the pages. His eyebrows creased. I drew a breath and locked my spine straight.

"Unfortunately, one of these conditions has been met," I said. "As of last night, I negotiated terms of surrender to the vampire, King Kadence Hendrick of Vari Kolum. My agreement with him negates any previous contract I had been bound by."

Reuben pressed his lips together.

"I don't understand," he said.

"I have surrendered. We lost the war. The vampire king owns us now."

"I don't see what that has to do with us getting married."

I sighed. "I don't have the authority to sign a marriage contract."

"That would have to be one of the terms of surrender."

"It was."

"He said you can't marry me?"

"It was agreed that any outstanding engagement would be terminated upon acceptance of the surrender."

An expression I'd never seen on Reuben's face flashed across his features. Normally, he displayed a mild temper and a level head. The glint that passed behind his eyes was something different, wild and aggressive. It was the face of a man whose best laid plans had just gone to naught.

Reuben smashed his fist onto the table. The wood cracked in half with a groan, shards scattered on the floor beneath. Papers flew. He stood, fast and agile. His face turned red, jaw clenched so tight, I could see the place where the joint and muscle met.

I sat still, hands gently gripping the rest of my pages and elbows resting on my knees. My heart raced. I had never seen Reuben angry or flustered. I had once heard he'd been stalked by a great cat during a hunting trip and didn't even increase his pace.

He glared at me. His blue eyes were hard, confused, but a coil of rage pulsed beneath. I reconsidered my decision to leave my weapons in my room. My fingers suddenly itched for a blade.

"I don't understand, Sal. We've been betrothed for twelve years. We grew up together. We sat through weeks of those horrible etiquette classes while your mother breathed down our necks. When your parents disappeared and people wanted to put a new family on the throne, I advocated for you. I fought for you. Now you're throwing it all away. Why?"

My tongue felt like lead.

"This isn't my choice, Reuben." I searched for the right words. "If I didn't surrender, our kingdom would be in flames tomorrow. Instead, everyone gets to live. We have a chance to survive."

He shook his beautiful golden head. "Has the council heard about this? What did they say?"

"Zavier is informing the council as we speak. The official surrender will be announced at the coronation tomorrow."

"That's when our wedding should be announced."

"There will be no wedding, Reuben."

"It's not too late, Sal. Maybe we can talk to the king. If he knows, if we can talk, maybe he would see reason."

"It's not about reason, Reuben. We lost this war and we lost it very badly. It's a miracle that the king didn't kill me last night. There's nothing to talk to him about."

Reuben dropped to his knees. He pulled the papers from my grip and wrapped his warm, soft hands around mine. He clutched them to his chest and stared into my eyes. His were red, swollen, as he held back tears.

"Please," he begged. "Please, Sal. I'll give anything, do anything. Please, talk to the king, or let me talk to him. I've waited for you. I'm ready to be your husband. Please, please." Tears tipped over the edge of Reuben's eyes. He dropped one of my hands to cover them.

This was the man I had expected to marry for over a decade of my life. He cried for us and I could not conjure a single tear. Reuben was everything I could ask for in a husband—tender, kind, honest, not much of a warrior, but I had soldiers for that. He understood his role as king would be secondary to mine as queen. He was comfortable and easy. We had courted at least once a month for the duration of our engagement. Each visit had been filled with jokes, laughter and whatever delicious food he had cooked that week to bring me.

My heart had never raced for him. The few kisses and touches we'd shared were simply pleasant. I had never wished to wake up with him the next morning. After seeing those flashes of anger across his face and my ruined table, I wondered if the tendrils of distrust were stronger than I'd realized.

As he cried, a voice whispered in the back of my mind that this was hard, but I would be okay.

"Reuben, look at me please."

His blue eyes, two perfect aquamarine stones set in a golden pendent, turned to me.

"I love you." The words were true. Reuben held a place in my heart.

"But I have obligations to my country and tomorrow, to my king. We will not be married and there is nothing we can do about that."

Reuben's face flattened and the tears stopped. He squeezed my hand, set it on my lap, and stood. His heavy steps pounded the floor as he strode toward the door. He paused and looked back over one shoulder, glaring down at the carpet.

"Did you surrender yourself in place of the country, Sal?" he asked.

"I did."

"You know what that means? What he's going to do to you?"

"I do."

He nodded, opened the door, and left.

Chapter Five

MY DRESS WAS RIDICULOUS.

Final preparations for the coronation were almost complete. Chairs lined the edges of the Great Hall for the ceremony and would be pushed aside to add tables for the feast. Massive platters of food rested between hot ovens to stay warm. There had been a small rehearsal and most of the guests had already arrived.

The council had avoided me since Zavier informed them of the surrender. They were insulted. The council traditionally approved a new ruler's coronation and I wasn't sure even the king's decree would change that custom. If the council rejected my appointment tonight, all would be lost. It would cause a rebellion and the vampires could pick off the unruly crowd. No need for a battle, my people would walk into their own slaughter. I hoped the council would see what was at stake beyond hurt feelings.

I was the last to get ready. I took a bath, which was much too short, and washed the grime and blood away. Saffa combed my hair, wrapped it into elegant, twisting braids, stuck them with diamond pins that caught the light, and brushed rouge and kohl on my face.

Then they brought out the dress.

Air hissed through my lips as Saffa and Elaine pulled on the silk cords that wrapped around my chest. The fabric tightened, straining my ribs.

"I don't know if it fits," Elaine whispered, barely six inches from my ear.

"I can wear a different dress." I suggested.

"Nonsense." Saffa pulled on the stubborn laces again. "It's tradition to wear a beautiful, expensive dress to your coronation." Pull. "The dress is a symbol of sophistication and wealth." Pull. "Plus, this one was Queen Estelle's."

My mother hadn't had a coronation, as my father was already king when they married. This had been her wedding dress.

It was broken into three layers. Beneath the dress, a tight slip convinced my body that it didn't need so much space. Over that, two petticoats scratched at my legs. The base dress was white silk, sleeveless, and corseted against my chest. It wrapped around my waist and flared into an elegant A-line. Hems embroidered with golden thread shone and diamonds sewn in here and there sparkled with every movement.

The top layer waited on my bed—an overdress of pure golden lace, woven so delicately that a strong breeze might unwind the fabric. It was long sleeved, would button under my breasts, and then fall against each side of the silken skirt all the way to the floor. The delicate fabric would probably rip the moment I stuffed my arms into it.

"There!" Saffa tied the last lace. She brushed her hands down the dress, smoothing any wrinkles, and fluffed the petticoats. We looked at my reflection in the mirror.

Elaine squinted her eyes and tilted her head.

Saffa pressed her lips together.

"Maybe it's the eyes," Saffa said.

"It could be the hair," Elaine said. "I'm not sure I like the side braids."

They reached for me, but I ducked out of the way.

"It's fine," I said. "It will look better with the lace overdress."

The girls smiled and nodded.

We all knew it wouldn't look better with the lace. The dress wasn't the problem, I was. Queen Estelle was dainty and petite and her dress wasn't meant to fit on my five-foot-eight inch frame. My mother had never held a sword and I used to practice twice a week with the soldiers. My arms were stronger and thicker than hers, my waist straighter than hourglass. I would have looked better in my armor, but my mother would have clicked her tongue at me for even thinking such a thing.

"Please find Zavier and tell him to come talk to me," I said.

The girls bowed and left the room.

I squinted at the mirror, trying to see my mother. Even wearing her clothes and about to take her title, I stood alone in the mirror. Familiar bitterness toward my parents blossomed.

They left us. They left me. They took everything we needed to survive and ran away in the night. There hadn't been a note. They hadn't even said goodbye. We had eaten dinner together and the next morning they never arrived for breakfast. Anger burned a hot fire inside me and every thought added wood to the flames.

Sorrow mixed amongst the embers and ashes. My soul ached that they would not be here tonight. My mother should be the one tying my dress and assuring me I looked wonderful. My father should pass his crown, instead of the circlet perching on the pedestal we had ground into the raised dais for the ceremony. This should be a happy, joyous, anticipated moment. Instead, it rained with dread and finality.

Hot tears poked at the corners of my eyes. I brushed them away before they could spill. Saffa didn't have time to reapply the rouge.

"Princess?" The door creaked open and Zavier peeked inside. He scanned my face and his brows tightened. He hurried toward me and I let him wrap me in a firm hug until the pain lessened.

"Why are you crying?" he asked.

I pulled back. "I'm not crying."

"Of course not," he said smoothly. "Why are you upset then?"

"I'm not upset either."

"Whatever you say, Your Majesty." He mocked me with a bow. I laughed and poked him in the chest. His eyes danced, but an edge of darkness lined them. He was worried about me.

"You are a vision, my princess," he said. "I remember when Queen Estelle wore this gown to her wedding. I dare say, you might rival her loveliness."

"I can always count on you for a laugh, Zavier. Has security been tightened in the Hall?"

Zavier gave a stern nod. "We've doubled guards at all entrances. If more assassins appear, we'll have a forewarning at least."

I tried to smile, but feared the expression turned to more of a grimace. Rogue assassins had become an unfortunate problem, desperate to end my rule before it even began. They appeared to know my schedule well and attacked in unexpected places. Zavier worried we had a traitor in the castle. I didn't disagree, nor was I surprised. In my experience, people tended to be more ruthless than one may expect.

I didn't need uninvited assassins trying to kill me at my coronation. The vampires would be enough to contend with.

"Did our guests of honor arrive safely?" I asked.

"Yes, my men and I met the king and his entourage outside the gate. We used the underground tunnels and staff passages into the castle. Nobody saw us," he said. "Although I would rather have left them outside."

"If we left them outside, they would catapult their way in."

He waved his hand, brushing away my statement. "The king is a very... stubborn man. It will be interesting to see how this plays out. We may all die yet, coaxed by him to do the deed ourselves."

"What did he say?" I asked.

"He's very provoking."

"I don't understand."

"You will, Princess. He wants to meet with you before the ceremony."

Of course he did.

"Please let him know I'll be there shortly. Send Saffa and Elaine back in. They have to persuade that jacket to fit me."

Zavier looked at the golden jacket spread across the bed and back at me.

"I'll wish them luck."

MY STEPS WERE SILENT ON THE STONE FLOOR AS I LED SAFFA and Elaine to the formal reception room on the ground level. The benefit of wearing a dress I was too tall for, was that I couldn't wear high heels.

The girls had slipped silk slippers onto my feet and I resolved they would be my only footwear from now on. Comfortable and flexible, they might be better in combat than my boots.

A guard opened the door to the staff passage behind the Great Hall. The Hall was full of guests and I didn't have time to mingle. The narrow spaces fit two people side-by-side and roamed the entirety of the castle. An obscure door opened at the end of the passage and we tumbled into a well-lit walkway behind the Great Hall. We turned right, toward the reception room.

A pair of soldiers guarded the wooden doors. The hinges were secured in the stone by sheer force and maybe some ancient magic. The guards opened the door.

I smiled.

Unlike the small one in my suites, this reception room was very large. White marble floors matched the Great Hall. My mother never let rugs cover a single inch. Two banquet tables sat at each end of the room, a tall throne at the head. A circle of couches gathered in the center, framed by a simple fireplace. A piano, cellos, and several violins scattered about. One never knew when a guest would request entertainment.

Four strangers crowded on the couch, backs to the fireplace, where they could watch the rest of the room. Zavier moved to stand to the left.

Rayhan lounged at the far end of the sofa. The warmth of the fire softened his face, making him look younger. Laugh lines creased his forehead and his full lips appeared eager to smile. He'd propped his feet on the table and held his axe in one hand.

Kadence sat between Rayhan and a woman I did not know. He wore an all black formal military dress uniform, double-breasted jacket, undershirt, and boots. Even the buttons on his uniform were black, although polished to a pristine shine. His dark eyes looked feral, a wild tiger locked in a cage. *You can touch me*, the tiger said, *but you won't like what happens next.*

The king looked me up and down and twisted his lips.

"You're wearing that?"

I bowed, as low as the constricted fabric would allow.

"It's a pleasure to welcome you to the Kingdom of Ededen, Your

Majesty." I gestured to my side. "This is Elaine and Saffa, and we are here to make sure everything is ready and comfortable for you tonight."

King Kadence leaned back.

"This is the head of my personal security, Cynthia." He gestured to the woman beside him.

Cynthia's face pinched with distaste. She was Asian descent, black hair falling straight to her knees. A black-and-white dress, flexible enough to fight in, fit her muscled figure, and a headband gripped her hair—tactical choices no doubt. Her hands trembled, as though they weren't used to being empty. My instincts said she was dangerous. She looked small and harmless, but if a confrontation started, I would choose the large, muscular man beside her as my opponent. I knew what to expect from him.

"This is Renee. She will be joining your personal staff after this evening." Renee was less remarkable with a plain face, flat eyes, and a barrel-shaped body lacking muscle tone. She wore a shift dress and flat, black shoes. She looked normal and boring, exactly as a spy should.

She stood and bowed.

"I am eager to serve you, Your Majesty." Her voice was light, monotoned.

"Thank you." I turned to the king. "Has Zavier finished reviewing the ceremony schedule with you?"

King Kadence eyed Zavier. My First Seneschal's face was rosy, and bore the same tight smile that he wore in battle right before someone died. I didn't need anybody to die tonight.

"We were just discussing that," the king said. "When does the begging-for-the-lives-of-your-people part happen?"

"I thought that requirement was fulfilled before we signed the contract."

"What time do you grovel on your knees and thank me for my endless mercy?"

The same time I shove my sword through your heart.

Lips pressed, I tried to keep my expression blank, but a sliver of anger tightened my face. "I haven't scheduled that in yet. Did you have a time in mind?"

"How many blood sacrifices have you prepared?"

"Zavier has a list of volunteers to donate blood this evening. Please let him know if the need arises." The king's questions searched for a fight, but I forbid that from happening. Nothing would damage this surrender. My people's lives depended on it.

"Have you prepared the seventy virgins we will carry away in the darkness after the coronation?"

I raised a brow. "If you need help finding a woman, Your Majesty, although the practice is discouraged, there are a few underground brothels in the city. I'm sure you could afford to pay to take someone home for the night."

The king stood, quick, graceful.

Zavier tensed and turned toward me.

My ladies, both trained in armed and unarmed combat, reached for their weapons.

I held a hand up. *Please, do not kill anybody tonight.*

The king stalked toward me with measured and precise steps. He was a silent predator, creeping above unaware prey. He stopped inches away. My dress suddenly felt much too tight. I couldn't breathe. I conjured my strength and met his eyes, afraid of what I would find in their depths. They flickered with a spark of amusement. Underneath, peeling back layers, the rage and hate burned hot.

"That's not very diplomatic to say to your new overlord."

I bit my tongue. He was right. Zavier warned me and I still let the king under my skin. My magic recognized his proximity as a threat and flared up. It brushed against him and licked the power on his flesh. It twisted and wrapped around his body, eager for me to attack, but beneath the call to battle, it gave an almost content purr. I pressed my lips and resisted tilting my head. I'd expected the magic to scream in hate at the king's presence, but it was...pleased?

King Kadence glanced down, then back at me. He raised his eyebrows. The magic moved too quick and the vampire felt it entwine around him. He was waiting, challenging my next move. I toyed with the options. I could bind, immobilize, or shock him, all of which would end badly.

I let the coils fall. The magic retreated and I stepped away from the wall of his body and bowed.

"My apologies, Your Majesty."

He turned back to the couch, but I caught the expression on his face. He looked disappointed.

"The ceremony is fine," he said, his back to me. "I'll see you there."

I bowed again even though he couldn't see it. I would focus on being more proper. My life, and more importantly, the lives of my people, depended on it.

Chapter Six

My pulse fluttered against the curls brushing my neck. I waited alone in the reception hall for the musical cue and the double doors to open, signaling the start of the coronation. Inside, my friends, council, marshals, royal guests, and an assortment of civilians waited for me.

The nausea turning my stomach didn't stem from the ceremony. It was an easy role for me to play. There would be a series of yes or no questions, I would sit on the throne that my father once occupied and have a crown placed on my head. Traditionally, I would take a moment to announce a wedding. Instead, I would announce the surrender, the end of our civilization as we knew it. Sweat beaded on my skin, despite layers of powder Saffa had brushed across my face.

The music began. *Oh, please no.* I wasn't ready.

The doors opened. I plastered a smile on my face.

The Great Hall looked magnificent. The white marble floor had been scrubbed until it shined and looked wet. Rows of rich wood chairs with white cushions lined the room, packing over two hundred people on each side of the aisle. Layers of white silk billowed from the ceiling, wrapped and twisted into hanging mosaics like an intricate spiderweb. Flowers lined the aisle, along with silken cloths, and flickering candles. It looked bridal, but instead represented the birth of a new rule. A blank slate for the new queen.

The weight of the responsibilities of the kingdom threatened to drag me down, push me lower and lower with each step. I forced my shoulders back, lifted my chin, and found Zavier at the back of the hall. His smile soothed ache soothed a bit.

At the end of the aisle, a raised stage held the magnificent golden throne. It towered ten feet tall, carved from wood, with gold inlaid in the swirls of the design, and a brilliant red cushion. A pedestal sat to the left of the throne, where my father should stand to pass the crown as a physical symbol of exchanging power. The golden crown perched alone on a red velvet cloth. Zavier stood beside the stand, a scroll in one hand.

I reached the dais and knelt before the crown.

Zavier read the script from the scroll. "Are you Salvatore Erica Isabelle Astor, Princess of Ededen, the one and only heir from King Tolen Chandler Astor?"

More attuned to the battlefield, the formality in Zavier's voice brought back all the anxiety and uncertainty I'd tried to suppress. I swallowed. I needed my people to trust me today and their wavering loyalty made me nervous.

"Yes," I said.

"Do you understand the responsibility the acceptance of the crown places on you? That the duty to your kingdom will supersede all individual dedications you may wish to pursue now and in the future?"

"Yes."

"Do you swear loyalty to your people and your kingdom, to do what is best in their interest as a whole?"

"Yes." I hoped my people listened to these words. I only had their best interests in my heart.

"Everyone, bow your heads as I recite the royal blessing."

I ducked my head, but movement caught at the corner of my vision. I turned a fraction of an inch and squinted. A flash of golden hair reflected in the candlelight. Reuben, dressed in white with a golden sword at his waist, scurried behind the back row of chairs. Guards were in place to manage trouble, but suspicion bubbled inside me. Reuben disappeared through the door of a staff hallway.

"Amen," Zavier said at the end of the blessing.

I lifted my head. Reuben had disappeared into the staff hallway. He could access almost anywhere in the castle through the halls.

"We will now pass the crown."

Two guards stepped on stage and handed Zavier a pair of white gloves. He tugged them on, picked up the crown and placed it gingerly on my head.

It wasn't a feather-light, decorative circlet for special events, made from twisted wire, small gems. This was a man's crown, a king's crown. It was thick and heavy and cold. Diamonds the size of my thumb, surrounded by rubies and emeralds, danced in the light. I struggled to lift my head.

Zavier's extended his gloved hand. I took it and he helped me stand.

When I was little, I played dress up with my mother's clothes. I would wrap myself in her prettiest dress, convince her heels to fit on my small feet. I would invade her cosmetics, rubbing rogue on my face until it was all pink. I felt so elegant, so regal, until I looked in the mirror and the reflection was just a little kid in too-big clothes.

This dress wrapped too tight and the crown forced my head down. I felt like a little kid again, looking in the mirror and seeing my dreams replaced with reality.

I sat on the great throne. The cushion was hard and ornate gemstones ground into my back. My father had never complained about the chair, but he hadn't seemed excited to sit in it either. The chair symbolized my new rule as queen. Beautiful and elegant but not truly where the power resided. My authority ended in this seat and the vampire's encompassed the rest.

"The council will now be asked to confirm your place as queen. Councilwoman Andrews?"

Dark skinned cheeks pulling tight as she grimaced, Jayne Andrews brushed locks of her hair from her wrinkled face. She had been a councilwoman for almost twenty years and a royal advisor before that. Slow to accept change, she had not taken the news of the surrender well.

My heart pounded and I curled my fists on the golden throne to hide the shine of sweat on my palms. Councilwoman Andrews would announce the council's decision about my rule. If they rejected me, the surrender would disintegrate around me and plunge my people into bloodshed.

I wanted to close my eyes, but pressed my lips tight instead. Quiet murmurs shimmered among the guests. An undercurrent of eagerness spread through the room. Some of the people desired my coronation to be rejected, so they would have an excuse to evict me from the throne. They didn't know their lives and the lives of their children relied on the next words Andrews would speak.

She pushed her frail body from the seat in the front row. Magic curled around her and her voice projected throughout the room. "The council has agreed that I will speak on their collective behalf." She picked up a folded piece of paper from her chair and smoothed it flat.

Uh oh.

"Princess Salvatore Astor," she began, "the council has watched you grow. From a child walking properly behind your mother's legs, to a teenager leaning over history books in the library, now a lost young woman blindly leading a kingdom, we have watched you. And we have been mostly disappointed."

Her words cut at me.

"Although smart and obedient, you spend more time with the troops than learning legislature. Your magic craves violence in a way that has never been seen in a ruler. Once your parents disappeared, your people were hesitant to see you on the throne. Many of your decisions have been questionable."

Whispers floated through the room. Everyone talked about the decisions I had made.

I clenched my jaw so tight that it ached. Interrupting the council was unheard of. I kept a straight face and my head high under the weight of the crown. The council had never rejected a ruler at a coronation, those years of scouring history books had taught me that. If they denied me the title tonight, we would all be dead. I held no doubt King Kadence had his army ready for war at a moment's notice.

Please, please let me save my people. Please let me try.

I hadn't had the opportunity to prove myself to them yet. Preoccupied with my parents' disappearance and the looming loss of the war, I'd put my people on a back burner. I needed the opportunity to prove my loyalty to them. If the surrender succeeded tonight, I'd finally have that chance.

Councilwoman Jayne Andrews lowered the paper. She locked her gaze, pinched with age and wrinkles, on me.

"We see now that the traits we had dismissed as notions of youth, the obsession with being on the battlefield, training regularly with the soldiers, practicing magic until you honed it in battle, are the traits that will be the most beneficial to this kingdom. We see a young ruler who needs to grow and deserves an opportunity to do that."

She dipped her head.

"Collectively, this council honors the sacrifices you have made and those you will make in the future. We are ready and eager to support you in your new responsibilities." Several council members wore scowls. Andrews might speak for them, but they didn't all agree. "Sir Zavier Croft, we formally accept Salvatore Erica Isabelle Astor as our queen."

Relief flooded me. My people were less pleased. The whispers stopped, but faces turned red, jaws and fists locked. They had hoped, maybe expected, that the council would reject me. It was fair. My parents had abandoned them and I had floundered with their problems while I'd juggled the rising threat of an imminent attack. I thought of the vampire king waiting behind the curtains. My people were about to be even more disappointed.

Councilwoman Andrews bent to put her paper down and she stood clutching a glass. She held it up.

"A toast," she said. "Long live Queen Salvatore!"

Some people repeated her words, but most remained quiet. I expected that, but now I had a chance to prove myself to my people.

Zavier picked up his scroll.

"As appointed by your birthright, bound by your vows, approved by your council, on this day forth, you are crowned Salvatore Astor, Queen of Ededen."

The orchestra erupted, proud music thundering through the room. Nobody moved. I gripped the arms of the throne until my fingertips turned white. To my right, the staff door opened and closed. A figure slipped through. The dim lights barely illuminated Reuben's face as he pressed against the wall, hiding amongst the shadows.

The song ended. I forced my gaze from Reuben. The coronation was over. I was Queen, and I wanted to throw up. Eyes scorched my back through the thin curtains. The vampires were waiting.

I stood, straightened the wrinkles from my dress and balanced the weight of the crown on my head.

My magic wrapped around me and my voice spread through the Hall. Every eye turned to me and I wondered how I appeared to them. If the rouge covered the paleness of my fearful face, or if they saw beneath the layers to a girl that barely knew what she was doing.

"It has not been an easy transition since the loss of my parents," I said. "We have seen heartache, war, death, and there's an army of enemies outside our gates. Calling these times rough or difficult would be an understatement."

The words froze on my lips. Familiar and new faces watched me. Young, old, warriors, civilians, they saw their new queen and hoped for salvation.

I only held their defeat.

"I have met with the council, our marshals, mine and my father's advisor Zavier Croft, and we have all determined the reality of our situation. We have lost the war."

Gasps and cries rose in the hall. Someone in the back stood and shouted. Guards swooped in before the upheaval could increase and pulled the man outside. I waited for the shock to wear off. Quiet spread like a disease through the room.

"When a war is lost before the final battle, the losing side has choices. I could choose to fight that battle. I could watch more of our soldiers die on the battlefield, brutally slain cut by cut. I could find bodies drained of blood, husks of our people scattered on the killing lawn. I could watch as the enemy sieged the castle, my home, until we ate the bodies of our own dead. I would say goodbye to friends, soldiers, children, everyone. We would all die."

I paused and let them imagine my words. War was brutal and ugly. Most guests were civilians or from high status families. Very few, except the marshals, had ever seen a battle. I wanted them to imagine holding their dead children, starving to the point of cannibalism. I needed them to have a glimpse of every thought I had struggled with for the past six months. They needed to be as desperate as I was.

"Or," I said as horror filled their gazes, "we could all survive. Maybe not thrive, at least not right away. Maybe not declare victory over the past two-hundred-year war, but we would be alive."

I went on before any protests could ring out. "The council has approved my decision, Zavier Croft helped negotiate it, and my coronation fulfills it. As of this evening, we have surrendered to Kadence Hendrick, king of the vampires of Vari Kolum."

People yelled, spilling into shouts. Someone screamed. The guards meandered, hands on their swords, and pulled more people from the room. Some stood, some shook their fists, but nobody offered another solution.

Magic flared, bubbling across my skin, making the hairs on my arms stand up. This had to stop this before someone got hurt.

King Kadence stepped from behind the curtain. He strolled toward me, surveying the unruly crowd, and smirked. "Do I have to stab someone to get attention around here?"

"That's not funny," I told him. But it might be true.

The people in the front row noticed the king first. They paused their shaking fists and their faces turned from red to white. Several sank into their seats and one folded his hands and offered a silent prayer to his gods.

King Kadence looked at me and raised an eyebrow.

I shrugged.

Shock spread through the room. People froze, drinking in the king's sharp stance, the silver sword on his belt, the pure power that rolled from him in waves. They recognized a predator in their midst and panicked. They turned into prey, looking for a place to hide, and only found their chairs. Some hardened warriors stood, hands gripping the hilts of their weapons.

"Thank you all for that warm welcome." The king's voice was smooth, with an edge of danger, a poison apple. "I have heard many things about your people and I am glad to see most of them are true."

He reached inside his jacket and pulled out a scroll. "As your new overlord, I have prepared a speech of the expectations I hold for all of you." He let the paper open, and it unrolled down, down, and down, making a paper puddle at his feet. "Don't expect your queen to intercede. She doesn't have much power now."

He sent me a dark wink.

I bit my lip until I tasted blood.

"First—"

A sharp shout cut him off. "King Hendrick." Reuben stepped from the shadows. The candlelight flickered across his white and gold outfit. He resembled a sparkling god. He raised his sword in front of him and his hands shook. "I challenge you to a fight for rule of the kingdom and the queen's hand in marriage."

My face grew hot. "Reuben, whatever you're doing, please stop."

"I always fight for you, Sal." He licked his lips. "I'm not giving up now."

"There's nothing to fight for. It's over."

"I have rights!" He turned back to the king, "According to your law, you can be challenged at any time. You can pick a champion in your place, if you want. But that would make you a coward."

The king smiled, a truly amused show of teeth that sent chills down my spine.

"You're quite right, young man." I clenched my jaw at his condescending words. They were about the same age. "The king can be challenged at any time."

King Kadence stripped off his jacket and dropped it to the floor. He pulled his great silver sword from the sheath and twisted it, warming his wrist. The vampire stepped from the stage and met Reuben in the center of the wide aisle.

"Please, stop," I begged. One of them would likely die in this fight.

"Relax, Sal." The king eyed Reuben. I recognized the look as he calculated his opponent's skills and compared them to his own. "This won't take long."

Reuben charged. His sloppy grip caused the weapon to bounce as he ran. The king sidestepped and Reuben sprinted past him, almost charging into the crowd.

"I'm over here now." Fangs peeked through the king's smile.

Reuben charged again, a battering ram aiming for a heavy door. The king stepped away, theatrically slow. He clashed his sword against

Reuben's golden blade and the force of the blow sent the smaller man to the ground. Reuben's sword flew and he crashed to his knees.

The king picked up the sword. He walked to Reuben and held the weapon out, hilt first.

"Next time, pretend to charge, and then stop at the last minute," he said. "Your opponent won't expect the sudden change and won't be able to dodge in time." The king's eyes sparkled with laughter. He had captured the audience's attention and was destroying Reuben's confidence while establishing authority in his new rule. He was enjoying it.

Fear settled in my gut as I knew the king would be indifferent, perhaps pleased, if this ended in Reuben's death.

Reuben slashed out, quick. The sword caught King Kadence's shirt before he jumped back. He put a finger through the hole.

"I liked this shirt." He studied Reuben with a new expression.

A shadow crossed my ex-betrothed's face. The same eerie expression that had splashed across his features when I ended our engagement. It twisted him, made him into someone else.

Reuben rolled to his feet and slashed again, fast, graceful. The sloppy swings and tactics he'd previously displayed melted away in a whirlwind of skill.

The king blocked.

Reuben smashed his fist into the vampire's exposed stomach.

The king bounced away.

Reuben adjusted his grip and swiped across the king's body.

He dodged and cut at Reuben, and the edge of the blade ran across the witch's arm. Red blood swelled, shocking against his white clothes.

Reuben looked at the vampire with death in his eyes. If his magic held any trace of fighting power, Reuben would have wielded it like a second weapon. Unfortunately, his magical talents laid elsewhere.

As the two men danced across the room, a ripple of anger swelled into a waterspout of rage in my chest. My entire life so far had been in preparation for this night. It was already in shambles. My dress didn't fit and the food was growing cold. Best of all, I had signed away my kingdom to the man now in a pissing contest with my ex-betrothed. This was ridiculous.

I pushed my magic out, a whip instead of a thread. Tomorrow, there might be fights and blood and death, but not tonight. Tonight was mine.

The magic roared, a terrible dragon building a fire in her throat, eager to turn everyone to ash. It wrapped around the men's legs, twisting on itself into layers. I built them thicker and thicker. Every breath the men drew settled more magic into their bodies. The two didn't even notice.

Reuben slipped, his formal shoes losing traction on the polished marble. He stumbled to his knees, head down, mouth open. The king raised his sword over Reuben's exposed neck. It would be a single hit kill.

I pulled. The magic solidified, turning both men to stone. I plunged the magic down deeper and deeper, imagining embedding them both into the ground. I wished it was real. I longed to see their bodies wrapped in thick chains, fighting against me, as my fury only wrapped them tighter. The king was strong. His power fought me, thrashing and angry, but his anger was nothing compared to my rage.

I walked down the aisle, sinking more power into the room with every step. People shifted in their seats. *Yes, I am mad and disappointed in all of you. I want you to feel it.*

I reached the men. Slowly, I unwrapped the magical bindings from Reuben's body. I lifted one arm to help him stand.

"Sal, we can kill him. We can kill him now," Reuben whispered. He was cut and bleeding. His breath smelled like liquor.

"Go home."

"Sal, we can end this, right now."

"Go home!" I yelled. All my frustration, all my molten fear and fury, poured over Reuben, spilling into my audience. I was on fire, my head spun. "Don't you see the mess you've made?"

Reuben's eyes widened. His cheeks turned red and tears spilled down them. He shrugged from my grip and ran from the hall.

I wrinkled my nose, relieved and annoyed at his departure.

Raising my voice, I turned to the crowd. "Don't you see the mess you've all made?"

The king wrestled against the layers of my magic. He was so strong. I wouldn't be able to hold him for long.

"You are the reason we are here tonight. My parents asked for more soldiers for years and none of you picked up a sword. My parents committed their lives to this kingdom and yet you wouldn't swear loyalty to their declared heir. You have fought me every step of the way, but I have sworn vows. I understand what a promise, what my word, means. It's time to learn what it means for you."

The king shrugged off my magic like so much cloth. He lowered the sword.

I dropped to my knees at his feet, both hands on my lap, neck bowed. I had taken his kill, let his prey free into the forest. There was only one repayment.

"I will stand in for Reuben's life."

I waited for the blade to bite into my neck. Wasn't my life supposed to flash before my eyes? I could see the king's feet, spread apart in a strike stance, unmoving. Time stretched on and on. What would death feel like? Hopefully quick.

"No one?" King Kadence's voice shook the Hall.

I lifted my head. He looked around the crowd. Everyone stared at the floor or their hands, anywhere except us.

"No one will stand in place or raise arms for their queen? She has offered her life for one of her subordinates and you would all watch her execution?"

He threw the sword to the ground beside me. The marble cracked.

"You deserved to lose this war."

He stalked away, peeling back the curtain behind the throne. I caught a glimpse of Cynthia before the silk fell.

I stayed on the floor. My hands were numb and dizziness claimed my head. Zavier knelt at my side. I hadn't seen him walk to me.

"Your Majesty?" he whispered.

"Send everyone home," I said. "There's nothing to celebrate tonight."

Chapter Seven

I KNOCKED ON THE DOOR THAT HAD BELONGED TO MY father's room. Nestled at the end of the long hallway of royal suites, the doors were the largest and most intricately decorated.

Frustration from the ceremony had fled, leaving me tired and empty. I forced myself to stand tall and walk with purpose. The queen was an example to her country.

Along with the exhaustion and disappointment came dread. It was a black sludge, growing thicker with each moment I lingered in the doorway. I did not want to speak to the king. The contract was signed and I would be expected to uphold my obligations.

I belonged to him now.

"Come in," the king finally called.

I pushed the door open.

Four great windows composed the far wall, each peering into the east side of the garden. The fireplace stood centered between them, painted with gold leaf. Above it hung a thick black mantle, bare except for an uncorked bottle. A fire, which I'd ordered lit hours ago, provided the only source of warmth in the room. The four-poster bed ate away at the space, great arms stretching to the raised ceiling, and billows of black silk cascaded down to brush the floor. The blankets and sheets were also black.

There used to be a couch against the opposite wall, but it was gone, leaving the rest of the room open. With nothing hanging on the walls, the space felt too large and too empty. The room, once so familiar, was now alien and dark. Nothing of my father's remained. I'd had all of his things emptied out earlier. I'd ordered the remodel in the typical vampire style, even though it felt dark and deary to me.

The king wore the same clothes from the coronation, his jacket still missing. He was barefoot and held a glass with an inch of red-black liquid resting at the bottom. He rested one forearm against the window as he looked into the garden.

I stepped inside and closed the door.

The king took a sip from his drink. The liquid clung to the glass like rouge on a woman's lips. *Is it blood?*

"Is your room all right?" I asked. "Did you see the attached sitting room?"

He took another sip, staring into the silver-coated garden.

All right, then. I twisted my hands.

"Are your staff happy with their accommodations? I saw Cynthia in the hallway. She didn't have any complaints."

Nothing.

I took a breath. Exhaustion pulled at me, and I longed for a place to rest. There wasn't anywhere to sit other than the bed and I didn't want him to think about the bed.

"I can come back in the morning."

"Did the coronation go as you expected?" His voice was flat, unreadable.

"Not exactly." The tone made me weary. He took another drink of the red liquid.

"So you weren't planning to interfere with a direct challenge against me? To force your magic over me in front of everyone? To let a political criminal run away free?" He turned from the window, fire in his eyes. "None of that was part of your plan?"

I had overstepped my authority, embarrassed him in front of his newly conquered kingdom and stolen his opportunity to discipline a subordinate. I had nothing to say.

"Come here," he said.

I didn't move.

He arched his brow.

"Are you going to disobey the first order from your king, Queen Sal?"

"No, I'm not." I stepped forward and the room swayed. The thought of toppling over in front of this man pulled me up. I stuck my chin out. I had pride and dignity. He couldn't take that from me. My feet moved, slow but steady, and I walked toward the vampire.

I stopped two steps away. I couldn't convince myself to take the final step.

He set the glass on the mantle and closed the gap between us. Muscles played through his clothes, strong and agile, toned from years on a battlefield. He stood less than an inch away. If I drew a deep breath, my chest would touch his.

I met his eyes. Rage burned within his gaze like a wildfire, years of anger built into the depths of his soul. He didn't stare at me as though he'd conquered a kingdom and held the victory above my head. His piercing gaze held more desperation, more personal pain, than a political triumph. King Kadence carried something heavy in his heart and blamed me for it. I couldn't fault him. Years of war had turned my heart bitter in some places, too.

He raised his hand, ran it along the side of my neck, and grabbed a handful of my hair. He turned, switching our places, putting my back to the windows.

His huge body pushed against me, forcing me backward until my back hit the cold glass. Our bodies connected, shoulders to knees. I wrapped one hand around the wrist at my hair, the other a fist by my side. The white noise of battle roared in my ears.

"What do you think would happen if I broke this glass?" The king turned my head until my cheek pressed against the cold window. His eyes bounced to my exposed neck, then back at my face.

"It would be easy." His breath floated across my skin. "Glass is fragile, highly susceptible to vampire strength. What would your country do if this window shattered and you fell three stories and died in the garden?"

I licked my lips. "They wouldn't do anything."

He pushed harder. The seal of the frame groaned. My heart thundered in my ears. I wanted to close my eyes, but I couldn't look away. If these were my last moments, I needed to see them.

"That's right, Sal," he whispered. "Your country, your people, they wouldn't do anything. You have given them peace and they don't care. Yet you came to me tonight. You expected the worst and you're here anyway. Why do you keep protecting them?" Did this anger sprout from his frustration with my people's actions toward me? I didn't dare hope.

"It's my duty," I said.

"Don't lie to me."

"I'm not. I took vows. I was raised for this."

"Your father was too, but he wasn't willing to make the ultimate sacrifice for his kingdom or his daughter. He abandoned you and now you're cleaning up the mess."

"I am not my father," I said. "I have fought in this war alongside soldiers that died. My father was a capable warrior, but he didn't understand the battlefield. He never held a comrade as they bled." He never wished to trade places with a dying soldier.

"How far will you go for these people, Sal?"

"These people now include your people, *Kadence*." I guessed we were on a first name basis. "I would die for any of them."

"You're a fool."

Anger slipped through the fear. "I am willing to admit defeat in a two-hundred-year war. I am willing to set aside the loss of countless loved ones, my birthright to the throne, my body and life if you choose to take them. I have fought next to soldiers better than me and I will continue to do that for my people, for your people, for any innocent that needs to be protected. If you think that makes me a fool, you should wish the title for yourself too."

His eyes sparked. I had fueled the flames. My instincts screamed to flee and hide, but there was no escape from his hard body pressed against me. He loosened the grip on my hair and slipped his fingers between the strands. I thought, perhaps, a flash of a softer emotion drew across his face, but he pulled the cursed silver bracelet from his pocket.

"Put it on." He held it out to me. No markings marred its matte silver surface. It wrapped into a three-quarters circle with a small opening wide enough to slip my wrist through.

Memories of the dread and hopeless feeling of the loss of my magic surfaced. My hand shook as I reached out and grabbed the bracelet.

Shock pierced me along with pain, a thousand sharp cuts through my mind. I forced my hands to move. Shaking, I put the jewelry on my wrist. Unlike when I touched it in the dim tent, I knew what to expect this time, and the pain ebbed. I let out my breath. My head cleared. The opening of the bracelet sealed and it became a solid cuff on my right wrist. A witch had certainly crafted this item. What traitor would make the vampires something like this?

Kadence watched me. I piled all the hatred, all the pain and anger into my gaze so he could see hellfire in my eyes.

One corner of his mouth turned up.

"Take the dress off."

"What?"

"Take it off."

"You want...me to do it?"

He nodded.

I fumbled with the single button of the lace cardigan. At some point while breaking the fight between Reuben and Kadence, the lace had ripped. The seams stretched apart, thread unraveled and hung like golden cobwebs on my arms. It took several moments for my shaking fingers to persuade the tiny button from the hole. The freed fabric dropped to the ground in a golden puddle. The strapless white dress underneath bared my shoulders and hugged my breasts and hips.

"I guess I can take it from here." Kadence grabbed my waist and pressed against me, hot compared to the icy glass on my back.

He wrapped one hand into my hair again and pulled my head back hard. His eyes, wild and unfocused, roamed my neck, my breasts, my lips. I put my hands on his chest, maybe to push him away, but I stopped. I wasn't naive. I would do anything to keep my people alive.

"What do you think, Sal?" His breath ran over my neck. His eyes bled to silver and twin peaks of white fangs poked through the dark smile. I couldn't feel the icy window anymore with his body pressed so hard against mine. "Are they worth this, the people that would have gladly watched me kill you tonight?"

I shut my eyes, too scared of the answer that may have slipped through my lips.

The vampire stopped. Breath froze in his chest and he turned to stone against me. One hand moved to my face and he rubbed my cheek with his thumb.

He was suddenly gone.

I collapsed to my knees, scraping my hand along the rough rock hearth to stop my fall. My breath caught in my chest.

"Leave, Sal," Kadence said from halfway across the room, his back to me. "Leave me."

I rose to my shaking feet. My head swam. More controlled than a sprint, but barely, I crossed the room, pulled open the heavy door, and slipped into the hall. Afraid of what I would see in the king's face, I didn't look back.

My mother's old room felt dark and foreign. Her bed had been replaced with my own, but the familiar headboard didn't eliminate the hollow echo saying I didn't belong here.

I turned the key in the door's lock, although it only created a faux assurance of safety. If the vampire wanted in, he would make short work of the iron lock. As it clicked in place, trapping my sorrow and grief outside, a new emotion funneled from my soul—loathing. A match against paper, it consumed me from the inside out and hungered for more.

I staggered away from the door and opened the chest at the foot of the bed. Nestled on top of armor plates and leather buckles, lay my sword. The familiar weight in my palm was the bandage I needed to help heal from this broken night. Dragging the weapon with one hand, I climbed onto my bed. The fire had died long ago and the bedding harbored a chill from the brisk air.

I settled the sword beside me and pulled the blankets up to my neck. My country may crumble, but if the vampire wanted another visit tonight, he would greet sharp steel first.

Chapter Eight

"IT'S MADNESS," COUNCILWOMAN SHANNA BOWDEN SAID, smacking her hand on the table of the council chamber. "The kingdom cannot hold half of the vampire king's troops. There is nowhere to put them."

"I don't understand why they want to be here." Councilman Eric Knox's bald head bobbed when he talked. I usually had to suppress a laugh, but frustration had created a headache and I didn't feel like laughing.

Rayhan huffed beside me and settled into his chair. He and Cynthia had joined the council for the last two days. Nobody had seen Kadence since I'd fled his room the night of the coronation. I didn't ask where he was. Renee, my new staff member and Kadence's spy, waited outside the council chamber with Saffa and the guards.

"Councilman Knox, you have read the fine print of the surrender probably as many times as I have," I said again. I almost had this speech memorized. "The vampires have the right to live in either kingdom, as do our own people. Many merchant witches are already planning to sell their wares in Vari Kolum, as long as the peace is maintained. The vampires are having the same discussion that we are right now."

He crossed his arms over his chest. "It just doesn't seem fair."

I bit my tongue. Surrender wasn't supposed to be fair. We were lucky with the terms Kadence had set. I would uphold them even if it meant arguing with children.

"Would you shut up, Eric?" Jayne Andrews said, her voice cracking in the middle. The rest of the room smothered a chuckle. "Maybe if you lot had listened to the queen earlier, we wouldn't be trying to fit six thousand vampires into the city."

The vampire army still settled in the valley beyond our gates. Half would return to their kingdom, but the rest would be relocated inside. Kadence needed to maintain a show of force and have soldiers to police his new people. Shuttling supplies to their camp cost time and money.

"Look," I started again, "we have the empty barracks from the five thousand troops that..." *My parents stole from us.* "...disappeared. That leaves about a thousand people to house. See these plots of farmland?"

A map covered the meeting table, an aerial view of the entire kingdom and the surrounding two miles. Sections of green farmland spread through most of the map, but clusters of houses, shops, and common areas nestled here and there. The castle grounds stood like grey blocks. I pointed to two brown houses at the top corner, less than half a mile from the edge of the castle's perimeter.

"The families on this land have been trying to sell for years. The property is sloped and water runs down the hill, causing irrigation to be irregular and unpredictable. They haven't had a successful crop yield in almost five years. If we buy the land and employ a temporary labor assignment, we can have two new barracks built in less than a year."

"And where would the displaced farmers go?" Knox asked.

I shrugged. "They could go anywhere, Councilman Knox. They would be able to afford new plots of land or to invest in a new business."

"Where will the vampires stay while the barracks are being built?" Councilwoman Bowden asked.

"I am open to suggestions."

Julien Amos, the son of a high-status family, sneered.

The flat end of Rayhan's giant battle axe smashed onto the table. The wooden surface groaned. The legs at the rear tipped up two inches and papers slid toward me.

"Do you have something to say?" Rayhan pointed a thick finger at Amos. "Because I thought I heard you say something."

"No, you fat leech." Amos showed his teeth. "I don't have anything to say."

Rayhan stood.

"Call me that again and you won't be able to speak. I'll carve out your tongue with my axe and my aim isn't that good."

Amos pulled a sword that I was sure had never tasted blood.

I reached for my magic and found only a ragged, gaping hole. I teetered at the edge, lost inside myself. I found my footing and drew back. The bracelet looked flat and innocent on my wrist, deceptive.

"Knock it off," I commanded. "You're both grownups. Put away your toys or go sit outside."

Councilwoman Bowden clicked her tongue. "That's not very professional, Your Majesty."

"A good queen wouldn't say something so brash. I wonder what that means about you," Cynthia said.

I wished I could threaten them all with my own battle axe.

The door opened and Zavier stepped inside, holding a thick stack of paper. He paused halfway and took in the room. Rayhan's axe sat on the table, Amos had his sword pointed at the larger man, and at some point Cynthia had drawn two dainty knives. I don't know where she hid them in the skin-tight black dress, but they were clearly well-used.

"I trust everything is going well, Julien?"

Amos lowered the sword. "Yes, sir."

"Rayhan?"

"Just a bit of fun." The vampire gave a toothy smile.

"My Queen?"

I smiled, but my face felt too tight for the gesture. "We were having a disagreement about where the surplus troops can be housed while the barracks are built."

"I had a thought about that." Zavier put his papers down, shuffled through them, and pulled one out. "Why don't they stay in the common centers?"

The kingdom had three common centers. One was on the castle grounds, behind the gardens. Two were at the public parks nestled in the city. The centers hadn't been used much since my parents left. The common center building at the castle could hold almost five hundred cots.

"But then where will the summer art gallery be held?" Bowden asked.

Zavier gave the woman a bright smile and her cheeks pinkened.

"I love your passion for the arts, Shanna." He turned to me. "My Queen, do you have any alternate venue ideas for the summer gallery? I know how important community morale is to you."

Zavier was doing it again. He was setting me up to look good in front of the council. I just had to say something smart and popular.

"We can host the gallery in the Great Hall," I said. "The castle could provide food and we can evolve the gallery into a gala, with a feast and dancing."

"That would be lovely!" Shana said. The rest of the council murmured in agreement. Excited whispers trailed through the room. "And the Hall is large enough that we could invite more artists to display their work."

"That's a great idea," I agreed. "We could include some vampire artists too, as a display of our unity."

The whispers stopped. The council gave a collective sigh. Zavier smiled wide.

"That's a perfect idea, My Queen." He shot a glance at the other council members. They ducked their heads, pretending to be properly chastised. It was a ruse. There would be more problems at the next meeting. "Is there anything urgent that needs to be addressed? The queen has to look over the barracks renovations before troops start moving in."

"I think the rest can wait until tomorrow's meeting," Andrews said, shooting glares at the other members when their mouths opened.

"Thank you. Your Majesty?" Zavier gave her a short bow and held his arm out to me. I grabbed his elbow and he led me from the room. Rayhan and Cynthia followed.

"I can't leave you guys alone anywhere," Zavier said.

"You heard them. They're impossible," I said. "They'd be happier getting everyone killed."

"I'd have liked to fight the little man," Rayhan said. "My axe hasn't tasted blood in days."

We all looked at the axe. It did look surprisingly clean.

"Do you want to join the queen and me in examining the barracks?" Zavier asked the two vampires.

"No, thank you." Cynthia's voice cracked like ice in unexpected sunshine. She sent me a dark glare. "We are meeting with the king tonight."

My curiosity spiked. What did he have to talk to them about? Why hadn't he talked to me in two days? I didn't dare ask.

Zavier led me down the stairs and through the glass doors that spilled into the garden. Saffa and Renee trailed behind us. The Royal Guards remained in the castle, as Zavier and the girls were more than competent at protecting me, should the need arise.

The gardens clung to fading blooms and blended into a tapestry of pastel color. Roses, daisies, other more exotic flowers peered at us from a nest of green and shined their bright faces to the world. Heady, sweet scents filled the air, tinged with the hint of approaching fall. Summer was trickling away and the flowers would drop soon. A stone path wound around the garden, worn to a shine. The sun warmed the back of my neck and my blue dress heated in the light. It was a bit too warm for a comfortable walk, but it was nice to be outside.

I didn't look at the windows as we walked under the royal suites and Kadence's room. The memories of two nights ago made my cheeks hot, and the sun had nothing to do with it.

The barracks buildings rose in the form of grey bricks stacked on the castle lawn. The three buildings were identical. They stretched long, with a slight bend in the middle, as though a great giant had twisted them in half. The entry doors lay in the middle of the bend and more doors settled at the end of each hall. People bustled in and out of the buildings, carrying paint, ladders, rugs, and tools.

"The queen!" Teri, the barracks manager squeaked as we approached. Soft grey locks framed a face full of laugh lines and smile creases. She bowed to me.

"Teri, it's nice to see you again. I'm sorry it's been so long since we've talked."

I hadn't checked on the barracks since my parents left. Another strike against my reputation.

"Not to worry, Your Majesty," she chirped. "We're almost done here.

We'll need a couple days for the paint to dry, but I think it's going to look real nice. We talked to the, um," she lowered her voice, "the vampire. He gave us some good tips."

I smothered a frown. The vampire?

"I'm glad to hear that, Teri. I have a new member of my staff, Renee." I gestured her forward. "She's going to give the rooms a once over and let me know what she thinks."

"Oh, good. I'd walk you through myself, but I have a delayed shipment of black rugs so I'm going to see if I can light a fire under their butts to get that here." The woman bowed again and hustled to the sea of contractors piling supplies on the lawn.

We walked to the front of the building to the open door. An empty security table stood straight through the door and a hallway split to each side. The identical halls stretched on and on, a never-ending illusion. I walked to the first room and opened the door.

When our troops lived here, the walls had been painted warm neutral colors that matched the carpet. The windows had been outfitted with simple curtains and white trim. Now, the room could be called a cave. The walls were deep grey, almost black, and thick curtains covered every inch of sunshine that tried to slip inside.

I stepped aside for Renee. "This is the right aesthetic?"

She peeked around the doorway and scanned the room.

"Yes," she said, her voice flat, no hint of emotion. "Vampires like to feel close and secure. Black shrinks a room, gives it the impression of being smaller. We want to feel like our room is holding us in a sanctuary."

"I know sunlight isn't a problem, so why are there blackout curtains?"

She shrugged. "We like it dark."

"We like the curtains to match our souls," a deep voice sounded behind me. I resisted the urge to jump, and instead I bowed slowly. *See? You don't scare me.*

"My King," I said. "You honor us with your presence."

He smirked. "I wanted to make sure you weren't screwing this up."

I smiled warmly. "Please, look for yourself."

He stepped into the room. I entertained the thought of shutting the door and locking him inside. Tempting, except he could easily beat through the thin wood.

He turned to me, his mouth open to speak. He paused and his face twisted, listening.

"Do you hear that?" He looked up.

I listened, but the vampire had better hearing than me.

"What?"

"It sounds like someone is on the —"

Dust and bricks crashed down. Two giant holes punched through the ceiling, one in the barracks room and the other in the hall. Two people spilled into the barracks room, blocking Kadence's escape, and four more tumbled into the hallway. They held a combination of swords and knives like they knew how to use them.

Zavier and I sighed at the same time. Kadence titled his head at me.

"Assassins." I shrugged. What could one do?

A brush of magic trailed up my skin. The assassins were doing spellwork. I pulled on my power, prepared to twist it around us. The magic bunched against bars on a cage, caught in the emptiness of its prison stemming from the cursed silver band on my wrist. I hesitated, two seconds, and the assassins' spell tightened.

"Zavier, can you control the spell they're doing?"

"I can probably do that."

Good enough.

The group attacked. Zavier took the two to the right side, spinning and slashing. His opponents moved together, a team, fighting in unison that came with practice.

Renee held a combat knife the length of my forearm. The thick and bulky knife wasn't graceful, and she wielded it more like a battle hammer than a blade. She smashed the hilt into one assassin's face and flipped her knife across his chest. Fear widened his eyes and he fled down the hallway, dripping a trail of blood. Renee chased him.

Kadence fought both assailants in his room. He didn't draw a weapon. Instead, he bounced and dodged with fists raised near his face, letting them tire out.

Five assassins were engaged, leaving one for me. The masked figure held a feminine shape. She spun her sword, warming her wrist. Her stance was wide and stable, and her eyes followed my every move. She'd seen battle before.

I mirrored her warmup, spinning my sword in tight circles.

She bounced on the balls of her feet.

Familiar static of the battlefield began to beat through my mind, but nerves twisted my stomach. This was my first fight without magic.

She slashed at me, her sword slicing from my left shoulder to right hip. I blocked and she skirted away, still bouncing. She came again, fast and low. I knocked her blade to the side and countered with an upward flick. She danced out of range.

My mind cleared. I didn't need magic for this. The weight of the sword and the woman in black were everything I needed in this moment. My muscles, familiar with battle, warmed quickly, moving together in a coordinated performance of cuts and strikes, ducks and dodges, until I panted and sweat dripped down my face.

Laughter bubbled from the part of me that craved battle.

My assailant stumbled back and wiped her hand over her forehead. She thought she was safe, thought she had a moment to recover, regroup. She underestimated my speed. I slashed across her arm. The edge of my blade came away with blood. Through the slit of her black hood, her eyes went wide with shock.

She stepped toward me and cut at my torso.

I sidestepped. Her blade chopped at my chest and I paused and let her sink into the blow.

She committed. Her weight leaned forward, her legs too far apart. I would take a hit, but she wouldn't recover in time. She tensed when she saw it, too late.

The sword cut into my chest. It ran a straight line between my breasts to my stomach, long and shallow. Lines of fire followed the gash, spreading out along the sensitive nerves. Pain roared through my mind and I soaked it up. I gathered each tongue of flame and stoked them into an inferno. It fueled my strength.

Her arms locked straight between us, sword tip embedded in the ground.

I punched her in the face. Blood sprayed from her nose, but she kept her grip on the sword. I hammered my knee into her stomach. Air and blood bubbled from her broken nose and she choked. Both hands clutched her face. The sword fell to her feet.

I sliced my sword across her throat, quick and deep. Blood poured onto the floor. She collapsed to her knees and fell to the side. I kicked her sword out of reach, just in case.

I felt Kadence watching me. Both of his opponents lay on the ground in bloody heaps. He'd never even drawn a weapon.

Exhaustion wrapped around me, but my soul sang. The fight would have been easier, quicker, with my magic, but I hadn't needed it. My body had recognized the familiar tune of battle and danced perfectly. Adrenaline made me high.

"Sal, are you all right?" Zavier appeared in the doorway. Blood splattered his face, but he remained in one piece.

"Assassins?" Kadence gestured at the carnage on the ground. "Neither one of you looked surprised."

Zavier and I glanced at each other.

"It's been happening," I said.

"They wanted to kill you?"

"Yes."

"And this isn't the first time it's happened?"

We shook our heads.

"Why?"

I shrugged. "You said yourself that the people are unhappy with my rule. It seems a rogue band may be determined to do something about it."

"You didn't mention that at the negotiation."

"I didn't think it mattered."

"It matters if you're not alive to uphold your country's end of the deal."

"I'm alive. See?" I spun in a circle. "I'm fine." The cut burned like acid on my skin.

"You're a mess. Your dress is slashed and you're covered in blood."

"And you're so perfect with..."

Kadence's long sleeve black shirt and breeches were spotless. His hair remained neatly combed as if it hadn't moved the slightest in the fight. Not a single drop of sweat shone on his forehead.

He gave me a smug smile. "You were saying?"

Zavier cleared his throat. "Sorry to interrupt this very important conversation, but I need to call a cleaning crew to take care of the bodies.

I'll have a physician examine the corpses and will let you both know when they're identified . I imagine that there will not be any obvious connections between the assassins, the same as the previous attacks."

He turned to me with a sinister twinkle in his aging eyes. "It's a lovely day. I bet the king would appreciate a tour of his new kingdom."

"That's a great idea. I'll have Saffa arrange a guide."

"Actually, My Queen." Zavier's smile could catch flies. "I cleared your schedule so you could take him. It would be best if he saw Ededen through the eyes of the person most invested in it."

Years of etiquette training, yet I only mustered a squeak from my throat. I had a lot to do today. I needed to check on the number of volunteers for the blood donation program, secure the land for the new barracks, and avoid the king as much as possible. Going on a tour of the kingdom with Kadence wouldn't accomplish any of that.

A body stared blankly at my feet. This would have been the fate of my country. It still could be. I needed the king to fall in love with this place and my people.

I nodded. "That does sound...good. Your Majesty?"

He smiled, but it didn't touch his eyes. "Yes, that would be...good."

"Wonderful." Zavier tucked my hand into the crook of his elbow and pulled me toward the door leading out. "We'll go to medical and get the queen patched up. She will meet you in the foyer when she's ready."

Zavier half-led, half-pulled me outside. I squinted into the morning sun. Renee leaned against the building, a body face down at her feet, her knife gone. She straightened as we approached.

"Thank you," I told her.

She nodded. Her beige dress hadn't caught a single speck of blood. I was the only one who had any wounds. I silently cursed the silver bracelet on my wrist. It would have been a better fight if I had my magic.

The gaping hole threatened to swallow me, but I pulled against it. I was more than that. I would learn to live without magic. I had to.

Chapter Nine

A WITCH IN OUR MEDICAL FACILITY PATCHED ME UP WITH A disapproving glance and told me to be more careful next time. I assured the nice healer that I didn't intend there to be a next time and he laughed at me.

Saffa helped wipe the blood off my skin and I buttoned on a new, emerald dress trimmed with cream lace. She wrapped my long, brown hair into a low bun, and I was ready for a tour with the king.

I found him in the foyer between the staircase and the hallway of the royal suites. He wore a different set of black clothes. I didn't see any weapons, but he had killed two people with his bare hands this morning. He didn't need weapons to be dangerous. As I walked down the hall he turned and his dark eyes scanned my body. My cheeks burned, but I didn't alter my stride.

"Why does it take you so long to get ready?" he asked.

My headache returned. I smiled.

"The stableboy prepared the horses, so we can leave if you're ready."

"I've *been* ready."

"Fantastic."

It would be a miracle if we both survived this.

Two horses waited for us. My usual mount, a young white mare named Vry with a brown stripe across her nose and four white socks on her feet pawed impatiently at the stall door. While not battle-trained, she was fast and reliable. The mare King Kadence had given us to ride home after the surrender stood in the aisle, saddled up and ready for him.

Kadence's face lit up at the sight of the horse. He touched the animal with warm affection and whispered softly to her. He brushed along her side, spending time scratching the itchy spots. A new look settled on Kadence's face. Beneath the layers of hardness, a glimpse of joy stared out. Once the horse seemed content, he leaped into the saddle, and the mare rocked as she adjusted to the weight.

"Her name's Juniper," he said as he smiled at the horse. When he looked back at me, his eyes dulled and the momentary joy fell into that burning fire of rage.

I turned away from all that anger and we mounted up. I set the pace, steering Vry along the well-trodden trail out of the stables and in the direction of town. She found a rhythm and the motion settled my twisting gut. A breeze tugged at my dress, cooler than I had expected, given how hot it was this morning. Fall would be here soon. Leaves scattered through the dense foliage. Animals scurried from their dens, already searching for food to store for winter.

The silence between the king and I gaped as wide as a cavern. It was uncomfortable, an itch on my back I couldn't scratch. I remembered how he looked at me in his room, the hate and pain. How he turned away from me so sharp and sudden. I didn't know what to say to this man, but the quiet felt wrong.

"Why is the horse named Juniper?" I finally asked.

"My dead mother named her."

"Oh."

Great job. The cavern spanned another inch as we both thought about his dead mother.

"Aren't you wondering why I sent you home that night on a horse my mother had named?"

"I wasn't going to ask."

The horses snorted at each other, reacting to the emotions of their riders. Vry flicked her ears back and forth, no doubt wondering if she should be concerned.

"My mother always wanted peace." Kadence rode stiff and upright. His eyes scanned our surroundings constantly and his hand lingered near his sword. "She worked her whole life for it. I thought if I let you ride home on her horse, maybe she'd somehow know that she had helped orchestrate that peace."

"That's a very nice thought," I said. My throat tightened. Maybe the fire and hatred he kept showing me hid different feelings of loss and loneliness, emotions he couldn't quite comprehend in himself. I turned my face from his to hide any rogue pity that may have sparked in my eyes.

"Is it?" Kadence's fingers played on his sword hilt. "It's a lie. My mother never cared about horses. She and my father plotted daily to wipe this kingdom out and kill everyone in it. She would be disappointed if she saw me today, riding alone in the woods with the witch queen and not even holding a knife in my hand."

Anger clawed at me. I should have known he didn't have a sincere bone in his body. My hands curled tight around the reigns.

"If you don't want to talk, you don't have to make up lies."

He raised an eyebrow. "Don't I?"

I clamped my jaw. I didn't have anything appropriate to say and several things I wanted to say might get me killed.

I dug my heels into my horse's hide and she sped to a trot.

The green of the forest spit us abruptly onto a cobblestone street. More horses, wagons, and pedestrians milled around clustered housing buildings, through an open market, and disappeared deeper into the town. The colorful buildings stood one or two stories tall, and were filled with the hustle and bustle of everyday life. One woman piled fresh bread onto her stand and another rocked a baby on the balcony of a second story.

There was a type of magic here, the magic of routine and dependability. The details may change—the woman might put out sourdough bread instead of white or wheat—but it was consistent. I could imagine myself as the baker's wife, selling our goods on the street, under the open air, and the house always smelling like fresh bread. I could almost feel the weight of a tiny baby in my arms, gentle cries filling my heart.

I wrapped the images up, put a beautiful bow around them, and cast them into the fire of my mind. I'd never had a simple, routine life and I never would. Pain dug into my soul when I imagined it.

We started down the street, our horses making soft clip clops against the stone road. People stared while we rode. A few bowed when we passed, but most awkwardly skirted away.

"Your people aren't very respectful." The king wore half a smile, but his lips were pressed together. I wondered if his jaw was clenched as tight as mine.

"It was different for my parents," I said. When our family rode to town together, people went out of their way to see them. By the time we headed back to the castle, the streets would be lined with people stretching their hands to rub my mother's cloak or catch a scent of my father's spiced perfumes. They used to smile at me, waving their hands until I waved back.

Six months in charge and I had lost them.

"What happened?" Kadence asked. The people that ignored us craned their necks to look at the vampire king after we passed. A wake of open-mouthed onlookers stood in the street behind us, blocking horses and wagons that also stopped to gape at the king.

I shrugged.

"I wasn't ready. I could have handled the people's problems or an amassing vampire horde. I couldn't do both, not right away. My parents had stolen our army and in a single night, we went from well-secured to defenseless. There weren't enough soldiers. I had to implement a draft."

There had been protests in the streets. Mothers made their children hold signs that said, 'I don't belong on the battlefield.' Protesters raided training camps, drafted soldiers stolen out of barracks and attempted to be smuggled over the borders to nearby kingdoms. I had to take away our fighting force, already outnumbered and at war, and use them to patrol our own city. Fighting on the battlefield myself didn't quench anyone's anger, not even my own.

I wasn't ready to spill that information to the king. He didn't know me and hadn't earned the right to criticize my rule.

"It was not a popular decision," I said, instead.

"What did your parents say when they left?"

I smothered a frustrated laugh and an awkward snort came out.

"They didn't say anything. I woke up and Zavier said half of our troops were gone, and he couldn't find my parents. There was no warning, no message, and no sign of anyone."

"Five thousand people don't just disappear without a trail."

"I know. We sent out our best trackers, witches whose magic could pluck a single feather from a flying bird. They couldn't even find what direction they went." I had sent my own magic combing through miles and miles of land, until I passed out in the woods in the middle of the night, and Zavier had to drag my freezing body back home. I had gotten a good lecture about that.

"Do you think they are looking for the Fields of the Dead?"

An involuntary shiver slipped down my spine. If my parents found the Fields, the vampires would be the least of my problems.

"I hope not. I hope they're not that stupid."

"They were stupid enough to abandon their half-trained daughter and their country. They might be stupid enough to look for the Fields," he said.

I waited to be angry at his words, but I could only conjure sadness. Thinking about my parents made my chest hurt.

"Why did you go into hiding after your parents died?" I asked. If my chest had to hurt, his should too. "Although you'll probably just lie to me again."

He shrugged. "I didn't really hide. I spent a lot of time in battle, but I killed everyone I fought. Lots of people saw me, I was just the last thing they saw."

Other words left my mind. I didn't want to think about him methodically slaughtering my people in battle. I shouldn't have asked at all.

"We're nearing the market," I said. "Don't stop or you will have to buy something."

The cobblestone path split into a fork and I led us to the right. It skirted along the tree line and then opened into the market. The market doubled the size of the Great Hall, stretching down and down along the street. Horses and riders trotted between thongs of people, yelling at each other to get out of the way. Hundreds of little tents and fabric canopies stretched across the paved ground, each portraying specialty items for sale.

Venders sold food, art, magical trinkets. Almost anything could be bought at the market.

Most people wore robes and dresses in vibrant colors, but I spotted a few dressed in black. Some of them were new vampire patrols, holding hammers, axes, and spears, but some were off duty soldiers milling through the stands and talking to salespeople. The vendors talked back, some sounding apprehensive, but never able to pass up a sale.

Kadence's mouth gaped a bit. He blinked before putting on a blank face. By the time he sent an arrogant smile my way, it was as though I hadn't seen his surprise. But I had, and the moment of vulnerability bothered me. It was easier to imagine him as a stone wall, annoying and unfeeling, than someone that could look at the splendor of the market and the blending of two nations, and actually feel something.

An old woman trotted to us, dangling charms and little potions filling her hands. She gave a halfhearted bow.

"Look, look, My King and Queen." She shook her arms so vigorously, the draping sleeves of her robe bounced. "These are a very good deal. Two charms for the price of one. I have charms for everything! You need luck?" She plucked a green token from the bunch. "You need money?" Another charm. "You need help in the bedroom?" She wiggled her eyebrows and gave us a toothy grin.

My face got hot.

Kadence laughed. "Yes, the queen needs that one. I'll buy all the ones you have!"

"Kadence, don't," I said through a locked jaw.

"How much?"

"For you..." She tapped her chin. "Two-hundred coins."

"That's ridiculous!" I said.

"Done!" Kadence fished through his pockets and bent down to hand her the coins. She held the gold pieces to her face and her eyes welled with tears. The vampire had handed her much more than two-hundred coins.

She bowed low and the tears rolled from her face and dripped in the grass.

"Thank you, thank you. Wait here, wait and I'll be back." She hurried to her tent and began stuffing charms into a woven black and white bag.

"What are you doing?" I asked.

He watched the woman blankly. "What? She said it would make you better in bed."

"I don't need to be better," I had to swallow, "in bed," I whispered.

"How do you know?" He winked at me, but turned back to the woman. "Besides, look how happy she is. She gets to impress her king and make enough money not to worry about her sales for the week."

The woman came back and pressed the bag into Kadence's hands.

"All of the charms you wanted, My King, and a couple extra."

The blush burning my cheeks felt as though it would never go away.

Kadence caught the woman's hand. He bowed his head over it and gave her wrinkled fingers a soft kiss.

"Thank you. I'll come back when the queen has more problems." He leaned over the side of his horse and whispered loudly, "I'm sure I'll be back often."

We rode through the market and Kadence dragged us to a stop at every other stand. He sampled food that vendors pressed against his lips and left golden coins in their hands just for the taste. He loaded his pockets with knives, blankets, and potions. When his pockets filled, he handed things to me, until both of our arms were weighed down with a small fortune of goods.

His dark features lightened with laugher. He flirted easily with the women and carried on, joking with the men. He recounted war stories to several veterans and it was as though they had been on the same side. Every stand that we left, the people smiled, and they waived as we rode away.

We exited the market and urged our horses into a quieter part of town, until the last few stragglers following us turned away.

Kadence's brightness slowly died and his smile faded. Deep circles lined both eyes and he sighed. I wanted to hold on to the man at the market, but with each step our horses took he transformed back into the vampire king. When he looked at me, his face was flat again.

"Is there a shelter we can donate these things to?" he asked.

I didn't compose my expression fast enough.

"Don't look so surprised," he said, "I need the people to like me, I don't need any of their junk."

I rolled my eyes. The sadness and compassion melted away. When would I stop trusting him?

"There's an orphanage on the way to our last stop." I looked at the artwork, blankets, and knickknacks clustered in our arms. "I think the children would enjoy most of this."

We dumped the haul at the orphanage stoop, knocked on the door, and rode away before anyone answered. Kadence didn't want the vendors to know he had chucked their stuff. It would have tarnished his budding good impression if the witches learned Kadence had tried to purchase a positive reputation.

We'd ridden through most of the city, excluding the expanses of farmlands nestled along the border. Zavier told me that Kadence needed to see Ededen through the eyes of the person most invested in it. Before I took the throne, that would have been my parents, and they had a special place we used to visit together.

Our horses panted as they trekked up the tallest hill in the inner kingdom. The hill climbed over the west side, directly opposite of the castle. Exposed branches and protruding rocks in the dirt path forced the horses to pick their steps.

"Are you finally leading me to where you're going to try to kill me?" Kadence asked. He hadn't spoken since we'd left the orphanage, over half an hour ago.

"No, unfortunately not."

The gradient of the hill flattened. One moment we only saw trees and dirt, and then the city spilled before us, a mosaic of land and life, stretching farther than I could see.

Most of the kingdom spread across flat fields and gentle slopes. The land was good for farming, though vineyards also found success. We imported most of our livestock, but some ranchers lived in the outer edges of the kingdom. The city walls spread like giant snakes, winding through town and trapping most of the population inside. Thick clusters of houses and buildings grouped through the inner space, with occasional breaks for parks and grandfathered farms. A small river snuck through the edge of town, peppered with bridges. Beyond the gates, neat sections of farmland reflected different colors at us. Rich golden wheat sprouted beside the wetlands of rice fields. Directly across from our perch point, the castle stood, tall and strong, the beacon of security to the kingdom. Its structure and consistency said home to me and I was eager to be back soon.

"The city looks bigger up here," Kadence said. The setting sun reflected in his eyes. His hands and shoulders appeared loose, relaxed as he looked over the land he had claimed as his own.

"Is this what your kingdom looks like?" I asked.

He shook his head. "It's different."

"How?"

"We don't have as much space."

My parents used to bring me here when there was a lesson I was struggling with. My dad would hoist me onto his horse, look over the kingdom and point out different buildings and crops. He reminded me that the people came first, that even if I failed a thousand history or strategy lessons, if I remembered the people, I would be a great queen. My mother's mouth would twist and she'd smack the back of his head, but I would see her smile when she turned away.

"This is my favorite place." I felt dumb as the words left my lips. He didn't care about me.

A breeze pushed over the hill and cooled the tears on my cheeks. When did I start crying?

Kadence watched me with his dark, unreadable eyes. He watched while I wiped the tears on my sleeves and then he turned away, back to the scattering of glowing lights beneath us. Silently brooding on our own thoughts, we watched the sunset.

Chapter Ten

I STILL HADN'T SETTLED INTO MY MOTHER'S ROOM. THE massive space dwarfed my four-poster queen bed frame. The arched ceilings were the highest in the castle, peaking in the center, framed with wooden beams and accented with hints of gold paint. Pale waterfalls of white silk cascaded over the beams. The portraits of my family had been brought in and they stared at me, still and cold.

It had been true dark when we arrived back at the castle. Saffa, Elaine, and Renee drew me a bath, which had chased away the chill of the night. I put on a thick cotton nightgown and a long robe. A large fire warmed the room. I curled on the blue-and-gold couch under a blanket, savoring its warmth.

I wrapped my fingers in the blanket, tugged them free, and wrapped them again. A weight sank in my chest, threatening to pull me down. I pushed against it. If I went down, I might never get back up.

Kadence would come tonight. I wouldn't go to his room again and hatred burned in his heart. He would come.

The silken edge of the blanket pulled along my fingers as unease tugged at me. Kadence at the market today had been different than Kadence in his room after my coronation. His face lit up at the sight of the people and true joy etched into the smile lines across his mouth. When he looked at my people, he didn't hold fire in his eyes, only when he looked at me. It was as though the man were two sides of the same coin—one side relatable and kind, the other pained and angry.

Anxiety twisted its serpent head in my chest. Which side of the king would find me tonight and why did I secretly hope for something besides hatred to burn in his gaze?

The creak of the door opening made me jump and clutch at my blanket. Kadence slipped inside. He closed the door, quieter than a pop of the fire.

The king had broken from his black ensemble and wore a white button up shirt, black breeches, and no shoes. He looked at my pile of blankets and found a half smile.

"You have too many clothes on." He reached into his pocket and pulled out a charm from the market. "This says you have to be naked for it to work."

The flames danced in his eyes, though if it was a reflection from the fire or that burning hatred, it was hard to tell.

"Why are you here, Kadence?" I asked. The blanket was soft. The fabric couch hugged me, enticing me to stay. Between the king and assassination attempts, constantly being on guard drew me to the edge of exhaustion. I'd like nothing more than to curl on the couch and sleep, although it would be impossible while the hungry gaze of a predator rolled over me.

Kadence stalked around the room. He ran a hand down the plush comforter on the bed, over the wooden vanity in the corner, across the top of the empty copper tub. I turned as he walked, keeping him in sight.

He paused at the portraits of my parents near the door. He pressed one finger lightly on the canvas picture of my mother.

"Why do you have their pictures up?"

"They're my parents," I said.

"They left you."

I shrugged. "They're still my parents."

He looked at me and that flicker of darkness crept across his face. The man from the market was gone, leaving the vampire in his wake. Kadence crossed the room, slow and careful. I didn't dare move. I didn't want to anger the beast.

Kadence plucked the blanket off.

"I was using that," I said, drowning my fear with sarcasm.

He grabbed my hips, drawing my feet to the floor. He stepped between them, demanding space from my body, and put both hands on either side of my head to grip the back of the couch. Inches away, he sucked the air from the room. His power brushed me, twisting and dangerous. I was sweating, but not just from the heat. Beneath the layers of logic screaming that the vampire stood much too close, something akin to desire stretched from my core. Kadence's smoke and earth scent twisted between us and I held my breath to prevent the intoxicating smell from overwhelming me.

"You always have too many clothes on." His breath trailed down my throat. There was a rawness to his tone, and even as the beat of my blood spread so close under his lips, I couldn't tell if hunger or desire colored his words. Maybe Kadence wasn't a coin with only two sides. Maybe a third side hid, waiting for the right person to draw it out.

He pressed the side of his face against mine. The rough edge of stubble caught at my skin. A shiver crept down my spine. He brushed his lips along the side of my face and pressed a kiss against my pulse. I couldn't move. I waited for the sting of sharp fangs and tried to decide if anticipation or fear made my heart beat faster.

He leaned back. "Are you going to cry again?"

"You're a fool." I pushed against his chest, but I may as well have been pushing against a solid wall.

He laughed, rich, low and rumbly. Something caught in my heart. This was a real laugh, not a cruel mock. The sound stoked the flames creeping low in my body, even as my mind tried to remind me that Kadence might still be my enemy.

Kadence's voice faded. His eyes widened, as though the laughter had surprised him too. Confusion and insecurity chased away the hate and rage in his face. He smoothed the traces of emotion, settling into a blank expression. Beneath that carefully painted look, a hint of desire peeked out.

He put one hand under my leg and the other around the back of my neck. As though I weighed nothing, he lifted me from the couch and traded places. He fell onto the plush cushion, pulling me on top of him. I squeaked and Kadence locked his arms around my waist, trapping me against his body.

His chest rose and fell with every gentle breath. He was so warm and he smelled like fire and horses. This wasn't the kind of rage that promised retribution at my coronation. This was the man in the market, bending his will to satisfy the people. I wondered if I could eventually coax him from his angry shell forever. For now, maybe I could relax here, curled and comfortable on the couch, and we could rest.

The king slipped the robe from my shoulders. Adrenaline cut through me, sharp. He brushed his hands down my arms, leaving behind tingling trails. His eyes searched my face, looking for something he might never find. His fingers grazed the back of my neck and he freed the band from my hair, letting curls cascade down my back. Kadence ran his hand through the locks, watching with those predator eyes as each strand fell. Sparks popped under my skin. My cheeks burned and air turned stagnant in my lungs.

I opened my mouth. To ask him to stop, or continue? I wasn't sure I could speak and feared which words would slip from my mouth.

"Why do you have the portraits of your parents?" His breath was feathers on my cheek.

"You want to talk about my parents right now?"

He nodded. His fingers played in my hair, twisting the damp strands, and I pretended it wasn't distracting.

"They abandoned you," he said. "They took everything. Look where their choices have brought you. Why do you want to see their faces every day?"

It was a good question. I didn't know how to put years of experiences and emotions into a simple sentence.

"They loved me." The words caught in my throat. They did love me, and that made their absence so much worse. They didn't love me enough to stick around. I squashed the thought and locked it away. "They are just people and people make bad decisions. I am angry and sad and confused, but I can feel all of those things and still love somebody."

"You can, but should you? They treated you like you're disposable,

Sal. They raised you and molded you and then threw you away. Why do you love them still?"

His brows were smooth, his jaw relaxed, but silver eyes exposed his pain. I searched his face, digging through the layers of protection, past the bloodthirsty gaze of a starving predator, and looked for Kadence buried inside.

I brushed my fingers over his cheek. My fingertips danced from his temple along the edge of his jaw. He closed his eyes.

"Who hurt you, Kadence?" My voice was a whisper, a gentle breeze between the two of us. The atmosphere between us shifted. I wasn't sure if the space separating our bodies, which had felt suffocatingly close moments ago, was short enough now.

"I—"

Three hard knocks beat against the door. It swung open before I could speak and Reuben stepped into my room. The firelight turned his white shirt to a gold that matched his breeches. He didn't have a weapon on his waist, but the fists clenched at his side suggested he may have longed for one.

Reuben stopped, halfway between two steps. His eyes locked on us and his jaw dropped.

I pushed from Kadence's lap and the vampire let me go. Putting both arms along the back of the couch, he crossed his legs. His eyes turned dark again as they scanned Reuben. The wheels of battle turned behind them. He was likely predicting how another fight between them would go.

I snatched the robe from the floor and tied the sash around my waist. My nightgown was modest, but I nestled into the soft fabric as though it was my armor on the battlefield.

"Sal?" Reuben asked in a small voice.

"You can come in," I said, rushing to shut the door. "Nothing was happening."

"Nothing?" Kadence watched us without betraying a hint of emotion.

"What do you want Reuben?" I asked, ignoring Kadence's burning gaze on my back.

"I came to apologize for the other night and to check on you. Zavier reported another assassination attempt to the council." He looked over my head to stare at the vampire. "The guard in the hall told me you were alone."

"She was not," Kadence said in a guarded tone, although hints of anger slipped through.

"I can see that," Reuben snapped.

"Both of you shut up." If I let this continue, they would decide to find some rulers and measure a few things out. "You don't have to apologize to me and you can see that I'm fine. You should go, Reuben."

He caught my hands and pressed them tight between his.

"Why are you even still in this castle?" I jumped at Kadence's sharp voice. "Shouldn't you be hiding in the woods with your tail between your legs?"

I suppressed the desire to roll my eyes. "Reuben is one of our statisticians. He helps determine the cost and personnel risk with certain strategies."

"Are you all right? Zavier told me you had to kill someone," Reuben ignored the king's question.

"I've killed a lot of people, Reuben."

"But this was a witch, one of your own people."

I gently plucked my hands out of his grip and stepped away.

"They're all my people now," I said.

"You know what I mean." Reuben's eyes were tiny pools of water inviting me to come and rest. They were so different from the invigorating black and silver of the vampire. After the desire that had sprouted between Kadence and me, I wasn't sure I wanted to rest now.

"Please leave, Reuben."

Kadence's silence began to worry me, but I didn't turn to look at him.

"Zavier identified the bodies," Reuben said.

I groaned. Why didn't Zavier tell me this himself?

"And?" Kadence almost growled the words.

"Two of them had stands at the market." Reuben talked to me as though I had answered him. "One sold fine clothes and the other general supplies. Neither of them had a known history of combat training. The four others were ex-military. They only had two-year contracts though."

"That doesn't explain why they all fought so well," I said.

"What does one of your soldiers learn in a two-year contract?" Kadence asked.

"Basic hand-to-hand and sword combat. If they have any magic, we'll train that up too. It would be beginner stuff. We're not going to focus a lot of time and resources on a two-year contract," I said.

"We send the short contracts to supply and transportation, unless they have a specific magical talent. Our army wouldn't have given these guys much training," Reuben said.

"So they learned combat from somewhere else?" Kadence asked.

Reuben nodded. I bit my lip and studied the implications. The rogue rebel group may have been stronger than Zavier and I feared. They likely had superior combat trainers in their ranks.

"Is that all you have to tell us?"

Reuben pressed his lips into a thin line.

Kadence stood from the velvet couch and walked toward us. Each step was deliberate, slow, as though it took the entirety of his self-control to walk instead of run. His hands hung loose at his side, but tension tightened the muscles in his arms. He stopped, two steps away. The beat of his power wrapped us in a deadly hurricane.

"You need to leave," Kadence said, low and dangerous.

Reuben looked between me and the vampire.

"Will you be all right?" he asked, reaching for my hand again. I stepped back, out of his reach.

"She will be fine," Kadence bit. "I cannot say the same about you if you choose to stay."

"Sal—"

"Go!" Kadence yelled.

Reuben's eyes widened. His face bubbled into a strawberry red. With one more glance at me, he fled.

Kadence grabbed the doorknob. The metal creaked under his fingers. All the vulnerability, the little trust we had built, fell away like wax dripping down a candle. The rage returned in its place.

"Next time we talk, Queen Salvatore," he said, "I'll remember what 'nothing' sounds like."

"Kadence—"

"Don't." He pulled the door open and escaped my room. The darkness swallowed him up and the door slammed shut.

I flinched.

My heart weighed heavy in my chest and pressure built in my head, but I refused to cry. I had shed too many tears already. The couch caught me as I fell into it and the softness of the blanket was the sweet caress I craved. I watched the fire until the flames died and I was alone with the glow of the embers.

Chapter Eleven

THE HALLWAYS HAD NEVER FELT SO LONG. PAINTINGS AND doors blurred as I ran past them. My shoes clicked on the stone floor and people jumped out of my way with quick apologies as I smiled and hurried by. My soft, simple black dress clung to my legs as I ran, slowing me down. My mother's voice told me that princesses don't run, but I told her I was the queen now, and she needed to be quiet.

Saffa stood in the hallway connecting the council room to the main entry room at the front of the castle. A neat braid of her blond hair hung down the back of her red dress. She straightened when she saw me.

"Queen Sal, I have something to tell you," she said.

"Can it wait?" I slowed to a fast walk and she fell into step beside me and matched my pace.

"No, Your Majesty, I—"

"I'm very late to the council meeting, Saffa. Is someone in danger?"

"No, but—"

"Dying?"

"No, Sal—"

The cool door handle chilled my sweaty palm. I pushed it open and stepped into the council room.

"I'm so sorr—" The apology fell from my lips.

"Your Majesty." Saffa said behind me, her voice more than a little smug. "I wanted to inform you that the king is joining the council today."

"Thank you, Saffa." I sent her a tight smile over my shoulder. "I see that now."

King Kadence sat in my seat at the head of the table. He leaned his chair back at a dangerous angle and both feet were propped on the wood slab. One hand held a stack of papers, and his dark eyes peeked suspiciously over them.

Julius Amos's face held a red hue, and Jayne Andrews looked between him and the king, smothering laughter.

Saffa mumbled under her breath. She would forgive me eventually.

I shut the door. The last open chair sat between Shanna Bowden and Eric Knox. They didn't acknowledge me as I settled into it.

"Thank you for blessing us with your presence, Queen Sal," Kadence bit off. "I expect there's a good reason you're late?"

I felt like a child being chastised by her mentor. Unlike the way I behaved in my studies, I bit my tongue. Kadence wanted to bait me and I needed to be sharp. This was going to be a nightmare.

"Is Zavier attending this meeting?" I asked.

"I told him not to," Kadence said.

"Why did you tell the First Seneschal not to attend a council meeting, which happens to be one of his main responsibilities to advise?"

"I didn't want him to interrupt us."

Frustration ripped through my chest like an ugly monster, but I smiled at the king. "What have I missed?"

"The King," Amos made the word a question, "was recommending pulling funding from our offensive troops."

"I wasn't recommending, I ordered it."

"That's not how these meetings work." Amos said through clenched teeth.

"That's how they work when I'm here."

I set both of my hands on the table. The wood grounded me. It was cold and firm, a contrast to the tense conversation in the room.

"Councilman Amos, why do you think the funding should remain unchanged?" I asked.

He reluctantly turned to me. He might hate the king, but I wasn't much better in his eyes.

"We have never cut our military budget in the history of our kingdom," he said. "The soldiers keep us safe from threats both out and inside the walls."

I pressed my lips at his comment. Amos implying the king may be a threat bordered on treachery. I side-eyed Kadence, but he'd fit a half-smug smile across his face and remained silent.

"We have always been at war, until now. We are cutting our troops in half. There is a committee dedicated to combining forces with the vampire army to protect and police our people. Why does our budget need to stay the same if our defenses are minimized?" I asked.

Amos's face darkened. He tried to kill me with his stare and if his magic was stronger, he may have succeeded.

"Because they're in our kingdom," he spat. "We need soldiers to keep us safe from the creatures you let into our home. My children have nightmares that the blood-drinkers are going to kill us. Telling them we have soldiers trained and ready lets them sleep at night."

Dark circles under his eyes and his slumping shoulders said that his children weren't the only ones losing sleep. Knox, Bowden, and even Andrews, sported similar expressions. My council was scared and I had missed it. Dumb, Sal.

My next words would balance across a fine line. Amos had basically called Kadence and the vampires a threat against the kingdom. Kadence could order him killed for that accusation and my hands would be tied to halt the execution.

The king's gaze remained fixed on Amos, but I felt his subtle attention crawl over my skin. He would fixate on my answer and I needed him to realize Amos's comment came from a place of fear. That inside, we were all a little afraid.

"My King." I lowered my voice. Everyone leaned closer. "How long has it been since the surrender was fulfilled?"

Kadence's face scrunched, but he didn't move.

"Almost two weeks. Why?"

"Before the surrender, we had five thousand active troops in the kingdom. They were split into three eight-hour shifts, so at any point one third of our forces were asleep."

Eyes flicked as they followed my math.

"When there wasn't a battle, our soldiers were training, scouting, preparing to fight at any moment. We maintained a force of roughly six hundred soldiers to protect those of us inside the kingdom walls. My King, how are our troops delegated now?" I asked.

Kadence shuffled through his papers, but I knew it was an act. He could recite the patrol numbers from the top of his head.

"Our combined forces top eleven thousand troops. The vampires maintain most of the external perimeters and the witches patrol the city. We split the defense of the main gate and the castle evenly."

"Thank you, My King." I turned back to Amos. I spoke to him, but the quiet in the chamber meant everyone was listening. "As you heard, all of our soldiers are now inside the walls. We have never had more of our forces available to protect our people. Please let your children know that if they are ever in trouble, it will be witches arriving to help them."

"It won't stay like that if the budget is cut," Amos said.

I forced my lips into a small smile. "Zavier is composing a five-year plan to manage the transition. The vampires will be here for a long time, so please don't expect immediate change. As our countries assimilate, the need for so many soldiers will decrease. We are not at war anymore. We do not need thousands of soldiers to protect us. Over time, the military budget will be minimal, and we will be equally safe. Our people look to the council for how they should react. I am asking you to be an example of peace and patience during this period. It will get better, I promise."

Amos's face returned to an almost normal color. He gave me a sharp nod and then twisted his expression as though the polite gesture had left a bad taste in his mouth.

"So nobody is going to cry over cutting the defense budget by ten percent in the next year?" Kadence asked.

"No," the council muttered.

"All right." The king dragged his feet off the table and they dropped with a thud. "Let's talk about the education budget."

We all groaned.

Miraculously, everyone survived to the end of the meeting. The council members filtered out, grumbling under their breath and ignoring the formalities of leaving like they always did. I smiled anyway and waited until the door clicked closed.

Kadence didn't move from the head of the table. He watched everyone leave, then turned his dark eyes to me. My skin crawled from the disdain in his gaze.

"I wanted to apologize for last night," I said.

"Don't. I don't care."

"It was improper. I need to apologize."

"Do you always do what's proper?" he asked.

"I try. Does that bother you?"

He shrugged.

"How old are you, five?" I snapped and regret unsettled my stomach. I had asked Amos to be an example of patience, but I couldn't control my own tongue.

The king turned to me, his face edged with anger.

Someone knocked on the door.

"Come in," he barked.

Renee stepped inside. In a pale-yellow dress with a white apron around the skirt, sensible white shoes, and her brown hair pulled into a tight ponytail, she would fit in with the kitchen staff, the medical crews, or my own ladies. People would take one look at her and forget they ever saw her. It was the perfect ensemble for a spy. She bowed and stood at a soldier's rest, staring straight ahead.

"Report," Kadence commanded.

"Sir?" Renee sent a subtle, pointed look at me.

"I don't care what she hears, Renee. Report."

Her voice came out flat, crisp. "The queen woke and took breakfast in her room. The regular staff, Elaine Sandore, Saffa Leblanc, and I assisted her in dressing. She did the daily inspections of the barracks and the training grounds. The soldiers spoke with her freely and there were no alarming conversations. In the late morning, there was an emergency call from the blood donation center. The queen left to assist and I was unable to attend with her. She returned back four and a half hours later and ran to the council meeting where she arrived thirty minutes late."

I pressed my lips together. Knowing Renee was a spy was different than having my day laid out clearly and methodically.

"The former betrothed never showed up?"

"No, sir. The queen met with her advisor, Zavier Croft, over breakfast and had no other visitors."

Kadence turned to me.

"What was the emergency at the blood donation center?"

"It's fine. I handled it."

"It was important enough to be late to a council meeting."

"Everything was recovered and it's fine now." Maybe if I smiled enough he would leave it alone.

"Tell me."

Guess not. I sighed.

"Someone stole a wagon that was loaded with donated blood."

"Vampires?" he asked.

"Unless a vampire can teleport a two-thousand-pound wagon, there was magic involved."

"Was it found?"

"Yes, the wagon was located in the park behind one of the community centers currently housing the surplus troops. Only a single bottle of donated blood was missing from the lost wagon," I said. The search had taken hours.

"How do you know there was magic involved?"

"The driver had just gotten off the wagon. He realized he forgot something and the wagon was gone when he turned around."

"Why would a witch steal a wagon and take one bottle of blood?"

"I don't know. We had to throw out the rest of the blood due to possible contamination." It pained me to think of the hundreds of bottles of donated blood going to waste.

"Update me if anything else happens," he said. "Renee, thank you. You're dismissed."

The woman bowed and shut the door softly.

"Both of our people are working to find the missing blood bottle," I said.

Kadence nodded once and stood from his chair. His tight black shirt somehow still managed to flex over his hard chest. His breeches were tucked into battle boots. He had dressed for the council meeting like he was going to a fight. The thought made me smile.

"If there's nothing else, Sal, I'm leaving."

He brushed past me. I caught his arm and he let me stop him. His strength played beneath my hand.

"I really am sorry about last night." I licked my lips. "I'm planning an art gala at the castle. It's going to be long and boring, and I would like it if you came."

For a heartbeat, he became stone, still and unbreathing. He looked down to my hand on his arm. I slowly lifted it and let him go.

"I don't care what you'd like, Sal," he said, ice in his voice. He left too, leaving me alone in the council room.

Chapter Twelve

"ARE YOU SURE THE BUTTONS WILL CLOSE?" I ASKED.

Saffa tugged hard and I waited for the rip of shredded fabric at any moment. I held my breath and Elaine pinched the sides of the dress closer together.

"This dress was made exactly for your measurements." Saffa huffed. "It will fit."

It sounded like she was trying to convince the dress rather than me. The dark-blue garment had thigh-high slit and was embroidered with shimmering jewels. The strapless neckline meant that if any assassins showed up, the entire gala would get a complimentary show. The dress had been made to my measurements, admittedly six months ago, before the stress of ruling and surrender, and when I had been sparring regularly in the practice arena. Saffa pulled my brown curls to one side and pinned them into a fancy ponytail. I wore only the cursed bracelet as jewelry.

"Got it!" The last of the buttons at the top of the dress closed beneath her agile fingers and my available oxygen was cut in half.

"Fantastic," I wheezed. I turned from the mirror and Elaine held up a pair of strappy black high heels.

"No," I said. "Please."

"Just close your eyes, My Queen," Elaine said. "It'll be over soon."

Rhythmic taps echoed down the hallway with my every step, but Zavier's sensible shoes were silent next to me. He wore a simple black ensemble that hugged his shoulders and narrowed at his waist. Zavier still sparred almost every day and it kept him healthy and fit. His attire showed that off. On one arm lay a sleek black walnut board holding paperwork.

"The food is prepared?" I asked.

"Yes, the servers are starting appetizers now."

"All the art was delivered?"

"One artist showed up late, but her work was relocated to the last galley and should be hung by now."

"The king?"

"He has not arrived," Zavier said.

"I don't think he's planning to," came Rayhan's voice from where he leaned against the double doors at the entrance to the Great Hall. His black armor carried new engraved symbols and the flickering candlelight gave the illusion of movement across his chest. His axe slung over one shoulder.

"Did he tell you that he wouldn't come?" I asked.

"No, Your Majesty, but he's been in the training field all day, and he wasn't slowing down when I left."

"I see."

"There's someone I want to introduce you to tonight." Rayhan studied the floor, avoiding eye contact. His hand clenched too tight on the hilt of the axe. The burly vampire was nervous. The realization almost made me smile.

"I have a few things to check on as the gala starts. Can I find you in a little while?" I asked.

Zavier eyed the checklist on his board.

Rayhan's toothy smile stretched from cheek to cheek and his eyes almost sparkled. Smiling, in the warm glow of candlelight, he was a juxtaposition to the terrible giant we had seen the first night, grinning harshly in the dark. The monster he'd appeared to be that night had faded away, leaving a man behind. Deep down I realized vampires weren't monsters any more than my own people. They had wishes, goals, desires, and people they loved.

"I'll find you." He switched the massive axe to the other shoulder as though it was as light as a feather. With a bow more graceful than expected from a man of his size, he opened the door and held it for Zavier and me. I waited for the shiver of tension as I walked through the door and left my back exposed to a man that would have been my enemy on the battlefield. Only the woosh of air crossed over my skin as the door closed.

Music spilled across the hall. A string quartet played a soft, fluttering melody that was light, but eerie and mysterious. Guests strolled across the floor, enchanted by the beautiful music. Long gowns skirted the white marble, some rich red or orange and others more melancholy tones. There were slightly more witches attending than vampires, but not many.

My stomach growled at the smell of food. Waiters in black uniforms passed around trays of mushrooms bursting with cheese and artichokes, lobster rolls stuffed into artisan bread, and caprese skewers drizzled with balsamic dressing. A buffet line curved around the back of the room.

Temporary walls composed of wooden rods and black canvas split the Great Hall into sections. Each artist had their own cubicle to display their work. A flexible walking tour weaved around the sections, allowing guests to enjoy the art at their own pace. Laughter and conversation filled the room, as light as the violin from the quartet.

"Here, Queen Sal." Zavier snatched appetizers from a tray and handed me a stuffed mushroom. Cheese and garlic hit my tongue, and my eyes wanted to close in delight.

"It's going...well," I said.

"Don't sound so surprised." Zavier smiled at me. "You worked hard for this."

We wandered through the art tour. The majority were paintings, but some booths had elaborate sculptures, poetry pinned to the canvas wall, and one artist displayed a leatherbound book on a pedestal.

One booth captured my attention. Splashes of colors across three canvases composed a single scene, split into thirds. Simple, precise brush strokes and the artful dancing of sunlight across the fabric portrayed an impressionist style. Loose, but recognizable, a twisting river seemed to flow in front of a distant, colorful city. I could feel the sun across my face, hear the tumbling river through the tall, grassy strands.

"It's beautiful, isn't it?" A short, stocky man in a black suit and red tie stood next to me, looking at the paintings.

"Very," I said. "Are you the artist?"

He shook his head. "No, but I know him."

The man's worn, calloused hands marked him as a laborer or a soldier. The bracelet stopped me from tasting him for magic. I didn't know if he was a witch, vampire, or human. Perhaps it didn't matter. Perhaps tonight, in this place, we were one kingdom combined.

"Please tell the artist we enjoyed his work."

He dipped his head. Zavier and I left the stall, circling the end of the row of displays.

"There you are." Rayhan appeared from the shadows. "There's someone I want you to meet."

He took the lead, bypassing rows and rows of artwork, shuttling us to the last cubicle. Shadows half-hid the division. People walking in front of us peeked into the space, their faces paled, and they hurried along. One man wrapped his arms tightly around a woman's shoulders. Their lips twisted and eyes wide, terrified by whatever lay beyond the black fabric.

The redheaded giant gestured toward the booth.

I stuck a smile on my face, but my heart hammered. What art could terrify people so much?

"The paintings are odd," Rayhan said. He settled one hand on each of our shoulders and they felt like heavy boulders trying to drive me into the earth. "But you need to talk to her."

"What?" I asked.

Zavier's hand lingered close to the hilt of his sword.

"Shh, you don't want to startle her." Rayhan turned his massive head to look behind us. "I'll answer questions when we're done."

We stepped into the cubicle. The art hadn't been hung on the metal hooks like the rest of the canvases. Instead, three paintings rested on the floor, leaning against the support beams of the faux walls. I caught a glimpse of the canvas. Tendrils of terror leaked into my soul before my eyes could comprehend the shapes and figures. Some long-forgotten instinct told me to stand up and run as fast as I could.

Thick and chunky paint stretched across the canvas in black, white, and shades of grey. The largest painting sat closest to me. Two grotesque and misshapen figures stood, one on each side of the canvas. A third figure, a man, sat in the middle, a silent scream etched onto his face. Each shadow figure had long claws connected to skeleton arms, and they ripped into the man, tearing organs and flesh and tossing them into the air in a snapshot of horror.

The second painting displayed a single humanoid figure, but too narrow and the limbs too long. It peeked through a doorway, and its black nails wrapped around the doorframe, blending gradually into darkness. The stark white eyes gazed empty and unseeing. It stared through me, into my soul. If I looked too long, I feared I may not come out.

The last painting was abstract streaks of black and white and grey, jumbled into a chaotic mess. Thick and thin lines slashed the canvas like strikes from a sword. It resembled the depiction of a scream, loud and long and terrible.

Individually, the paintings were creepy. Together they were hell personified.

"It's okay." Rayhan smiled into the dark corner of the room. "You can come out. These are the people I told you about."

Tension locked my back.

Zavier's hand gripped his hilt. If one of these shadow creatures from the paintings appeared, the gala would turn to bloodshed in an instant.

A woman stepped from the shadows. The size of a young child, with her arms folded close to her body, she looked at the ground while she shuffled from the darkness. The grey hair and sagging skin revealed her advanced age. She squinted against the light, as though the flickering candles pained her.

"This is Grace," Rayhan said. "She's the artist."

Zavier bowed and I nodded in greeting.

The woman stared pointedly at our shoes.

"Your work is..." Horrifying. "Unique." I tried to smile.

"Very skillful," Zavier followed up.

"Do you want to tell them about your paintings, Grace?" Rayhan asked. The last thing I wanted was to provoke this poor, trembling woman to talk about the dark forms on the canvas.

Grace remained silent.

"You told me that you would tell them," Rayhan's voice turned hard.

I shifted on my feet and glanced at Zavier. Lips pressed together, he watched the two.

The old woman looked up at the large man, but her expression remained as blank as the creature's eyes she had painted. Slowly, painfully, she lifted a slim hand and pointed a finger to the creature peeking through the doorway.

"Qu—" She cleared her throat. "Queen."

My face pinched. The figure didn't look particularly royal.

"That's the queen?" Rayhan asked and Grace nodded.

"Queen Cameron Carter Hendrick," her gravel voice whispered.

Kadence's late mother. Chills danced over me.

Grace pointed to the largest painting, where the man was bleeding as his body was pulled apart. "King Loren Ellis Hendrick. And the queen."

"And that one?" Rayhan gestured at the mess of black and white.

"Me." The word was barely audible.

She turned from the paintings and a flash of silver ran through her eyes. Grace was a vampire. I tried to smother the shock that threatened to creep across my face. I'd never seen a vampire age so poorly. Even those in advance years looked timeless and beautiful. What happened to this woman to strip her lifespan so severely? Tears tapped on the floor and Grace scurried back into the corner, fading away in the deep shadow. Rayhan let her go, without lifting a hand in comfort.

He looked at us, his blue eyes the size of serving saucers.

"Do you understand?" he asked.

Zavier's face was as confused as mine. The old man shook his head slowly.

"I'm afraid I do not, Rayhan," Zavier said.

The vampire studied me and grimaced.

"Listen." He looked around again and dropped his voice. "Kadence would kill me for telling you this. He banned all of us from talking about it."

Rayhan grabbed both of my shoulders and jerked me toward him with unprecedented strength.

I swayed on my feet and Zavier half drew his sword. I held a hand up. We didn't need to rekindle the war because Rayhan had grabbed me too fast.

He leaned his bearded face close to mine.

"I need you to understand, Queen Sal," he whispered, but there was an edge I hadn't heard before—fear. "There has to be peace. We—I really need this peace to last. Nothing is more important. We need you and Kadence to work together. The way it has been, the way he's been acting, it's going to fall apart if you don't."

My heart jumped. I knew things with King Kadence weren't great, but I didn't realize he was on the verge of plunging us back into war. Visions of bodies and blood swam through my mind. The thought of walking another battlefield, stepping through dead and dying, of watching our kingdom fall one soldier at a time, sent an ache through my bones. I needed this peace much more than Rayhan did. My people needed this peace.

"Kadence is angry," Rayhan continued as though my world wasn't grinding to a halt. "Every time he sees you, he becomes more and more bitter. He spars with the soldiers all day, stopping only for barracks and blood donation updates. He's sent three of our own men to the infirmary with broken bones. I think," the vampire licked his lips, "I think if you knew what happened, it could help."

I gently lifted his hands from my shoulders. I put them together as though he was praying and held them between my much smaller hands.

"If Kadence doesn't want me to know," I whispered, "you shouldn't tell me."

"I don't care what he wants, Queen Sal. I have pledged my life to that man and I would die for him a hundred times. I have never fought beside a more loyal and devoted soldier, had a fiercer friendship. Before, I wouldn't ever talk to you, but I have someone—erm—something else now. Something more important." His blue eyes bore into mine and we both swam in his desperation. It was like a dying soldier begging for company on the battlefield and I couldn't turn him down.

"Ok, Rayhan. Tell me, and I'll see if it can help."

Relief flooded his face like rain on a dry field.

"Kadence's mother, Queen Cameron Hendrick, lost three sons to the war. When Kadence was old enough to pick up a sword, she vowed not to lose another. Desperate to end the bloodshed, she started looking for the Fields of Death."

Oh, no.

"Tell me she didn't, Rayhan."

"She found it," he said. "Do you know what happens to someone in the Fields?"

"We all know the stories."

"They're true." His eyes glossed over and he didn't see me anymore. He returned to someplace else, someplace where blood spilled in the halls and hell screamed in the night. "She invited a demon into her body. It tore through her, ate away at her soul. She looked like herself, the same skin, the same eyes, but inside was evil. She had brought her maidservant with her."

"Grace," I said.

He nodded.

"The queen came back to the kingdom. The guards let her through. How could they know? She approached King Loren and told him what she found. She said the demons were the answer. They were strong, healed instantly, too fast to see. She told the king that they could win the war. He said no. He told her to leave and that kind of evil was not welcome in his kingdom."

"What happened?"

"Whatever was left of the queen died. Her husband's disapproval killed her, and the demon swelled up, strong and angry. The one inside Grace also took control and they tore into the king, ripped him to shreds. Kadence was hiding under the bed. He was eight years old. They killed the king and turned to the rest of the castle. Room by room, they murdered everyone inside and then spilled into the village. It was a slaughter. It took our people two days to gather enough soldiers to finally trap the demons. The queen...they tore her apart. They ripped her body to pieces and the head laughed at them until they set it on fire. They burned all of her and scattered the ashes into the sea."

"How did Grace survive?" I asked.

"The demon saw what happened to its comrade and it fled. Grace was in a coma for two weeks. When she woke up, she didn't remember her life before the possession. She started to paint."

I shivered at the twisted ball of darkness and chaos. Hearing horror stories as a child about the Fields was different than seeing the visual remnants of suffering they brought. Kadence's mother had been possessed by a demon and killed his father. The thought of having something so vile and terrifying trapped inside my body made my stomach turn.

"It was reported that the queen and king had died in battle," Zavier said.

"Lies," Rayhan said.

"Why are you telling me this, Rayhan?"

"I have someone to protect now, My Queen." A hint of a smile tugged at his lips. "When you showed up at the gate, asking for the king, and posed as the perfect target for our archers, I thought you were crazy. Now, I understand what's worth that sacrifice. Kadence blames your kingdom for killing his parents. This war is the reason his mother found the Fields. Kadence's rage is going to convince him to kill you. Your kingdom will retaliate, despite the turmoil they feel with you on the throne. It will be a bloodbath and every witch loyal to your name will die." His eyes darkened. "I can't let that happen."

Rayhan's voice tightened at the word 'witch.' I glanced at the enchanted symbols spread across his breastplate. When we'd met Kadence at the vampire siege camp, there'd been evidence they had a witch in their midst. Chances were it was same one Rayhan thought of now.

I pulled our combined hands to my chest and bowed to Rayhan. I didn't know how this information would help me with Kadence, but I had to try.

"Thank you," I said.

He bowed back, lower.

"No, thank you, My Queen. I hope it helps."

Me too.

Pins pricked the back of my neck. The music paused, and so did the conversation and gentle flows of laughter. Silenced stretched through the Great Hall similar to my coronation when I waited for Kadence to decide to behead me or not. This couldn't be good.

I circled the end of the booth, happily leaving the demon paintings behind. There was nothing I could do for Grace. She had new demons to fight now.

People gathered into tight groups, whispering amongst themselves and daring to look over their shoulders at the front doors. A dark figure lingered in the open doorway. Moonlight spilled around the shape, silhouetting him in the rich gala light. It took a moment for my eyes to adjust from the darkness in Grace's booth.

Kadence stood at the entrance of the Great Hall and everyone avoided him as though he carried a plague. Even the vampires, his own people, gave him a wide berth, fear pinching their faces. Rayhan said Kadence had hurt his soldiers during training. The rumors must have spread. The vampires shrank in fear from their king.

The musicians gaped at the man in the doorway and didn't see my approach. I wanted to bind them in magical ropes and send a shock through their empty heads to wake up their common sense, but my magic lay out of reach.

I snapped my fingers in front of their shocked faces.

"I know the king is exceptionally handsome, boys." I raised my voice so the people around could hear. "But I am not paying you to stare at him."

"S-sorry, My Queen," one man with dark skin and a receding hairline stammered. He gestured and the others picked up their instruments and resumed playing, as though the interruption had been part of their performance.

"My King." I bowed to Kadence.

He stood, unmoving, his eyes dark and cloudy. My people, our people, needed me to put out the fuse to his anger.

I held out my hand. We didn't have much ground to stand on, but I prayed there was still a ledge.

Kadence took my hand. He had fresh blisters and new callouses, which his vampire powers should heal quickly. Perhaps he'd worked himself into exhaustion and his healing abilities suffered for it. I tucked his palm into my arm and led him from the door, toward the art. Stiff and stoic, he let me pull him away. Slowly, as the warmth of music filled the room along with the satisfaction of good food, conversation rolled through the court again.

"What are you doing?" Kadence clenched his teeth.

"There is lots of lovely art here tonight. I thought we could look at it together." I smiled. People scrambled out of our way. We pretended not to notice.

"I didn't come here to look at art with you," he said.

"Then why are you here?" We paused at a booth of delicate watercolor paintings.

"I didn't have anything else to do."

"You ran out of soldiers willing to spar with you?" I kept my tone casual.

He tensed.

"Who told you that?" His voice was quiet, but I heard the rage. "It must have been Rayhan. I'll have his head for that."

"Nobody had to tell me, Kadence. Look around."

We walked, pausing at each booth. Kadence watched the people around him. They darted away when they saw us coming, turned their eyes to look anywhere else. Several soldiers put a hand on their weapon, as though expecting a strike. I smiled and tucked Kadence tighter into me, but his anger rolled out in waves.

Finally, he sighed.

"They're scared of me." There was an edge to his voice, but I couldn't place it.

"They loved you at the market," I said. "What changed?"

"I was passing out coins then."

"I'm sure it wouldn't hurt if you tossed a few coins at people."

"We both know it's more than that," he said.

We neared the end of the loop and I pulled the vampire away from Grace's booth. He didn't need a history lesson tonight.

"I don't know what to do." The clouds had left his eyes, replaced with clear exhaustion. The king's shoulders drooped and I recognized the slouch of a soldier that had overtrained. I had felt the same heaviness in my own body.

"You need to show them that you're okay, that you're not here to break any of them," I said. "Come dance with me. Normal people dance."

He looked down at me. "I don't want to dance with you."

"I don't care what you want." I echoed his own words from days ago. I tugged on his arm. We both knew he could refuse my invitation. If he did, this fragile peace would soon break. I was the glue between kingdoms. The vampires were ingrained through our city now. Their people slept in our community halls, under our guards, and patrolled with our soldiers. If

Kadence killed me, there would be a rebellion. The vampires would win the war, but they would pay a heavy toll.

His face pinched as he reached the same conclusion. It may not save my life, and our people, indefinitely, but it was enough for tonight. He let me pull him to the dance floor. We were the only ones there, and neither of us pointed it out.

I wrapped his arms around my waist. I waited for my stomach to turn, for the bitter bite of fear in my mind. Nothing. I imagined Kadence as a child, gripped with terror as his own mother murdered his father. Kadence wasn't born a monster. Years of desperation changed his mother into something unrecognizable, and he'd lost her and his father in one night. Alone in my castle, filled with enemies that indirectly led his mother to her decisions, Kadence was lost. I felt sorry for him. We twirled in poor, offbeat circles, the warmth of his hands sinking into my skin.

I stood on my tiptoes in the awful high heels and put a hand on his shoulder to balance.

"I thought we had a deal," I whispered into his ear. My breath moved the dark hair nestled at his neck. "You could scare me as long as you didn't scare the people."

"I've managed to scare everybody." His voice was cold.

"It's not too late. You care about them. You have to remind them that they come first."

"How do I do that, Your Majesty?" I ignored the thick layer of sarcasm.

"You have to show them."

I leaned my head against his chest. My heart pounded, but this close, skin to skin, I could hear his beating just as fast. I wrapped my arms around his solid waist, feeling the muscles taunt and thick under my hands. It was like hugging a warm, unyielding tree. A spark fueled between us as we pushed away the tension and uncertainty of the past few days, the past years. The man I once loathed wrapped his arms around me, and a new feeling twisted in my core, very different than hatred. I didn't dare think what the heat pulsing through my body might mean. Kadence's fingers drew tiny circles on my back. Adrenaline and desperation made me pull the man closer, and we spun under the candlelight to the lullaby of a string quartet.

Eventually I pulled back enough to study his face. He hadn't shaved and the stubble sharpened his jaw. He looked dark and dangerous and delicious. I should leave, hide in my room and face the consequences tomorrow. I slipped from his grip and captured his hand instead.

"Walk me to my room?" I whispered, peering at him from under my lashes.

He pressed his lips together and nodded.

He led me from the dance floor, through the wave of dancers that had joined us. Heavy gazes burned my back. Whispers spread like wildfire as people wondered where we were going and what we were going to do.

We slipped into the darkness of the staff's hallway. The door cut off the side looks and rumors, and we were alone.

Kadence caught my wrist. He pushed me into the stone wall. A single candle illuminated the hallway, fluttering frantically at the opposite end. The king's jaw clenched and his eyebrows furrowed. He pressed against me, solid muscle reminding me that a hand-to-hand fight would be futile. His free hand caught my jaw and forced my head up. His eyes searched mine.

"What was that?" he asked.

"It was a show," I said within his tight grip. "Everyone saw you. They saw you escorting me to look at art. They saw us dance together. They saw me smile at you and leave with you. I didn't flinch or look afraid. We showed them that you don't scare me, and they will learn you shouldn't scare them either."

"They think we're going to go sleep together."

I shrugged, feigning indifference.

"Is that what you want?" he whispered. The hand on my jaw turned soft and his gaze skirted down our pressed bodies.

"I will honor the terms of our surrender," I said and wondered if being with Kadence would fulfill much more than our agreement. If it would stoke the new, bickering fire in the pit of my core.

He bent down, his body pressing me tighter against the wall. His hand shifted to the back of my neck and pulled my face toward his. Those full lips hovered inches from mine, his breath sending tingles over my skin.

"You care about all of them," he said. "My people were just as afraid as your witches, and that show was for them too."

"*Our* people come first," I said. "They have to."

He kissed me and it was not gentle. His lips claimed mine, and he forced my head up for a better angle. He growled into my mouth and pushed my legs apart. With shaky knees, I made space for him. I tried to match his demand, but he didn't want me to kiss him. He wanted to take me, angry and impatient. He wanted to taste my fear on his lips and my blood on his tongue.

I could give him one of those.

That flame inside me turned to a burning inferno. His aggression and demands should have angered me, but it reminded me of the rapid chaos of the battlefield. My soul ached for the fight, for the triumph.

I grabbed his waist and pulled his hips hard against me, an invitation he didn't expect. His eyes turned silver as his control slipped. I ran my tongue over his lip and he invited me in. The hand behind my head turned to steel, blocking any escape. Good, I wasn't looking for one.

Skirting the edge of his breeches, I ran my hand up his shirt. Despite the layers of muscles and the callouses on his palms, softness hugged his sides and back. Hard ridges lined his body, but caught by surprise, they sought out my touch.

I licked along his lips, exploring him. The perfect, neat row of his teeth were broken only by twin fangs, long and sharp. I rubbed the side of my tongue across a pointed tip. The skin caught on the edge, a tiny cut, spilling blood into his mouth.

Kadence froze. His silver eyes widened and he groaned. I caught it between my lips.

The rage left, turned to a new hunger. He shifted the grip at my neck and softly ran his fingers through my hair. He pulled me closer.

My head spun. The kiss was fire and I was kindling. A spark lit between us and stoked higher and higher with every soft caress until a blaze tore through my body.

Then suddenly he was gone. The fire stuttered, leaving me blinking in the cold hall.

"Why did you do that?" Kadence asked from three steps away. He looked at me, his eyes black again, suspicious and confused.

Anger, frigid compared to the faded firestorm, wrapped over me. "Whether you like it or not, whether you're the overlord, and I'm just a pretty puppet on a throne you control, we are a team. We have to work together if we want our kingdoms to survive."

Kadence stared, but he didn't see me. Maybe he was a child again, watching the demon in his mother's body kill his father piece by piece. Maybe he was on the battlefield as his people died over and over in a war he'd inherited. Maybe he was back at the first night we met, wishing he had killed me before I'd had the opportunity to become a martyr. He blinked and came back, focusing on me in the dark hallway, the scent of my blood in the air.

His eyes narrowed. "I hate you."

The vampire turned and disappeared through the door at the other end of the hall. I sank to the hard floor, ignoring my body's complaints, and held back tears until my eyes burned from the effort.

Chapter Thirteen

"HAVE THE SCOUTS SEEN ANYTHING?"

"No," Zavier said. "King Kadence went to his kingdom to take care of some business. He is obviously not finished yet. As I told you last week Sal, I'll let you know as soon as he's sighted."

I pressed my lips together. I held onto Zavier's elbow and he led me from the grassy field where we had tied the horses near the blood donation building. The single-story building stretched long and flat. Composed of mostly light brown bricks, the color of caramelized butter, the building looked about its age—old.

Mr. Jon Chan, the director of the donation center, held a bright red door open for us. A sheen of sweat beaded beneath his short, thinning black hair. The collar of his shirt gaped open, as though he had been fussing with the buttons, and the fingers of his free hand tapped against his leg.

"My Queen." He bowed hastily. "Mr. Croft. Thank you for coming down here, but like I told you before, we really do have the situation under control."

The narrow hallway stretched before us. The doors had been removed, so the openings cut into individual rooms, outfitted with matching beds, medical supply cabinets, and standard blue sheets. Patients peered out of a couple rooms and I tried not to look at them.

"Please tell me how losing five wagons and six bottles of donated blood in two weeks is under control," Zavier said. "Not to mention the two hundred gallons of blood we've had to throw away due to possible contamination."

The hallway opened into a wide room. Tall cabinets lined the back wall and an old table sat in the center of the room. The black paint on the tabletop began to peel away, revealing a dark stain underneath. I sank onto one of the seafoam green chairs clustered around the table and the thin, worn cushion inset in the wooden frame. Zavier sat beside me, flattening his face, likely to hide his discomfort.

Mr. Chan grimaced. "It is unfortunate to lose all that blood, but we replaced the supply quickly and are meeting all quotas consistently and safely for our patients."

That was true. We were maintaining the minimum amount of blood despite the setbacks from the robberies. As we passed two months since the surrender, repeat donors had started to arrive.

"The first four encounters happened to your employees, correct?"

Mr. Chan clenched his jaw. I saw the process in his face. Denial, anger, depression, and acceptance. We weren't going anywhere. It was out of his hands. He sighed and turned his palms up on the table, looking defeated.

"Yes," he said. "The last incident happened to me, though. I was in the yard, doing the final checklist to send the blood to the offsite storage facility before it gets distributed. We have an enchanted cold room here, but it's not big enough for long-term storage. The driver had to use the bathroom, so I double-checked the paperwork before he left. The wagon was there, I checked off a few boxes, and the wagon was gone."

"The horses?" I asked.

"They were still here, tied together in a perfect line."

"Did you see anyone nearby?" Zavier asked.

Mr. Chan shook his head. He glanced around the room and leaned over the table.

"Here's what bothers me," he whispered, "my magic has an affinity toward transportation. I have an innate sense of navigation and direction.

I could tell you the best route between two places that I have never seen. When the wagon disappeared, I didn't feel anything. I didn't sense any magic and I couldn't feel the wagon's location. I don't think a witch did this."

Zavier pressed his lips together. "What do you think it could be, Mr. Chan?"

He pushed back in his chair. "I don't know, but I don't think this will be the last missing wagon."

"Thank you, Mr. Chan," I said. "We're going to put a security detail on the donation center and every wagon that drives onto this property."

"Your Majesty, do you think that's necessary? This facility strives for privacy for our patients."

"The safety of our people has to be my priority." I smiled. "We will make sure that our staff, patients, and drivers are well defended at all times."

Mr. Chan smiled back, a hard line of teeth. He couldn't argue about protecting his staff, but he didn't have to like it.

"Thank you for your generosity, My Queen." He bowed.

Zavier and I showed ourselves out. Mr. Chan disappeared into one of the rooms, lost in the sea of sterile supplies and paperwork.

I blinked in the light and held a hand over my eyes. The building was nestled in the tree line on a patch of red clay. A dirt road cut through the forest, the only path in and out of the clearing. Overhead, branches layered through the canopy.

"Could the thieves have flown the wagon out?" Zavier asked, cupping his hand over his eyes too.

"The wagon is too big. It would have ripped right through those branches and left broken tree limbs or piles of fallen leaves." I shrugged. "There's nothing."

Zavier scraped his foot along the ground, walking around the perimeter of the dirt patch.

"There's no remnants of symbols," he said.

We both stared at the ground. *Tell us your secrets, dirt.*

It remained silent.

I kicked at the ground. "This is dumb."

"It is dumb." Zavier nodded.

"It's all dumb. I'm dumb."

"Now, now, Sal. It's been a rough week, but there's no need to degrade yourself."

I rubbed my fingers through my sun-warmed hair and gripped fistfuls of the locks. An ache settled in my head, only partially from the stress of the missing blood.

"First, I ruin everything I'd carefully built with Kadence. Then, he runs away. Now, I have six bottles of blood missing and I don't know how or why. I don't think you can call the truth 'degrading,' Zavier."

"Come here." Zavier wrapped his arms around me.

I rested my head on his shoulder. He felt warm and familiar. I matched Zavier's breath. In and out. In and out.

"You didn't ruin everything with the king." He patted the back of my head. "You and all your people are still alive and you have been taking excellent care of them in his absence. The missing blood is puzzling, but we will get to the bottom of it."

"I hope so."

I held him tighter and then pulled away. Kadence's absence gaped like a fresh wound. He didn't inform me he wouldn't be attending, instead sending a messenger with the news. He'd left without a word to me, the same way my parents had fled, and I wondered if any of them ever planned to return.

Zavier and I turned and walked away in defeat.

As we approached the field, a figure lingered beside our horses, holding the reins to a third horse. Cynthia's form sharpened as we neared. Her braided hair brushed the back of black boots that stretched over her knees. She wore a tulip-cut, black jacket and black athletic breeches. She stood strong, confident, with a natural arch to her back. Her dainty fingers looked like they would be as comfortable plunging a knife into a man's throat as they were holding the leather reins.

She turned as we approached, a miniscule movement that said we had her full attention, despite the fact she didn't acknowledge us.

"Cynthia," Zavier said warmly. He could make his voice sound like he had been reliving a fond memory about the very person he was talking to. "What can we do for you?"

She tightened her lips, but there was a hint of a smile.

"Zavier." She turned to me with a sneer, but didn't greet me. She talked to Zavier. "You have noticed the king's absence."

"He's been gone for over two weeks," I said.

Her dark eyes sharpened at me, then flicked back to Zavier.

"I assumed you had gone with him, Cynthia," Zavier said. "Nobody had seen you either."

"I did go with him." She nodded. "We were supposed to come back together, but he sent me ahead." She shrugged. "He does that sometimes. He likes to travel alone. That was two days ago."

A chill went through me. "You haven't seen him for two days?" My voice was flat, hard.

Cynthia lifted her upper lip, fangs exposed. "I don't obey you," she hissed. "You're the reason he left. You've been driving him to insanity."

"I have been trying to keep this war from starting again."

"You should have groveled at his feet and let him run this place like a true king! Instead, he treats you as an equal. You control the blood supply, you're overseeing the barracks for our people." She spat at my feet. "You lost this war. He should make you act like it."

I stretched my arms out. "None of those are my decisions, Cynthia. Read the contract. He decides what I can and cannot do every single day."

"Ladies," Zavier said calmly, "it's more important that we find the king than fight among ourselves. I'll organize some soldiers into search parties and we'll comb a grid five miles out from the kingdom. We can stretch it farther if nothing turns up. Cynthia, can you gather groups to look along the paths from our kingdom to yours?"

She nodded.

"Sal, please find the best scouting and transportation magic users and have them report to me."

"Wait." Cynthia put up her hand. "I hear something."

We froze. I held my breath, straining to listen. A gentle breeze rustled the leaves of the trees. Squirrels or chipmunks scuttled through foliage and over branches, chattering to each other. Our horses made soft noises while their velvet lips ripped up grass and their teeth ground the plant away. The blood rushing through my head sounded a steady rhythm.

"I'm not hearing anything, Cynthia," Zavier said.

Figures dropped from the trees. All four landed on their knees in unison, one hand on the ground. Their skin varied from paper-white to rich brown. Shiny, smooth skin revealed recently shaved heads. The men were shirtless, wearing only black shorts. Even their feet were bare.

Red symbols of spellwork swirled across their exposed skin. Every inch of uncovered flesh bore red mosaics of shapes and signs. Crosses, circles, and lines marred their flesh and almost glowed in the bright sunlight.

I pulled the sword at my waist. The hilt fit my hand perfectly. Years of experience flooded my memory. I hadn't practiced in a long time, but my body fell into a comfortable position. My breathing steadied and my mind cleared. I curved my lips into a harsh smile.

The four men snapped their heads up in unison and red eyes bore into us. They smiled and pointy fangs peeked out.

"Vampires," Zavier said.

"We don't have eyes like that." Cynthia had pulled two short daggers from somewhere in her skin-tight outfit and held them like extensions of her arms. They reminded me of short, black claws. "These are something else."

The four didn't wait for us to determine their origins. They charged, splitting nicely as they ran in a practiced and coordinated movement. Two went for Zavier, one for Cynthia, and one for me. It was a good strategy. They would keep Cynthia and I busy while the two killed Zavier, then they would team up against Cynthia and me. Age hadn't slowed Zavier down though and they were in for a surprise.

The red eyed creatures didn't have weapons, but they did have vampire speed and strength. I reached for my magic and fumbled at the gaping hole. It didn't get easier. Distracted, I dodged a punch. Too slow. The hit ricocheted my arm, spiraling tingles down my fingertips.

"Don't die immediately, Queen," Cynthia said. She blocked blows and retaliated with quick, precise strikes. "I'd like the opportunity to watch."

"I'll do my best." I dodged another punch. There was no time to raise my sword. My opponent turned to a blur of skin and symbols dashing at my body. I had moments to prepare for my next maneuver.

A low groan escaped from the man Cynthia fought. He doubled over, and she shoved her dainty blade in his neck. He grabbed at her wrist, fingers trailing blood across her pale skin. She sliced through the side of his throat. A torrent of red rained down, and his head fell to the side, the spinal column no longer supporting it. His body collapsed.

The remaining three vampire-like creatures didn't hesitate. One stepped away from Zavier and engaged Cynthia.

Something warm and familiar slid across my skin. A light whisper, a baby's breath. I recognized the texture of magic, but something twisted inside the pale strands. Something dark and dangerous. They were vampires who did magic. Some type of hybrid.

"They have magic!" I yelled. "Zavier?"

Dodge. Duck. Sidestep. Still no room for a strike.

The magic thickened, growing stronger.

"I can't fight and contain it at the same time." Zavier said through clenched teeth. "It's getting stronger."

Duck. Turn. *Ouch, too slow.* More pins radiated through my arm. The hybrid didn't pause or revel in his strike. He kept coming and I was the only one getting tired.

"Cynthia?" I yelled.

"On it!"

We moved closer to Zavier and our opponents followed. Cynthia swept her feet under the hybrid she fought. He bounced away, off balance. She used the moment of hesitation to plunge her dagger into the back of Zavier's remaining hybrid. The creature turned, spit dripping from his mouth, and struck at Cynthia. She led him away from the witch, now dueling two enemies.

Zavier dropped his blade. He bowed his head, and the force of his magic stretched around me, looping through the foreign threads from the three hybrids. I used to weave my magic into wire or strings or cloth, flexible and strong. Zavier's magic was like a brick wall, stacking one layer on top of another. He built the wall higher and higher, an invisible mosaic of baked clay. Slowly, he pushed his wall away from us, laying new bricks one at a time, blocking out their magic.

Zavier was sandwiched between me and Cynthia, as protected as possible. I focused on my assailant. He hammered blows at me, continuously, rhythmically, and a pattern formed.

Dodge. Duck. Step. Dodge. Duck. Step.

He was fast. There wasn't a drop of sweat on his forehead. His breathing remained steady. My lungs burned as though my heart couldn't carry enough oxygen. He would outlast me in this fight, but speed and endurance were not the same as agility and accuracy. Though the hybrids displayed battlefield tactics, their movements held a stale quality. I bet this hybrid had never been to battle. Forming a pattern on the battlefield would get you killed.

I settled into the rhythm, a dancer warming up before a performance. Dodge. Duck. Step. Dodge. Duck. I was a ballerina, gasping and bloody, and this man was going to watch me dance.

I struck. As his fist went back, preparing to punch into my chest, I soared forward, sword first. His eyes widened, but he waited too long to pull the strike. He tried to step to the side, but my blade bit into his waist. Exhaustion damaged my aim and my sword caught on his spine, grinding to a halt. Sloppy.

I pulled the blade from his body. Blood dripped into the grass. He watched it roll off the tip of my sword and his red eyes narrowed.

Now that I could read his body, I recognized each motion before he completed it. I raised my sword. Muscles in his legs tensed, the creases at his arms deepened. He came at me, a blur of black and red. His fist smashed into my stomach and pain tumbled through me in hot waves. Bile rose in my throat, blocking my breath. I choked, coughing and heaving, but the end of my sword had cut through his chest like butter. The hybrid's eyes widened. He grabbed at the blade, already sagging from my weak grip, and tried to pull it from his chest. His hands cut to shreds, but the weapon stuck firm between his ribs.

I turned the sword. Trapped between ribs, it couldn't move much, but it was enough. His heart got a new gaping hole and he dropped at my feet.

Sweet air expanded my lungs. My stomach still thought it needed to exit my body. I brought the sword down on the fallen hybrid's head. It rolled away.

Zavier stood motionless behind Cynthia. His magic stacked around me, still expanding.

Cynthia was death in motion. She twisted and turned, never doubting where her strikes would land. Narrow red slices covered her opponent's exposed skin. She was bleeding them out, one cut at a time. Joy, true joy, radiated across her face as she smiled while she fought.

These two hybrids had a better strategy than the one I'd killed. One charged in a quick strike, and the other would wait, taking a moment to rest and recover. Once she landed a blow, they switched places, like runners in a relay race. Cynthia would tire before they did.

She underestimated them too. I could see the arrogance etched across her smiling face, even as her energy drained. These hybrids had established a pattern, like the one I had killed. Patterns were dangerous for more than one reason. Once fighters found a routine, they didn't expect it to be broken. As Cynthia fought one hybrid, the other tensed, prepared. He was in her sightline, but she wasn't paying attention. She didn't expect him to attack until she hit his partner. The battle rhythm had trapped her.

I ran. I was too far away. My stomach cramped and my muscles screamed for rest. I would never make it. I ran faster.

The hybrid was already there. He sprinted behind Cynthia and hammered a hard punch into her back, in line with her kidneys. She froze, her red mouth a pale circle. She flipped the dagger and stabbed it into the hybrid behind her, but the one in front didn't slow. He punched her in the stomach and she doubled over.

The second hybrid grabbed a handful of hair and cranked her head up. He was going to break her neck.

I made it. My body groaned, but I lifted my blade and cut at the weak junction of the hybrid's wrists and arms. His hands fell to the ground under a waterfall of blood.

A scream tore from him, low and harsh and primal. He staggered away, bloody stumps already healing thanks to his vampire powers.

His partner moved on me with a fury of jagged strikes.

"You saved me?" Cynthia chimed from behind. "You should have let me die."

"Why?" I asked. This vampire moved slower. I sliced with my blade and it came back wet with fresh blood.

"I hate you. I insulted you. I've tried to convince Kadence to kill you since you stumbled into our camp."

Sidestep, slice. Duck, slice. This was going much better. The vampire bled all over the ground.

"I swore to protect all of our people in exchange for peace." Slice. Duck, cut. "You are one of my people whether you like it or not."

"I would have let you die."

Ouch. That was worse than the gut punch, although I shouldn't have been surprised. Her job was to protect Kadence. She blamed me for the king's self-inflicted torture.

"I signed a surrender when my own people would have preferred that I died," I said. "It doesn't matter what you would have done."

Slice. Slice. Slice. The hybrid wavered on his feet and collapsed to his knees. My sword cut through his neck.

Cynthia flipped one of her daggers and launched it at the handless hybrid that had wandered away. It struck the back of his head and he fell face first into the grass.

The hint of magic slipped away. Zavier opened his eyes and looked at the carnage in the field. He sighed.

"What were they trying to do with the magic?" I asked.

"I couldn't tell," he said. "But it felt very foul and would have been bad if they were successful."

Cynthia held up an arm from one of the bodies. "What are these markings?" Blood peppered the red swirls twisting across the limb. The glow had faded. We all bent down for a closer look.

"I don't know," I said. "I recognize some of the symbols. This one represents obedience. But this swirly one strengthens spells across distances. Together, the symbols don't make sense."

"Are they painted in blood?" Zavier asked.

Cynthia leaned down. Her nostrils flared as she sniffed the body.

"No. It has an earthy smell. Some kind of spice, maybe? I'm not familiar with it."

The whiz of an arrow shot passed my head. The projectile embedded in the ground, inches from my hand. Soft plucks of fingers on string sounded from the trees.

"There's more!" Cynthia yelled. Her dark eyes brushed over me and Zavier and then the field. She could run with inhumane speed, but we were open targets.

"We'll have to run," Zavier said. "We have to get to the—"

His voice garbled. He palmed his chest and it came away red. Zavier's blue eyes, wide and startled, caught mine. Blood leaked between his lips and he took a sharp breath, mouthing the air.

"Don't talk, it's ok, it's ok." I wrapped my arms around his body, but he was too heavy. His eyes rolled back in his head and he collapsed. The feathered shaft of an arrow protruded from his back like a broken compass point.

Cynthia threw her other dagger at something I couldn't see. A groan of pain came from the forest and the arrows paused.

"It wasn't a killing shot," she said. "But it bought us a minute. Apply pressure to his wounds, I'll get the horses."

She disappeared toward the field.

Zavier's chest moved up and down, and blood spread through his clothes. I ripped his vest away at the impact point and tied it around both sides of the arrow, locking it in place. He groaned and shook, as though cold with fever.

"Get on the horse and I'll lift him to you," Cynthia said.

I jumped at the sound of her voice. If she'd been an enemy, I would be dead.

I convinced my numb feet to climb into Vry's saddle. A metallic taste stained my tongue. Zavier's blood chilled my hands and I held them up. I didn't want to touch anything. Cynthia lifted Zavier effortlessly and draped him over the horse in front of me.

"Hold the arrow still while we ride. I'll tie your horse to mine."

"All right," I said. White noise smothered my emotions. Part of my brain said I was in shock, but it was a fleeting thought, unimportant and dismissed. I pressed my hands against the wound, trying to stop the bleeding without touching the projectile.

Cynthia mounted and an arrow struck at her horse's hooves. The animal didn't flinch. She tied off our reins, and we rode, more arrows peppering our wake.

It was impossible to hold Zavier steady. His body bounced with each step and my arms burned with the effort to keep him on.

Cynthia looked back. Long strands of hair slipped from her braid and flailed wildly in the wind.

"Can you do any magic?" she yelled. "His heart rate is dropping."

"I bound my magic as part of the surrender." I had never felt so helpless, so unbearably small. My support, the man that I trusted most in this world, was bleeding out in my arms. "I can't do anything."

Her eyes raked over me and narrowed as though she didn't like what she saw.

"We'll ride faster then." She set a new, groaning pace.

Chapter Fourteen

ZAVIER SURVIVED THE JOURNEY TO THE INFIRMARY. THE healers started working on him before they even pulled him off my horse. They promised to send a messenger with any updates and disappeared inside.

Cynthia and I stood outside the white stone medical building. I couldn't halt the tremble in my hands, although I wasn't cold. I had passed the point where I wanted to cry, but my eyes burned. My body felt like a lead weight, emotionally and physically exhausted. Blood soaked my dress, one eye was starting to swell from a hit I must have taken, and my hair swung loose and ragged. My bones creaked in protest when I moved.

Cynthia didn't wear a drop of blood, her flawless skin glowed, and her long nails bore no evidence of the hand-to-hand fights she had won—or lost.

"I'll take care of finding the king." She didn't look at me. "You have enough to worry about."

I bit my lip. It would be irresponsible to avoid searching for Kadence, but he was the last person I wanted to see. If Kadence had been here, if he hadn't run away from his own feelings, Zavier might not have gotten hurt. Another part of me wanted to find him, to ring his neck myself. Duty and desire warred.

Cynthia crossed her arms. "Go to bed, Queen Salvatore. Get some rest and I'll update you on our findings later. If Kadence is in trouble, he can handle himself for a couple more hours."

Her logic was flawed, but sincerity stretched across her face. She knew that worry and guilt for Zavier would render me useless in her search.

"All right." I wrapped my arms around myself.

Cynthia shot her hand out, fingers extended.

I twisted my mouth, confused.

"It's a handshake," she said. "You were a good partner to have by my side today." She gripped my bloody hand in a firm, confident grip. I hoped she didn't feel it shaking.

"Thank you," I said.

She nodded and left, barking orders at the guards on her way to the castle.

The sun was past its zenith and it baked the castle in a fiery glow. Shapes and shadows of people moved through the windows, busy with the routine of life. I couldn't bring myself to take a step toward the grey stone structure. The thought of sleep drifted through my mind like a sweet lullaby, but I knew it would not find me.

Zavier's cold blood covered my hands and clothes.

The healers said they would send a messenger if anything happened to him. I didn't want to know. They would go to my room first, then through the rest of the castle. If I wasn't in the castle, maybe they would never find me.

My legs carried me away from the infirmary, the vampires and the witches, the council, the rooms where my parents used to live. A trio of Royal Guards followed my steps and I ignored them. I ignored everything. As I walked, the landscape blurred. The trees became a single green streak. Buildings and houses faded away. I didn't notice when the cobblestone road became a well-worn dirt path. The sounds of chatter slipped away, replaced with a harmonious blend of orders and yelling.

I had wandered into the training arena, although calling it an arena was generous. The space was nestled in a valley between two hills and flooded whenever it rained. The ground had been flattened to dirt from endless marches, sparring matches, and formations. Three hastily constructed wooden bleachers formed a semicircle at the back end where soldiers learned to fight. Metal racks held blunt training weapons.

A unit of soldiers split into sparring groups. Two people fought and an officer critiqued them. Jeers and shouts spread across the field. The familiar sounds drove away the memory of Zavier's body on my horse.

One young officer caught sight of me and did a double take.

"Attention!" he yelled in a slight accent. The soldiers, some with weapons raised, froze at the command. Their heads turned and they snapped into a quick formation.

An older man with rich brown skin stepped from the crowd as I approached. He wore a loose fitting camouflage battle uniform that was clean and neat, despite the sparring practice.

"Queen Salvatore." He smiled and genuine warmth lit his face. He bowed and I nodded in greeting. "It has been many months since you've come this way."

"Marshal Forster. It has been too long," I said.

"You are busy. Your parents, the war, and now managing a peaceful surrender. Some of us wonder how you do it."

The secret was to not do any of it very well.

"I was wondering if I might join in a spar?"

His brown eyes studied my face.

"It looks like you already did, My Queen."

I resisted the urge to touch my swollen eye.

"My opponent is dead." My voice sounded flat in my own ears. "I need to practice with someone that's not trying to kill me."

Marshal Forester had been on the battlefield many times. He knew the difference between fighting for one's life and for one's sanity. He scanned my tattered dress and the dried blood flaking from my palms.

"Commander Greer, find the queen a partner."

SOLDIER RHODES STOOD TOO WIDE, PUTTING HIS SHORT AND stocky body off balance before he even realized it. His arms lacked the definition that came with years of fighting and he gripped the practice sword with a loose fist. The brown-and-green uniform gaped at the sleeves, bound to get in the way of his movements as he fought. Rhodes wiggled his eyebrows, portraying more confidence than I knew his skills would prove. Commander Greer had given me an easy opponent.

I stood with my feet shoulder width apart, knees slightly bent, sword up. The training sword felt familiar in my warm hand. Pain, confusion, and worry faded away as a fresh wave of adrenaline coursed through me. The world pinpointed to me, my opponent, and our weapons.

I remained still, water on a flat surface.

Rhodes tilted his head, like a confused puppy. His big, brown eyes squinted at me as I watched him. It wouldn't be long. Men were never very patient.

He charged, the tip of his blade out from his body, two hands holding the sword like a rope in a game of tug of war.

I held my place. *Wait. Wait.* A shadow of doubt flashed through his eyes. *Now.*

I sidestepped. He tumbled through the space where I had been, tripping over his feet and catching himself at the last minute.

"Don't overcommit to a strike," I said. "Keep your body loose and your knees bent. It'll make you flexible."

Rhodes straightened. His mouth pinched into a line. Behind the blank face hid an edge of anger. There was hope for him yet.

"Try again." I smiled.

He charged, this time balancing on the balls of his feet. He held the sword like a club, deciding to swing at me rather than stab.

I stepped again, and he followed, quick and decisive. *Good.* He sliced down, expecting the hesitation of metal on flesh, but my sword was already there. His blade bounced against mine and the impact pushed him back. I raised my sword to his neck. He dropped his weapon, the universal sign of defeat.

"Don't hesitate when you take a bad block. It leaves you open," I said.

A crowd of soldiers had assembled. They clapped and whooped at us.

I picked up the fallen sword and handed it to Rhodes, hilt first. "Again."

I struck first. My sword arched overhead, aiming for a simple downswing.

His face flickered in surprise. He lifted his blade and blocked me, a chime of metal scraping metal.

The crowd cheered.

"Good," I said.

I cut from the side and he blocked again.

"Faster. I pulled the strike at the end."

The soldiers urged him on, chanting his name and shouting tips.

Pulling the sword up, I feigned a high swing, turning it into a stab at the last minute. He blocked and cut my strike down. His face lit in triumph, a real smile caught at the edge of his lips.

I punched him in the face. His air rushed out and he staggered two steps back.

The audience groaned.

"What?" I spread my arms. "You guys don't do hand-to-hand training anymore?"

Standing nearby with his arms crossed over his chest, Commander Greer smiled and shook his head. "We sure do, Your Majesty."

"Then he should have been able to block that."

"Yes, he should have."

"I'm done," Rhodes said, holding his nose and lifting one hand in the air in surrender.

The tight ball in my chest faded. The smell of sweat and blood, the sound of metal on metal, the feel of dirt sticking to my skin, all without the risk of dying. I had missed this. The stress of the surrender, the possibility that Zavier may die, none of that existed out here. It was just the weapon in my hand and trust in my body.

"Anyone else?"

One by one, soldiers came from the crowd to spar with me. One by one, they returned, sporting a black eye or a new bruise. As my victories increased, my fear and worries subsided until the only thing I thought about was the next place my sword would land. I felt lighter than air. I was flying.

Two soldiers struck at me at once, learning to work as a team. I ducked between their blades and kicked the legs from under one of them. He toppled into the dirt and his partner stabbed at my open back. I fell forward, rolled and popped up next to him. A strike to the gut from the side and he was out.

The first guy picked himself from the dirt and charged. He had good speed and a strong stance, but I had more practice. I dodged, swinging my blade around for a final strike at his exposed chest.

My blade hit metal unexpectedly and bounced off. I staggered, unbalanced. A sword from a new opponent struck from the right and I parried it easily.

I retreated two steps to reset and catch my breath.

Kadence smiled at me. His back turned to the sun, casting shadows on his face. His eyes danced with delight at my surprise. I scanned his all-black attire. He appeared to be uninjured, in one piece. The crowd went ramrod straight to attention, watching with curious stares.

Weight and frustration crashed back onto my shoulders. Fear turned to anger at the man that had caused so many of my problems. If he hadn't gone missing, Cynthia wouldn't have looked for us. We wouldn't have lingered in that field and the hybrids wouldn't have attacked us. Hate and rage bubbled like lava in my stomach, and I let it fill me with hot determination.

Kadence took a step forward, and I backed away. We circled each other, assessing the invisible lines of our bodies, waiting for the first tell.

"It's lovely to see you, My King. It's been too long." *Where the hell were you?*

"Likewise, My Queen."

"I trust you didn't get lost on your journey home?" *I know you've been missing for two days.*

"It went exactly how I expected." He wasn't going to tell me anything. *Fine.*

I let him see the tension grip me, the weight shift on my feet. Moving into a defensive stance, he prepared for a front strike. I took two steps, sword raised, and cleared the distance. He tracked me, until the last moment, when I dashed to the side and through his defense. My dull sword slipped across his clothes.

"First blood," I said, behind him now. Due to the dull practice weapons, there wasn't any, unfortunately. I would have been happy seeing his blood on my blade.

"It wasn't a killing blow," he said, but smoke smoldered in his dark eyes. He hadn't expected me to score the first hit. He'd underestimated my motivation.

"No, it wasn't." *But the next one will be.*

He spun and struck, fast and sly like a snake. In terrible, rapid precision his sword clashed against mine. I danced away, but he kept coming, tireless. He hadn't spent the day fighting the hybrids creatures. He was fresh and I already gasped for air.

Unlike the hybrids and new recruits, Kadence fought with purpose and determination. He knew where his blade would land before he struck. He calculated my most likely position and adapted his moves accordingly. I managed to stay ahead of him, remain slightly unpredictable, but I couldn't keep it up for long.

My foot slipped as I retreated, opening my defense. He struck, sure and fast. I scurried away, but his sword licked the fabric of my dress.

"Second blood." He smiled.

Anger, rage, hatred, everything dropped from my mind. I entered the space reserved for life and death fights, the ones where hopes were low and prayers were whispered between strikes. White noise cut through my ears, the steady pulse of my blood a constant companion urging me on.

Kadence studied my face, and I let him see the pain, suffering, fear, disappointment, and depression I had fought for weeks. Like fresh snow on the first day of winter, my mind became clean.

A snap of doubt clouded his face. He would lose this fight and he knew it.

I cut at his wrist. He pulled back, but I was inside his defenses. My blade spun, a tornado of strikes and stabs, which he blocked over and over again. I poured more strength into my strikes, grunting with every swing. He blocked, but each became a microsecond slower to meet my blade.

I burned. My muscles were past the point of exhaustion. I wanted to fall on my face and sleep in the dirt of the arena. The sweat and blood and soldiers would be comforting and familiar and I might actually sleep, unlike the tossing and turning I'd done in my mother's room. My arms protested each time I lifted the sword, but training and discipline forced them in line.

Strike. Block. Strike. Block. Again, again, again.

Kadence slowed. One block was sloppy and the next barely met my blade. The third, he was open.

He was mine.

His eyes widened and he tensed in preparation of the impact of the blade. He calculated his options, examining me for a mistake, for a chance that he might get another strike. His face settled as he realized there wasn't any.

Joy bubbled through the static in my head. My arms locked and I planted my feet for the final strike.

Movement caught the edge of my vision. The soldiers had broken attention and stared, their mouths agape. They watched as we plundered each other, one broken royal against another, and they were about to see me claim victory in this fight.

It would ruin everything. We had lost the war. *I* had lost the war. Kadence was the king of both nations. Cutting him down would destroy all the report we had built.

I caught Kadence's gaze. I slowed my strike.

He readjusted, moving out of my range, and bounced my sword off his. Metal on metal sent sparks in the fading light. I'd shifted my weight too far forward during the strike. I hadn't anticipated the weightlessness of missing my target. Hard ground met my knees as I fell, catching my hands in the bloody dirt. The cool touch of Kadence's sword found my neck.

"Killing strike," Kadence said.

I nodded. I didn't have the air to speak.

He looked down at me, dark eyes lined with silver. He threw the sword in the dirt.

"I'll see you tonight." He turned and started down the ragged path toward the castle. He walked slow, careful, but anger leaked from the lines of his body.

I slid back until my butt hit the ground. I stretched my sore, tired, bruised body onto the dirt and looked at the dimming sky until the first stars peeked out. Helpful hands from my soldiers reached for me, but I waived them away. The dirt and darkness were the only comforts I wanted.

Chapter Fifteen

I STOPPED TO CHECK ON ZAVIER. THE HEALERS SAID HE WAS stable, but his body had taken a lot of damage. They claimed it would be too distracting for him to see me and I was too tired to argue. They patched up my black eye and bruises and sent me on my way.

I staggered to my room and found Kadence already there. He had lit a fire and stood next to it with a glass of deep red liquid, a mirror to the night of my coronation. He had changed into dark breeches and a black button up shirt, the most casual outfit I had seen him wear.

In stark contrast, my dress was covered in blood, dirt, and cuts where blades had sliced through the fabric. My hair cascaded down my back in dirty curls, sporting leaves and sweat. My body ached. I had abused it to its breaking point and beyond, and it would punish me tomorrow.

Kadence raised his eyebrows. "What happened to you?"

"Assassins, and then you," I said.

"Assassins? Again?" he avoided the second part of my statement.

I nodded. "They're dead."

"You let me win that fight," he said.

"Yes." I didn't see a point in denying it.

His lips twisted to a snarl. "Why?"

"I'm too tired to do this." I turned away from him.

Someone, probably Saffa, had spread night clothes across the bed. If Kadence wanted to argue, he could do it while I was comfortable. I pulled cream colored silk breeches up under my dress. My fingers fumbled with the dress button at the back of my neck, cramping from overuse. I turned away from the vampire watching me like injured prey. The fabric slipped down my arms and off my hips. I left on my neutral brassiere like an armored plate and slipped the shirt over it.

"I would have liked to take a bath," I said.

"I'm not stopping you." Fire burned in Kadence's eyes. He took a sip of that red liquid.

I ignored the implication of his words. "Where were you?"

"A messenger informed you that I went home to take care of my own kingdom, Sal."

"I mean for the last two days, Kadence. Cynthia told me you went missing."

"Did she?" Another sip. "I'm surprised she did that. She doesn't like you."

"Have you talked to her? She's running a search party to find you."

"She knows I'm back." Kadence's face tightened and he looked away from me. He had a secret he didn't want Cynthia to know.

My patience unraveled like a spool of spilled yarn.

"If you don't want to talk to me, then just leave," I snapped. "I'm tired and I'm hungry. I'm not in the mood for you to bother me tonight."

"Is that what I'm doing? Bothering you?"

"Yes. You're leaning against my window as though there weren't a hundred people searching for you all evening. You're sipping your blood or wine or whatever it is, as though you haven't a care in the world! I'm sick of it, Kadence. Go to the market, go throw coins at people until they like you. In the meantime, I'll sit behind your smug face and make sure this kingdom doesn't fall apart."

I felt the draw of his power before he used it. He suddenly stood in front of me, less than an inch between our bodies, and I hadn't seen him move. If he had used his power during our fight, it would have been over immediately. We had both pulled our punches.

"Do you think this is blood, Sal?" His voice sounded quiet and dangerous. He held the glass between us and ruby liquid shimmered under the candlelight. A bitter scent slipped from the cup, but I held my breathe in fear the metallic edge of blood may follow.

"I don't know." My heartbeat picked up. I swallowed, but my tongue stuck to the roof of my mouth. He was too close. The heat from his body along with his power rolled around me, a whirlpool threatening to drown me.

His eyes turned to silver coins with an eerie black center. Twin fangs poked between his teeth. There was no control here.

"Why don't you try it?" He offered me the glass.

"No, thank you."

His hand caught the back of my head. He twisted his fingers through my hair and pushed against me. I stepped away, but Kadence planted his foot behind mine. My weight shifted, tilted off balance, and I toppled backward, except his hand on my head grounded me and trapped me in place. His palm was the only thing holding me up.

"I insist." He smiled.

The cold glass settled against my lips. I pressed them together, but the liquid seeped in, past the barrier of my teeth. Red wine, sharp and fruity, spilled into my mouth. I sputtered and choked, and the vampire laughed.

Like a wineskin that had been empty too long, I snapped. I was so tired—tired of the fear that angering this man would hurt my kingdom, tired of being afraid in my own home, of making sacrifices that nobody appreciated. I was done, so very done.

I punched Kadence in the throat. My arm was weak, but my aim was true. He sputtered and choked and instinctively put both hands on the injury. He released my head and I tumbled to the floor, rolling closer to the bed.

I fumbled against the bottom of the bedframe, feeling for the hidden sheath there. My fingers caught against cool metal and the latch popped open.

A strong hand wrapped around my ankle and yanked me from under the bed. I came out with a knife the length of my forearm. I slashed at Kadence's wrist. He swore sharply and let me go.

He took two steps back and eyed my knife.

"What are you doing?" Wildness edged his silver eyes. The vampire realized he wasn't the only predator in the room and he didn't like it.

"Are you mad that I let you win earlier?" I pushed from the ground and twisted the blade. "Don't worry. I won't do it again."

He reached behind his back and pulled out a stubby dagger from an unseen sheath. "Let's see it then."

I lashed out. Rage and fear and frustration fueled my strike. I slipped close, and danced away, barely avoiding the edge of his blade.

"You missed," he said.

"Did I?" I held up a single black button. The front of his shirt gaped open. He ran a finger across his unbroken skin. When he looked up, a fire burned in his gaze, and it was more than eagerness for a fight.

"There are easier ways to take my clothes off, Sal."

Then he was on me, striking with his dagger. The short blades forced us close. My knife gave me a longer range, but his dagger offered more precision. My magic was locked away and I was exhausted. Kadence was primed, ready, his rich power a tornado whipping through the room. This would likely not end in my favor.

I dodged his first barrage and slashed the knife across his chest.

"Where"—*slash*—"were"—*slash*—"you?"

The last slash brough me close to his chest. His smokey scent twisted around me, drawing my mind from the battle for a moment, to darker and more forbidden places.

He took two steps back, breaking my thoughts. We circled each other.

"Why do you care?" he asked.

"What you do affects my kingdom and my people." *And your absence hurt me.*

He dashed into my range, flicked his blade, and was gone. The right side of my shirt fell, severed at the shoulder seam. He gave me a half smile.

We met again, our blades connected and slipped apart, reflecting flashes of the fire.

"I spent the weekend at the coast, in a nice brothel." He aimed a punch at my torso, but I dodged.

"Lie." I ducked his swing and took a stab at his exposed stomach.

He turned and my blade hit air. "I spent two days planning an orphanage since we can't even get a barracks building constructed here." He spun toward me, invading my space.

I backpedaled and my balance tipped. I embraced the fall and caught one hand on the stone ground.

"Lie."

I kicked Kadence in the tender spot inside his knee. His leg collapsed, forcing him to kneel. I lunged up and he rolled to avoid my blade. I followed his body, straddling his waist and pinning his arms under my legs.

He bucked and I pushed my knife against his throat until his pulse became visible against the blade. He stilled.

I tried to ignore the feel of him between my legs. The rhythm of his chest rising with every breath. I tried to pretend it didn't drive me crazy in more ways than one.

"Tell me the truth." My lungs hurt. My hand shook. This wasn't a dull training knife. I might slit his throat by accident. I pressed my knee into the tendon cluster of nerves on his hand between the thumb and the wrist.

His face twisted as his fingers were forced open. He dropped the dagger.

"I went to see my mother's grave." His eyes had lost the edge of frantic danger. I searched the depths of his gaze, and for a moment, saw a pool of deep sadness. He buried it away and I was left with my reflection and the dance of the fire behind me.

I hesitated too long. I could have killed him or demanded a surrender, but that flash of emotion stole my focus. He freed one hand and pulled the knife from his throat. In a graceful turn of his hips, he flipped us. My back collided with the floor and Kadence's silver eyes consumed my vision. They burned with a steady mix of pain and desire. Did he see the same in mine?

"Your mother was cremated," I said.

Kadence caught both of my wrists and secured them in one hand above my head. My knife had gone missing and I was too tired to fight more anyway. A pounding in my head blended into the array of aches and pains until I felt numb. Kadence's stark silver eyes almost bled to white and he looked at me the way he looked at his glass of wine—like he couldn't wait for a taste. The final shred of his humanity disappeared. The vampire stared down and tilted his head.

"Who told you that?" He leaned his weight onto my wrists, locking them tightly in place. My heart jerked and I tried to convince myself it was fear and not the eagerness of the vampire's next move.

"Does it matter?"

"I'll have to kill Rayhan." He didn't look like he wanted to kill Rayhan. He watched my throat and his eyes bounced with my pulse.

He bent down, the intensity in his gaze increasing with every beat of my heart.

I closed my eyes. "Does it hurt?"

His lips grazed my throat, light and soft.

"Do you want to find out?" he asked in a husky whisper.

I tensed, waiting for the pierce of fangs into my flesh. I was dizzy and exhausted. I shouldn't have picked a fight with him. I had made my own bed, and I had to lie in it. For the first time, I wondered what it would be like to lie in it with Kadence.

Hot breath tickled my skin when Kadence opened his mouth.

The door to my room crashed open. Wood splintered from the overstressed hinges and the knob slammed into the wall. Stone dust showered the floor.

Renee stood in the doorway, a dark silhouette with candles flickering behind her. Kadence lifted his head from my neck. Renee looked right through us.

"I have news," she said.

"Zavier?" My breath caught.

"No." She swayed on her feet. "Your parents have been sighted. They found it. They found the Fields of Death."

The fear I had been too tired to feel swelled from the depths of my soul and spread through me in a swift, paralyzing wave. Kadence's face went white and the deep black of his eyes slowly returned. Renee turned and disappeared, leaving us in stunned silence.

Chapter Sixteen

A FLURRY OF PAPERS, MAPS, AND PANIC ERUPTED FROM THE meeting room. People milled around, picked up pages, and put them back down. They wore blank or angry faces and everyone waited for answers we may not have.

I had thrown on a new, light blue dress, but my hair was still dirty, and dried sweat had left salt crystals on my skin. I pushed the exhaustion and my complaining muscles to the back of my mind and trapped them there with mental ropes. Saffa handed me a cup of steaming coffee. It tasted better than Kadence's red wine.

The vampire took in the state of the room. Rayhan sat in the back corner, observing the mass of witches as they flurried about. His axe rested on one armored shoulder.

Kadence raised his eyebrows at the man.

Rayhan stepped to the meeting table and smacked his axe on the wood with a loud thump. One day, he was going to break my table. Sharp inhales spread through the room and everyone looked wide-eyed at the axe.

"All right." Kadence walked to the head of the table and put a hand on Rayhan's shoulder.

A bit of tension eased from the giant's form as he lifted his weapon and stepped back like a towering bodyguard. Both the gentle touch and placating effect Kadence had on the man surprised me. Rayhan mentioned they were friends, but I found it difficult to imagine what a friendship with Kadence would look like.

"What do we know?" Kadence asked the room in general.

The council members and other experts stumbled into seats around the table. I picked the chair across from Kadence, closest to the door. The cold wood was a comfort on my sore legs.

Marshal Hale stood. In the latter half of her fourth decade, her blond hair sported hints of grey, but youth still stretched across her round face. She had served in our army for over twenty years and commanded our scout units.

"Sir, we confirmed the marching of five thousand troops from the north early this evening. Our scouts were over a week's ride away, but sent a messenger via an emergency transportation spell."

"How do we even know they found," Councilwoman Shanna Bowden lowered her voice, "the Fields? What proof do we have of demonic possession?" She ran her hand through her frazzled brown hair again.

"The younger, weaker demons can't hold their human bodies together for long," Marshal Hale said. "There were already several half-forms."

"I don't understand," Bowden said.

"I'll explain," said Tatianna Gaines, a petite redhead wearing a deep-green dress and glasses too large for her dainty face. She pushed her lenses up. "As a professor of history and geography, I've studied the lore of the Fields and the effects of demon possession for years."

She looked to Kadence and me, awaiting permission to go on. We both nodded.

"The Fields of Death are a place where the connection between our realm and the realm of the dead is exceptionally thin. It is rumored to be a literal field, a flatland where the two places meet, but nobody who has been there has survived to confirm that. Legends say that if one enters the Fields, they have an opportunity to accept a demon into their body in exchange for limitless power."

Arms crossed, Bowden scowled in her direction. "If it's an entrance to the realm of the dead, why don't they get possessed by angels or ghosts or something better than a demon?"

"Great question." Tatianna's eyes sparkled as she talked. "Our best guess is that morally good beings would not do such an evil act as to possess someone." She put both hands in the air. "Again, that is just a personal guess."

"Are all these demons going to have limitless power and magic?" Marshal Hale's face turned white. "We'll be killed immediately."

"Demonic history suggests that possession overrules a witch's innate abilities. They shouldn't be able to do magic."

"Shouldn't?"

Tatiana shrugged. "It's never been recorded in the lore, at least."

"What's a half-form?" I asked.

"Yes, My Queen. The older a demon is, the more power it amasses. Living bodies are very weak. It takes great power to stuff two souls into one body and keep it together seamlessly. When a demon doesn't have that ability, their natural form spills through the human skin. They turn into a monster, of sorts. Imagine a human covered with boiling black tar." Tatianna looked almost giddy while everyone else turned sickly green.

"Thank you, Tatianna." I turned to Marshal Hale. "These half forms were confirmed by the scouts?"

"Yes, My Queen."

The door opened. A tall, blond healer pushed Zavier into the room in a wheelchair. Reuben hovered behind him in the doorway and tried to slip inside the chamber unnoticed, but I caught Kadence's lips press tighter.

"Zavier!" I jumped, but hesitated, remembering myself. I didn't want to rush into his arms if his body was still healing. Zavier's jaw clenched and his fists balled on the arms of his chair. Pain tightened the lines of his face, but he smiled at me, and warmth chased away my sorrows for a moment.

"My Queen, it is a pleasure to see you tonight." His blue eyes sparkled with hints of concern. "I wish we were gathered under better circumstances."

"What's he doing here?" Kadence's dark gaze fixated on Reuben. The man had combed his blond hair back and his beard looked freshly trimmed. He wore black breeches, a white button down shirt, and a white jacket. His polished black shoes shone from where he lingered in the doorway, as though unsure if he wanted to remain in the room.

"Mr. Emerson is one of our best statisticians and I think his expertise would be beneficial in these circumstances," Zavier said. "Despite any unfortunate personal feelings."

Kadence nodded once. Arguing with Zavier would make him look insecure and lacking confidence. The council needed a calm and decisive leader who put his kingdom before his feelings. I respected that he held his tongue. He eyed the rest of the attendants and a softened look crossed his face. He didn't like when his people were afraid.

Reuben took a chair beside me and gave me a sly smile. I kept my face blank as the witch and vampire both watched me.

"What are our stats with the kingdoms combined?" I asked.

Councilman Knox dropped a thick stack of papers and scrolls onto the table with a thud.

"I've been working with Rayhan." He eyed the giant, but a hint of amusement twinkled in his eyes. "The vampires brought twelve thousand soldiers here, but they really only have a fighting force of about ten thousand. There's a good number dedicated to logistical and medical assignments. We have five thousand prepared to fight, one thousand in reserves, and could muster another two thousand from a draft."

"Getting two thousand people battle trained in a week would be very difficult," Reuben said.

"Your Majesty," Marshal Hale said. "There's more to the report. The army of the damned wasn't marching this way."

"Which way are they going?"

"To the east."

I leaned back in my chair. "What's to the east?"

Metal on stone thundered through the room. Rayhan turned paper white and his axe shattered the stone floor where it had slipped from his grip.

Kadence looked calm and poised, but his hand fisted on the table and his lips pressed into a grim line. "They're marching on us. Our home is to the east."

I shook my head. "That doesn't make sense. You always attacked from the west. In the past we've sent scouts out west looking for your kingdom."

"It's called 'deception,' My Queen," Kadence said, but his heart wasn't in the insult. He was miles away, imagining an army of demons ravaging his village and killing his people.

"Natalie's there," Rayhan choked.

"She's okay," I said, though I didn't know who Natalie was. "They're not there yet. How far east is Vari Kolum?"

"Three days journey from here," Kadence said.

"Marshal Hale, how long before the demons reach the vampire kingdom?"

Her face twisted. "Two weeks. Maybe a day or two longer."

Two weeks. It wasn't a lot of time. We wouldn't be able to fully train new recruits. My fingers drummed the table.

"There isn't enough time for everyone to train and travel," Kadence said.

"Councilman Amos?"

Peering at us from within dark circles that appeared to be trying to swallow his eyes, Julien Amos spun his fingers on a blank piece of paper in front of him and one side of his mouth tilted down.

"We could make it happen with a transportation spell." Amos said slowly, as though each word caused him physical pain. "We could transport soldiers in waves. It would take a few days to prepare the spells and some witches will have to go on foot to set up the entrance sites."

"What does that mean?" Kadence asked.

"Spellwork is inherently magic," I said, "But there's a lot of trial and error and extrapolation involved. I wouldn't call it science, but there are similar principles." I spread my fingers on the table. "Transportation spells are very complicated. Mass is not expected to move outside the laws of gravity, and it has to be done carefully or else physics interferes."

"We can't just pick up a cluster of people, close our eyes, and blink them somewhere else, Your Majesty," Amos explained bitterly. "That's how people get cut in half."

Kadence raised his eyebrows.

"Nobody will be cut in half," I tried to reassure him, but all his experiences with magic would have been trying to survive it on the battlefield. "Only our top experts handle troop transportation magic. Transport spells have designated exit and entrance sites. You must tell the spell *this is what I need moved* and *this is where I want it to go*. We would have to send witches on foot to your kingdom to establish the entrance site there."

"Then we can transport all the troops instantly?"

Amos interjected. "Almost instantly. With these numbers, we would set up multiple sites and funnel people through in groups of a hundred or so. It would be a process."

"I'll tell our people to prepare for the influx of soldiers," Rayhan said.

It had taken a demon horde to reveal the location of the Kingdom of Vari Kolum. The fear in Kadence and Rayhan's eyes wasn't worth it. I would rather their home remain a secret to me forever, than watch them endure this new blast of morbid uncertainty.

"I'll get started on implementing a draft." Amos stood.

"Wait," I said. "Ask for volunteers first. If we don't meet the quota for volunteers by tomorrow, then we'll enforce a draft."

"You'd be losing precious time, Sal," Reuben piped from his chair.

Kadence jerked his head to the man. "She is your queen, Emerson, and you should remember to call her as such."

Reubens eyes darkened and I could almost see Kadence's death twisting in his irises.

"My Queen," he said, although the words offered a challenge.

I spoke quickly, before a fight over something so minuscule could break out. "If we crush morale immediately, this fight will be over before it begins." I had already made this mistake. It wouldn't happen again.

Amos bowed and slipped out the door.

"Your Majesty, I will go too," Marshal Hale said. "There's a lot to prepare."

At a nod from Kadence, I gave assignments and duties, and people shuffled out one by one. The panic and dread in the room turned into hopeful chatter, and the room felt lighter as people left.

"Rayhan stay here," Kadence said.

"Tatiana, can you stay too, please?" I asked.

The two sat down.

"I promised to kill anyone that told Sal about my parents." Kadence looked at Rayhan with fire in his eyes.

Rayhan shrugged. "She needed to know. You were hurting yourself and your soldiers. I knew it would help her, and I would do it again."

"You're an idiot." The words lacked menace. Kadence squeezed Rayhan's shoulder. "Natalie's going to be okay."

Rayhan nodded, but his blue eyes reflected doubt.

"Kadence," Zavier's soft and warm voice felt like velvet on a cold day. "I think you need to tell us about your mother."

Kadence's face was calm, but a flicker hid underneath. For a moment, he was not the fearsome king who conquered a country after generations of war. He was a child, hiding in the dark, afraid of what he'd seen.

"My mother," he said, "was tired of the war. She watched her parents die, her brothers and sister, her other children. She would do anything to end it. But my father had limits."

He didn't look at anyone in the room. He gazed over our heads, in a different place at a different time. My heart ached for him, surprising me.

"She disappeared," he said. "She was gone for weeks. I was young and I didn't handle it well. I started sleeping in my father's room, on his floor. I was there when she came home. She was different. I could see it right away. I was afraid of her, so I hid under the bed, and she didn't see me. Grace, one of our servants was with her."

Throat working, he swallowed hard. Compelled by something deep inside, I reached under the table and placed a hand on his leg. He didn't respond to my touch, but he didn't pull away.

"Mother walked up to my father and told him she found a way to end the war. He asked who she was and what the demon had done with his wife. It threatened him, said it wanted blood and death, and he wasn't going to deny it that. It said that if my father wanted to avoid bloodshed in his kingdom, he would gather the armies and march on the witches immediately. My father said no and it laughed. The demon laughed as my mother's fingers became claws and she reached into his chest and came out with handfuls of his flesh. She and Grace tore my father into pieces while he screamed and they mocked him." Muscles in his jaw tightened. I squeezed his leg and he glanced at me. Although his mind focused on memories miles away, his hand found mine beneath the table, warming me with his war-beaten palm.

"They went out into the village. The demon wore my mother's face and people flocked to her, celebrating her return. Men, women, children gathered at her feet and kissed the tattered edges of her skirts. The demon slaughtered them all. It was a bloodbath. The stairs of the palace soaked in blood and bodies and every soldier that approached it was added to the trail of carnage. She ventured into the village, and for two days, people fled to the woods or hid in secret places of their homes and prayed she wouldn't find them."

When it seemed Kadence wouldn't go on, Rayhan spoke for him. "It took three units to bring her down," he said. "My father was one of the commanders. They baited her with children and managed to corner her. They ripped her head from her shoulders and the demon laughed at them while they threw parts of it into the fire. My father only talked about it after a night of drinking, when the depression and weight of war finally caught up with him."

Children used as bait. My stomach turned. They must have been desperate.

Kadence sat up straighter. "The demons didn't just kill, they played with, and tortured people. In two days, a quarter of our population was either dead or had run away. That was only two demons. This..." Kadence stretched his arms out. "There are five thousand."

"Tatiana," I said, "what are your thoughts?"

She pushed her glasses up. Her fingers twisted into knots. "According to the legends, one demon alone could take down two or three hundred people. They left their hosts only when there was a great enough threat to flee. To face five thousand?" Her lips twisted. "It is an unlikely feat."

"They wouldn't be fighting normal people, though," Zavier said. His skin had taken an unhealthy pearly white tone. "We would have battle trained soldiers on the field and spellcasters working alongside them."

"That would help," Tatiana said slowly, "but it wouldn't be enough. Not by a lot."

Nobody said anything. Dread twisted my heart. Panic warred with exhaustion. The adrenaline faded, replaced by the long-term sense of impending doom. I couldn't stop imagining tiny faces twisted in fear while a demon stalked toward them.

Swaying in his chair, Zavier shook his head. "The outlook appears grim." He needed to go back to the infirmary and rest.

"I must return home," Kadence said, his hand pulling from mine.

"They need more than just you, Your Majesty." Rayhan's gaze locked on me like an archer on their target.

"We'll put together an advanced team." I looked to Zavier. "You and I will go with the best transportation witches to prepare an entrance spell at your kingdom." Either the exhaustion or the sheer determination to survive ignited anger in my soul, and it burned like acid. "We might not survive, but we will damned well fight."

"Yes, My Queen, yes we will," Zavier said. "But not tonight. I'm afraid I must rest some more. This old body isn't used to these injuries and my sweet Lily is waiting downstairs."

Calling Zavier's wife, Lily, sweet was like calling a rabid bear cute. She was a short, black-haired woman with a sharp face and sharper wit. She ran her house the way a Commander wished he could run his unit, with discipline and unconditional love, but mostly discipline.

Zavier squeezed my hand, then his healer rolled him out the door.

Kadence dismissed the others and everyone followed Zavier out, leaving us alone with Rayhan.

"I have to send a messenger to Natalie," Rayhan said.

"Make sure she doesn't tell anyone else," Kadence warned. "I don't want to start a panic, at least until we're prepared."

"Yes, sir," Rayhan said, already halfway out the door.

For a moment, Kadence and I sat in silence.

"I have to go," he said.

"I know." I shuffled some of the abandoned papers on the table. "Are you staying here?"

"For a while. I have things to look over."

"You need sleep."

"Are you concerned for me?" I already knew the answer. I knew his feelings had changed when he grabbed my hand tonight. Maybe we weren't in the same place as that night in my bedroom, before Reuben interrupted us, and my rushed words damaged our forward momentum, but Kadence didn't hate me as much as he wanted to.

"My kingdom suddenly depends on your troops and you have their loyalty," he said. "I need you to be alive and mostly healthy." The sharp words didn't hide the true concern on his face.

I rolled my eyes, letting him see the fragility behind the motion. There was no menace between us tonight. There couldn't be, with all of our people's lives hanging in the balance. "Thank you for caring. I'm fine, you can go."

I scanned the papers again. Maps and numbers blurred. After a moment, the door opened and shut, and I was alone.

I pressed my palms into my eyes. My shoulders weren't strong enough to carry the weight of two kingdoms. My people were finally safe, savoring peace after generations of war, and an army of doom decided to march our way. My lungs felt small, each breath a struggle. Weeks ago on the battlefield, I had been tempted to let the vampire win, to let everything go. Now, having touched the edge of peace, I would do anything to keep it. Even if the effort consumed us all.

The dark wood desk was cool and inviting. Tonight, there would be emergencies for someone else to handle and questions I wouldn't be able to answer. If I went to my bed, they would look for me there. They wouldn't look here. I curled my arms under my head and closed my eyes.

Chapter Seventeen

As news of the army of demons spread, I tried to prevent mass panic. There was chaos, of course, but I placed people carefully to keep it organized.

"Your Majesty, we've had many volunteers join our army," Councilman Amos said. "But we haven't met the quota yet. I suggest implementing a true draft to round up the stragglers."

I subtly looked behind him at the line of people that stretched out the meeting room door. Everybody hustled about and there wasn't time to call a formal meeting. Unfortunately, there were endless questions and problems I needed to solve. I was parked at the head of the table and people filed in looking for me.

I had been here all morning and still couldn't see the end of the line.

"We've had a great turn out then, Amos," I said. "Let's give it until sunset and if the numbers aren't there, we'll start the draft immediately."

He pursed his lips. "You're wasting time, My Queen."

"I don't think giving our people a chance to process this challenging situation is a waste of time, Amos. I would rather have soldiers in my army that want to be there than are forced to be."

He opened his mouth, but thought better of it. He bowed low and left.

Next.

Marshal Hale stepped forward. Dark circles lined her eyes and her armor sagged as though she hadn't taken the time to buckle it properly. She bowed.

"Marshal, I am sorry you had to wait," I told her.

"I understand the demand for your time, My Queen."

"Is there news from the scouts?"

She shook her head. "It's the same from last night. The army continued their eastern march. It appears that the demons' fleshly bodies must eat and rest. They move barely faster than our own forces would."

That was good news. It would buy us some more time.

"What do you need?" I asked.

"I would like to pull some of the new recruits with an affinity for transportation magic to join our scout teams. Our charms supply is dwindling and they're not the most reliable form of magic anyway. If we had a transport witch on every scout team, we would have immediate updates," Marshal Hale said.

I tapped my chin. "We might already have some soldiers with transport skills. Check with Marshal Curtis from Supply and see who he can spare. The new recruits won't be battle-trained yet. They'd be in your scouts' way if anything happened."

"My scouts are well trained in defense, Your Majesty. I'm confident they could protect or evacuate any untrained personnel quickly and efficiently."

"Check with Marshal Curtis and if you need more people, pull from the recruits," I said.

"Thank you, My Queen."

"Stop by the kitchens on your way and grab something to eat," I told her. "We all need to keep up our strength."

She smiled, bowed, and left.

Next.

An elderly man scooted to the front of the line. His white, long-sleeve and overalls were peppered with dirt and a well-used leather tool belt cinched his waist. Although lean, dense muscles along his arms suggested years of manual labor. He bowed and was a little slow to straighten up.

"How can I help you, mister...?"

"Patrick." His voice was gravely, as though he smoked a pipe. "Patrick McGee, Your Majesty."

I smiled. He wasn't in the army or part of Kadence's team, here to bother me. He was a civilian with a civilian request. One of my first.

"Mr. McGee, how can I help you?"

He pulled on his fingers and glanced around the room from the side of his eyes. Most civilians didn't venture this far into the castle.

"Your Majesty, with the demons and the war and such, I'm sure this project is the last thing on your mind, but all of my workers joined the army. I don't think I can finish his build as soon as the king wanted." He scratched the back of his neck and grimaced.

I smoothed my face. What project? What build? Years of training made me bite my tongue. *If you don't know what's going on*, my mother's voice whispered, *just pretend that you do.*

"What timeline did the king suggest?" I asked.

"Well, Your Majesty, he wanted it finished in about six months. He said the barracks would be done soon, and more workers would come help after that, but I'm sure the barracks people are in the army now too." He licked his lips.

The barracks project had been put on hold. We wouldn't need to house extra troops if we were all dead.

"Look," Mr. McGee continued, "I myself would cut the project. We don't need to use supplies and people for building when there's a war coming." His face turned white and he backpedaled. "Um, Your Majesty, I mean, Queen Salvatore, since it was the king himself that ordered the project, I felt I needed to ask before stopping."

Kadence had found this contractor and ordered something to be built. I had to know what it was.

"I'm going to need to see the site in person to decide." I motioned to the guard beside me and he leaned in. "Send for Zavier, he can take over here."

Patrick McGee met me on the edge of the kingdom on a plot of land pushed up against the border wall. The ride from the castle had been pleasant in the cool afternoon. The trees dropped their leaves and the promise of winter hung in the air. A knit shawl settled over my thin cotton dress and fought the chill of the breeze. It was a relief to step outside and breathe fresh air, teemed with a hint of evergreen.

"There isn't much to see yet, Your Majesty. We only broke ground two days ago," Mr. McGee said, gesturing to the field in front of us. It had been tilled to rip up the grass and the ground was in the process of being leveled. A skeleton crew of older men shoveled dirt here and there and stomped down the piles.

The field was quite a far ride from the castle. It wasn't close to a water source, so it wouldn't be suitable farming. A landfill didn't require the ground to be cleared and level. What was Kadence doing?

"Can I see the blueprints?" I asked.

Mr. McGee's face twisted. "Didn't the king show them to you?"

"Of course," I lied with a smile. "But I'm having trouble visualizing it now that I'm here."

The old man squinted at me, but turned toward a tent propped up at the edge of the site. A little square table covered with papers and tools squatted in the shade of the structure.

The stone wall of the city's boundary cut around a looming hill. Geographically, this was an awful location for defensive or offensive structures. A watchtower would only see one direction. A permanent catapult would launch into our own kingdom. Unless Kadence planned to kill a very specific section of our people, this location was useless.

Mr. McGee returned and pressed the thin velum paper into my hands. I oriented it and studied the drawing.

"It's a house?" I asked.

The sketched building was divided into two stories and split into subareas. Each area contained four bedrooms circling a large living room, with bathrooms dispersed accordingly. One kitchen ate the majority of the downstairs space. There were twenty bedrooms and five living rooms, a rather large facility.

"Yes, Your Majesty." Mr. McGee looked at me from the corner of his eyes. "It's the new orphanage. And here are the drawings of the garden next to it."

He ruffled through the papers and put a new one on top. Tiny swings and wooden play structures scattered the page. A shallow pool and an intricate playhouse, complete with a real door and running water, nestled at the edge.

I struggled to remember when we dropped the goods from the market at the orphanage. Kadence hadn't done or said anything that made him sound interested in it.

"Did the king mention why he's displeased with the old orphanage?" I asked.

"He had the building inspected last month. It passed, of course, it's in good shape, barely ten years old," Mr. McGee said.

Then why would Kadence want to build a new one?

"He did say he wanted the children to have more space to run around," Mr. McGee said, breaking through my thoughts. "There wasn't room at the current orphanage to add a garden and play area."

It clicked. Kadence was an orphan. I was sure the vampires hadn't put their prince in a public orphanage, but he would have been under constant supervision. An image of a young Kadence, one I had never seen, staring out the window and longing to play, broke my heart. His circumstances had hardened him, but he saw our orphanage and decided the kids needed a place to play.

If we survived the next two weeks, I'd make sure this was built.

"The king really wanted to find the perfect spot too," Mr. McGee continued. "He spent two days dragging me from place to place. This one's too small, he'd say, or this is too far from town, and they'd need a quick road to get supplies. He was real careful before he decided on this old lot. He said it was a good spot, easy to fortify."

"This is a good sp—wait," I said. "How long did the king look at land?"

"It was about two days, I'd say." Mr. McGee rubbed the white whiskers on his chin. "He also hovered over the architect while the plans were done up. I don't think Tommy's ever drawn so fast in his life as with a vampire breathing down his neck. Maybe I ought to hire one of those things, that'd be real handy actually."

Two days. Cynthia had headed up a search party of hundreds of people, and Kadence was touring plots of land to build a new orphanage. He hadn't told her. He hadn't told anyone. Except, that wasn't true. When I questioned him in my bedroom, Kadence had said he had been building an orphanage. I called him a liar. Guilt shot through me as swiftly and as painfully as an archer's arrow.

"Mr. McGee," I said, "unfortunately I won't be able to provide any more people to this project. The orphanage we have now is in perfect condition and the children are in very good care. This will be a lovely home for them, but I have to prioritize the war. We are short on volunteers for the army and will likely implement a draft tonight. Troop training starts tomorrow, and by the end of the week, we will be transporting thousands of soldiers to prepare for battle."

Mr. McGee nodded. "I heard all that, Your Majesty. My boy's thinking about signing up. He's just turned eighteen though and his mama's real worried."

"We could use him," I said gently. "We need everyone right now. I'm going to be honest with you, Mr. McGee."

"Call me Pat, Your Majesty."

"Pat," I gave him a small smile, then quickly snatched it away, "it doesn't look good. We have numbers on our side, but what's marching toward the vampire kingdom aren't our loved ones anymore. They may wear familiar bodies, but they're monsters, and if we lose this battle, they won't stop. Our kingdom will be next. Your son will have to face the demons sooner or later and I want him to do it with the best people supporting him."

Pat's head bobbled again.

"I'll let him know," he said.

"Please do. As for this project, if there's anyone left after the draft, then you can try to build. If not, it will be a top priority when we return. I'm afraid I have a lot to handle back at the castle. I wish I could stay longer, Pat. This place has a lot of promise."

The breeze sang a soft song through the trees and the rock wall danced in color under the autumn sun. Nature stirred something particularly special here. Kadence had chosen well.

Pat caught my hand as I turned away. Warmth filtered from his skin, which felt like worn leather and was calloused from years of work. He gave me a gentle squeeze.

"Your Majesty," his eyes searched mine as though he was looking for his words in them, "I was worried when I came to see you. People talk and these days it's not such good things." He grimaced and shrugged in apology.

"I understand," I said. I knew what my people thought of me.

"But you're not what they say." He reached his other hand to scratch the back of his neck. "You came out here and saw the plans and you...you care about my boy."

His voice tightened and he looked hard at the ground.

I squeezed his hand.

"Of course I do. I care about all my people. That's what I'm here for," I said.

His head wobbled and he shuffled his feet in the dirt. I pretended not to see the tears trailing down his face. "I'll remember that," he whispered to our feet.

Pat pulled himself together with a deep breath and flashed me a toothy grin.

"Thank you, Your Majesty. Have a safe ride home."

Chapter Eighteen

KADENCE WAITED, MOUNTED ON JUNIPER AT THE CASTLE entrance. He wore all black under a layer of flexible leather armor, with a large battle hammer strapped to his back and a longsword at his waist. I remembered the dagger he had pulled in my room. How many more weapons was he hiding?

"Where were you?" His voice was hard, frustrated. "I was looking for you."

"Why? Did you have something to tell me?"

"No." His face pinched. "Should I?"

Was he not ready to tell me about the orphanage, or did he hide it for another reason? "It doesn't matter." I waved it away. Kadence would tell me eventually, I'd make sure of that. "What do you need?"

"Zavier wants us to meet at the training arena. He said to wear armor and bring weapons."

"Fine," I said, wondering what fresh torture the old man had in mind. "Give me a few minutes."

I tied Vry outside and Saffa helped me change from my long green dress into a simple black uniform. The flexible cotton knit material wicked sweat and other less pleasant liquids from my skin. My leather armor wasn't as durable as the metal set I wore into battle, but it was more maneuverable and comfortable. Putting on the armor felt like coming home after a long absence. It hugged my body, tight and reassuring.

"You're very strange, Sal," Saffa said, stowing the green dress with the rest of the dirty laundry.

"Why?"

"You're the only person I know that smiles putting on their armor. Most people wait until they get to take it off."

Laughing, I wandered back downstairs and hopped into the saddle.

"What does Zavier want?" I asked Kadence.

Vry sashayed under me and whinnied at Juniper, who made horse noises back. The sun had crested in the sky and slipped toward the horizon. The countdown to a mandatory draft was coming and with it would come displeasure and backlash from my people. If we survived the war with the demons, I may be kicked from the throne afterwards.

"He didn't say."

We spilled into the meadow before the arena and a cluster of five people crowded the rugged bleachers. Zavier, wearing what looked like a healer's outfit, was propped in a wheeled chair. He had more color today and the bags under his eyes had faded. A blond nurse stood behind him, also wearing a similar outfit.

The other three were soldiers. Two men wore the standard witch uniform with infantry patches. They were both tall and lean, and one man had a scar that stretched up his cheek to his forehead. The third woman wore a vampire uniform, all black with a battle axe in one hand. Her rich red hair, probably not natural, was twisted into a bun.

"I hope you don't mind that I borrowed one of your soldiers, My King." Zavier smiled when we approached and dismounted. "Soldier Barton here was describing some of her battle experience."

"I've seen Ocean Barton fight in person." Kadence smiled. "I wouldn't want to be on the other end of her axe."

"Well then, you're not going to like this." Zavier sent me a wink and Kadence's eyebrows shot up. "Tonight we will have the bulk of our army assembled and tomorrow we will begin to train thousands of civilians to become decent soldiers in two weeks. It will be even more difficult because our armies have never fought together before."

Zavier continued. "We know a lot about killing each other, but not how to survive united. I don't want soldiers getting hurt because they weren't familiar with their teammate's fighting techniques. There will be plenty of dead without friendly fire."

"Why are we here?" I asked as Kadence said, "What do you want from us?"

Zavier kept smiling.

"You two are the heads of our kingdoms. King Kadence may hold the true title, but these people have been following Sal, and her parents long before that. So far, the only thing they have seen you two fight, is each other. Yes, Sal, I've heard about that."

Protests lined the tip of my tongue.

Zavier sent me a stern look and I swallowed my words.

"If our people see you as individuals on the battlefield, it will be a bloodbath. If they see you as a team, we will at least have a chance."

"What are they doing here?" Kadence eyed the soldiers. His mouth pinched as though he tasted something sour.

"These soldiers volunteered to attack you, for training of course. It wasn't difficult to find willing participants. It seems everyone wants a chance to beat one of you up." Zavier said and I was suddenly three years old again, being chastised in my mother's room. Even Kadence pressed his lips together.

"Well, go on then," Zavier said.

I barely had time to prepare before Soldier Barton turned into a streak of black as she lunged at me. I dodged, barely missing the edge of her axe. I pulled my sword and held it across my chest. These weren't training weapons. Adrenaline streaked through me like aged, rich wine, and I welcomed it.

Grunts and groans of battle echoed behind me as the two witches attacked Kadence. The sounds grew closer. They were pushing us together.

Barton swung the heavy weapon and I jumped backward. I slashed, but she was already gone.

We faced each other. Barton swayed the axe from side to side. She scratched my body with her eyes, probing for a weakness. She charged, axe low and prepared for an upswing.

I held my ground. *Closer. Closer. Wait.*

Now.

I sidestepped and ran into a breathing, brick wall. I bounced off Kadence and caught myself before face planting in the dirt. The impact ruined the vampire's stance and timing, and one of the witches cut into his arm. The smell of blood wafted around the arena.

"Sorry, Your Majesty," the witch said.

Kadence turned to me. "What were you doing?" he snapped.

"Sorry, I didn't expect you to need the entire arena for two opponents. Would you like the rest of us to leave?"

"This is your fault." He held out his injured arm, which had already healed the minor wound.

"I'm sorry, My King. Do you need a bandage?"

"Children." Zavier smiled. "Reset, switch opponents and try again."

Frustration stole the edge of excitement. The two witches squared up against me, spinning their swords. Their bodies held a line of tension. Weight shifted forward. A moment, a single breath, passed as the man with the scar pressed his back foot into the ground and lunged at me.

I was gone.

He slipped by.

I swung at the second man, catching him by surprise. I hammered a swift punch to his gut and he keeled over. I lifted my sword for a killing strike, but his partner was back.

The scarred man's sword became a blur against mine. Strike. Strike. Strike. He drove me back, but sweat beaded on his forehead and his breathing grew ragged. He would tire before me.

Something hard and heavy struck the back of my head. Lights exploded behind my eyes. When had I closed them?

I fell to my knees, fighting for consciousness. The lights faded to a black tunnel and I followed it, wondering where it might end. I heard a low groan and realized it came from me.

"The Queen!" Zavier's voice sounded far away.

Hands pressed against my head, sending ripples of pain like shards of glass through my skull. Magic puddled around us, heavy and glowing, and struck into my skin. My head healed, blood moving too fast, nerves repairing at alarming speed. I wanted to scream, but my throat pinched closed.

The pain ended. I turned on to my hands and knees and retched in the dirt.

"What happened?" I asked, wiping my mouth on the back of my hand. *Gross.*

"Kadence swung his hammer at his opponent, and you were behind him. He struck you in the back of the head."

"Ouch."

I touched the tender spot and came away with blood.

"Sorry," Zavier's nurse said. "The skin was split before I could heal you."

"We get the point, Zavier." Kadence put his hammer on the ground and leaned on the hilt. Agitation tightened his muscles even as he feigned indifference. The frustration likely stemmed from his own mistake of accidentally striking me. "What do you want us to do?"

The old man raised his grey eyebrows.

"Practice, My King. You two need to become an unstoppable team. You must be the very definition of unity. I don't care what happens behind closed doors. If you want to keep harassing each other every other night—yes, I know about that too—then by all means, go ahead. But in public, you are all but married. Or get married! Do anything that tells your people you, together, are confident in a victory."

My lips curled at Zavier's haphazard suggestion of marriage. Kadence's face mirrored mine. As much as I hated to admit it, my First Seneschal was right. We had been showing our people how to avoid each other rather than work together.

Kadence sighed and looked at me. He held out his hand. I grabbed it and he helped me stand.

Our hands connected and more than sweat heated between us. It brought me back to the fight in my room, when Kadence's eyes burned with the desire to best me, but also the desire for something much, much different.

"Again," he said.

Several matches later, and one nick to Kadence's arm from my blade, we found our rhythm.

"Left," Kadence called his position as I dodged a swing from Barton's axe. I stepped to the right to give Kadence more space.

Barton lunged at me, fast and hard. I sidestepped and she tumbled forward. I cut against the back of her head, pulling before contact.

"Dead," I said.

"Coming at you." Kadence turned, bringing his opponents with him. He swung the hammer as though it were a sword, calm and calculated. His eyes scanned his opponent's body, watching for tells, determining where the hammer would hit before he committed. One witch aimed a fatal strike to Kadence's back, but I was already there. I blocked the blade with a shower of sparks.

The novelty of sparring had worn off. Exhaustion, sweat, and the craving for a bath I wouldn't get tonight remained. There would be one more council meeting to determine the outcome of recruits and then a draft would be announced.

The thought of a draft spurred anger, strong and hot, like boiling water in my soul. I channeled it.

My people would hate me.

Strike.

They would call for my throne after this battle.

Strike.

No matter what I did, I'd failed them. I had failed them again and again and again.

Strike. Strike. Strike.

The soldier's eyes widened under the flurry of my blade. He stumbled backward and fell in the dirt. One hand blocked his face as though the flesh would protect him from my sword.

I stopped, inches from his throat.

"Dead," I said.

Kadence echoed behind me, "Dead."

Zavier slow clapped our victory from his wheeled chair.

Exhaustion and dread made me giddy. I helped my soldier up and we shared a stressed laugh.

"Good one, My Queen," he said.

"You too, soldier."

"That was much better," Zavier said. "Now if only you could work together in real life."

"You're becoming dramatic in your old age." I grabbed the towel he offered and patted sweat from my face.

Kadence watched the dirt path from the castle, tracking something in the dark I couldn't see. "Someone's coming," he said. "It looks like a messenger."

A young man trekked out of the shadows. He wore a tan shirt and brown shorts with jagged hems. He bent to put his hands on his knees and drew ragged breaths. "A message," he said between gasps. "For the Queen. From Councilman Amos."

"Spit it out, lad," Zavier said.

"He said the quota has been reached." The kid shuffled through his clothes.

"The volunteer quota?" Shock and disbelief jolted through me. I sealed my heart against them. Hope felt too distant.

The boy pulled a paper from somewhere in his clothes. He handed me the creased, tattered page. Amos's perfect cursive was scrawled across it.

2,000 troops required

2,500 recruited

500 pending

"What does it say?" Kadence asked.

I passed him the note.

"We did it?" Zavier asked.

I nodded. I couldn't speak. The weight of my people's disapproval sank away with the appearance of these numbers. I drew a deep breath, my first one in almost two days.

"It won't be enough." Kadence looked at the paper in his hands like he held a body of a loved one. His mask disappeared and fear leaked onto his face. Desperation and memories impossible to forget stared at me from within his eyes. He was a child, an orphan, alone.

My arms wrapped around the vampire before I decided to move. The thick armor sat between us and sweat clung to our skin, but it didn't matter. Kadence was strong and solid, and he smelled like fire and leather. After a moment, he put his arms around me and buried his face in my hair.

"It's enough for tonight," I whispered.

When I looked up and stepped away from the king, we were alone.

Chapter Nineteen

MY HAIR REMAINED WET AFTER MY BATH AND COOL WATER soaked into my long black dress, but I didn't have time to let it dry in front of the fire. I hurt. Sleep hadn't chased away the beatings from sparring last night, and the knock on my head pounded with every movement, despite the speed-healing I'd received at the arena. The council was having an emergency meeting, the third one today, and two scouts from the field would be there with an updated report. Marshal Hale had teamed new recruits that had transportation magic with the scouts to facilitate quicker updates, but they weren't battle-trained and the worry gnawed at me.

Someone knocked on the door. At my invitation, Saffa poked her head in.

"Mr. Emerson is here," she said.

I sighed. "He can come in, but leave the door open."

Reuben strode into the room as though he owned the place. He was in a button-down white shirt, white breeches, and a black jacket. He looked ready to join his friends for a pleasant carriage ride through the countryside and not like he was plotting against an army of bloodthirsty demons. He saw me and smiled ear to ear.

"You look good today." He scanned my body. "I like that dress."

"What do you want, Reuben?" I asked, resisting the urge to cross my arms over my chest. His stare burned me with discomfort.

He crossed the room and extended some papers to me. "I have the numbers from the most recent estimates. Transporting troops and supplies would take upward of twelve hours. We recommend dividing it over two days. Half the troops and half the supplies one day, the rest the next day."

"We have a council meeting in an hour. Why don't you just tell us this altogether?"

His perfect eyebrows dipped. "I thought you'd want to know."

"I do, but everyone needs to know."

He reached for my hand. I stepped back.

"I wanted to tell you personally, Sal." His blue eyes misted with a veil of tears. "We never talk anymore."

"We're not betrothed, Reuben. It's been months," I said softly. It felt like kicking a puppy.

"We used to talk a lot. We made time for each other. I miss that."

I missed it too. Life with Reuben would have been simple. I would have handled the kingdom and the people, and he would have managed our home life. We would have been a good team. Now that the engagement was over, there was a guilty sense of relief. I now imagined my future and a pair of much darker eyes looked back at me.

"I have to keep my promises to the king," I said.

Reuben's lips twisted into a snarl. That darkness I'd first seen months ago when I had ended our marriage returned. A cold, calculating shadow etched beneath the surface. I had a sinking suspicion Reuben held a secret I would soon discover—and dislike.

"I don't know why you worry about him so much. He treats you badly. He doesn't care about you, he wouldn't care if we were together."

"I think Kadence is learning how to care," I said quietly.

"What?" Reuben asked.

"Never mind. What matters is that I care. I signed a contract and I gave my word."

"Even if it means you're about to throw away your entire kingdom to save the bloodsuckers?" Reuben said.

I narrowed my eyes. "What do you mean?"

"The dead are marching on their kingdom, not ours!" Reuben pointed out the window. "We would be fine! They'll leave us alone. We should let the vampires lose their own battle and then we'd be free." He took another step toward me and I backed away. "We could be together, Sal."

"Reuben, do you understand what you're saying? The vampires are part of us now. We are one people. These creatures marching on us are demons—they crave blood and death. They're not going to destroy the vampires and decide to go home. You're a fool if you think we wouldn't be next."

His eyes turned dark, the color of the sky before a storm. His face flattened. I had never seen Reuben look so cold, so deadly.

"You don't know that," he said.

"I do," I said. "You need to leave."

He tensed. A tremor vibrated through his arms. The hair on the back of my neck stood up. I had a knife hidden under the coffee table in front of the fireplace. If Reuben attacked, I wasn't confident I could get there first. Reuben had height and speed on his side, but he wasn't trained and his magic was weak. If he caught me before I reached the knife, a hand-to-hand fight with a man of his size would be difficult.

He scanned me as though calculating his odds. Reuben had never been to battle, of that I was confident, but there was fighting knowledge splayed across his body. Had he learned to fight and never told me? It didn't sound like the Reuben I knew.

I balanced on the balls of my feet, waiting for a tell.

"Your Majesty." Saffa stuck her head back in.

I jumped.

Reuben dragged his eyes from me to look at her.

"Yes?" I asked casually. *Just two old friends having a nice conversation, no cause for alarm.*

"Jon Chan just sent a messenger," Saffa said. "There's been another theft."

"The missing blood is going to have to take a back burner," I said. The army of demons had to take precedence.

"He says it's gone, Sal," Saffa said. "He said all the blood is gone."

Shock rolled down my back, colder than the wet hair through my dress.

"All of the inventory? Are the guards alive?"

"He said nobody was hurt and nobody saw anything. There's evidence of spellwork in the chilled storage room."

Very few people had access to the storage room. Someone on the inside was involved.

"Tell Mr. Chan not to touch anything. I'll be right there." I grabbed a coat. "And tell the council Zavier will speak in my place for this meeting." I doubted I'd miss anything new at the third meeting of the day.

"I'll go with you." Reuben's spine snapped straight. I thought I saw the edge of a grin on his lips.

"That's not a good idea," I said.

Saffa looked between Reuben and me.

"I'll go too," she said. "People keep trying to kill you and I keep missing it. Let me get my sword." She disappeared down the hall.

Reuben smiled and I resisted the urge to bury my face in my hands.

WE'D ABANDONED THE ROYAL GUARD AT THE CASTLE DOOR. They were content with Saffa and Reuben accompanying me. Two regular soldiers flanked the entrance of the blood donation building, swords in their hands and their faces grim. They bowed when we approached.

"Your Majesty, we apologize for this occurrence." The short, wide man wore a higher rank emblem on his shirt. "We remained at our post and there was no evidence of an intrusion. We will accept any punishment you deem suitable."

I smiled at them. "Your presence here is the reason this theft didn't happen sooner. I appreciate the work you've been doing."

The door wrenched open and Jon Chan emerged. He appeared disheveled in a wrinkled blue shirt and a dark jacket. There was a stain on his slacks. Circles settled under both eyes and his wild gaze locked onto us.

"You're here." He clasped his hands together and lifted his face toward the sky. "I cannot handle this. This is above my station. Come on, come on."

Saffa and I shared a look. We followed Mr. Chan down the hallway, Reuben at our heels.

"This isn't ordinary magic," Mr. Chan said. "This is something very dark. I don't want anything to do with it. You're going to have to find a new director. I can't keep doing this. I don't sleep anymore. My wife is tired of me being up all night."

"Mr. Chan," my voice was calm, "I'm afraid that I don't understand."

"That's right, My Queen, you *should* be afraid."

We reached the meeting room with the seafoam colored chairs. A door settled behind the aged table and Mr. Chan put his palm against it. Prickles of magic swirled across my skin as he pushed his power into the door. Invisible locks clicked and the hinges swung open, revealing a dark vault. The space beyond was inky blackness.

"This is a magically cooled room," Mr. Chan said. "I, and six members of my staff, have access to this door. It's warded on the outside and there are no windows or internal access points. We have witches that come by every week to update the cooling spell. The blood must be chilled to a particular temperature. Magic is finicky at best, so we check the temperature every two hours, day and night."

He reached into the dark doorway and blindly patted the wall. He pulled out a slim wooden board with a paper pinned at the top and handed it to me.

"This is the log of everyone who checked the temperature yesterday and today. You can see that no employee checked it twice in a row, except during the night shift. The theft happened sometime between six and eight this morning." Mr. Chan started into the blackness. "I don't know how they had enough time to do this," he whispered.

"Have any of your staff been acting strange?" I asked.

Mr. Chan shook his head. "Darla was away on leave, but she came back yesterday."

I scanned the clipboard. Darla's name was at the bottom.

Reuben craned his neck to peer at the list over my shoulder.

I passed the log to Saffa and sent him a sharp look.

He smiled sheepishly.

"Mr. Chan, we need to look inside the vault," I said.

He tensed and backpedaled from the door.

"You go ahead, but I can't be here. I'll be outside with the guards." He scampered away with a final look over his shoulder. The color had drained from his face. There was a distant sound of a door opening and closing.

We stared into the gaping hole. Nobody moved to turn on a lantern. Unease gnawed at me. Mr. Chan drew and collected blood for a living. I was not eager to confront anything that generated so much terror. I bit my lip and side eyed Saffa.

"Do you want to—"

She shook her head. "Nope."

Reuben had already taken half a step away. No point asking him.

"Fine." I sighed. "I'll do it."

I forced my feet to move and shuffled forward. I reached inside. The smooth, cold wall brushed my fingertips. I held my breath, prepared to scream if something grabbed me. I found the round edge of a lantern and felt for the knob. It twisted and a spark caught against the accelerant, sending an orange glow through the room.

The blood stood out first. Trails of the red liquid lined the walls, the floor, parts of the ceiling. It had dripped into puddles on the floor. The cooling spells were still intact, so the blood hadn't started to smell. Globs of thicker liquids and chunks of flesh were scattered across the ground in haphazard piles. Under the blood and guts, familiar red symbols swirled along the tiles. The hybrids we fought had worn the same ones across their skin. The rest of the vault was empty.

Saffa peeked her head around the corner and studied the room.

Reuben looked inside, then pressed his elbow over his eyes. He stumbled out, retching.

"What is it?" Saffa asked.

"I don't know," I said.

We crept inside. There was no sense of magic on my skin.

"I'm pretty sure the spell is inert," I said. "The magic was already used up."

Saffa toed a pile of organs with her satin slipper.

"These are chicken pieces." She wrinkled her nose. "And not a fresh, young hen either. This is an old bird."

"How do you know?" It just looked raw and bloody.

"Look at the muscle, it's lean and ropey. A young chicken would have more fat." She gestured to the sinewy pieces of meat.

"What does that mean?"

Saffa shrugged. "It means it was an old chicken. I've never heard of a spell where a sacrifice's age mattered."

The word fell heavy between us. Sacrificial magic had been illegal for centuries. Magic harvested from suffering and death was potent and wild. Witches that used it tended to crave more and more power, eventually losing their mind in the pursuit. When a witch was proven to be using sacrificial magic, justice was swift and final.

I leaned closer to the symbols on the floor. Not a single mark had been muddled with blood from the chickens. The splatter pattern on the walls and ceiling didn't match the layout of the carnage on the floor. It looked like someone had taken a bottle and splashed the blood onto the surfaces.

"I don't think the chickens are a sacrifice," I said. "I think they're a distraction. Look, none of the blood touches the spellwork."

Saffa leaned close, her brows creased. "What are they distracting us from? They left the entire spell here."

I bent and touched one of the symbols. The red powder clung to my fingers. I rubbed them together, but there was no smell. I waited. Nothing happened.

"I think it's all a distraction."

"That can't be right. They stole the blood here and the bottles of donated blood out of those wagons," Saffa pointed out.

"But they stole the whole wagon too. They stole all the blood to distract us from looking too closely at the bottles they actually took. We need to look at who donated the missing blood."

"We already did. There wasn't anything special about their blood. None of them had a rare blood type, any diseases, or abnormal counts. They were perfectly normal," Saffa said.

The blood, the animal parts, it didn't have any place in this spellwork. The real clue was the symbols on the floor, and I didn't know what they were. But what did they take this time?

"I need a list of all the donors." I gestured Saffa out of the room. "I have to talk to Mr. Chan."

Reuben slouched at the meeting table, his head in both hands. He took measured deep breaths and hummed quietly.

"The door's closed, Reuben, you can't see it anymore," I said.

Beads of sweat peppered his pale brow.

"Thank you," he said. "How-how many died in there?"

"Probably three or four," I said.

Reuben swallowed hard, his Adam's apple bobbing up and down.

"So many?" he whispered.

"Yeah, you might have an egg shortage for a couple of days. You'll probably want to grab some at the market." I patted his back.

"Wh—what?"

"They were just chickens. You can relax."

I followed the others down the hallway. We couldn't collect and store bottles of blood as long as the thieves remained at large. Killing, even chickens, meant they were becoming more violent. I would have to recruit fresh donors, which wouldn't be a popular idea. The kingdom would pay them, but it was a bandage on a gaping wound. The thieves would have to be handled, after I cleaned up the five thousand demons marching our way.

Reuben opened the door. A black shadow fell from the roof onto his head. The man collapsed in a flurry of black and white, screeching and batting at the hybrid creature that sat on his shoulders.

I drew my sword, and Saffa was already swinging hers. The blade bit into the back of the hybrid's neck. It missed his spinal column, but stunned the creature, and he scurried away, dazed.

Another hybrid hissed thirty strides to the right, crouching over the broken and bleeding bodies of Jon Chan and the two guards. A third hybrid lie beheaded to the left of the door. The guards had taken one out before they died.

The hybrids looked the same as before. Their heads were shaved, they wore loose athletic breeches, and red symbols had been painted across every bare inch of their bodies. The symbols glowed and shimmered as they moved. Ruby eyes shone at us.

"What are these?" Reuben's high-pitched voice drew me from the blank space of my focus.

"They're magical vampires. Hybrids." I scanned his body. "Do you have a weapon?"

"N-no," he stammered.

The hybrid to the right lunged and I met him part way, swinging my sword across his body. He edged back, patient and observing. *Oh great, they're learning.*

"Why don't you have a weapon?" I dodged another strike and stabbed at the beast. Missed.

"I'm never out alone," he said. "There's always a guard."

Grunts and groans drifted behind me as Saffa engaged the second hybrid. My opponent punched at my face. I dodged, but his second fist drove into my gut. I stumbled back, fighting for air.

"Sal! Be careful!" Reuben said.

I clenched my teeth. "I'll get right on that."

Magic pricked against my skin. Cold, alien magic that shouldn't exist. It swirled around me, capturing my space, replacing the air. It filled my lungs like sand, and I drew a heavy breath.

"Reuben!" I creaked. "Magic!"

"What?" His blue eyes streaked with panic.

"Magic!" My oxygen disappeared.

I swung my sword blindly, sloppily, the pinpricks of magic choking me from the inside. My own power beat against its internal bonds, begging for freedom. I scratched at the bracelet, searching for a seam or a clasp. The cold metal remained smooth and perfect. My magic was behind a door without a lock, and it would kill me. The panic that swirled like whitewater in my head settled down. I understood death. Death would be calm and peaceful. As more sand filled the open places in my body, the sweeter death's lullaby sounded.

"Oh," a familiar voice said from far away. I recognized the voice, but I couldn't remember who it belonged to. "Magic. I can do magic."

The sand consumed me, all encompassing, devouring, complete. I turned to it and embraced it. Rest was good. I needed to rest.

Air seeped into a tiny hole in my lungs, burning and real. Pain flushed the static from my head. I gasped like a fish out of water, sucking in as much oxygen as I could. My vision cleared in time to see a roundhouse kick coming at my face.

I raised my sword to block and the blade cut into the hybrid's leg. He screamed and lobbed a flurry of hits that I ducked and dodged.

I blocked and we circled. He lurched, feigning right, and I pretended I didn't notice. At the last second, he turned left, and my sword was already there. It stabbed through. Blood and fluids leaked down his chest. The symbols stopped glowing. The hybrid's red eyes turned golden brown, clear. He grabbed the sword, slicing his hands on the blade, and pulled it deeper into his body. Inches from my face, his final words were a caress on my cheek.

"The traitor," he whispered. His eyes darted about before the light of life left them and he slouched, dead. I let his weight drag him to the ground and I pulled my sword from his body.

Shock and confusion twinged in my chest. The vampire had told me something very important, but I didn't know what it meant.

Saffa's vampire perched on his knees. She lifted her sword, aimed at his neck. The symbols on his body dimmed and he raised his deep blue eyes to her for a fraction of a second, then squeezed them closed.

Her concentration broke. Her blade hesitated.

The hybrid peeled one eye open.

"Um, hello?" Saffa said.

"What are you doing?" the bloodsucker hissed. A raspy edge lined his voice, as though it hadn't been used for a long time. "You have to kill me."

Saffa raised an eyebrow.

The hybrid dragged himself toward her sword and pressed the blade against his throat. His hands trembled while he held it there, eyes shut again.

"Please, please, miss, just do it. I don't know how long I can be like this. They could come back at any moment." Tears broke through his closed lids and trailed down his face, smudging the red symbols on his cheeks.

"I'm not going to kill you," Saffa said.

The hybrid's eyes snapped open and locked onto the witch.

"You have to, or I'll kill you. Or her." He pointed a shaky finger at me. "I'm supposed to kill her."

"How about *if* you try to kill any of us, *then* I will kill you?"

He looked up at her. "You promise?"

She nodded, her dark bun bobbing at her nape.

"All right, that's all right," he whispered. He fell to his knees, arms down at his side. His chest heaved as though it hurt to breathe.

"Who's making you try to kill me?" I asked.

Saffa sent me a sharp look. "You could at least ask his name first."

"My name is Remi and I need to talk to the queen before they come back," the man said. Without the glowing symbols and red eyes, he looked tired and sad.

"Before who comes back?" I avoided Saffa's pointed glare.

"I don't know who it is, who they are. They kept us locked up in a dark cage."

"Us?"

"There were several others with me, but I don't know how many. There was never light, never anyone to see. I could hear the others, but I couldn't see anything."

"Shouldn't hybrids be able to see in the dark, if they're half vampire?" I asked.

"I'm not sure what a hybrid is, Queen Salvatore. I was born a vampire and we can see in the dark. It must have been magic. They came every couple of days and force-fed us blood to keep us alive. We were bound and there was no way to avoid it. Some days they brought new vampires into the cage. Sometimes, I heard them drag others out and they never came back."

His gaze hollowed and I knew he was back in that cell, beside the sounds of tortured people, remembering helplessness.

"They came for me. They shocked me with something and I woke up in a chair. My head was shaved and they painted symbols on my skin. Once they were done, they forced more blood into my mouth and chanted something. Then," Remi shook his head, "then my body wasn't mine anymore."

"Like possession?" The word left a bitter taste in my mouth.

He shook his head. "I had my thoughts and my mind. But I couldn't move. My body was on fire with these symbols and I realized they controlled me."

"Like mind control," Saffa said.

Remi nodded quickly. "Yes. Yes, like that."

"That's impossible," I said. "There isn't a spell for mind control."

"Apparently there is," he said. "Also, I can do this."

He stretched his hand, palm out, and a blast of magic hit the nearest tree. The torrent of power ripped through the thick trunk, sending pieces of bark through the air. The great pine split in half, teetered for a moment as though warring with gravity, then crashed behind us, thundering into the open clearing.

My jaw fell.

"We should kill him," Reuben said as he pondered the remains of the smoldering tree truck. I had almost forgotten he was there. "We should definitely kill him."

Remi looked at his hands as though he didn't recognize them.

"I don't know what they did to me," he whispered.

I didn't either.

Nausea ripped through me. I clutched my stomach and the world spun. Bile burned the back of my throat, but I swallowed it down. I swayed on my feet, rocking, and fought to remain upright. Sweat beaded on my skin.

"Sal?" Saffa frowned. "Are you all right?"

Cool air, tinted with the smell of fall, filled my lungs. The nausea slipped away.

"Yeah, I'm fine." I straightened my shoulders. The illness faded as quickly as it had come. "Reuben, ride toward the castle and send the first soldiers you find. Then go to Zavier and tell him to come out here right away."

"Why do I have to go?" Reuben crossed his arms.

Saffa made a face at his disrespectful tone, but she didn't say anything.

"Because we have a possible enemy prisoner and you're the only one who didn't bring a sword."

He stuck his lower lip out and looked between me and Saffa, whose blade hovered close to Remi's neck. Just in case.

"Fine." Reuben stomped to the horses, skirting around the blood and the bodies. "I'll do it for you, Sal."

His eyes caught mine as he pulled the horse around. A shadow flickered through them, dark and bitter, the same expression he had in my bedroom earlier. He looked at me the way he would look at a cow at slaughter. Distasteful, sad, but with a hint of anticipation. He turned and rode away.

"He's going to be a problem." Saffa narrowed her eyes at Reuben's retreating figure.

"Yes." I sighed. A problem I would deal with later. There seemed to be a lot of those stacking up.

Jon Chan stared blindly at the sky. His throat was a torn mess of flesh and blood, and evidence of teeth marks suggested he had been chewed on after his death. Blood wet his wrinkled clothes. Gently, I put my hand over his eyes and closed them, letting him rest. His skin was still warm.

"I'm sorry," Remi said. Silent tears washed away the chalky red symbols in twin rivers that flowed down his cheeks. "I don't know if I killed him, but I know I helped."

"It's not your fault," Saffa said gently.

I dragged the guard's bodies next to Jon, lining them up in a neat row. They had been killed cleanly, all their necks broken. They had quick deaths, painless. Maybe that would bring me comfort when I tried to sleep tonight.

I didn't touch either of the dead hybrids. The symbols on their bodies were almost pristine and I needed my historical spellwork experts to look at them. But my heart ached. These innocents had gotten caught as collateral damage in a vendetta against me, a result of the escalating assassination attempts. Their families were missing them, as they were locked away in the dark and hopelessly waiting for rescue. We didn't even know any vampires had gone missing. It was unacceptable and I vowed it wouldn't happen again.

Tears brushed against my own cheeks and I wiped them away. There would be more to cry for in the coming days. I couldn't spare any tears now.

I stood and the world tipped. I rubbed my face and splashes of color stole my vision. Sweat trickled down my forehead and my back, seeping into my black dress. Nausea returned and I couldn't fend it off. I staggered to the tree line and threw up in the grass.

A sliver of something vibrated through my bones, a faint hint of an alien magic. The taste of sand stung the back of my throat. Strong and fierce, like an ocean wave, my magic beat against the bonds restraining it. I clawed at the silver bracelet again, blindly, frantic. My fingertips became slick. I had scratched into my skin, leaving bloody nail marks on my arm.

The foreign magic swelled again, eating into my body like acid. A scream cut through the wind. It might have come from me, but I couldn't feel anything. Just the pain, a torrent of burning and ice swirling through my body, searching for my soul.

Someone flipped me over. When did I fall? I blinked in the bright sun and Saffa's pale face stared down. Her hands fluttered over my body, searching for a wound.

"M-m," I whispered, gasping through the icy jaws trying to smash me, "magic."

Her hands stilled. The warm flickering of her power traced across my skin, a momentary relief to the pain devouring me. It splashed against me, unable to break through the strange magic inside.

"I can't do anything, I don't have an affinity for healing," she said. "Just hold on, Sal. Help is coming."

Maybe I closed my eyes, or maybe my sight faded, but the world turned black. Voices became muffled, as though spoken through a cloth.

"I can carry her," a man said.

"You're not going to eat her or anything, right?"

"I don't think so."

"Okay," a woman said. Her voice was familiar and comfortable, but I couldn't place it.

Strong arms lifted me and then everything disappeared.

Chapter Twenty

A FLASH OF LIGHT. A WAVE OF NAUSEA.

"She's going to throw up again," a voice said.

"She's too hot, we can't cool her down."

I was freezing. My body shook uncontrollably. Icy water splashed against my skin. *Please, no more.* I couldn't handle more cold.

My muscles locked, a scream frozen in my throat.

"She's seizing. Help me turn her. Is there a suction bulb nearby?"

The cold slipped away.

"Someone get the king."

I welcomed the darkness back.

THE LIGHT DID NOT RETURN, BUT THE SOUNDS DID. VOICES buzzed in my ears like honeybees. They grated against my thoughts and I wanted them to stop, but I couldn't move. I couldn't tell them to go away.

A door opened on squeaky hinges. The voices hushed.

"My King," a man said. I pushed through the mud that was my brain and a name stumbled forward—Zavier.

"What happened?" A dark, angry, powerful new voice echoed through the room. I wanted to shy away from it, but I was intrigued, captivated. What would he say next?

"Poison, my Lord. The assassins attacked again and one of her opponents had an affinity for poison magic. It saturated too deep in her body before we figured it out. We've had our best healers working all day, but..." His voice trailed off. "She's dying."

In my blindness, I felt the power move across the room. It settled next to me, cold but inviting, a refreshing drink on a hot day.

"Is this something her magic could heal?" the man asked. My brain scrambled for a name, but it slipped through my fingers like water.

"No," Zavier said. "Her magic has never been able to heal and the healers have tried everything. There's nothing we can do."

Fingers brushed my forehead and coolness soaked into my skin. Part of my mind realized it must be my fever, but the rest reveled in the touch. The fingers trailed across my face and tucked a piece of hair behind my ear.

"I can help her." The man's power pressed against me, threatening to drown me. I should have been afraid, but I craved another touch. "It won't be pretty. You all need to leave."

The room fell silent. Not even a breath was drawn.

"Would your help turn her?" Zavier whispered. "Would she become a vampire?"

"Can you decide that for her?" Power cascaded around my body, a waterfall of strength. It recognized me and pulled a name from my broken mind. Kadence, this was Kadence.

"I don't know," Zavier said.

"Can you decide if she would rather die now, quickly in her own bed? Or would she rather survive this as a vampire, the enemy she's fought against her entire life? Which would you choose for her?"

"She would want to live," Zavier whispered. "No matter what. She would do anything to be there for her people."

"That's what I thought," Kadence said. "But I'm not going to make her a vampire. Now leave, so I can help her."

A moment later, footsteps faded and the door closed.

Kadence sighed. His hand wrapped around the back of my head and he lifted me from the soft mattress. His strong arms cradled my body in his lap, and the rhythm of his breathing fought the panic in my mind. Power brushed over me, a thin veil lighter than air. He pressed into my body, sharing his strength. The blackness faded away. The pain receded enough to crack open my eyes.

He studied my face, lips curved into a half smile.

"You look like hell, Sal," he said.

I licked my dry lips and tried to speak.

"You too," I croaked. *Gee, yes, that's a good one.* It wasn't even true. His black hair was neat, his shirt didn't have a thread out of place. The warm, sturdy arms wrapped around me were the most comfortable support I'd had in a long time. He would have to kill me before I admitted that.

"I can help you, but you're not going to like it."

His power had chased away the pain, but it ebbed and flowed like a tide. Each time, it swelled up stronger. My voice faded again and my head lulled. I wouldn't be able to hold onto consciousness for long.

Kadence shifted his hand and held up a small knife. It spanned barely three inches, plain silver, and undecorated.

I pushed the sand from my lungs, fighting for a gasp of air.

"What are you doing?"

"You'll see."

The knife slit Kadence's skin like paper. He sliced vertically down his right wrist, three or four inches into a vein. Blood spilled, deeper than red wine.

"The knife is silver. It won't heal right away." Kadence brought his wrist to my face. "You have to drink it."

I turned, but his strong hand locked my head in place.

"I don't want to," I whispered, my voice broken. The sound scarcely escaped.

"Don't worry, Sal," he said, "I've got you."

He pressed the blood against my lips. I squeezed them shut, but the liquid flowed through. It slipped across my tongue like fresh honey, sweet and delicious.

A growl ripped through the room, stolen from my throat. I grabbed at Kadence's wrist, pressing it closer with both hands. My mouth sealed around the wound, and I guzzled the liquid, panting as I swallowed. The blood was warm and metallic, the power inside intoxicating. It was life and love and every beat of his heart pumped more and more into me. The sand in my lungs melted, no match for the vampire's strength.

My mouth soon pressed against solid skin. Silver slowed down a vampire's accelerated healing, the same way it slowed our magic, but it didn't stop it. His wound mended and the blood flow ceased. It felt like when I had first touched the bracelet and my magic had been ripped away. A hole gaped in my soul, searching for more blood, more power.

"It's healed, Sal," Kadence said softly. He had shifted me, cradling my head against his chest, and his hand stroked my hair. "There's no more."

"No," I cried. Tears fell from my cheeks onto my chest, pooling between my skin and his shirt. I cried for his blood, for Jon Chan's eyes staring sightlessly into the sky, for my parents who had wandered away and were now returning to condemn us all. I cried for Kadence, an orphan alone in his own kingdom, then alone in mine. I cried for my people, about to fight for their lives and for the ones that I knew would lose.

Kadence rocked me and ran his hand through my hair.

I cried until I fell asleep.

Chapter Twenty-One

A SOFT LIGHT BRUSHED AGAINST MY EYELIDS AND I PEELED them open. I groaned and my throat hurt, as though I hadn't had water in days.

"Sal." Zavier sat up from the chair beside the bed. A stack of papers spilled to the floor, forgotten in his haste. "Can you hear me?"

"Yes." I squinted in the dim light. The familiar view of my mother's room sharpened – my room – tucked into bed. Someone had changed me out of the bloody dress and into a clean nightgown. My head pounded with every movement.

"I feel awful," I said.

Zavier laughed and grabbed my hand.

I smiled, ignoring the ache his touch sent to my head.

"Kadence said it would take a few days for you to fully recover."

Days?

"How long has it been?" Panic caught my heart. How much time did we have left?

"It's only been two days," Zavier said. "Everything is okay. The new recruits are training well and the Army of the Dead are advancing as predicted. We've managed to hold everything together without you, although I'm not sure for how much longer. This is the most lucid you've been. Usually you wake up mumbling and then pass out right away," Zavier said. "Are you hungry? Thirsty?"

My stomach revolted at the thought, but my throat ached.

"Just a sip of water."

He lifted a cup to my lips. The cool liquid spilt into my mouth, but nausea made me choke.

"When does the advance party leave?" I asked to distract myself from throwing up.

"In two or three days," Zavier said.

That gave me plenty of time to recover.

The room blurred. I fell into the pillow and the open arms of unconsciousness beckoned me. I pulled away, twisting and bucking in its grasp.

"It's okay, Sal," Zavier patted my hand and smiled. "You can rest some more."

"Remi?" I asked as my vision became a black tunnel.

"He's fine. We have people studying the symbols. You'll be interested to know…" Zavier's voice faded. Sleep pulled me back into the darkness.

I JOLTED FROM THE PILLOW, SITTING UPRIGHT, AND SEARCHED the room. Adrenaline pulsed through me, heightening my senses. The smell of fresh baked bread masked a lingering foul stench. A shadow moved in the darkness and I locked on it, scanning for a threat.

The shadow turned the knob on a lamp and gentle light flooded the room. Kadence stood next to the bed and raised an eyebrow.

"Are you going to throw up again?" he asked.

Warmth filled my face. That explained the sour smell.

"What are you doing here?"

"Going over the latest update." He held up a handful of papers. "They send new ones every few hours now."

"In the dark?"

"Are you worried that I might strain my vision?"

I rolled my eyes but the motion set the room spinning. I closed them for a moment while the world settled.

When I opened them again I found Kadence watching me. He wore a blank look, but an edge underneath betrayed his worry. My heart pounded harder, for a reason unrelated to my illness. Was the vampire concerned for me?

"What does the update say?" My head ached and the turning in my stomach grew worse. I leaned against the pillows.

Kadence walked to the other side of the bed and sat. He slid close to me, leaning against the headboard. The blankets already bore creases. Someone must have been lying beside me.

His power slipped across my skin and I shuddered. Memories surfaced from the murk of my unconscious mind. A flash of a knife, his blood on my tongue, his hands in my hair. The power filling my body, cleansing it from the inside out. My throat closed as he settled next to me, as though it had never happened. Had it been a dream?

"These are the new reports." Kadence passed a sheet of paper. "The scouts have a final estimate and it's lower than we expected. According to Tatiana, some bodies aren't good hosts for a demon. A few of the soldiers must have died at the Fields."

I scanned the paper, but the text was a blur. Had the blood been real? If not, what other fever-induced dreams did I have?

"Are you listening to me?" he asked.

"What?"

Kadence sighed. "Do you want to talk about it?"

"About what?" My face got hot again. If I kept blushing, it might stay that way.

"About drinking my blood," he said. "Do you want to talk about how much you liked it, Sal? How you begged me not to stop? Do you want to talk about how you cried for more, like a child?"

Anger flashed through me.

"No, I don't want to talk about it with you," I snapped.

"Did I make you mad?" he asked. "Good, because you're better mad. You're stronger and smarter, and we need that right now. After this is over, we can talk about the blood and the craving, but right now our people need you to be sharp."

Rage and annoyance twisted, because I knew he was right. If I went down the spiral of almost dying, leaving our people alone, and the sudden desire for another taste of Kadence's blood, I would be useless. My lungs filled as I took a new breath. The stretching strengthened me, grounded me.

"How many are there?" I asked, setting my feelings where they wouldn't get in the way.

"Roughly, four thousand and five hundred soldiers."

"They lost five hundred people?" I whispered. Those soldiers had family here. We had lost so many people and the battle had yet to begin.

"We don't know how many died due to the possession, or if anyone refused and was killed," Kadence said. "It's not great news, but it's good news."

"How is the training going?"

He shuffled the pages, bringing a new one forward.

"It's going well," he said. "The new recruits are learning abbreviated self-defense..."

My eyes were so heavy. It wouldn't hurt to rest them for a moment.

"Sal?"

"Hm?"

"Are you asleep?"

Something warm cradled my head. It wasn't particularly soft, but there was a space hollowed just for me. Kadence's heartbeat steady in my ear.

"Oh!" I jerked my head up from his shoulder. Spots claimed my vision.

"It's okay," the vampire said. He pressed his palm against my cheek. "You can rest with me."

My body felt too heavy and the spots danced. I let my head fall and he was there to catch me. The worries of the upcoming war faded as Kadence held me tight against him.

"How did we get here?" I asked, fighting the urge to fall back asleep.

"Here?" Kadence's eyes peered across my chambers. "Well, I walked, but I'm sure someone carried you."

Exhaustion stole every witty response from my tongue. Death had called for me and Kadence warded away the reaper with his blood. Surely, we were past rival insults. Surely, our future was leading somewhere else now.

"Here, the war, being strangers and also being enemies," I said.

Kadence tensed against me, but his fingers found a steady rhythm running through my hair.

"Lore says the vampires and witches once resided together," Kadence said. Shock rolled through me at his serious tone. Not even a hint of sarcasm marred his words. "Until the witch queen murdered her vampire husband in a fit of jealous insanity. The rest of the witches fled, facing execution if they remained."

I licked my dry lips. "Our myths claim the vampires began the war, with unprovoked attacks on surrounding kingdoms. We stepped in to protect those less able."

"It's a nice story," Kadence turned and his breath brushed over my face, wrapping me in that smokey scent that was only his. "I think that's all the myths really are—stories. The truth lies in what comes next, what you and I and our people will become together."

As my breathing steadied, Kadence's body softened. His heartbeat slowed, and I thought I felt the press of a kiss on my forehead, but sleep claimed me before I could be sure.

Chapter Twenty-Two

"CAN YOU EXPLAIN EVERYTHING ONE MORE TIME, PLEASE."

Juno Williams tapped a pointed stick against one dark=skinned palm and narrowed her eyes from beneath curls of black hair that had come loose from where the mass was pinned atop her head. High heels tapped the floor in disapproval and she looked as though she may have strangled me if I wasn't her queen.

"Of course, Your Majesty," she clipped, catching herself before she rolled her eyes. She pointed a finger at a line of chunky geometric symbols painted on the naked, decapitated body of one of the hybrid creatures suspended waist high on a table. The blood had been cleaned around the red marks and a white sheet covered the headless stump.

"These symbols are reminiscent of ancient script from the Awriba Dynasty, which ceased to exist in the third millennium or so."

She raised her eyebrows at me, despite the four other people in the room.

"That means that they're very old," she said.

I bit my tongue at her impolite comment. It was my fault for not catching this information during her first lecture. I felt like I had been trampled by horses and the animals had turned around and trampled me again. My body ached, a light fever came and went, and I had almost thrown up three times since we'd walked downstairs to the morgue. I missed Juno's first explanation due to a mysterious ringing in my ears. Zavier watched me from the corner of his eye, but he hadn't argued yet. He couldn't say much, since his arm was in a sling, and healers tried to trail him through the castle.

"Thank you for clarifying," I said, "Please continue."

She pursed her lips. "Anyway," she said, like it was two words. "These are the same symbols from the captive."

"Remi," Saffa said behind me.

Juno clenched her teeth. "The symbols match the ones from the captive, *Remi*, and have clear indications of spellwork. It took a while to recognize them. Luckily, we have the best historical linguistics scholars on our team, and they identified the Awriban symbols. However, they don't all make sense. This script," she gestured to a series of triangles with lines scratched through some, "is a deviation of power or control. It could be a foundation for the mind control the captive—*Remi*—described. But this symbol," she pointed to a square box on top of two rectangles, "is nonsense. It doesn't mean anything."

Lanterns flashed on the walls of the windowless room. The smooth grey stones didn't retain any heat from the stories above and I wrapped my shawl around my shoulders. Chairs had been dragged in from the adjacent laboratory and the room resembled a classroom. Instead of a large slate at the front, there was an examination table. The body looked ghostlike, the red symbols shocking on his pale skin. Juno smiled down at the dead like she knew a secret. Zavier and Kadence sat next to me. Saffa and Remi behind us.

The body blurred. I blinked and it sharpened.

"What are the symbols drawn onto the victims with?" Zavier asked.

Juno smiled wide at the old man. I guess it was just me that she didn't like.

"It's powdered dye from the roots of the madder plant. The plant prefers warmer climates, which we hypothesize is connected to the Awriban words. The Southern civilization used to reside in a humid location. However, it's a hardy plant and could easily be grown here, by a skilled botanist."

"It stains." Remi frowned. He had been cleaned up too. Dark stubble broke through his bare head. He wore a short-sleeved black tunic, breeches over his thin, fit frame, and a pair of slippers. We weren't sure if the mind control could come back, so he was comfortable, but under guard. The red powder had been washed away, but the symbols stained his skin.

"Can you still perform magic?" Zavier asked.

Remi grimaced. "I keep destroying your trees. My apologies."

It was impossible not to imagine his power ripping through the stone walls and bringing the castle down on top of us.

"We think that as long as the stains remain, he will have access to magic," Juno said, a little too excited.

"What does this all have to do with the blood donation building and the missing blood bottles?" I asked. Jon Chan's blank face flashed in my mind. His funeral occurred while I was unconscious. I tried not to think of his wife and children, mourning for their father and asking questions that didn't have any answers.

Juno's gaze sharpened and her smile fell.

"The captive—"

"Remi!" Saffa said.

Juno turned pink. She pointed a finger at Saffa.

"If all of you never stepped into my morgue, it would have been too soon. *Remi* said he was forced to drink blood as part of the spell. We tracked down the donors of the blood that went missing from the wagons. They all belonged to powerful witches, including one with a particular poison affinity."

Like the magic that had poisoned me.

"So what does this mean?" I asked.

"It means the rogue assassin group stole a bunch of blood from powerful witches. Then they kidnapped some vampires. They cast a spell and forced the vampires to drink the powerful blood and the vampires could do magic."

I shook my head. "I still don't understand how it helps us, though."

Juno bent the stick in her hand until it broke with a pop.

"It means," she bit, "that we might be able to derive parts of the spellwork and apply it to our vampire allies. We'd try to avoid the mind control aspect, of course."

She waited. I wasn't the only one giving her a blank look. Juno pressed her palm to her forehead.

"We can take the magic symbols," she pointed to the body, "the magic plant root, and the magic blood, and put them on a good vampire, and the good vampire will have magic powers."

"Thank you, Juno, for explaining that," Zavier said.

Kadence eyed the body with his arms crossed. "How will you avoid the mind control part?"

Juno turned to him. "We won't include those symbols."

"But you don't know what all the symbols mean. How can you avoid them?" Kadence asked. Doubt pinched his brow.

"We would have to find volunteers and do some tests."

"What happens to the volunteer if the spell goes wrong?" Kadence asked.

Juno smiled a harsh line of teeth. "It won't go wrong."

"Your Majesty?" Remi said, "I'd like to be a volunteer to test this spell. What my kidnappers did to me was awful, but the army of the dead will be worse. I was there when it happened to your mother, sir. I was young, but it's not something to forget."

I saw through Kadence's blank face to the flash of pain underneath.

"These demons don't feel for us," Remi continued. "If we can give our troops these powers, we might have a fighting chance." He looked at his stained palms. "If that means some of our people will be hurt, or even die trying to make that happen, it's worth the risk. My family died in the war. I lost my parents, my brother, his wife, two nephews. I won't pretend there isn't pain between the witches and our vampires. After years of war and loss, part of me dreamed of revenge."

His blue eyes met mine. Rage and hurt and regret filtered through them. I didn't look away. He deserved to look his enemy in the face.

"But peace is better," he said. "Children get to keep their parents now. We have to make this peace last, and surviving the demon horde at any cost is the price for that. Others will feel the same."

Meaningful sacrifices, my mother's voice whispered and I ignored her. There wasn't time for grief and aches now.

"How many volunteers do you need?" Zavier asked.

Juno tapped a fingernail against her chin. "As many as possible."

"How much madder plant do we have?"

"We don't grow much here," Juno said. "We have to import it."

"I'll approve all expenses for imports from the emergency budget," I said. "Zavier, put out a request for people to donate it from their personal supplies. We need to get started right away."

The others stood, but Kadence lingered, no doubt to ask Juno more questions before offering his vampires as test subjects.

I stacked my papers and left the morgue with the group, ignoring the lines of black bags sitting on the sides of the room. The laboratory resided next door, and several witches gathered around low tables, whispering to each other. They didn't turn toward us, consumed with the beaker of bubbling liquid in front of them.

Dizziness made my head swim. I slouched up the stairwell, balancing one hand against the rocky wall until the world stilled.

Zavier caught my arm and tucked us into an alcove. He searched my tired face. This was the longest I had been out of bed since Kadence had chased away the poison with his blood. Sweat beaded on my forehead. Sleep beckoned me.

"Are you sure you're well enough to travel tomorrow?" Zavier asked.

No, I wasn't sure. Thinking about being on a horse made me want to throw up. "Yes, of course. I'm feeling a lot better." I smiled.

"It's a three-day ride to Vari Kolum." Zavier raised an eyebrow. "You can rest more here and come with the first wave of troops."

I needed to be there when my soldiers arrived. Walking into our enemy's land would be unfamiliar and frightening. I had to be an example of stability and support. They needed to see me and know everything was okay, even when it gravely was not.

"I'm well enough to travel."

A dark shape moved in the hallway. Kadence rounded the corner and stopped when he saw us.

"Everything all right?" he asked.

"I was just making sure the queen was well enough to travel tomorrow." Zavier said.

Kadence looked me over. A shiver ran down my spine and not from the fever.

"What did she say?" he asked.

"That she will be able to ride."

"But you disagree?"

"I would like the queen to prioritize her health." Zavier said carefully, diplomatically.

Kadence pressed his lips.

"If the queen says she can ride, then she rides." He turned away. "I'll see you both in the morning."

His footsteps faded away, but the warmth that his confidence sparked low in my chest did not.

Chapter Twenty-Three

THE ROCKY TERRAIN BLURRED AS WE RODE. WE HAD PASSED through a thick forest and were trudging up and down foothills nestled at the base of a great mountain range. Kadence had assured us there was an easy pass between the looming mountains that looked like giants through a haze of fog and he led us over the twisting roads.

A winter chill had claimed the land, setting frost across the grass. At some point during my recovery, the trees had dropped their golden leaves, and evergreens now wore a pale layer of ice. The blue sky promised peaceful weather, although the brush of a cold breeze slipped against my exposed face.

I had managed to stay on Vry, although the first few hours were uncertain. I rode sandwiched between Cynthia and a female transportation soldier named Bryn. Maybe it was the fresh air, but I felt better today. The rocking motion of riding didn't make bile burn the back of my throat. My strength was coming back. Progress.

Cynthia's black hair hung stick straight and brushed against the small of her back as she sat in the saddle. Her eyes wandered the landscape, scraping back and forth, scanning for threats. In black leather riding breeches and a blood red jacket over a white shirt, she looked both professional, and fierce. Her mount, a jet black stallion, snorted any time Vry got too close.

Cynthia reigned her horse in, slowing him, until he walked next to me.

"I'm surprised you're still alive." She sneered, but the expression didn't touch her eyes. She'd already cracked open her hard exterior when she'd trekked Zavier's bleeding body to the infirmary building. We were more than soldier and ruler now, though less than friends. "Rumor was you were almost dead."

"Guess I'm just hard to kill," I said. Kadence must not have told her about healing me with his blood.

I snuck a glance at Kadence, but stared ahead atop Juniper. I wondered if he grappled with returning to his kingdom engaged in a new war. He carried a heavy weight to defend his people and I knew how it felt.

Rayhan's giant horse had white-and-ginger hair that matched Rayhan's golden-red dreadlocks. He called the horse Forseti, usually in an angry tone. The engraved symbols on Rayhan's black armor swirled and twisted in the faint rays of sunlight. The hilt of his axe pointed forward, toward his grip on the reins.

"Don't start anything, Cyn," Rayhan said. "I might have to finish it."

Her blood red lips curled.

"You can try."

Three witches trotted behind us, dressed in standard issue uniforms and wearing the coat of arms of the transportation branch. They weren't new recruits, but they weren't trained to fight battles. The woman, Bryn, had brown hair, cropped short. A scratchy beard scattered across Halliday's chin, and the last man, Fellows, was tall and bald. They were close in age, late twenties or early thirties, and they carried swords that none of them had ever drawn in battle.

Zavier took the rear. He sat straight and confident, but the corners of his eyes pinched. He refused to wear the sling and flinched with his horse's every step. Tendrils of the morning sun reflected from his silver hair. He was getting too old for long rides. I would see to it he retired after this. I knew it was what he wanted. He and Lily would build a nice cottage in the country and watch their grandchildren grow. I would rule hidden behind Kadence and alone. I cut the thought short.

"I'll finish you both if you keep bickering," Kadence said. Juniper flicked her ears at the tone of his voice.

Rayhan and Cynthia were like siblings too far apart in age. They each wanted the final word and whined when they didn't get it. Although exhausting, there was a familial edge to their arguments. They interacted with both disdain and fondness in a way that I envied as an only child.

"Tattletale." Rayhan stuck his tongue out.

"Idiot."

Kadence turned toward them, a look of distaste creasing his brows. Dust from the horses' steps lifted on the breeze and swirled in front of Juniper's hooves. The debris caught on a twine rope stretched across the trail, hovering about three inches off the ground.

I opened my mouth and reached for my magic. The gaping hole that imprisoned my power tried to swallow me. I hesitated, clawing my way out.

My words were too late.

"Kadence, stop!"

Juniper's foot dragged across the string. Kadence looked down, his eyes wide, and an explosion of rock and sand pelted us from the left.

My ears rang. White filled my vision. Vry neighed and sidestepped under me, almost jostling me from the saddle. The hot sting of blood swelled to my skin where jagged rocks lodged into my flesh. For a moment, the explosive rendered me blind and deaf. My magic beat harder against the spellwork of the bracelet, but the silver band was too strong. Like a prisoner strapped in the guillotine, there was no escape.

Screams, and the distant sound of metal on metal, broke through the silence. I blinked, willing my vision to clear.

Come on, come on.

Shapes formed, first in black-and-white and then hints of color returned.

I wished they hadn't.

Zavier and Rayhan fought a monster. It would have been over six feet tall, except its back bent into a ninety-degree angle. It had all the parts of a human: a head, two arms, two legs, but it was like different puzzles smashed together, and they didn't fit right. One leg stretched too thin, the other twisted backwards, and the hip pulled inward, forcing the creature to lean to the right. Six-inch claws sprouted from the fingers on its elongated arms. Black welts and blisters bubbled on its skin, opening as it fought and dripping pus to the ground.

The creature was fast. It darted past Zavier and Rayhan with its broken body, perching on a ledge to peer down at us. Its black eyes locked on me and it smiled, all jagged teeth and a splash of a red tongue.

Juniper screamed. The horse had taken the brunt of the explosion. She whinnied, struggled to stand, but staggered with a loud cry. Kadence, bloody and covered in dirt, set his hands on the animal. She calmed under his touch.

"The scouts didn't say a demon left the main march." Cynthia had a dagger in each hand.

"Maybe they sent him before we saw the army." Zavier spun his sword in a circle, warming his wrist. "The timing would be right."

The demon's beady eyes bounced back and forth between speakers. It studied us the way a wolf watched a wounded deer—with absolute confidence.

"Hhhe can hhhear you," the demon's voice scratched at our ears.

Silence stretched after its words. It was one thing to know such a vile creature was sentient and could think and speak. It was another to watch words spill from its blackened lips.

"Who can hear us?" Zavier asked.

The demon locked on the old man and tilted its head.

"The man who gave me thisss body." Its voice had a mechanical edge, a clock with a bad gear. If one listened too long, it would drive them mad. "We can hhhear you. I can read his thoughtsss."

The demon whirled away, a blur through the grass. I slipped off my horse and drew my sword. We forged a rough circle surrounding the three transportation witches. Their magic burned against my skin, but it feathered uselessly. They couldn't help here. All of the emergency teleportation charms had been distributed to the scouts and there hadn't been time to make more. The demon would attack before any spellwork could be completed. And I'd seen enough bloodlust in its eyes to know it would attack.

The dark head popped up to my left, thirty feet away. A black blister burst on its forehead and a trail of green and grey fluid flowed down its face.

"Hhhe saysss hhhelp me. Hhhelp me." The demon titled its head again. "Do you want to hhhear him?"

The creature's eyes rolled back. The body seized, locked in a crouch. It blinked and clear green eyes stared from the nightmare. Its mouth gaped, as though unfamiliar with the motion.

"P-please," he rattled in that same grinding hum. "Kill me. Kill me."

The man fell to his face, his bent spine preventing him from standing. He crawled toward us on his arms, crying into the dirt.

"Kill me, kill me, kill me."

He looked up and screamed, raw and primal.

A dagger struck the middle of his forehead. Cynthia's face remained cold and calculated, her next blade prepped for another throw.

The man dropped, unmoving.

"Is he dead?" Rayhan asked. Nobody dared take a step closer.

Laughter, sharp and piercing, like shattered glass, cut through me. The demon picked its body up and plucked the knife from its forehead. Rich, red blood appeared striking amidst the black ooze.

"Did you think we can die ssso easily?"

The demon flipped the knife in its hand and threw it, fast and smooth. It sailed between me and Zavier, inches from our faces, and buried itself in Juniper's eye. Her cries stopped. Her body went limp under Kadence's hands.

For a moment, Kadence was ice. An inhuman stillness captured him, and his power flared out, wild and hot and angry. The vampire looked up with death in his silver eyes. He pulled the hammer from his waist and charged the demon in wordless rage.

Power lent him speed. A heartbeat passed, and he had closed the distance, lifting the weapon for his first strike. We watched, eyes glassy and mouths open. The hammer swung down as the demon laughed from the ground. At the last second, almost invisible in its speed, the creature spun away, and struck at Kadence's legs like a viper. It scurried out of range and disappeared among the foliage.

Kadence fell to one knee.

Adrenaline dissipated the fog of panic and disbelief. I lagged one second behind the others. Cynthia pulled her blade from Juniper's body and raised it over Kadence, while he found his footing. Blood leaked from his wound, but it began healing as I watched.

Zavier, Rayhan, and I protected the cluster of witches. They had drawn their swords and found competent stances, but their eyes were wide, and their chests heaved with heavy breaths. Fear. They had never been in direct combat.

The panting of scared animals and our boots scuffing the dirt sounded around us. We waited. Where was it?

"Behind you!" Cynthia called.

Rayhan grunted. The demon's nails were sharp as knives, cutting in and out of Rayhan's reach. It sliced at the giant man, and he swung his axe, a second too late. The creature's claws dashed across the engraved chest plate. Strong magic flared and struck at the demon, a bolt of fiery blue lighting. With a shattering scream, the nightmare scrambled up the ridge, a safe distance away.

"Interesssting." It turned its head. "I want that."

Rayhan adjusted his grip on the axe.

"Come get it," he snarled.

The demon pounced off the rock, a haze of black and blood, and landed on Rayhan's shoulders. The giant fell to the ground and the demon clawed at his throat.

Stepping forward, Zavier cut into the creature's hand. Three fingers fell in a pool of blood, severed down the center of the palm. It hissed and abandoned Rayhan, turning to Zavier.

The demon swiped impossibly quick. The old man spun his sword in a tight circle, defending the space in front of his body. Tendrils of magic filtered through his hands, amping up their speed until his sword turned to a streak of grey metal. It wasn't enough. Every cut Zavier deflected was followed by another. Several slices split the witch's skin, marking him with blood.

I ached to join Zavier's fight, but the three witches took priority. If I abandoned my post to help Zavier, the demon could easily jump over us and slaughter the three. This was our only opportunity to set up the transport spell and get our troops to the vampire kingdom. If the witches died, our precious time would be gone, our soldiers would have to march on foot, instead of training, and we would be slaughtered.

Kadence's leg finished healing. In a sprint, he ran the back of his sword across the demon's knees. It severed the hamstring and pale muscle peeked through the skin. The blow would drop another species to their knees. The demon didn't waiver. It slashed at the vampire and Zavier simultaneously, scoring hits on both. More wounds, more blood.

Zavier, Rayah, and Cynthia chopped and struck at the monster, taking two hits for every one they scored. Sweat beaded on their foreheads, but the creature's pace remained steady. It twisted and turned, and every cut excited it more.

In the dance of mayhem, its black eyes found me. A shadow shifted in the iris, darkness a curling storm inside. Its lips turned up into a bitter smile. Its clawed hands never paused, though it didn't watch the fight.

"My Queen," it whispered. Its tongue was the color of the blood on its skin. "I wasss told not to kill you yet." Those eyes flashed to the three soldiers beside me. "They didn't sssay anything about them."

It jumped, but I was ready. My sword, raised in front of Bryn, cut into the demon's shoulder. It howled and swiped, catching my arm. Hot pain flared. My brain recognized it and adrenaline washed the ache away.

The monster circled me, it's gaze darting between targets. It lunged again, this time at Halliday, but my blade bit into his claw. It severed halfway, leaving a squared fingernail in its place.

"Fiesssty," it said and a new, more terrifying fire burned on its face. It looked up and down my body. "I like that."

I did not. I charged. It bounced away before my swing arched, sneaking around behind me. Its claws danced out and I tensed for the hot cut of pain.

Bryn blocked the hit. The vibration of impact rattled her arms and her mouth made a small circle of surprise. She hadn't expected the sheer force of the repercussion and it stunned her.

I recovered, back swinging the blade, but it was too late. The clawed hand, arched in the middle, snapped into Bryn's chest. Blood spilled down her uniform. Bubbles popped on her lips, but no words escaped. The creature smiled while it dug inside her chest and pulled out her heart. It raced away from our blades, quick and agile. Bryn fell in a lifeless heap. Her eyes stared up, empty. It happened too fast for her to be afraid.

The demon perched on a rock, wounds closing rapidly. It bit into the heart and red liquid leaked down its face and hands.

Pain and anger pulled me. Bitterness cut through them both. My parents had brought this filth here. They had stolen our people and sacrificed them for evil. Bryn's blood was on their hands, the same way it dripped off the demon's.

Instinct made me reach for my magic again, but it remained captive, a gaping hole I couldn't reach, locked in an inescapable prison. As the demon chewed and smiled, something else brushed through me, a word, a whisper.

I threw my sword in the dirt. It was useless.

The whisper spoke again. A string, an invisible thread, tugged me.

I walked toward the demon. He had something of mine.

"Sal!" Zavier's voice echoed Kadence's. The two staggered toward me, but the demon moved far quicker. It smiled at me. The pair circled the creature from several feet away, but they couldn't attack while it was so close. It would kill me before they finished the first swing. I catalogued their actions and disregarded them.

"Hhhave you come to sssee me?" The demon licked its bloody lips.

"Yes," I said.

It tilted its head. "Why?"

"Come here." I beckoned with one hand. "Find out."

It rushed at me, a blur of nightmares, and stopped at my feet. Hunched over, it was shorter than me by a full head and had to crane its neck to see my face. The scent of decay leaked from its body, covered by the metallic smell of blood.

The thread tugging through my mind grew stronger as the creature neared.

The demon's eyes twisted into my soul, and from somewhere in the darkness, a voice called me. I reached a hand out. It flinched, but held still. I pressed my hand against its wet, blistered cheek and closed my eyes.

My magic screamed and twisted from where it was held tight, pounding inside my head, but it couldn't escape. That was fine. I had been trying to push the magic out, but now I needed to lock something else in.

The demon's mind opened under my touch, a tangled mess of violence and destruction, death and damnation. The strings of chaos were unsortable. I grabbed one, and it pulled me, a wagon heading straight to hell. I let it go, plucking a new string. Each one led me farther from the exit, trapping me inside the depths of the demon's mind, wrapping coils of darkness tighter around me. I didn't fight it. I let the creature carry me through the terrible places of its memory, where heads rolled and babies cried. It took me to the space that was instincts and survival, and pulled me in deeper and deeper until I didn't know where it ended and I began. I might never escape and I wasn't sure I wanted to anymore.

There. The thread, the whisper, the voice that was *mine*. I grabbed it and the darkness tried to snatch me away. I fought, and twisted, following the thread until I saw a flicker of white. The light battered against a wall of darkness, tearing at it uselessly—silent screams from a lost voice. The demon's mind was an ocean and this bright speck was a thimble of water, tossed in and forgotten.

I wrapped around the pale light like a blanket. I offered a caring touch, but the brightness grabbed at me, a drowning man pleading for salvation, and pulled me closer. I enveloped it and held it tight. The spark of the soul that belonged to the witch, to one of *my* people, clung to me with desperation.

Don't worry. I have you now.

Pieces of my mind slipped between the black strings of the demon's existence. I wrapped myself around those strings tinted with death and gore. I spread through them, grabbing as many as I could, winding them together into thick ropes. Each new twist wrestled against me, demanding more and more of my strength.

The bracelet on my wrist prevented magic from escaping. It hadn't stopped the hybrid's magic from poisoning me and it wouldn't stop the onslaught I planned to trap inside, either.

I gathered the thick fibers of the demon's essence and pulled. I pulled the inky blackness into my mind, shoved it through the bars of the magical cage, stuffing it deeper and deeper into the abyss of my power.

The demon screamed. It buckled under my hand, but its fight was useless. It had accepted my connection. We were locked together, mind against mind, and I sucked its life away.

As the black strings thinned from the demon's mind, the bright light grew bigger, stronger. New chains and threads appeared, trailing through the cleared and open space.

The demon beat against my magic. My jaw clenched with the effort to hold it in place. My magic rippled against the ambush of vile power, but the cage wasn't full yet. I pushed the demon deeper and deeper, drinking away its grip on the witch's body and drowning it in my magic.

I ripped the demon from its shell, locking it into my mental prison. The white light filled the body beneath my hand. His knees buckled and he fell.

The creature trapped in my magic, alongside my own soul, raged against me. One of us had to go and it wouldn't be me. I almost felt the twist of a smile cross my lips. My magic cut like a knife through its being, slicing away at it. Without a host, the demon held no power. Its life flickered with each strike, and I cut it into a thousand tiny specks, until it turned into a faint smudge trapped in my power. The magic swallowed and the corrupt soul was gone.

I opened my eyes. The witch's body remained twisted and broken. His fists clenched tightly, his teeth a harsh line.

The ground crunched when I fell to my knees. I brushed a strand of dark hair from his face and he looked up.

"It hurts," he said.

This body would never be healed. The demon's power hadn't been strong enough to sustain it. This man was given a death sentence the moment the creature entered him, but he wasn't sentenced to more pain. The demon was gone. There was plenty of room in my cage.

"Shhhh," I said.

My fingertips barely grazed his skin, but he flinched at the touch. His pain ran red-hot through his body, a spiderweb of connections. I took them all. Aches and fever spilled into me, along with regret and terror. Memories of things I'd never done splashed through my mind— ambushing a band of merchants on the road, eating through the tender flesh of their stomachs, searching for the cries of a child, eager for young blood on my tongue, and the horror as the demon pulled away at the last minute, letting Elis taste the bitter bite of a human heart.

Elis. That was this man's name. I took Elis's pain and suffering into my cage and my magic cradled it and held it close. One by one, it ate them away, tearing them into pieces too small to ever find again.

"Thank you." Elis closed his eyes and rested under my hands.

"Knife," I said. My throat burned.

Cynthia crept closer, watching the crippled body next to me. She handed me a dagger.

I trailed my fingers down Elis's chest and found that sliver between his ribs where his heart beat. The knife cut, quick and true. His eyes never opened.

"It's done," I said.

Exhaustion clawed me. I wasn't strong enough yet for a battle like this. My stomach heaved and I threw up next to Elis's body.

"The demon is gone?" Kadence asked. "You were able to use your magic?"

"No." I wiped my mouth with the back of my hand. "He invited me into his mind and I pulled him out instead. He's dead."

Dizziness forced me to the ground. The sun crested in the sky, warming me. When did I get so cold?

"We have to ride straight to the castle," Cynthia said. Voices blurred, fading at the edges. "It's not safe to stop for the night."

"That was one demon." Rayhan's face held a red hue and tension leaked through his voice, barely covering a trace of terror. "There were eight of us and we barely survived one of those bastards. How many are coming?"

"Four thousand, five hundred at the last estimate." Zavier sounded grim, but it was hard to tell. My mind couldn't quite decipher the words.

"I'll carry the queen on her horse," Kadence said. Strong arms lifted me from the ground. I fought for a moment, sanity warring with exhaustion, but my body gave out. Despite the surprise of his tender touch, I settled into the king's warmth and listened to the rhythm of his heartbeat.

One thought danced in my head, unbound and floating.

Four thousand, five hundred. Four thousand, five hundred.

Chapter Twenty-Four

THE HUMID AIR SAT HEAVY AGAINST MY BARE SKIN, CHILLING me to the bone. Two days of horseback riding without sleep and minimal breaks left me battered and sore. I abandoned my coat inside and the cold soothed my aching muscles.

The balcony off my room peered over an open field, solitary trees scattered across it, like wooden ghosts. Their leaves had dropped, and they were prepared for the first snow, which would come any day. A fire crackled behind me, spilling warm light onto the balcony. The castle's rich red-and-orange stones bathed the spacious room in comforting hues. Rugs stretched the entirety of the room, cushioning each step. The thick bedspread, the leather couch pressed against the wall opposite the fireplace, even the tapestries, were woven from shades of black and grey. Splashes of red popped in unexpected places, a bloodred vase on the bedside table, a single red rose resting on the pillow. I expected the dark decor to make me feel trapped or secluded, but I was beginning to like it. The room felt like a nest, someplace safe to curl up.

My first glimpse of the Kingdom of Vari Kolum had been at the peak of night, visible only by the moon and torches from an entourage of guards that escorted us into the castle. My window faced away from the city and I didn't dare wander the castle to sneak a peek. My authority didn't reach here. This was Kadence's kingdom, and I was a guest. I didn't need the residents to eat me in the hallway.

Ruby, one of Kadence's staff with strawberry-blond, curly hair, had brought me a black dress with red buttons trailing down the back. Composed mainly of thick wool, it was lined on the inside to avoid scratching my skin. The tight top exposed a generous amount of cleavage and the bottom fell to a straight hem.

Jon Chan. Two guards. Bryn. Elis. Dead. Dead. Dead. Dead.

I didn't want to start a list, but the names rolled through my head. I was not a stranger to death. It is a constant companion on the battlefield, sometimes foe and sometimes friend. These last few deaths weighed on me. We had found peace, only to have it snatched away.

I hadn't heard the door, but cushioned footsteps toned behind me. Kadence hesitated in the balcony doorway. He wore a formal uniform, a jacket with two rows of silver buttons over a collared shirt, the same one from my coronation. His breeches were tucked into black boots that reflected the firelight. He looked like an officer ready for a celebratory ball, rather than a king at war.

His gaze brushed me up and down. My cheeks were already stained pink from the cold and I was confident he couldn't see a new blush highlight them. Fire smoldered in his eyes, and just for a moment, the predator saw more than its prey. He smoothed his face and the expression faded like the last days of summer.

"I thought you'd like to see the city." He kept his voice flat, professional, afraid I might catch an edge of emotion. I could tell by that tone it was important to him that I saw his city and that I liked it.

Kadence cleared his throat.

"For strategy and tactical reasons, of course," he said.

He wanted to pretend he didn't care. Fine.

"Of course." I brushed past him and shrugged into my new coat. It fit perfectly and was warm. Feeling flowed back to my numb skin.

Kadence led us down a stone hallway that opened into a common room. Bookshelves and chairs nestled in the corners, leaving an open space to walk through. The tapestries and paintings here wore colors. An abstract canvas caught my eye, odd against the rugged castle walls.

Kadence led us to a winding staircase circling up to one of the castle's spires.

He must have felt my hesitation and glanced back.

"This way has the best view."

It could also be the best place to push an annoying queen to her death. Memories of Kadence shoving me against the window that first night flooded my mind. My steps faltered. Did I trust him enough to follow him?

I couldn't deny the nagging feelings building in my chest every time I looked at the man. In the few months we'd been together, the hatred that used to burn in his gaze had settled to a different kind of flame. Perhaps returning to his childhood home, where his parents had died, and where his blame toward my people began, would rekindle old biases. Had these emotions between us grown a firm foundation, or were they still spider silk waiting to collapse at the next breeze? I bit my lip, wondering if my bravery was strong enough to find out.

Kadence heard the change in my pace. He paused and stepped down.

"Almost there." He held his hand out.

I searched his face, looking for the rage and pain he once poured onto me. His expression remained hard and focused, but something sparkled in the depths of his black eyes. Something hopeful.

His hand felt warm in mine. He pulled me up the last flight of stairs and an open doorway spilled us onto a wall walk. The chill grew stronger up here, unprotected by the castle walls, and noisy too. Birds screeched as we interrupted their perching and a symphony of voices floated from the grounds below. The sun shone on my head, but its rays didn't beat away the cold.

"Over here." Kadence turned.

The bulk of the castle stretched before us. The blocky, rectangular structure ate away any open space for gardens. The building climbed five stories, two more than my home, with four spires like giant arms reaching to the sky. The stones outside matched the ones inside and the winter sun highlighted the warm tones.

Vari Kolum stole my breath. Buildings stacked six or seven stories tall, casting shadows onto the castle grounds. Grass peeked through cut divisions where parks peered between structures. Open pavilions housed market stands, barely visible from our distance. Most shocking was the plethora of color. Each building sported a bright, vivid color. Some buildings switched halfway, as though the top had been constructed later. A river rolled behind the city, cut off by the sprawling structures. The perimeter wall was short and less extensive than ours, designed to keep out wildlife rather than catapults. Farmland stretched in the peripherals, spanning too far to see.

Words caught in my throat.

"What do you think?" Kadence's flat voice held a cautious tone.

I couldn't deny its beauty, nor did I want to. The vibrant colors reminded me of life and laughter. I imagined children running through the playgrounds, the sky painted rainbow, feeling safe surrounded by stone guardians.

"It's so colorful," I said. "From your interior decorating, I expected something darker."

"If you stepped inside any of these buildings, your expectations would be fulfilled. We like to feel close and confined, comforted and safe," Kadence said. "Some historians speculate that it's an evolutionary trait. When our species first emerged, we had to hide in caves during the day and only venture out at night to avoid being killed."

"Do you think they're right?"

He shrugged. "I think sleeping in a dark room is more comfortable than sleeping in a cave."

"Then why does everyone wear black?" I asked.

"Fashion changes, Sal." A hint of laughter colored his tone. "In ten more years, clothes might look more like the outside of the city than the inside."

My country had tried to find this kingdom for centuries and I was glad we never did. The thought of these great structures, people's homes and livelihoods, torn down and the foundations burned stirred my heart with sadness. We had less than a week before the army of the dead marched on these walls. Determination grounded me like steel. They were my people now, whether any of us liked it or not. We might not defeat the demon horde, but we were going to try, together.

"What are you thinking?" Kadence whispered behind me.

I turned to face him.

"I'm thinking about the battle," I said. "We'll need to build up the walls so the demons can't scale them. The mountains will be a natural barrier, but we could dig trenches to funnel them into one area. They'll breach the gate and the walls eventually, but we could have a good number cut down before then...What?"

Kadence's blank stare disappeared. He searched my face with a look I didn't recognize.

I crossed my arms. "We don't have to do trenches, if you have a better idea."

"Forget about the trenches, Sal." Kadence shifted, locking both of my arms in his hands. At this distance, the heat of his body pressed into mine through the bulky coat. A knot twisted in my chest—expectation, apprehension, uncertainty.

"Do you know what I was thinking?" he whispered. "I was thinking about when you walked toward that demon, unarmed and blank, like you were in a trance. I thought I was seconds away from watching you die. I have imagined your death for years, in hundreds of different ways, preferably by my hand. When it was right there, in front of me, do you know what I felt?"

I shook my head. His scent filled my lungs, fire and smoke and new leather.

"I felt scared. And then angry. I wanted your death, for me, for my parents, for the thousands of my people that had been slaughtered in the war. But in that moment, I would have given anything to keep you alive."

His eyes locked on mine. "I felt like I was betraying my people and I didn't care."

Kadence's gaze shifted to my lips. He bent slow, as though asking permission, giving me time to pull away. My heart leaped into my throat. Fear and desire warred, freezing me in place. He slid one hand under my chin, lifting my face to his.

His lips were soft. He kissed me warm and tender, asking instead of taking. I couldn't move, couldn't think beyond his hands on my body. The knot in my stomach loosened under his touch and something hungry took its place.

I tilted my head and kissed him back. I claimed his mouth with mine, inviting him for a deeper taste. My hands trailed the edge of his jacket, fumbling with the buttons.

Kadence growled against my lips. I gasped and he caught it in his mouth, wrapping his hand behind my neck and pulling me closer. His skin burned like fire against mine. A distant part of my brain recognized that my coat had tumbled to the ground.

I plucked at the buttons and stripped Kadence's jacket off. He released me and pulled the shirt over his head. I caught a flash of a sculpted chest, toned and chiseled, before he pressed against me.

He kissed me harder, demanding. He was a spring rain and I was dying in the desert. He was sweet and safe, and strong and terrifying. I gave him everything, and he took it.

He abandoned my lips, setting kisses down my neck. I leaned my head back and gave him room, exploring his body with my hands. He softened under my touch, arching for more. His fingers found the buttons on the back of my dress and the fabric fell off my shoulders. Bitter cold bit at my skin, but his hands chased the chill away.

Kadence lifted me to the wall walk, his arms my only anchor against gravity. We perched so high, the fall would be fatal. He stepped between my legs, one hand holding me around the waist, the other searching for the clasps of my brassiere.

I leaned into him, eager for his touch, eager for everything he was willing to give me.

Someone coughed.

We froze.

A young man in black overalls lingered in the doorway. "Yo—Your Majesty." His cheeks painted red and he studied the floor. "You told me to tell you when the advisors were ready."

Shame at being caught in such an improper position burned my cheeks. I ducked my head and push against Kadence's chest. He lingered, hunger in his eyes, and I thought he might not move. After a moment, he took a reluctant step back, and I turned away from the boy, pulling up my dress and blindly latching the buttons.

"They're, um, ready, Your Majesty." The boy hesitated a moment longer and then running footsteps faded down the stairs.

Kadence sighed.

I straightened the dress and ran a hand through my hair. Curls bunched in my fingers. It was hopeless.

He watched me, his expression turning hard again.

"Kadence," I said softly.

"Don't. I'm sorry if that was embarrassing for you."

"I did not say that."

Sharp anger cut through his face.

"You didn't have to." He grabbed his clothes. "Let's go."

His bare back retreated down the stairwell, leaving me confused and alone in the cold.

Chapter Twenty-Five

I TUMBLED THROUGH THE UNLOCKED DOOR, SWEATY AND OUT of breath. Kadence was long gone by the time I clambered down the spiral staircase, leaving me to search for the meeting room alone. The castle resembled a twisting maze. Some hallways led to dead ends, others slipped onto balconies through solid wood doors. I flagged down a maid in the hall, who had looked at me with wide, scared eyes and stammered directions in a whisper. Maybe my status as the enemy queen frightened her, or maybe my anger at Kadence had seeped into my face.

Everyone in the room stared at me. I forced a smile, smoothed my dress down, and slipped into the nearest open seat. Zavier waived from the front. Rayhan, who sat next to the old witch, lifted his chin. My pulse slowed as the familiar drone of a council meeting resumed.

"Now that everyone is here," Kadence avoided looking at me, "what's our status?"

Chairs lined both sides of the room, facing the center. A thick black carpet lay underfoot, but the natural stone walls remained unpainted. A podium stood at the front, but Kadence sat in a simple chair beside it, his feet stretched out and crossed in front of him. His hands were folded on his lap, and he looked peaceful, comfortable. I fought the urge to slap him.

Zavier stood.

"Our witches have begun preparing the entrance locations for the transportation spell," Zavier said. "Unfortunately, we lost one spellcaster on the journey here, which will slow our troop transport."

Bryn. My heart stung at the memory of her death.

"How much will it be delayed?" a petite woman with long black hair asked. She sat near Kadence and was almost two heads shorter than him. Her height made her appear young, but creases at her eyes and mouth put her at about forty, though vampires aged very differently than witches. She wore a dark-brown dress and a wool shawl draped across her shoulders. A natural rosy glow filled her face.

"We expect an additional ten hours to move all the soldiers, Madeline," Zavier said.

"That's manageable," Madeline said in a crisp voice.

"Has housing been prepared for the troops?" I asked.

Kadence's dark eyes cut to me. The mood in the room shifted. Everyone suddenly found something else to look at.

"Are you doubting my ability to provide for your people?" he asked, a dangerous whisper.

"I am verifying that *our* people have places to stay," I said.

"My King?" the black-haired woman chimed in.

Kadence's face softened. "Yes, Madeline?"

"I don't know what has gotten into you, but you need to shake it off," she said. "The queen has made a long, dangerous journey to a new land. She's trusting you to provide for her army. The last people she trusted with that task stole them away and damned them to a life of suffering. You need to watch your tongue, before it leads you beyond return."

Kadence's face twisted, then flattened. "You make an excellent point."

"Perhaps she deserves an apology?" Madeline said.

Kadence didn't appear angry at her words. In fact, I recognized the slouch of his shoulders like that of a chastised child. If it were proper of me to place bets, I would put coins down that Madeline had a hand in Kadence's upbringing.

His eyes flicked to my face. "Perhaps later."

She didn't fight him, but turned her rosy, shining face to me.

"Please excuse my king's manners." She shot Kadence a side look that didn't hold malice. "He doesn't have any."

Kadence pressed a palm to his chest. "Straight to the heart, Madeline. Like always."

Madeline turned that sharp gaze to me. "I'm Madeline, King Kadence's Royal Administrator, similar to Zavier's task in your council, it appears. Let me introduce you to everyone. Anthony Cortez, in the back, handles our supply and transportation routes."

A dark-skinned man raised one hand.

"Marshal Chole Price manages military personnel and risk assessment."

"It's a busy time of year," Marshal Price said. She wore civilian clothes, her blond hair pulled back into a loose ponytail.

Madeline nodded. "Unfortunately, it is. And last is Lukas Brock, he does whatever we tell him to do."

The room chuckled, and a tall, thin man waved.

"Kadence never mentioned his advisors before," I said.

"You never mentioned us?" Madeline raised an eyebrow. "We've written to him daily since he's been gone. You let her think you were doing this all alone?"

"It made me look more intimidating." Kadence shrugged. His light-hearted flippancy might have made me smile if I wasn't so furious with him.

She pointed a finger at the king. Her muscles were defined, strong. It wasn't hard to imagine her with a battle axe in one hand and the head of an enemy in the other.

"Now, the reason we're all here," she said. "The updates."

Marshal Price stood. "We estimate the demons will arrive in four or five days. They've picked up speed according to recent observations. We've combined our scout teams with the witches so we have near constant updates now."

"Our forces?" Madeline asked.

The Marshal straightened. "Zavier has requested as much time as possible to train our troops to fight together and I agree. We aren't going to survive if we hurt each other. Everyone that can't fight will be on defense preparation. The walls need to be improved, among other things."

Kadence looked to Cortez, who stood.

"Our supplies have to be inventoried and rationed," Cortez said.

"Once the witch marshals arrive tomorrow, teams will be assigned to make those decisions. Supply routes are too dangerous to run right now, we've halted all merchant entrances and exits into the city. We have enough food and medical supplies to last almost a week."

"It will be over well before then," Rayhan said.

Madeline's green gaze swung to me while council members finished scribbling notes.

"Now, what we really want to know," she said. "How did you kill the demon?"

The scribbling stopped. Dozens of eyes squinted at me, quills poised to write the first word I said.

"Err—" quills scratched on parchment. Wonderful.

"I'm not sure." I admitted. "I felt drawn to it, to something that lived inside the vile creature. I knew that if I touched it, something would happen."

"Kadence said you dropped your weapon and walked toward the demon alone," she said. "Just because you knew 'something' would happen?"

Murmurs flooded the room, people snuck side looks my way.

I shifted in my seat. I probably shouldn't tell them I had heard a voice whispering to me. "It does sound silly like that."

Kadence raised his hand and the room fell silent. Disbelief swirled in me. My council would have been up in arms over my lack of manners. Kadence's advisors settled in their seats.

"It's not silly, Your Majesty." Madeline smiled. "We don't understand magic very well. We've mostly studied how to destroy it." Her voice turned apologetic. "We want to learn how to work with it."

"Magic is like a child," Zavier piped in. "There are rules, and it knows the rules. But it does whatever it wishes anyway. Every magic is different. I can heal a little, and use it to help in battle. It makes me faster. I can amplify my voice. But I can't do what Sal can."

"That is correct," I agreed. "My magic is strongest in battle, but I don't have an affinity, a specialty. It doesn't heal, I can't transport anyone, I can't detect poisons or use it to enhance my senses."

"Do different witches have different amounts of magic?" Madeline asked.

"Yes." I shrugged. "My magic is strong, but my family was bred for generations with magical abilities in mind. It was designed to be strong." In fact, they had been disappointed with the blandness of my magic. My mother never appreciated battlefield magic.

"I'm not a powerful magic wielder," Zavier said. "I rely more on my skill with a weapon."

"But her magic killed a demon?" Madeline asked.

At the mention, I felt the black stain of its corrupt mind in my memory.

I held my hands out. "I didn't know I could do that. I have never faced a demon before. Did it happen because of the strength of my power? Maybe. Was it because I have an affinity for destroying demons? I don't know." Was it because of Elis's voice that called me through his damaged mind, one of my own people reaching for me?

"If we put you on the battlefield, how many demons could you kill?" Madeline asked.

"I don't know. Certainly not enough."

Madeline cradled her chin in one hand. Kadence looked at Rayhan, who studied the floor.

"Could Natalie do it?" Kadence asked.

The blood rushed from Rayhan's face. His jaw clenched at the name, hands balling into fists. "I don't know," he grunted.

"Will you ask her to come?" Kadence asked, though a hardness in the words revealed it wasn't really a question.

Rayhan pulled himself from the chair as though it physically hurt. He shuffled out of the room slowly.

The door hadn't closed before he turned back. A young woman followed him.

"She was waiting in the hall," Rayhan said through clenched teeth, sending her a sharp look. "Even though we agreed she wouldn't do that."

The woman lifted her chin defiantly.

Natalie's big brown eyes stared at me within a round, soft face framed by a few strands of mousy-brown hair that had come free of her braid. She wore a simple dress with a white apron around her waist and thick soled, black shoes. While pretty, she wouldn't stand out in a crowd. Her eyes had the hollow gaze of someone used to being overlooked that had suddenly found unwanted attention.

Two puncture marks sat in an open display on her neck, slightly bruised at the edges. A vampire bite.

She scanned the rows of chairs. Despite the attention, her shoulders were relaxed, hands open at her side. She had been in this room before, perhaps recently. People nodded at her and she smiled.

Her gaze landed on me. She paused, choices clearly turning in her mind. Her face flattened with decision and she dropped to kneel on the ground at my feet, head down, a prisoner waiting for execution.

As she moved, power swirled around her like a heavy cape. It pressed into me, pushing against my magic like a piston. It demanded the room and filled it, hungry and confident, a wild animal that had never been tamed, could never be tamed. It stole my breath. My instincts screamed to get as far away as possible because I could never fight this magic and survive.

Natalie was a witch, the most powerful one I had ever met.

Memories tumbled forward. The etching of spellwork in Rayhan's armor and the brush of power the piece emitted. I thought we had a traitor witch working with the vampires and the roll of Natalie's magic made me think I'd just found her.

"My Queen," she spoke to the floor, "I surrender myself to your judgement as a traitor to our kingdom."

Rayhan choked. "Natalie." He grabbed her arm. "Get up."

She shrugged him off. "I told you how I felt about this," she snapped, sinking to her knees again.

"And I told you not to do it."

"You're not in charge of me, Rayhan."

"Perhaps I should be when you act like this."

Natalie's incredible power swirled in response to her anger. She could have forged a tornado, a hurricane, and killed everyone in the room. Instead, it licked lazily against Rayhan, rubbing over him like a content cat. It liked him.

"Children," Madeline called. "Rayhan, as you've been told before, Natalie is an adult. If she recognizes her queen's right to judge and sentence her, she's allowed to do that."

"Exactly," Natalie said. "Go sit down."

Rayhan trudged to his seat and slumped into it.

"My Queen." Natalie bowed her head again. "The vampires found me in the woods when they were still our enemies. I was with my eight-year-old sister. They threatened our lives and I gave myself as captive so she could go free. I have done terrible things against our people, but my family and I are loyal to the throne. I understand duty and honor, and it would have been right to lose my sister to protect the kingdom."

A thickness clung to her words. I knew if she had the choice again, she would make the same decision.

"I am not asking for mercy," she said. "I deserve only punishment."

"What crimes have you committed?" I asked softly. "Protecting a loved one? Being a captive during wartime? These are not crimes."

"I have used my magic against my people." Her face paled, her eyes empty. She stared into her past and regret peered back. "I have made terrible things."

Her gaze lifted to the bracelet on my wrist. Her power slithered toward me, a silken snake, strong and dangerous. It wrapped around the band, recognizing its own touch. She had made this bracelet and the prison trapping my magic, a part of my soul.

Anger and bitterness surged, a wildfire hungry for revenge. My magic roared, searching for a sliver of escape. Natalie's prison remained iron tight. I studied the girl in front of me as a judge would study a dangerous criminal.

She appeared healthy and well-cared for, but old scars settled into the skin on her wrists. She had once spent a lot of time bound, likely by silver chains which prevented her from healing. She acted timid, but not afraid. No resentment lined her face. She had forgiven these captors long ago. I pictured her in the woods, smothering her power, promising anything to save her sister's life. I would have done the same. If creating this bracelet kept Natalie alive, I was happy to wear it.

"If we sentenced everyone that has done terrible things to protect a loved one, we would have an empty kingdom," I said. "Please stand up, you're making Rayhan nervous."

The vampire's fingers opened and closed on his axe hilt. He sighed when the little witch stood and took a seat beside him. If I had punished her, he may have tried to attack me.

Natalie folded her dainty hands, flooded with bands of magic, on her lap. "How can I help?"

"We need to know if you can kill demons," Kadence said.

Natalie flinched at his voice and averted her gaze. She twisted slightly away from the man. The king had frightened her at some point.

A flash of regret peeked through Kadence's face at her subtle motions, before he flattened them again.

"Why do you think I can do that?" she asked carefully.

"Because I did it." I spoke before Kadence could. This woman could possibly kill the entire room in a moment, but my soul longed to protect her. "I don't know if it's an unusual affinity or just the strength of my magic."

It felt like a mockery to call my magic strong when hers coiled around the room like a dragon, ready to devour us all.

She dipped her head low in a bow and tapped one square nail against her chin. "I would have to search my mother's books, but it was unlikely to be any kind of affinity." Her large eyes fixed on the wall behind us, looking at something we couldn't see. "Demons don't have a physical form. Their entity is wrapped into pure power. They must have a host to use that power, so the possessed body is a demon's greatest strength. If you pulled a demon from a host, it would be easy to dismantle the life force. What did you say led you to touch the demon again? It was a bit hard to hear it all through the door."

I pressed my lips. "I had a feeling that if I touched the creature, something would happen."

Natalie nodded, apparently unsurprised by my decision to approach a demon with little foresight of the consequences.

"We won't have time to explore it before the demon army arrives, but my mother's books reference a specific type of affinity attuned to the royal family. The Affinity of Responsibility. You bare a responsibility to your people and your magic enhances to that. That feeling calling you to touch the demon, was the witch inside the beast recognizing your presence, your ability to protect them." She still didn't look at me, fixating on the wall. "Of course, killing the demon would simply be an act of pure power."

"I was exhausted after killing the one," I said. "If I killed a demon on the battlefield, I wouldn't be able to hold my sword after."

"Death should always bare a hefty toll," Natalie said, her voice hollow. She continued staring for a few moments while we held our breath.

"Yes." She straightened. "I think I understand the principle of it, in theory. I've studied the mechanisms at least. I think I could kill demons. I'm fairly confident of it."

"Fairly confident is all we have," Zavier said. "How many could you kill?"

"I'm not sure. I will have to do some practice spells, experiments." Her face pinched in thought. "But I'm almost useless after using my power. I would have to be very close to the demons, to kill as many as possible all at once."

A moan escaped Rayhan's throat. A sheen of sweat shone on his brow.

Natalie looked like she wanted to reach out and comfort him, but she restrained her touch.

"The problem is," she continued, grimacing, "I'm an awful fighter. If you dropped me on a battlefield, I'd be dead in moments."

"We could lay a trap," Zavier said. "We gather many demons in one place. Then we form a protective formation, the best of our people, around Natalie. If she can kill some of the creatures, maybe the rest would flee."

"No," Rayhan's voice cut through. "No, it's not happening."

"Rayhan." Natalie tsked. "Of course, it's happening. I'm the only one who might be able to kill enough of them to persuade the rest to leave."

The giant dropped to his knees in front of the witch. He grabbed at her hands, pulling them to his face. Tears swelled from his eyes and he let them flow down his cheeks.

Natalie softened and she leaned closer to the vampire.

"I can't lose you," Rayhan said. "You are everything."

She freed one hand and wiped the tears from Rayhan's eyes, cradling his large face in her small palm. "You are everything for me too," she whispered, searching his soul through his eyes. "That's why I have to do this. If I can take away a piece of their troops, there's a higher chance you'll come home to me after the battle. If I don't, we will lose everything. There has been too much death at my hands. Give me a chance to save lives."

The vampire pressed a kiss against the back of Natalie's fingers. He rose on shaking knees and strode out of the room, red dreadlocks disappearing through the doorway.

Natalie watched him. "He'll be all right." She looked around the room. "What else do we need to plan?"

It wrapped up like a normal council meeting. Duties and assignments doled out, scrolls stacked into piles, and a buzz of conversation followed the exodus from the room. Kadence and Zavier stayed in their seats, chatting about defensive options.

I waited for them to finish. I had given my opinions during the meeting and trusted Kadence to make the right decision, even if anger still pulled at me from his actions on the wall walk.

Natalie approached and bowed deeply before me. "May I sit with you, Your Majesty?"

While she had betrayed me, my kingdom, and our people, it hadn't been her choice. I held no animosity for her over it. And besides, I was alone in this place.

I nodded and beckoned to the chair next to me. "Please, sit."

We watched the pair talk.

"Vampires, huh?" she said. "King Kadence is a handful, I'm sure."

An unexpected smile tilted my lips. "You could say that. Rayhan is pretty smitten."

She sighed. "He's like a kitten in a bull's body. He has good intentions, but tramples his way through them. He thinks that because I don't have super-strength, or immediate healing, that I'm fragile." She cut a sharp smile. "He would be surprised."

Her magic—a part of her aura—curled around us, a great serpent too respectful to eat me. Rayhan would be very surprised indeed.

She tilted her head, exposing the puncture wounds on her neck. They were two neat circles, slightly scabbed with a tint of a dark bruise hugging the edges.

"Does it hurt?" I asked in a low voice that made her lean closer.

"What?" She followed my gaze and jerked one hand to her neck. Her fingers trailed the wound and a blush highlighted her cheeks.

"I'm sorry." I snapped away. "I didn't know it was personal."

She suppressed a laugh and lightly settled one hand on my arm. "It's fine," she assured me, but the blush grew. "You and the king haven't...?"

She sent a glance at Kadence, who was side-eying our hushed conversation.

"No." I shook my head.

"Oh." Her eyes widened. "I'm surprised. The way you look at each other. And there have been rumors..."

It was my turn to blush. We had been found in some compromising positions. Secrets never stayed secret in the castle.

"No," I said. "I haven't been..." The word caught in my throat.

She rubbed the mark again.

"It doesn't hurt." She dropped her eyes to the floor with a tight, embarrassed smile. "It feels good."

I opened my mouth.

"What are you two doing?" Kadence's voice cut through my thoughts and I jumped. His lips twisted in a half-smile.

"That is none of your concern," I said at the same time Natalie said, "Nothing, My King." She looked hard at her hands. Whatever Kadence had done to scare her, it left a deep scar. He studied the witch, his eyes cloudy, then turned to me.

"Zavier says your spellcasters are ready."

I jumped from the seat, too fast to be appropriate. I smoothed my dress down, slowly. "I'm ready."

THE SUN SET AGAINST THE BACKDROP OF THE RAINBOW buildings. Its golden rays did nothing to drive away the cold and it was chillier than it had been that morning. The sky was clear and blue, but black clouds built along the horizon, promising a winter storm.

"We'll have snow tonight," Zavier said.

We gathered in the vampires' training area, which they called the Lists. It was easily twice the size of our field arena. A roof covered the sitting area, while the center remained open. Battles rarely took place inside and it didn't benefit soldiers to train without facing the elements. Rows of black bench seats stacked against the walls, over ten feet high. Today, they were empty, but I imagined hundreds cheering on an underdog warrior and the groans with a final blow of a horn.

The two witches set the entrance spells in the back of the Lists, leaving enough room for troops to walk forward once they arrived. Herbs were ground into powders, then mixed with pigment and a binder to create a special paint, unique to that spellcaster. The paint let the witch see their symbols as they drew, helping avoid mistakes. Errors in transportation spells weren't usually fatal, but it would be bad if our soldiers came through missing limbs.

Twin circles spanned side by side, stretching probably twenty strides in diameter. Small, blocky symbols scattered the outer edge, and a second, smaller circle embedded inside. Halliday's circle shined in emerald paint and Fellows's was royal blue. Once the witches injected their magic, the circles would be permanent. When the sky dropped inches of snow into the Lists and covered the paint, the spells would still be functional.

Natalie rose on her tiptoes for a closer look.

"Who's coming through first?" Kadence squinted at the shapes on the ground. "I want to make sure my people won't be split in half if this doesn't work."

"We promise nobody will be split in half, Your Majesty." Halliday stood next to the king and studied his circle. "We've been doing these spells for the better part of ten years. I've only cut someone in half once, and we found a good healer to fix him."

The witch smiled, but Kadence looked at him flatly. The smile faded.

"My staff and the laboratory team are coming first," I said, lightly touching Kadence's arm with my fingertips. He didn't flinch. "And they're bringing the council."

A guilty part of me wished they would get cut in half.

"Laboratory staff?" Natalie perked at my words. "Do they study magic?"

"Yes, among other things." I thought of the stacks of bodies that had been waiting in the morgue.

"How long will it take to bring everyone through?" Kadence asked.

Halliday rubbed his chin. "You're looking at fifteen thousand soldiers. We have two entry points and we can teleport probably one hundred people per circle. We're only human, sort of." He shrugged. "We have to eat and rest. It'll be a solid two days."

"How long do we have?" I asked.

"The latest scout estimates give us four to five days," Kadence said.

The army of the dead would stand against this city within days. Demons would ravage the streets, seeking out blood and children and flesh. Panic roared into an ocean threatening to drown me, but I let it flow away. There would be plenty of time to panic later.

"Will the defenses be ready by then?" I asked.

"They'll have to be." Kadence's tone was grave.

The demons would be here either way.

"Your Majesty," Foster addressed me from where he stood next to his blue circle, "are you ready?"

Kadence and I nodded.

"Let's do it!" Halliday yelled.

Natalie stepped back, her wide gaze brushing over the spellcasters, consuming their every movement with a look of hunger. For one with so much power, she seemed very eager to study magic.

The two closed their eyes. Magic pushed from their bodies like a breeze before a tornado. They built the magic up and up, contained within themselves, but stoking it into a great storm. The power buzzed across my skin, familiar yet uncomfortable, the scratch of a wool sweater where the soft lining ripped. They grew the magic to a boiling point and spilled it out, sinking it into the circles. The paint looked inert, unmoved.

"Nothing's happening," Natalie said.

"Shhh," I whispered.

The witches pressed the last of the magic into their circles and cut it off. Everything became still.

Air rippled inside the painted markings, as though steam rose from the ground.

Kadence leaned forward.

The swells grew, turning through the space until they became thick and dense, mist instead of steam. The mist found solidity, and figures emerged, real and alive.

Saffa and Remi stepped over the circle, Elaine and Renee at their heels. Behind them, the council stood dazed, searching for familiar faces. Juno's heeled-boots sunk in the dirt. And she pressed her lips toward the ground disapprovingly. A team of white-cloaked people, arms full of beakers, scrolls, and books, followed in her wake. All bowed deeply to me and then to Kadence.

The other circle spilled soldiers in uniforms, broken into sections by platoons. Marshals and Commanders led their groups from the circle, and Zavier met them with directions.

I caught Saffa's eye, but Juno reached me first.

"Where can my team set up?" she asked in a hurried tone, another thought clearly spinning on the edge of her mind. "We are close to a breakthrough, but not if we have to construct our lab in the dirt." She squinted at the open ceiling. "It's cold here. Nobody said anything about it being cold."

"We have a space designated for your research," I said. "How close are you to a discovery?"

"Just look at him." She pointed to Remi. New symbols peppered his arms, drawn clear and precise this time, unlike the ragged etchings scrawled by his kidnappers. His hair had grown, half an inch peaking on his round head.

"He can destroy the trees again," Juno said.

"I didn't know that ability had gone away."

She nodded. "Once the symbols faded, the magic left. We brought it back, but there's a couple more kinks to work out."

"Like what?" Kadence asked.

Juno dipped her head low in a short bow to him, but I caught the grimace on her face . "It doesn't matter. I'll fix them."

Zavier found us, leaving Cynthia to organize the troops. He bowed to Juno and pressed a kiss to the back of her hand.

"Let me show you your new laboratory." He tucked her hand into the crook of his arm. "I think you'll be very satisfied."

"May I come as well?" Natalie's dark head poked up behind the taller woman.

Juno jumped, one hand pressed to her chest, and looked Natalie over. "Why?"

"I've only practiced spellwork from books. I would love to learn more from such a bright, intelligent woman like yourself. Plus, I have a little project you might be able to help me with. I have to learn how to kill demons."

Juno's face flattened and a hint of a smile tugged her lips. "Well." She pulled her hand from Zavier's arm and wrapped it around Natalie's elbow. "Let's see what we can do."

Zavier led the women away and Juno's team followed.

A hint of blond glistened under the sun. Standing inches above the tallest council member, Reuben peered at me through the crowd. He smiled and gave a little wave, looking for an opening to get through.

Kadence tensed beside me.

"This will be good." He palmed the hammer on his belt.

"Your Majesties," a voice called behind us, gasping for breath. A scout slumped in the gateway of the Lists. His hair was tousled, his uniform soaked with sweat. He gripped a spent transportation talisman.

"I have news from the field." He staggered toward us like he was drunk.

"What's wrong with him?" Kadence asked.

"The talismans aren't as seamless as the entrance spells." I ducked one shoulder under the scout and Kadence grabbed him on the other side.

Reuben reached us.

"Who's this?" he asked.

"Shh." I looked around. Everyone else was busy organizing the troops and preparing for the next wave. Even the Royal Guard's distracted looks filtered between us and the amassing troops with a sort of awe across their faces. "He just came from the field."

"What do you have to say, Soldier?" Kadence asked.

The man's head lulled.

"King Tolen and Queen Estelle have broken from the main camp." He paused, catching his breath. "They—they're on the way here."

Shock grabbed me, anchoring my feet. My parents, possessed by demons, were on the way. Fear and dread warred with grief and longing. Without the main march, they would be faster. Much faster.

"When do you estimate they will be here?" Kadence asked.

"Tonight," the scout said. "They'll be here tonight."

"The rest of the troops?"

"Days away." The scout's voice faded and he slumped between us, chin to his chest, breathing light.

"What does that mean?" Reuben's eyes widened. "Does the battle start tonight?"

"No," I said, though my heart was not in the word. "The rest of the army will be days behind still. But the king and queen will arrive tonight."

Kadence looked at me over the unconscious soldier. A wild, fearful look filled his gaze and I knew it matched mine.

My memories stretched to the single demon we'd faced on the road, when five witches and three vampires had barely taken the creature down. The two approaching now, wearing my parents' bodies, would be much more powerful.

It would take a miracle to defeat them and I wasn't sure we had any of those.

Chapter Twenty-Six

"YOUR MAJESTY," RUBY PEEKED HER CURLY HEAD THROUGH the door, ending the few moments I'd found for a short respite, "the prior king and queen were spotted less than five miles from the gate."

"Thank you, Ruby," I said.

She disappeared with the soft echo of cushioned steps.

I dragged myself from bed. The black I darkened the room, but Kadence was right when he said it was like sleeping in a warm, secure space. The room held the heat of the dying fire and the black blankets were calm and peaceful. I didn't want to leave.

Saffa had surprised me by taking the pictures of my parents with her through the transportation spell. They sat at the foot of the bed, peering up stoic and serious, mocking me with traces of life. I ran a finger over my mother's cheek.

Grief swelled into an ocean threatening to drown me. I missed them. The last thing I wanted was to meet them in the night, look into their eyes, and see evil gaze back at me. Tears burned. Their betrayal was too heavy. I wouldn't be able to carry it.

A knock sounded against the doorframe. Kadence hesitated in the opening.

"I'm almost ready." I wiped the tears before he could see them.

"They're still preparing the horses. We have a few minutes," Kadence said. We were going to ride out and head off the demons at the road. We didn't want the pair near the main gates.

He stepped into the room wearing the black uniform and armor of his army. He cradled a white silk bag in one hand.

"This is for you." He held the bag at arms-length as though it made him uncomfortable.

The soft bag almost floated across my fingertips and the ties opened like fragile spiderwebs. Golden lace pooled inside, clean and vibrant and bright. I pulled the garment from the bag and delicate lace dripped to the ground—my mother's golden jacket, worn at her wedding and my coronation, ripped to shreds when I intervened in the fight between Reuben and Kadence. I thought it had been destroyed.

My throat tightened.

"How did you get this?" I touched the threads lightly, afraid they would shatter at the lightest pressure.

"You left it in my room after your coronation." Kadence stepped closer. "It was important to you, so I found a weaver that was able to repair it. I thought that since it was your mother's and you're going to see her body tonight...maybe it could be something to remember her by, the real her."

New tears stung my eyes.

"If you don't like it, you don't have to keep it." Kadence squinted. "I can have the holes put back."

"No." I dropped the lace on the bed and grabbed his hand. Gratitude and despair were too much. My heart wanted to explode. "This is perfect. I thought it was beyond repair."

"I plan to give you an opportunity to wear it again," he said. "I had the sleeves widened, so if you have to wear it to another fight, it shouldn't rip this time."

"Thank you." Ugly laughter caught in my chest, half-snort and half-sob. "Thank you so much."

Kadence shifted his weight, averting his gaze. He caught sight of my armor spread across the bed.

"I'll help you put this on, if you want." He lifted the plates.

Sheets of metal composed the armor, secured with leather straps and ties. The thin material protected my body without weighing me down. They wouldn't stop a well-placed strike with an axe or hammer, but it could handle arrows and blades. I had been putting on my own armor since I first walked the battlefields, but I bit my tongue. Something delicate spun between us and I was afraid to ruin it.

My hair already braided and twisted into a tight bun. It was feminine, fierce, and wouldn't get in my face during a fight. A golden circlet was pinned in my hair, a testament of my status as queen.

Kadence lowered the armor onto my shoulders and it settled heavy and familiar. He searched out each clasp and buckle, hands drifting across my uniform as he found the connections. His fingers brushed over my ribs, my shoulders, my back, starting fires with each touch. The straps tightened at his touch until they were snug and sparks danced down my spine.

He fit the vambrace onto my arm. His fingertips trailed across the bare skin on my wrist. The faint pulse there caught him captive. Anticipation burned me and a deep longing that I tried to lock away beat against its bonds.

Kadence brushed against the silver bracelet, the one binding my magic, creating an endless pit stretching across my soul.

"I've been wanting to take this off." His voice went soft.

I tilted my head, but pressed my lips together. We'd come a long way, Kadence and I. The first time he'd held me, pushing me against the glass windows in his bedroom, I'd felt only fear and apprehension. Now, under the soft glow beneath his protection in his castle, new feelings twisted through me. Trust brewed between us, that much was obvious, but whether it was absolute, I wasn't sure.

"I've trusted you to keep my people safe in a kingdom not my own, before I even had reason to rely on you. Now I trust you to defend my kingdom, the very enemies that plagued you with war for two hundred years, against those that wear your parents' bodies." His fingers tightened on mine, slipping across the protective metal of the vambrace. "I want you to be yourself, and whole, when you see them tonight."

Kadence traced his fingers across the silver band, tightening on a place as though a secret latch resided.

I held my breath. My heart beat in my ears, excitement at the thought of having my magic and being free. Without the angry spell trapping my powers, I could help our people so much more.

The band remained.

Kadence's face turned red. He grabbed at the bracelet again, anger turning his fingertips white.

The bracelet didn't budge.

I waited for the wash of sadness or anger to bubble through me, but calm resignation remained instead. Something held Kadence back from trusting me, and though disappointing, I understood. Two hundred years of death and suffering couldn't be overcome in a few mere months.

I cradled Kadence's face in my hands. His rugged skin scratched against my palm, and he turned angry eyes to me.

I smiled. "It's okay." I whispered.

He tried to turn his face away, but I tightened my grip. "It's not. I trust you, Sal. I don't understand why it won't come off."

I trusted him too, which was why I remained unworried. It would come off eventually, when whatever wound lingering in Kadence's heart finally closed.

He looked at me, an edge of silver in his eyes. His scent slipped around his armored frame, smoke and forest and a deeper scent that was only Kadence. This close to me, his power danced between us, lighting new flames in my core with each pulse.

I set my other hand on his cheek, framing his face. He tried to flatten his expression, but I saw the edge of desire slip through. A half-smile tilted on my lips.

I stretched to the tip of my toes, trapping Kadence's head in place, and pressed my lips against his. For a moment, he stilled, then softly kissed me back.

Kadence broke the contact much too soon. He slipped the second vambrace from the bed and tugged one of my hands from his face. He settled the armor in my palm.

"I think you'll have to finish this," he whispered, turning toward the door.

I didn't want him to leave. I had spent weeks avoiding this man, terrified he would collect on the contract we had agreed to. He had threatened me, scared me, but had never hurt me. It seemed ridiculous now. I sacrificed so much to make this peace work, but had been blind to the sacrifices Kadence made—his happiness, his future. We weren't married, he could take another woman or a wife, but I knew he wouldn't. He would avoid anything that would unbalance this alliance.

He let my hand slip.

I grabbed on tighter. "Don't go," I said. "Don't leave me."

"We have another date planned tonight, Queen Sal."

"Yes, but after"—if we were still alive—"will you come back to me afterwards?"

Kadence shook his head. "Being with you tonight wouldn't be good for either of us. I've neglected my hunger for too long. I would make bad decisions. I could hurt you."

I waited for the flood of fear, but it didn't come.

"I don't think you'd hurt me, Kadence." His name sounded like music on my lips.

He turned. "Not tonight, Sal."

Ruby appeared in the doorway. She saw Kadence and stumbled into a bow. "My majesties, the horses are ready. The demons are almost to the fourth mile marker."

"Thank you, Ruby," Kadence said. He looked at me over his shoulder. The moment was gone, but longing remained in his eyes.

"I'll see you there." He disappeared through the door.

I sighed. I strapped the second vambrace into place, repeating the interaction in my mind. Where had I gone wrong, again?

Save for my guards, the hallway was empty. Almost everyone worked to prepare the defenses. Ten feet of sharp wire and pointed stakes were being added to the perimeter walls. The farmers on the outskirts of the kingdom had been pulled into the main city, along with early harvests of their crops for more supplies. Trenches and moats were being dug, explosive traps would be set, and Juno was almost done with her magical vampires. We had our footing and maybe even some extra time to rest up before the entire horde arrived, assuming the demon king and queen didn't slaughter us all tonight.

Voices trailed at the end of the hall before the stairwell that led to the main floor. I started in that direction, my two guards falling into step behind me.

"No, I told you, this one needs to be more square," Natalie's voice drifted toward me.

"This is a square," Rayhan said through clenched teeth. It sounded like an old argument.

"Who taught you to draw a square, then? That's clearly a rectangle. The symbol won't work as well if it's a rectangle."

"Maybe you should take the armor off and draw it yourself," Rayhan said.

"I told you, this particular symbol has to be set while the armor is on." Natalie's patience sounded thin.

I rapped my knuckles on the open door and they both turned to me.

Rayhan sat with his legs crisscrossed on the floor and Natalie perched in his lap. His black armor sagged on her much smaller frame. The straps were fully tightened, but the leather rubbed against her skin and it would chaff if she wore it very long.

"Your Majesty, Rayhan is just finishing this symbol for me." She nodded to me in greeting, then craned her neck over her shoulder. "But if he gets it wrong, it might kill me instead. Is that what you want? Do you want to kill me?"

Rayhan paled and his hand shook.

"I'm only joking." Natalie winked at me. "It won't kill me. Maybe just maim me a bit."

"I'm done." He put down the engraving tool. "I'm going to say it again: I don't want you to do this."

Natalie turned in his lap and pressed her palm to his cheek. There was another bite mark on her neck, red and fresh.

"I have to do this, Rayhan." She leaned forward.

Rayhan sighed and put his forehead against hers. He shut his eyes and drew a deep breath.

I bounced on my feet. I was interrupting a private, intimate moment, but I couldn't look away. Something sweet blossomed between them. It drew me in, ignited a craving in my heart.

Natalie broke away and stood up.

"Omph. This is heavy."

"It's too big," I said. "It's not going to be very protective."

She shrugged and grimaced at the weight. "Thank you for your concern, but, it's the magic in the symbols that will protect me. I've been working on this for over a year. It's almost done, but it's tuned specifically to Rayhan. It's not happy that I'm wearing it."

"I'm not either," Rayhan said.

I studied the symbols scrawled across the black armor. I recognized very few of the enchantments.

"Where did you learn these spells?" I asked.

"From the catacombs—"

"Natalie!" Rayhan yelled.

Natalie's face turned a hint of pink. "Oops. Sorry."

"Listen, girl," Rayhan said, his grip tightening on her arms, "you're not even supposed to know about those."

Natalie grimaced. "They've been destroyed now, anyway. I don't see the problem."

"The problem is—"

Natalie interrupted what sounded like the beginning of Rayhan's well-versed speech. "Please, Your Majesty, let's go before he decides to stop me."

We left Rayhan sitting alone on the floor.

"Are you going to be able to ride in that?" I asked.

She hefted the chest plate up.

"Yes, I can handle it."

The look on her face argued otherwise, but I didn't challenge her. None of us were ready for this.

Three horses stood saddled outside, their reins tied to a post. They weren't our regular mounts. They were younger and less trained. A ping cut through me. These animals were disposable. They wouldn't be missed if they didn't make it back.

Zavier stopped adjusting a strap and caught me in a tight hug.

"Good luck tonight, Sal," he whispered. The embrace drew me back to the night of the surrender, Zavier next to me while we walked toward almost certain death. He stood by me then and he would be there tonight if I allowed him to be. Someone needed to lead the battle if Kadence and I died.

He pulled back and held me at arm's length.

"It's going to be hard, but remember they're not your parents." He searched my face. "The demons inside of them are too powerful. The king and queen won't come back."

I nodded. My mind knew this, but my heart still bled hope.

The storm had come and gone. Snow glistened like white crystals, untouched beyond the stables. The frosty breeze had settled to a chill, but not biting. The moon reflected rainbows into the ice on the trees and fences. My uniform and armor wouldn't keep me comfortable, but they would be warm enough to stay alive. The horses' breath turned to mist in the night.

"Ready?" Natalie asked.

Kadence and I looked at each other and nodded.

We set out across the pristine snow, leaving behind Zavier and the Royal Guard to avoid the possibility of additional casualties. We marched forward together and I feared each step brought us closer to destruction.

NATALIE'S TEETH CHATTERED WHILE WE WAITED IN THE SNOW. She wrapped her dainty arms around herself, trying to trap her body heat under Rayhan's heavy armor. She didn't complain, but Kadence and I shared a worried glance.

Next to us, the signpost said we were three furlongs outside the city. Our last report placed the demons at the fourth furlong, walking slowly through the snow. They should be here by now. The wait gnawed on me. I tapped my fingers along the armor on my arms. Kadence paced between the horses, checking and rechecking the saddles.

"Can you do magic to keep yourself warm?" Kadence asked Natalie, breaking the silence, evidently tired of watching her shake.

"I'd rather save my strength," she said, pulling a woolen cloak tighter around her shoulders over the sagging armor. "Sometimes the magic comes out in a whoosh."

I didn't want to see what a whoosh of her magic looked like. It didn't sound like something we would survive.

Snow crunched.

Our heads snapped to the road.

Two figures emerged from the darkness, each holding the reins of a horse. The horses weren't saddled, instead carrying large pack bags draped across their backs.

The couple saw us and stopped. Moonlight illuminated their faces.

My heart skipped a beat. Time froze, as cold as the snow on my skin.

Queen Estelle Marguerite Astor, my mother, stood in front of me, barely more than ten paces away. Unlike the demon that had possessed Elis's body, these looked perfect, pristine.

Blond locks fell in gentle, sculpted waves around her face and shimmered in the moonlight. Her big eyes were icy blue and her lips pursed. She wore a simple dark-green dress, pinched at the waist with a gold belt and plain, black flats. The snow crept to her ankles, but there was no shiver in her stance. She tilted her head to the side, studying me.

Memories shattered the dam in my mind, flooding me – sitting on her lap while she brushed my hair and I recited the memory phrases for that day's lessons. That same head tilt when I explained why the staff had dragged me to my room after skipping class again. Mirrored pain while she wiped tears from my eyes. Agony and longing crashed together, threatening to rip me apart.

I don't know what I'd expected—tattered flesh, fangs, claws, blood—but this wasn't it.

Tolen Astor, or at least the body of my father, was thicker than when he had left. He had always been lean and fit, but new weight softened his gut. His beard was longer, neat and clean. He wore the formal uniform of our kingdom, white with red capped sleeves, the outfit he had disappeared in.

My father stepped forward, arms out as though to embrace me.

Kadence and I drew our weapons together.

Natalie faded quietly into the background.

The demon in my father's body swept his eyes over us and dropped his hands.

"Salvatore." My mother's voice was hard. "What are you doing? You know better than to disrespect your father."

My training said to apologize and seek forgiveness at my father's feet. But these weren't my parents. Waves of darkness twisted around these pristine shells, the same feeling that Elis's possessed body had when we fought on the mountain pass. Though they peered through my parents' eyes, it was not their souls that looked out. My sword didn't waiver.

"I see you wear a crown," the demon Tolen said. "Have you stolen our titles, too?"

"I have stolen nothing from you." My voice came out strong, confident, like I wasn't dying inside. "I have taken the title given to me as my birthright, after the death of my parents."

"Death?" The demon Tolen gestured at his body. "You see us right here, with your own two eyes." He held his arms out again. "Come, embrace me, daughter. It has been many months."

"I'd just as soon strike you down." The words were sharp, a dagger in my own heart.

"Fine." The voice from my mother's throat wasn't hers anymore. It was deep, ragged, the edge of a wound that could never heal. "We thought you might see reason from your own parents."

"We see that was a mistake." My father's face distorted, twisted, a flash of something less than human peeking out.

"Why are you here?" Kadence asked. The two demons turned in inhuman unison to study him. "Why did you break from the main march?"

"We're faster this way," the male hissed. His eyes flashed, fire behind the brown irises.

"Are you here to offer surrender?" Kadence asked.

The pair laughed. Chills slithered up my spine, leaving a cold trail. The noise turned to static in my head, sharp and heavy. It tried to convince me to drop the sword and run, while logic said I would never be fast enough. I ground my teeth.

"There will not be a surrender in this fight," the demon in my father's body said. "We will take our children and slaughter you all. We will eat the hearts of your young, drink the blood of your most innocent. Our claws will pierce through the chests of soldiers and abandon their crumpled bodies in the snow. When we find you and hold your heads in our hands, maybe then we can speak of surrender."

"What do you wish to achieve tonight?" Kadence asked.

"We wanted to see the woman who killed one of our own." My mother's eyes struck me.

It's not her, it's not her. Maybe thinking it enough would make me believe it.

"We felt his life crumple before us, and we thought only a powerful witch could have done that." She flicked her gaze up and down my form. "It appears we were wrong."

Even in her death, I couldn't gain my mother's approval.

"Here she is." Kadence pointed his hammer at me. "You can go now."

The demon Tolen's face split into a smile, exposing sharp teeth.

"But we brought gifts. It would be rude of us not to give them." He pulled the horses forward.

"We don't want anything from you." Kadence's lip curled.

"You'll want this," the demon Estelle said.

The demons dropped the reins and slapped the horses. They bobbed forward, the weight unevenly distributed in their packs.

Kadence grabbed the leather straps, never looking away from the demons.

"In the bags," my mother's demon said.

I took the reins and Kadence covered me with his hammer. Leather bags draped across the horses' back, one large bag on both sides of the animals. They were full to the point that the leather was stressed and the straps stretched. I persuaded the cold metal buckle from the strap.

I flipped open the bag and a severed head stared at me. A man's face, white skin and blue lips. His mouth hung open, blue tongue protruding between white teeth. Green eyes were half-closed under heavy lids. The neck wound was smooth, revealing that the decapitation had been clean, efficient.

My face stayed blank. I let myself blink at the head three times before lifting my gaze. The demon pair smiled at me, eager with anticipation. They wanted a reaction and as they waited, their features flashed, dashes of evil looking out.

"What is it?" Kadence tried to see from the corner of his eyes.

I opened the other bag. Two more heads. One of the neck wounds was not as clean. Jagged skin suggested it had taken several hits to free the head from its body. I recognized him. It was the scout that brought news of the demon king and queen's approach this morning. He must have gone back to the field after recovering.

Each bag could fit about four heads and there were four bags. Sixteen of our people had died. Our scout units were divided into four or five soldiers, depending on their mission. These bags contained four of our teams, all of our active scouts.

"They're heads," I said. "Probably sixteen dead."

"Seventeen actually." The demon Estelle gave a wide smile. "One of them got a little squished."

"You asked us why we're here," the demon Tolen said in that piercing voice. The hair at the back of my neck stood up. "We're the distraction. Your most recent update is half a day old and you don't have any scouts in the field. Our masses have been marching all night and you've had no idea. We have feasted on the countryside for days. We're full, rested, and at our most powerful."

"You thought you had three, maybe four days?" the demon Estelle asked. "We'll be here tomorrow."

Fear drove through me and I couldn't chase it from my face. Tomorrow? The walls were half-built, the trenches barely begun. Our city would never be fortified by tomorrow. Flashes of the dead rolled through my mind—Saffa, bloody and sliced. Zavier, his throat ripped out. Kadence...Bile climbed up my throat.

"That's right, Queen," the demon wearing my mother's body said. "It's over. Tomorrow, we will feast on your kingdom's bones."

"Unfortunately," the demon Tolen said, "you will die tonight. We can't let you spill our secrets to the rest of your people."

The demons' claws, over a foot long, sprouted from the ends of their fingers. They wielded them like master swordsmen, cutting across our bodies, expecting to feel flesh split between their razor blades.

Instead, a wall of gentle magic blossomed between us. From behind us, Natalie's power flowed into the wall, building and strengthening it, until it shaped into a towering, impervious fortress. The demons slugged through the depths, then bounced backwards as though ricocheting from an explosive charge. They caught themselves, stumbling in the snow.

"Interesting." The demon Tolen brushed his claws against the magic, a precise slice, an experiment. His gaze flicked to Natalie.

"You hid this much power?" he asked, voice filled with awe.

"You haven't seen anything yet," she said. Pieces of light flowed through Rayhan's armor on her body. One by one, the symbols illuminated, casting a complicated weave of spellwork onto the snow. She was the night sky, twinkling with a million stars.

The demon turned back to me.

"You were foolish to bring her here," he said.

"She will be dead on the field with the first wave tomorrow," the demon Estelle promised.

"You fools," Natalie taunted like a child would. "Let me show you the gift I have been making you."

Magic poured over the pair, drenching them like a summer storm when the skies opened and the gods cried from above. The demons held their hands out, as though they might catch the magic on their fingertips. Natalie wrapped the rain around them, drowning them in her power. She squeezed, suffocating the corrupted souls locked in their stolen bodies.

Shock rolled across their faces. The pair backpedaled, gasping.

"How can you do this?" The demon Estelle arched her spine, fighting against Natalie's magic. "It's impossible."

"Watch this," the witch bit out, her face scrunched.

The magic tightened. The rain turned to icy sleet, trapping the demons in a frozen prison. She tightened it, smothering them. The sparks of the demons' souls sputtered and flared, fighting to survive.

"We will kill you all," the demon Tolen said between gasps. "You will wish you had died here tonight."

The pair turned and fled, faster than any human feet.

Kadence tensed as if to pursue them, but he froze, hesitating as his gaze shot back to me. He studied my face as I watched the demons retreat, and a blend of confusion and something softer twisted in his eyes. Their steps soon faded, as did Natalie's magical grip.

"They're too far." She slumped. I wrapped one arm under her and she leaned on me, panting. "They knew the magic had a distance."

"You couldn't kill them." Kadence watched the direction of their retreat.

Natalie shook her head. "They were so strong, but I almost had them. I understand their life force now, how it feels. Juno has been teaching me some amplification spells. If she can help me find the right one, I can kill the weaker demons, a lot of them."

"How many?"

Her face pinched. "Probably two or three...thousand."

Kadence's draw dropped.

"That would...help," he said.

"Those two were incredibly strong, and I almost had them," Natalie said. "If I can get close to the bulk of them, I can take out half their army."

"Maybe that would scare the rest enough to leave," Kadence said.

"Like Grace." I nodded. Maybe we wouldn't need to fight every demon.

"I'm not feeling well." At the last word Natalie's eyes rolled into her head and she dropped. I slowed her fall and lowered her to the ground.

"She did say she was useless after using her magic." Kadence lifted her from the snow and draped her over one of the horse's saddles.

My feet dragged beneath the weight of what I did as I tied the two new horses, carrying the burden of the dead, onto mine. We would take the heads home for identification and so their families could bury them. My hands shook against the straps. I felt like I had been poisoned all over again. Physically, I was fine, but my limbs dragged like lead, and my foggy mind bogged me down.

"Sal," Kadence said and I jumped.

"Apologies." I ran a hand over my face. "I'm tired. What's up?"

"How do you feel?" Kadence searched my eyes and I considered my next words. His expression, so carefully blank, told me that he searched for a specific answer. I knew he wasn't asking about my physical health. We had a shared experience now, seeing the bodies of our loved ones worn by cursed souls.

"I've been better." I shrugged. "I knew they were gone, but..."

"It was different to see them in person?" Though he stood beside me, his mind was leagues, years, away. "When they look so alive, so real? When you know an embrace would feel exactly the same?"

Sorrow ran through me like glacier water, ripping apart my heart and carving a new crevice. My parents were gone, but I didn't have bodies to bury. I was an orphan, but demon's wearing my parents' faces had tried to kill me moments ago. We would meet on the battlefield tomorrow and we wouldn't all walk away.

A sob tore from my throat, unexpected and loud. I couldn't hold it back, and more followed, one empty wail after another. Tears burned down my face. My lungs struggled for air.

Warm arms wrapped around me. Wood and fire filled me, and I sucked in as much of the scent as I could. Kadence was real and alive and his heart beat against my ear. He knew how I felt. He was the only one.

He rubbed circles on my back and held me as the sobs turned to silent crying. The cries faded to exhaustion and I sagged in his embrace. The horses' calm noises, and the rise and fall of Kadence's chest, settled me.

Finally, Kadence squeezed me and let me go. With a lift from him, I swung into my saddle. When I turned to check on Natalie, she'd awoken and sat upright on her horse.

"How do we know they won't turn around and follow us?" Kadence asked.

"I can still feel their life forces," Natalie said. "They're very far away."

A hot fire and a warm bath beckoned me. There was so much to do, but I needed a moment to breathe and settle. I had to be calm and secure for our people.

"We need to get back to the castle so we can rest and strategize. Let's go." Kadence set a punishing pace toward the castle, and Natalie and I followed.

Chapter Twenty-Seven

WATER SPLASHED AS SAFFA AND ELAINE DREW MY BATH. WE had informed the council of the new timeline and handed the heads of the dead scouts to Marshal Hale. She had closed her eyes and said a quick blessing before leading the horses away. The council members took one look at me and declared me unsuitable for their needs. I had explicit orders to take a bath and rest before returning to my duties.

The fire danced in red and amber hues. Its flickering arms hypnotized me, drawing me from my memories. If I closed my eyes, the warmth could be from Kadence's body, standing too close and too demanding. A whisper of longing trailed through me.

I missed him.

"Your Majesty, the bath is ready," Saffa said.

I slipped into the hot water. Saffa wet my hair and trailed shampoo through it, rubbing my scalp.

"How's Remi?" I asked.

Saffa's face turned pink. "I'm sure he's fine. Why do you think I know?"

"I was just curious."

"She knows you've been sleeping with him." Elaine handed me a bar of soap. "But she can't say that because she's the queen."

Saffa choked.

"I am not...sleeping with...him." Even the tips of her ears were colored. "We should be talking about the queen and king getting caught pawing one another on the roof," she said with good-natured cheekiness.

My cheeks heated.

"Tell me more." Elaine leaned forward.

"It wasn't the roof," I mumbled.

"The wall walk, then." Saffa rolled her eyes. "The stableboy said you were almost naked."

"Sal!" Elaine gasped.

"I was fully clothed! Mostly."

The two giggled.

"Besides..." I sunk in the water and let it dissolve the memory of Kadence's skin on mine. "He doesn't want to be around me. He told me to stay away tonight."

"Are you crazy?" Elaine dumped fresh water into the tub. "When you are in a room together, he can't look anywhere else. What did he say?"

"He said he would make bad decisions."

The two looked at each other.

"You have to see him," they said together.

"What? I can't. He told me not to."

Saffa waived her hand. "If you show up tonight, he won't refuse you. He can't. He's crazy about you."

I remembered his eyes as he kissed me, the hunger when I kissed him back. He didn't want to stop. Saffa was right. He wouldn't turn me away.

My heart skipped a beat. Butterflies beat in my stomach, in time with the anticipation and uncertainty that turned my gut.

"I don't know what to do," I said.

"Do you want to see him?"

The warmth of the water accented every chill that slipped over my bare skin. I felt his chest against mine, his power a curling whisper of smoke, the taste of metallic honey in my mouth. A fire stirred in my body, a spark with the possibility to become an inferno.

"Yes," I whispered.

"I'll get Renee." Saffa disappeared through the door.

Elaine rinsed my hair and combed it to a shine. She wrapped me in a thick robe and I sat with the fire to my back while the heat dried the wet strands.

The door opened. Renee wore a simple black dress and her hair twisted in a bun. She carried a satchel on one shoulder and a bag in the other hand.

"Your Majesty, please stand up," she said. Her brown eyes scanned me. I wanted to scrunch under her gaze, but forced myself straight. "Turn around."

Renee dragged a chair next to the coffee table. "Sit here, please."

She opened her backpack and sorted the supplies into neat piles on the table—rouge, charcoal, brushes, dyes, and other products I didn't recognize. She studied my face, twirling a brush in one hand the way she would spin a sword.

"What would you like?" she asked.

"I'm going to see the king tonight." I was past the point of blushing. My face felt permanently red.

"It's about time." Renee ran a brush through a tray of kohl. "Let's see what I can do."

Elaine and Saffa peered around to watch.

MY THROAT TIGHTENED WHEN I KNOCKED ON KADENCE'S door. He had been overseeing the defense preparations, but Renee said he recently returned to his room.

The girls hadn't let me look in the mirror, but I caught a glimpse of my reflection in a silver planter in the hall. Renee styled me in the traditional vampire way. Thick kohl lined my eyes, cutting up to a sharp edge. She'd painted my lips blood red. My hair was tasseled into big, wavy curls that fell soft across my shoulders. The woman looking back at me was fierce, confident. I didn't recognize her.

Renee's second bag had housed dozens of scanty outfits, all black, some more revealing than others. She recommended a dainty two-piece that a strong wind could blow away. I settled for a plain silk slip. It clung to my body, ending midthigh, leaving little to the imagination.

I pulled my black satin robe tighter and glanced down the hallway again. Empty. The Royal Guards attended to defense preparation, leaving our care to competent staff members. The same ones giggling in my room as I'd left to meet the king.

"Who is it?" Kadence's voice was muffled through the door.

"It's Sal."

I waited.

"Come in."

Kadence's room looked similar to mine. More artwork decorated the walls, vivid paintings of landscapes, some picturesque, others abstract and modern. His large, simple bed blended into the decor rather than controlled it. Double doors lay open and a stone balcony spilled outside. I could see his dark silhouette in the night.

I shut the door and ventured to the balcony. The snow had been swept away, but the rocks chilled my bare feet. Winter broke through the thin robe and brushed across my skin. I wrapped my arms around myself, to fend off the cold and my nerves. It didn't help either.

Kadence leaned against the railing wearing black breeches and a white button-down shirt, half undone as though he hadn't finished dressing. He looked over the open field below, past the trees and the mountains in the distance. I knew that look. It was one I'd worn often. He already saw the battle. Death and blood would take over the pristine grassland, leaving bodies and grief behind. I could almost see the thoughts, strategies, and techniques spinning in his mind. The same ones ran through my own.

"Kadence."

"I told you that I didn't want to see you tonight." He continued to scan the landscape.

"Did you expect me to listen to you?"

He let out a harsh laugh. "I guess I did. My mistake, Queen Sal." He turned and his gaze rolled over me. Almost forced, as though pulled against his will, he searched my face, my hair, my body. He ran a hand over his jaw and surprise turned to something darker. His eyes bled silver.

"What are you doing, Sal?"

My fingers fumbled at the knot on the robe. The sash was stubborn in the cold, twisting in my shaking hands. The fabric finally gave way and I peeled the robe from my body, letting the winter air touch my skin. The silk puddled at my feet.

Kadence turned his back to me.

"I am ignoring what you told me."

"You need to leave." Tension strained his voice, as though he held his breath.

"No."

Power splashed against me and Kadence moved in front of me in a heartbeat. He grabbed my arms, pressing them to my side. His grip was careful, and his hands shook with the effort of control. The strength in his grasp ignited an aching need I had kept buried. His eyes raked my body, as though he couldn't look away.

"I don't want to frighten you again." Hints of white fangs showed between his parted lips.

"Kadence." I pulled one arm free and pressed my palm against his rugged cheek, enjoying the warm skin beneath my hand. I cupped his chin, pulling his gaze to my face. \

"Do I look scared to you?"

He searched my eyes. I knew he would not find fear in my gaze.

The vampire brushed a finger across my cheek. His touch burned my skin, scalding through the layers of flesh, and burying somewhere deep inside me.

"No," he whispered, "you don't look afraid, but you've terrified me. Tonight, when your parents stood before us, the demons a perfect image of the pair, I had a terrible moment where I imagined you'd walk away with them. That you'd choose those who loved you, raised you, over me and the kingdom we are building together."

I shook my head, trying to track Kadence's thoughts.

"Going with them would only lead to death, Kadence. Why would I choose that path?"

He grew distant. "My mother chose that evil over my father, over...me."

"Your mother chose to protect you the best way she knew how." I ran my thumb across his stubbled chin, but Kadence caught my hand and wrapped his fingers around it. "Queen Cameron's choices were wrong, but the intention behind them was not."

"What are your intentions, Sal? Tonight, after this battle, when everything you've worked for has finally been achieved. What then?"

I had a lot of plans for the future of our people, though I hadn't thought about them in the weeks building up to the battle. I knew Kadence didn't want to hear about my desires to explore surrounding kingdoms, to advance our feeble science outside of the war effort. He wanted more.

"I plan to be where you are," I said, letting him see both the want and need in my gaze. "Always."

Kadence closed his eyes and ran his hand up my arm. His fingers pressed against the silver band around my wrist and an almost mechanical clicking flicked between us.

I froze, my breath caught. I didn't dare hope that the noise meant what I wanted it to.

Kadence stroked his hand across the bracelet. A faint latch, almost invisible to the naked eye, appeared down the side of the jewelry. The latch snapped open and the shackle clattered as it fell against the stone floor.

Magic burst through my mind and body, a flood from a broken dam. The power was strong, so sharp, it threatened to cut through me. For a moment, pain and darkness blinded me, and as the magic settled, I found the point where my soul met the power, and my mind climbed through that opening, pulling me back into my body. I welcomed the magic, wrapping it like a fur coat, and settling into its soft caress. I relearned its feel and it danced for me.

I gulped for air and opened my eyes. When had I closed them? I was doubled over, kneeling on the stone floor.

Kadence held my shoulders, worry etched in his face.

The cold air settled my rolling stomach.

"Are you all right?"

Joy floated through me. Months without my magic had dulled the pain of its absence. I couldn't imagine living without it again.

"I'm great." My wrist looked naked, free without the matte silver cuff. "Thank you."

Kadence helped me to my feet. Relief and freedom rolled through me, but a sliver of doubt plagued my mind. The bracelet could only be released once Kadence trusted me implicitly, once he knew I bared him or his crown no threats. I knew he pictured a world of us ruling together, of our people being one kingdom. The bitter guilt grew and his vulnerability cut at me. I had to repay that trust. We deserved a clean slate.

"I lied," I said. "When we met for the surrender, and I said destroying our people would ruin your supply train, I lied. There's no such thing as magical residue. I have no idea where any of those boxes came from."

Tension twisted in the inches between us. I waited for his anger, his doubt. I should have told him long ago, with the first tendrils of trust. I hoped it wasn't too late.

Kadence laughed. "I know." He brushed a light hand through my hair. "I personally approve all trade routes. I knew exactly where those supplies came from."

"If you knew I was lying, why didn't you kill me?"

"I didn't expect the princess to trudge down to our camp in the middle of the night and demand a meeting. I was intrigued. I wanted to see what else you had up your sleeve." He shrugged. "Plus, we gained a lot more supplies by not destroying your kingdom and keeping the laborers. It was a mutually beneficial situation for all, really. Except for you, of course."

"Of course," I echoed.

"You want to talk about supplies right now?"

"No, I don't," I whispered.

I caressed his cheeks, his forehead, across the bridge of his nose. He closed his eyes and let me explore his face. My heart pounded harder with each touch, a fire stoked in my soul. I ran my fingers through his hair and pulled him closer to me. Soft breath brushed my face, and he held perfectly still, watching through half-closed lids. Smoke and leather enveloped us, every breath I drew filled me with more and more of him.

Our lips touched. A groan escaped me. I tilted my head, capturing his mouth, claiming him with my kiss. He sighed, and I claimed that too, drinking him like fresh water in the midst of a firestorm. I would never get enough.

He kissed me back, but it was different than before. He was careful, controlled. Immobile and frozen, still holding my arms, Kadence turned to a wall of stone, ice to my heat.

I pulled away.

His jaw locked, eyes squinted closed. He stood steady, as though he hadn't noticed my sudden withdrawal.

A dagger of hurt and pain cut through my heart. He didn't want me. I'd thrown myself at him, would give him anything, and he was a boulder, cold and unmoving. Tightness caught my throat. Tears I hadn't expected to shed tonight choked me.

I looked at the black slip and the robe at my feet. The fabric clung to my breasts, nipples peaked in the cold air. My hips swelled, and my legs were shapely from decades of good breeding and years of sword fighting, but I wasn't anything special. He had prettier girls in his court.

"Oh." Embarrassment highlighted my face. I scrambled to pick up the robe. "I'm sorry. I'm so sorry."

I jolted toward the door.

Kadence caught me, one hand wrapped around my bicep. It was not a gentle touch. He held me tight and firm and offered no escape.

"Do not run from me," Kadence growled. The black in his eyes had faded, silver moonlight filled his irises. His face was hard, hungry.

I recognized the predator in front of me. The vampire had finally caught his prey. I stilled, deciding whether to fight or flee. Kadence's sword would be in his room. Was I fast enough to reach it?

He jerked me against his chest, capturing both of my wrists in one hand and wrapping the other in my hair.

"What were you thinking before you ran, Sal?" His lips brushed my cheek. "Did you see the vampire in my eyes and it scared you?"

"N—no." I whispered, barely a breath.

"Did you regret coming to me tonight?" He kissed the other cheek.

"No."

"Did you think I didn't want you?"

I didn't answer.

"That's the one. I pulled away and you assumed I must find you lacking. Do you want to know the truth, Sal?" He kissed the corner of my mouth and chills spilled down my spine. "The truth is, predators move slow when they see their prey. They don't want to scare them away."

He smiled, sharp fangs and silver eyes.

"But I've caught you now."

He kissed me, wild and free, and I kissed him back. His body was a ship in the sea, and I was drowning. I clung to him like he was my last hope, the only thing keeping me afloat. He pushed me against the stone wall, and I wrapped around him, inviting him closer. His lips took my mouth and demanded more.

He stepped away and pulled his half-buttoned shirt over his head. I loosened his belt and his breeches fell to the stone floor. His body was a sculpture, carved from a block of pristine marble, and I wanted to feel those muscles against my hands, my breasts, my tongue. He was strong, confident, and he wanted me. Lust and hunger lurked as his eyes roamed my black dress.

"Do you want me to take it off?" I asked.

The hunger deepened. "No."

He caught my waist and lifted me. I wrapped my legs around him, the black slip bunched at my hips. I thrust against him, rubbing his cock against me. He groaned into my neck. One hand balanced my body tight against him, and the other pushed at the strap, baring my shoulder and freeing one breast to the winter chill. I gasped and he caught it with a kiss.

His fingers trailed across my breast. He massaged me, catching my nipple between his fingers. I arched toward his hand, searching, begging. Need built inside me, and Kadence stoked the fire.

He was relentless. The dress gave up and tatters fell around us. He teased my skin, my lips, until the pressure tipped, and then he backed away, leaving behind icy cold. I ground against him, the feel of him between my legs became intoxicating. I wanted more.

With a gentle, but firm tug, he pulled my head back, exposing my neck and the pulse beneath my skin.

"You have to tell me what you want, Sal." He kissed the sensitive spots. Chills and pleasure and anticipation followed his lips.

"I want you." I rubbed against him. He buried his face in my neck and moaned. "I want all of you."

He twisted his hips, and I wrapped tighter around him, searching for his cock. I rubbed against him, and he suddenly filled me, stretched me. He thrust, and the sensation threatened to tip me to climax.

His lips traced the skin on my neck. Fear caught me and for a moment, I almost asked him to stop. My mouth opened, but no words came out. I already knew that I trusted him, with all of me.

His fangs pierced my skin, sharp and quick, followed by a layer of his rich power. It was so much stronger than when I drank his blood, more delicate, more sweet. Euphoria ran through my body, chasing the pain away. Kadence sucked at my throat, replacing my lost blood with his power. I drank it down, twirled it inside me like fine wine. He was a drug and I would always crave more.

My mind twisted into a fog of pleasure and power. I moved against Kadence, driving him deeper and deeper inside of me. We were a raging inferno, an inextinguishable fire. There was no logic, no reason. We would burn anything in our path.

The fire grew and grew until I exploded from the inside. A scream of utter bliss built in my throat, but I swallowed it down. I didn't have any air to scream. Kadence drove into me harder, locking me in place with his strength. Each thrust sent new pleasure down my spine and I climaxed again, digging my fingers into his shoulders. He arched and spilled into me. He broke the seal at my neck, leaning his head back.

He held me as though I may fade away if he let go.

Eventually Kadence stepped from the wall, balancing my weight in his arms. He staggered to the bed and we collapsed onto it.

The fire warmed my icy skin. When had my teeth started chattering?

"Are you all right?" Kadence brushed a dark strand of hair from my face.

"Yes." I smiled.

"Here." He pulled the thick blanket over us.

Exhaustion drew my eyes closed. An army of demons marched our way, but Kadence's arms were safe. He rubbed circles on my back. Tomorrow, people would die. Tomorrow, there would be blood on my hands. Tonight, I tucked myself against the king and closed my eyes.

Chapter Twenty-Eight

Juno strode across the Lists toward us. She bowed deeply to both Kadence and me. "Your Majesties. I'm afraid there's only time for a brief demonstration."

Remi and two other vampires stood in the middle of the Lists. Their exposed skin made me shiver, but they acted indifferent to the cold. Snow had piled in through the open roof and had been flattened under the boots of training soldiers. Vampires, witch council members, and marshals sat together in the stadium, along with Juno's team and the demon expert, Tatiana Gaines. Kadence, Zavier, Cynthia, and I stood in the center of the arena.

An internal clock ticked away in my mind, counting down to the demons' arrival. New scouts, partnered with transportation and infantry soldiers for increased security, observed the demons at a distance. They were close. Last reports put them in Vari Kolum before sundown.

Tick, tock.

"We were able to replicate the magic in several volunteers," Juno said. "These three reacted the strongest."

Remi and the unnamed male vampire stood shirtless, wearing training uniforms. The female wore a more modest, similar outfit. Red powder painted their skin, but far fewer symbols marked their bodies than those who had attacked us.

"Most of the symbols on your attackers had been nonsense," Juno said. "The spellcasters either didn't know what they were doing or purposely tried to distract us. Either way, we are much smarter than them."

Tick, tock.

"Subject One, demonstrate your abilities for the king and queen."

Remi turned from the audience, toward a table that had been set up across the arena. The table bowed under the weight of a giant stone that stretched taller and wider than me. He raised one hand and a blast of magic pulsed through him. The magic exploded, directed through his outstretched palm. It cut into the rock and shattered it. Powder and pebbles rained on the seats behind.

The audience gasped.

"Subject two."

The woman stepped forward. A dead pig stretched across her table. No blood dripped from the animal. It must have been bled out before being dragged here. She focused on the carcass, her eyes half-closed. Her magic formed a single blade, sharp and pointy. The pig's body shuddered. A layer of skin fell away. Her red lips tilted in a smile. She sliced at the pig, stripping skin, fat, and muscle into paper thin layers that tumbled to the ground like diced meat. Her magic cut into thick organs and peeled them away as easily as orange skin, dividing bone and tendons and sinew.

A physical power with an affinity for bladework. It was rare.

The vampire stepped back and a swirl of joy ran through her magic. She liked it.

I had to suppress a shudder.

"Subject three."

The third table was empty. The last man raised both hands and closed his eyes. He turned one wrist, palm facing the sky, and curved his fingers as though holding a glass. His magic wrapped around the table in gentle tendrils, filling the space atop it. He pulled on the power, coaxing it into a shape. The magic hardened. The distinct figure of an axe shimmered on the table, an outline, a suggestion. He pushed more power, willing the weapon into existence. The magic fell away, and an axe smashed onto the table with a thud.

The man's eyes rolled into his head and he collapsed.

Three witches in healer's uniforms hurried over.

"You see, Your Majesties?" Juno beamed at us like a proud parent. "They're perfect."

Kadence raised an eyebrow. "He just passed out."

Juno squinted at the vampire. "Well, maybe not perfect. But it's what we have."

"I expected more."

Juno flashed her teeth at him before dipping her head in a delayed show of respect.

"Have we located any of the other missing vampires?" I asked. It hurt that some of our people were still lost to whoever was forcefully creating these hybrids.

Zavier shook his head. "No, My Queen. And we've been forced to halt the search until after this battle to preserve forces. That likely means there will be another attack by whoever is orchestrating this rogue group."

I nodded, putting the thoughts in the back of my mind for now. The approaching demon horde had to come first.

"How many can be enchanted before nightfall?" I asked.

"We've taught more witches how to perform the spell. It's rather simple, really. You could probably learn too, My Queen." She bit the word in half, making it two syllables. "We can prepare a thousand or so soldiers."

I expected more too, but we were out of options.

Tick, tock.

"Get started right away," I said.

Juno gave a half-hearted bow and shuffled off with her subjects.

"One thousand won't be enough," Jayne Andrews said from the stadium. Dark circles lined each wrinkled eye and she shivered despite a thick shall over her shoulders. Two guards hovered in case she needed help to stand.

"Tatiana?"

Tatiana Gaines sat between two other council members. Her red hair was a beacon in the dark bleachers. "The demons will be hard to kill." She pushed her glasses higher on her nose. "They can heal any wound."

"Decapitation?" I asked.

"It may take a few hours, but if they can find the head, they can heal it."

"These powers are useless then?" Julien Amos gestured to the abandoned tables alone in the arena. "Have we wasted our time?"

"We're not trying to kill them all, right?" Tatiana asked. "We just need to slow them down until Natalie can complete her spell. Decapitation will do that."

"It is impossible to decapitate an opponent with every strike," Amos said.

"I am open to other ideas," I said.

"Your Majesty, there are no more ideas," Councilman Eric Knox voiced. "We have a strong offense and defense. It's up to fate now."

"Marshal Price, what's the troop report?" Shanna Bowden asked. Her cheeks were pink, her jaw locked. She had children in the army.

"Our troops have been training together," Marshal Price said. "It's going well enough."

"I don't think we'll have too many friendly casualties," Cynthia agreed.

"There have been some incidences of the head banging variety," Zavier chimed in. "The vampires have difficulty determining how long their axes are."

The back of my head throbbed in sympathy.

"I have been impressed." Madeline looked me over, lingering on the marks on my neck. I hadn't tried to hide them. "I am glad we're not fighting the witches anymore. Under this leadership, they would have been formidable opponents."

Her words sparked pride in my chest. Our soldiers trained hard and learned quickly. We had turned half an army and a group of new recruits into a competent fighting force in very little time.

"I am also impressed," Amos's voice was so quiet, I almost missed his words.

Everyone turned to him. He cleared his throat.

"Your Majesties." He bowed to us and spoke louder. "I am very impressed. The troops are doing well, our defenses are strong, and the queen..." He swallowed thickly as his gaze shifted to me from beneath his brows. "The queen is an inspiration to her people."

My throat tightened.

"We have all watched her bloom this season," Jayne Andrews said. "She matches our sacrifices with her own."

She raised one shaking fist into the air. "Long live Queen Salvatore!"

The Lists filled with chanting as they all shouted my name until it echoed off the walls, filling and expanding the space, thundering like the crowd was of a thousand, instead of a feeble band of people gathered in the cold.

I couldn't breathe. My name became more than a chant on their lips, it was a battle mantra, a cry for blood and death. They chose me to be the motivation for this fight, for their kingdom. The knot in my stomach uncoiled. I had worked so hard to keep them alive and there was more to do. I would give them anything.

The chants stopped and the echoes faded. The silence in the Lists was stark, sudden.

Tick, tock.

"My Queen." Kadence tucked my hand into his arm. "We have a battle to prepare for."

THE WALL WALK WHERE KADENCE HAD KISSED ME WASN'T AS enticing in the snow. The sun touched the horizon, spilling ember glows across the sky. Our last recon put the demon horde ten furlongs from our gates. We pulled all our troops in from the field and waited for the first of the enemies to crest the top of the main road.

The tension and stress from the past weeks faded to the familiar beats of the battlefield. The weight of my sword in the sheath at my waist was comfortable. I wore a simple white tunic under my armor and black breeches, lined with sheep's fleece, to keep me warm and flexible. My boots were insulated with wool socks, but the winter chill beat through my clothes. I ignored it. The thought of cold would fade when the battle began.

From my vantage point, I could see the roughly constructed addition to the city's walls. Sharpened stakes ground into the stone between hastily poured layers of mortar. Beyond the main gates, cut halfway into the thick forest trees, two carefully arranged layers of grass covered deep trenches on each side of the road. If the demons marched in a wide formation, they would lose the edges of their troops to vats of enchanted acid. We could only hope.

Voices floated up the open stairwell. Kadence rounded the corner. He wore all black, and light armor, with his battle hammer secure on his waist and a sword slung across his back. His eyes were sharp, focused. He walked as though we had already won the fight.

He came to stand next to me and leaned over the wall walk. "Is everyone ready?"

No, and they never would be.

Instead, I said, "Juno and her people are finishing their spellwork." Kadence wore long sleeves, so I couldn't see if his arms bore any of Juno's symbols. "Did she cast the spell on you?"

Jealousy poked at me. Thinking about Kadence drinking the blood of another witch and gaining their magic wrapped me in a layer of anger. I kept my face blank, letting the feelings settle in my chest.

"Are you offering your blood again, My Queen?" His voice was raspy and eagerness spread in his dark eyes.

My cheeks burned and the king laughed, low and sexy. My body tightened, desire and the anticipation of war colliding like milk and honey.

Kadence brushed a strand of my hair from my face.

"Don't worry, Sal. I'm not borrowing your magic or anyone else's. My people need to see me lead them to battle whole and unaided. They need to be confident in my abilities."

I wrapped my arms around his waist, sucking in the scent of polish and armor. He held me against his chest, and his heart hummed a soft song. If we survived this, I was never leaving his arms again.

He pressed a gentle kiss to my hair.

I turned my face up, forcing his lips to meet mine.

He kissed me, one hand on my waist and the other delicately cupping my cheek. His lips were soft and sweet, begging rather than demanding. He was the first apple plucked from a promising harvest.

"You have to survive tonight," he whispered against my lips. "You have to make it back to me. If you have to kill, maim, poison, run—I don't care. I can't lead these kingdoms by myself and I don't want to do it without you."

"I'll do my best, if you will, as well."

He nodded.

I kissed him again, giving him my heart through our touch. This was the moment I would remember with every slash of my sword, every breath I struggled to draw on the field. I would come back to his arms again.

Trumpets erupted through the silent winter night. The first sighting of the enemy.

We moved apart, straining over the wall to see them. Nothing moved on the road.

Zavier and Cynthia stepped from the stairwell, sweaty and breathing as though they had run here.

"All the troops are in position." Cynthia's armor was solid black, darker than Rayhan's. Her black hair fell down her back and at least six sheathed daggers hung across her chest. Everything about her was designed for stealth and killing, and I was relieved that she fought on our side.

"They will send the weakest demons first, the most disfigured," Zavier said. "They want to shock and scare our soldiers and send them running from the battle before it begins."

"We are prepared," I said.

"Yes, we are."

The smell came before the demons. Bitter, but sweet, like rotting flesh, the scent boiled through the city, a horrific wave of vile expectations.

Bile rose in my throat.

Zavier turned a shade of green.

Shadows moved in the distance. Screeches pierced the dusk. Shrill screams, impossible from human throats, stabbed into my ears like ice picks.

Our forward defense waited outside the main walls, rows of soldiers blocking the entrance at the gate. The very front row held large shields as a barricade against the onslaught—a combination of witches and vampires, side by side. Archers watched from the roofs. Black-and-green uniforms painted a picture of unity and preparation. I hoped we would fight with the same principles.

The demons appeared at the top of the road.

The first wave scurried on their hands and feet, like broken, disfigured rats. Too far to see, I could imagine the bodies full of black boils and popping sores that oozed pus.

Our rows shifted, anticipation driving through them. The creatures scampered forward, a flood of evil and nightmares. Thirty strides away.

Marshals of our armies looked back to the castle, to us. From the parapets where we stood, Kadence and I held our hands up, giving the command for the forces to hold.

The demons stayed on the road, a straight line aiming for our troops. They ran past the covered trenches. That was fine. We'd get them later.

Fifteen strides away.

Hold.

Chants rang from our people. War cries, promises to defend their loved ones. The demons screeched, glass in our ears, claws sprouting from their fingers.

Five strides away.

The demons spilled across the front shields. Soldiers kept the defense, stabbing around the shields to cut bodies down where they stood. Heart and flesh wounds didn't slow the creatures, but decapitation forced them to halt. It was hard to form an offensive strike without a head.

"We need to persuade the rest of their army to come fight," Zavier said.

Our first shield went down. Guttural noises and sprays of rich red blood accumulated at the front line.

The demons zoned in on the broken point, slashing through people and driving a wedge into our forces.

Witches and vampires filled the gap, magic bloomed, and hammers hit their targets with sickening crunches.

The demons were ruthless. They pushed through the hole faster than we could fill it.

"Archers," Kadence called.

Cynthia raised her hand, two fingers up. Pinpricks of fire illuminated archers on the roofs for the barest of moments. They shot flaming arrows into the swarm of demons, at the heart of our broken line. The monsters screeched and wailed. Several scampered away, weakening their onslaught. Our people filled the gap.

Kadence and I exchanged a look and I nodded. He raised a hand again, giving the sign to engage. Our forces marched forward, driving the demons away from the wall. They began a slow trudge, stabbing and stepping over punctured, writhing bodies, to push the horde away from the kingdom.

We gained five strides.

Ten.

Fifteen.

"Where are the rest of them?" Zavier tapped his fingers on the half-wall. "This should be enough to draw them out."

Under a barrage of screams, the demons wearing my parents' bodies appeared at the top of the road.

My heart skipped a beat.

Even from this far, I recognized the spread of my father's shoulders, the precise stance of my mother's form. My father raised his arms. Thousands of soldiers spilled around him. They ran like a mob, disorganized and impulsive. Long, black claws sprouted from their fingers, barely visible in the sinking light. They ran down the road and through the forest. Thousands of them tumbled around each other, racing to the battle.

The outskirts of the horde reached the trenches and hesitated. One demon slowed too late, lost its balance at the lip, and tumbled through the thin layer of grass. The acid rippled for a moment, then settled. The demon didn't have time to scream.

The rest hesitated, eyeing the vat. They skirted around, avoiding the disturbed ground. The length of the vat forced them deeper into the tree line, shrinking away from their reinforcements.

"Calvary," I commanded.

Cynthia held three fingers to the sky.

The riders were invisible and their horses silent through the trees. Screams drifted to the castle. As quickly as they had run into the forest, demons were driven out of it. Our riders were death in the dusk, swinging scythes atop pristine horses. The bladed weapons took the heads from a demon before the rider reached striking range of their awful claws. Hooves trampled the removed appendages while they still screamed.

The demons fled the calvary. They flung themselves toward the road, but the trenches of acid lay in the way. One by one, they tumbled in, dozens of demons swallowed by the steaming liquid.

A scream tore through the demon Estelle's throat.

"I think we've angered them," Kadence said with a smile.

Confined to the main road, the demons pressed against the center of our troops, driving a punishing force through them. Flaming arrows punctured the horde, but the onslaught continued. More and more creatures filed along our lines. They took back the ground we had gained, pressing our soldiers against the stone wall. Most of the shields had fallen.

The gates held. Our people took hits, cut down by bleeding black claws, dark eyes and evil the last thing they saw.

I bit my tongue. Kadence had to make the next call.

Blood soaked into the ground, turning the dirt to red mud. Swords and claws met as sunset faded to night. Lanterns lit across the main wall, illuminating the carnage. Demons laughed with every kill, driving spikes of fear and anger into my gut.

Kadence's face remained blank. I tapped my fingers on the stone wall. Cynthia and Zavier waved away messengers from the front lines, waiting for Kadence's orders. Impatience beat at me, but I trusted Kadence to give the next order. He would know when the time was right.

My parents joined the charge. Their claws grew longer than the others. My father slashed across three soldiers, cutting them down in one swipe. Anxiety pricked my palms. They were pushing us to the brink.

Kadence put his hand in the air, a closed fist—the sign to retreat. Tension flooded his eyes. Lines of pain warped his mouth.

I grabbed his hand and he clenched mine tightly.

The main gates groaned open. Our people scampered in, cutting down demons in their retreat. The horde rushed through the gates, bottlenecked like sand in an hourglass. Archers hurried from rooftops, jumping ahead of the monsters.

Eerie chuckles drifted from below. Demons tore through buildings, searching for prey. Black bodies moved from window to window and we waited while they filled the empty city.

"There's something satisfying about watching this when they have no idea what's coming," Cynthia's mouth tilted in a thin smile.

"I wish there had been another way." Zavier's voice was grim.

"This was the only way." Kadence watched demons ravage his city. Furniture fell through broken windows. Smoke billowed as fires sprouted.

"Do you think they've realized the buildings are empty?" Zavier asked.

"They're about to," Kadence said.

The city exploded.

The castle walls shook with the force of it. Buildings trembled as supports fell, before cascading into rubble and debris. New flames licked the collapsed walls. Water poured into the street as pipes buckled.

One by one, the towers of the rainbow city fell. Buildings toppled as fresh charges erupted under their neighbors, shaking the ground. Dust billowed through the wreckage, casting the city in an earthen haze.

Kadence's hand shook.

"They're safe," I reminded him. "Our people aren't here. They're almost to my kingdom, and they're safe."

"It's still hard to watch," he whispered.

I squeezed his hand. He was right. I imagined my city falling apart one explosion at a time and shuddered.

The rest of our troops spilled out the castle gates, invading the shattered city with war cries. They picked off the stunned demons, sending body parts through the street in sprays of blood. The monsters continued through the open gate, filling the space with more and more, trapping themselves in the thin opening.

Natalie said she needed proximity. They would never be closer together than this.

"It's a shame the explosives won't kill the demons." Zavier scanned the buildings as dark shapes began to pick themselves from the ruins.

"Trapping them under thousands of pounds of debris will have to be enough." Cynthia plucked two knives from her sheaths and twirled them in her fingers. "Are you ready?"

Zavier palmed his sword. "After you."

The two disappeared down the hall, heading to the battle for the final assault.

Kadence watched the ruins of Vari Kolum with a blank face. Words tumbled through my mind, but I bit my tongue. There was nothing to say.

"Natalie's waiting for you," he said.

"Our people are waiting for you."

"I need a minute," The king said, looking down at his kingdom destroyed at his feet.

I kissed the back of his hand before leaving him alone on the wall walk.

Chapter Twenty-Nine

"Queen Sal," Rayhan's voice thundered through the halls. "We are ready."

Buckled in his armor with black beads replacing the golden ones in his red dreadlocks, he looked fierce. His huge hammer was polished to a shine and another, smaller hammer hung on his belt.

Natalie peeked around Rayhan's shoulder. Her armor fit snug and secure. She had a sword in one hand, but she held it from her body as though she was afraid it may turn around and bite her. She gave me a half wave.

A crowd of ten men stood in a semicircle behind them. Rayhan had hand-picked his team to defend Natalie. Mostly vampires, but two witches waited in the back. These men stood tall and confident, years of war etched onto their faces. Red symbols painted across some of their skin. Magic swirled, hot and thick in the air.

"Fancy seeing you here." Natalie smiled with quivering lips.

"I told you this was serious, Natalie." Rayhan said.

"I am being serious." She crossed her dainty arms across her chest plate, the heavy sword dragging one side down. She looked like a little doll. "In fact, I couldn't be more serious than I am right now."

Saffa and Remi rounded a corner. She saw us and dropped his hand.

"Begging your pardon, Your Majesty, but what are we waiting for?" Saffa asked.

"A signal," I said.

"What signal?"

Shouts echoed through the main hall.

"They're outside the doors," Rayhan said.

"That must be the signal." Saffa plucked her sword from her belt.

"We'll clear the way." I told Rayhan. "Don't be too long."

The double doors shook. I smiled.

"Let's go!"

We pulled the doors open and several demons spilled inside. They recovered, swiping at us.

Saffa blurred, her sword a dash of silver. Two heads rolled, leaking blood along the stone floor.

Remi sent a burst of magic through one creature's chest and the impact stunned him.

I ran my sword through the demon's neck, another body on the ground.

The ten soldiers behind us cleaned up the rest.

Every weight I had carried—maintaining peace, pining for my people's approval—disappeared with the blood that dripped off my blade. I could think clearly for the first time in months. I wanted more.

We charged through the doors. Chaos greeted us. Vampires and witches fought in teams of two, slashing across possessed bodies, cutting them down one limb at a time. Demons dashed through the cobblestone streets, illuminated by flickering lanterns and rouge fires, shadows of nightmares cast onto the walls. Blood dripped down their claws.

One saw me and darted closer. She scampered on three limbs, one hand a bloody stump. Blisters popped under her weight, trailing black slime. She smiled, white fangs in leu of teeth.

The taste of battle was familiar, the weight of my sword comfortable. My magic coiled, slow from months of disuse. I wrapped it around the creature as she crept near. The magic listened, thirsty for revenge.

She slashed me with her claws.

I sidestepped.

She turned, too late. The magic weighed her down, bolting her feet in place. Her eyes widened and she screamed, a grueling sound that ate away at my eardrums.

Beneath the sludge of evil, a tiny spark shimmered. The current underneath the demon's mind flashed at me, called to me. I recognized the feeling now. It was the same that reached out when Elis was possessed and I'd torn his demon to shreds. Natalie had called it something—the Affinity of Responsibility. The witch inside the demon recognized me.

My heart ached as the spark beat inside the demon's mind. I couldn't stop and kill this demon the way I killed Elis's. It would drain my power and there were several thousand people depending on me for this battle. Her broken body would be beyond repair. We would experience losses in this battle and each one would hurt my heart.

All I could do was follow the plan Kadence and I had created, and hope Natalie's spell worked.

My sword bit through her neck. The body fell, and the head rolled away, mouth still moving in a silent scream.

I'm sorry, I thought as I turned from the body.

Despite the emotional pain, the motions of the battlefield fell over me like a warm blanket. Another demon approached and I cut through him. My muscles settled into the routine.

We pushed slow, steady, the three of us carving a narrow passage for Natalie and her force. She needed to be in the heart of the city, the very center of Vari Kolum, where the most demons were clustered and couldn't retreat through the narrow gate.

Two demons scurried down a back alley.

I raised my blade. *Yes, come closer.*

A ripple of magic exploded over my shoulder and struck the pair, disintegrating the bodies in a heartbeat. Smoke rose from Remi's outstretched palm.

"Apologies." He grimaced. "That was a little close, no?"

Any closer and I would have been dust.

"You're still learning..." Saffa jerked her sword into a demon's gut and sliced up. Its body split in half and sagged. She cut off the head. "But please try not to kill the queen."

Rayhan's team appeared, forming in a wedge around Natalie. Rayhan took point, cutting into demons as they began to fill the space we had cleared. Eight men remained. We had traveled less than four furlongs and already lost two soldiers. We joined their formation, cutting through enemies in the rubble heaps of town.

"I can feel their life energy," Natalie said. "We're almost to the middle, where I can kill the most at one time."

"Almost sounds like a long way." Sweat dripped down Rayhan's face into his ginger beard. Blood and ooze stained his axe red and black. He side-swung and smashed a demon's face with the blunt end of the weapon. The demon staggered to its feet, a perfect indent in the side of its head. Rayhan's lips curled and he swung again. The creature stayed down.

"Here!" Natalie froze in the middle of the street and I backpedaled to avoid hitting her. "This is as close as we can get to the heart of the demons, where my magic can reach the most of them."

We were at the edge of a green field, scattered with bodies and blood. Dust and smoke clouded our visibility. We wouldn't see a demon until it was on top of us.

"Are you sure?" I asked. Shapes twisted in the shadows and an eerie quiet enveloped us.

"Yes." Natalie crouched on the ground, tracing symbols into the dirt. "This is the best spot. I'm going to need a few minutes to set up the amplification spell."

Rayhan looked at me and I shrugged. It was a defensive nightmare, but... "Whatever she says."

Footsteps echoed down an alleyway. The sound turned, following a side street. Whispers floated in the air, impossible to pin down. I let out a breath I didn't realize I was holding. The steps thundered toward us. Whatever it was, it was running.

I lifted my sword. The others did too.

Reuben stumbled from the carnage. He didn't see my sword until it was inches from his chest. He swore and stepped backward, tumbling into the dirt.

Tension in my gut loosened.

"What are you doing, Reuben?"

His chest heaved, his face red and sweaty. The longsword in his hand dripped with blood.

"Looking for you!" He pushed to his feet and glanced over his shoulder. "They've broken through the back gate!"

A natural mountain pass blocked entrance through the back gate. It was almost impossible to reach from the direction the demons had come. Due to the low threat, only a single team of infantry and archers defended the entrance.

"I didn't hear the signal." As the words left my lips, trumpets rang through the night in a repetition of three notes. The signal that the second gate had been breached.

"Sal, we have to go." Reuben held his hand to me. "There's not enough defense at that gate! If we wait too long, they'll diverge more forces that way."

If enough demons swarmed the back gates, they would trap us between two fronts. Our only option was for Natalie to kill as many as possible and hopefully the rest would flee in fear. If our lines grew too thin, she wouldn't live long enough to finish the spell.

"Natalie, how long do you need?" I asked.

She traced patterns with her eyes closed.

"A few moments, but if you give me several, I can make the spell stronger."

"Sal, we need you here." Saffa's eyes were wild. "Don't go with him."

Several moments would be impossible fighting on two fronts. The gate had to be defended.

"I have to, Saffa."

Mud streaked across Reuben's face, blending with a different, darker fluid. The golden tassels of his hair ran straight with oil and grime. He didn't look like the prince in my foyer. He looked like a soldier.

"Let's go." I ignored his extended hand and led the way, sprinting through the city.

Spellwork buzzed over my skin. Every corner we rounded revealed witches and vampires locked in combat. Demons dodged spellwork, though were occasionally caught and sliced away piece by piece. I cut and slashed when I could. People yelled in gratitude as I sprinted by them. Reuben stayed on my heels, breathing hard.

We stumbled to the gate. It stretched higher than the stone wall supporting it, to the top of the parapets. The entrance gaped open and demons spilled through the hole. I cut at two and heads rolled down the steep hill to the right.

Demons trickled through unhindered.

"The infantry's gone!" Reuben's panicked tone made me grind my teeth.

Thick metal chains pulled the gate open. Each chain wrapped around a turnstile, held in place by a sword through the center. Two more demons approached and I slashed them to pieces.

The metal turnstile chilled my fingers as I wrenched the sword from its place and pushed against the handle. The gears groaned, but the gate didn't budge. The two had to be pushed together.

"Reuben, turn the other one!" I jerked the sword from the second coil of chain.

Dark laughter pressed around me. Reuben stood between the two turnstiles, twenty steps away from me, laughing. He shook his head.

I froze. I recognized that tone, the sound of something dark and sinister. I had heard it in his voice twice before, once in my room and again on the battlefield next to Jon Chan's body. My hand wrapped tighter around the hilt of my sword, the leather warm and comforting.

"What are you doing?"

Reuben rubbed his face with one hand, smiling between his fingers.

"Do you know how long I've tried to get you alone?" Reuben raised his voice in mockery. "Oh no, the vampire might be hurting my once betrothed that I can't get over. Help, the blood building has been attacked. Ugh. It took a war to finally get you to myself."

His blue eyes cut at me.

"Do you know why the infantry's not here, Sal? Because I sent them away. Do you know why the gates are open? Because I opened the damn things myself! The final chance to get you away from the king. My last moment to take what should be mine!"

He gestured wildly with every word. Sweat broke across his forehead, but his smile remained wide and perfect. Red stained his fingertips. I'd seen the same dye spread across half our vampire's chests tonight and on the hybrids that had tried to kill me.

"You're behind the assassination attempts," I said. "You've been drawing spells on kidnapped vampires."

"The assassination attempts?" Reuben held his arms out. "Give me some credit, Sal. I couldn't have done that alone. You have a team of rebels working against you. While your council chants 'long live the queen,' we've been plotting your death."

"Is this because I had to end the betrothal? I did that for our people, Reuben."

"The betrothal!" he spat. "Look how stupid you are. You think this started because you ended our marriage? The marriage was supposed to end you! All those rumors about you, your incompetence, your determination to enforce a draft, to kill our children. Where do you think those came from, Sal?"

Rage began to eat away at the battle static in my head. "You've been spreading lies about me?"

"Since the ink dried on our betrothment paperwork, sweetheart. Or maybe my parents started before that. Once we were married, you would have had an unfortunate accident. The people hated you. They would celebrate your death." He raised his sword to the sky. "They would welcome me as the new king of Ededen, ending your family's line on the throne."

He lowered the sword slowly, his face hard.

"Then you brought that vampire home. And the people grew to love him. The rumors I spent years building fell apart in my hands. They loved him, and they loved seeing you with him, especially these past weeks of war preparation. It ruined everything."

The darkness I had seen in his eyes... "You tried to kill me at the blood building."

"But your stupid maid had to come along. My witches got scared and that vampire broke the mind control. But don't worry. We've fixed that."

Reuben held out both hands, palms up.

Renee and Cynthia stepped from the shadows, painted with red madder powder. Cynthia walked behind Reuben and placed a hand on his shoulder. Her eyes flashed as red as the symbols on her skin. Her armor was missing and blood dotted her exposed flesh, although I didn't see any wounds.

"Your friends aren't here, Sal. They can't break out of our improved spellwork, since that awful scientist fixed all of our errors. And if you kill them, they're never coming back." Reuben smiled. "But they're not worried about killing you."

I tightened my grip on my sword and bit the inside of my lip. I didn't want to kill them and would avoid that outcome at almost any cost. The thought that I'd failed the pair, two people under my protection, drove a sliver of pain into me. Beneath that, though, a spark hotter than anger flared in my chest—rage. Reuben would pay for this ultimate betrayal. Once I incapacitated Renee and Cynthia as delicately as possible, Reuben's body would bend at my feet.

My magic flailed like a whip around me.

The women's eyes were glossy and vacant. Renee had a sword and Cynthia gripped two daggers—blades meant for me. I spun the magic around me, driving in more energy to strengthen the binds until it coiled like chain.

I bounced on the balls of my feet.

Cynthia's wrist flexed and she flung a dagger at me, quick, precise.

I dodged the weapon, and the two drew nearer, saliva dripping from exposed fangs.

That's right. Come closer.

They waded into the magic and I bound it around their limbs. I pulled them down, but the lack of use had weakened my magic. Cynthia's feet ground to a halt, but Renee shrugged the power off like a snake shedding its skin.

Surprise froze me and she darted in. Sharp pain cut through my wrist and blood pooled at the surface. I backed away, leaving a red trail in my path.

I blocked her strikes again and again, while Cynthia wrestled against my bonds. Renee cut at me with an overhead swing, and I dodged.

I dashed into her open arms and slipped my blade across her ribs.

She danced back, out of reach. Blood soaked through her shirt.

"Tsk, tsk," Reuben said. "Could the king ever forgive you if you killed his favorite spy?"

Could I forgive myself?

Cynthia slipped through my magic. She cut at me fast and low. Her blade slashed across my ankle and I fell to one knee. She aimed for my face, and I rolled away.

Renee was already there, her sword a blur. I fell to the side and the blade cut into the dirt. She plucked it out and stabbed again. I smashed a kick to her face, popped to my feet, and backed away.

A trickle of new spellwork brushed against my skin. Natalie's careful web of magic had finally spread to the outskirts of the city. It was light as a feather, a fresh snow to cover the layer of death and pain on the battlefield. How much more time did she need?

I pooled my magic again, but had no energy to fuel it. I was tired. My wrist and ankle hurt. My chest heaved to catch my breath. I just had to survive long enough for Natalie to finish the spell.

I spun the sword and wiggled my fingers.

Come get me.

The two attacked as one. I elbowed Renee in the face and she stumbled. Cynthia caught an opening and plunged a dainty dagger under my armor, into my stomach. Bile rose in my throat, and I swallowed it. Twisting away, I pulled the dagger from my gut, flipped it, and stabbed it into her arm. She screamed. I wrapped layers of magic around her and pulled her down.

Renee punched above the deep puncture from Cynthia's blade. Lights stole my vision. My breath hissed out.

Reuben laughed.

A hard kick to my ribs and I was on the ground. The lights faded. Renee aimed her foot, but I caught her ankle and pulled. Her mouth made a little 'O' as she tumbled to the dirt. I pressed my sword to her throat. Cynthia thrashed in my magic, weakening it with every pull. I pushed more and more energy to hold it tight around her.

Renee smiled at me. "Kill her," she said, her voice echoing as though spoken in an empty room.

I punched her.

Renee's head snapped to the side, air rushed from her lungs, and her body went limp. Her chest rose and fell. The blow hadn't been fatal.

I staggered to my feet. The world spun. Shapes moved, and suddenly Cynthia stood in front of me, her dagger aiming for my throat.

Maybe dying wouldn't be so bad. Surely the throbbing pain in my side would be gone. This was a better end than being eaten by demons anyway.

My mind found the edge of insanity and brushed against it.

"Why don't you try it?" Kadence's voice drifted through my fragmented thoughts. A dim, ghostly image of him held out a dagger hilt first.

He was shirtless, muscles playing across his chest and stomach. Black breeches hugged his hips and I longed for what I knew was under them. Fire of desire lit in my body. Sparks pulsed through me. His lips tilted up at the edges, the way they did when he found me amusing. He raised one eyebrow and gestured with the dagger again.

Did he want me to die?

"No, thank you." My lips moved on their own, tracing familiar words. "I must insist."

He pushed the dagger into my hand. It disappeared, leaving only the remembrance of power and sweet wine in its place.

Kadence's phantom image faded and Cynthia's face hovered inches away, her blade prepared to cut through my throat.

Power swelled in my chest, but not my own. There was no magic in the heavy and strong power, but there was fuel. I grabbed the foreign strength, struggling under its weight, and dragged it into my magic, funneling more and more power. The magic rolled and twisted, flexible chains becoming iron bars. I wrapped it around Cynthia and pulled her down, the magic an anchor in a deep and wild sea.

Her hand froze, the blade caressing my throat.

I forced my feet to move, circled behind, and elbowed her in the back of the neck. It wasn't enough to kill her, but her eyes rolled as she passed out. I released the magic as she fell.

Reuben pressed his lips into a thin line.

"Fine." He rolled up his sleeves. "I will do it myself."

The wound in my side trailed fresh blood as I moved. Pain shot through my wrist and ankle. Adrenaline pulsed in my veins, but my mind began to catch up, the aches becoming distracting.

Reuben twisted his sword in the air. "You didn't expect me to know how to fight, did you Sal? I made sure to keep you in the dark about a lot of things."

I was too tired for his gloating.

He charged me, a quick and efficient strike.

I stepped to the side and he recovered. His blade clashed against mine and sparks flew between us.

"I will kill you, then that stupid vampire." His eyes held an edge of madness. "I will take the throne."

He pushed against my blade. I had more training, but I was wounded, and he outweighed me. If this turned to brute strength, he would pulverize me.

I flicked his sword down and backed away.

He lunged. His hands turned to a flurry of sword strikes and punches, and I barely dodged them. Exhaustion and blood loss made my head spin. He fought harder and harder, until his face reddened and sweat seeped through his white shirt. Practice kept me one step ahead, but my wounds slowed me down.

His fist caught the corner of my jaw. Black stars exploded in my eyes. My recovery took too long. He punched me again and my head snapped to the side. Blood filled my mouth.

"Goodbye, Sal." His voice sounded distant.

Goodbye? I still had a lot to do.

Anger bubbled in my chest and spread over me, a sweet wash of clarity. He wanted to take my people from me. He wanted to kill Kadence. Death might be a welcome rest, but I had to live for my king and our kingdoms.

I pulled magic from the depths of my soul and wrapped it in the power that Kadence's blood had given me. They mingled together, two sides of the same stream. I molded them, shaped them into a blade of their own.

Reuben's sword cut down. His gaze intense, focused, dark. He caught sight of my face and hesitation stilled his hands.

I knew my eyes were silver coins and death stared out of them.

I drove the magic into his chest. There were no wounds, no blood, but it cut through his body like paper, ripping him to shreds from the inside. Pain twisted in me, but I stammered to my feet. I put a hand on Reuben's hot cheek and found his groomed beard soft. I screamed and poured more magic, more power, into him, filling him until his body couldn't hold anymore. Even as his heart stopped beating, I couldn't stop the flow of power. It ate through him and an empty shell collapsed at my feet.

My knees buckled. My vision turned black.

The subtle weave of Natalie's magic suddenly halted. It hovered through the air, beads of power frozen in place.

Something was wrong.

My body felt numb. It was beyond the point of pain, which I knew was bad, but the relief felt so good. I curled my fingers, but they didn't move. I willed my legs to stand, but they rested on the snowy ground. I didn't feel the cold seeping under my armor. Natalie needed me, but I couldn't remember why.

"Are you sure someone's alive out here?" Voices whispered through the quiet.

"Yes, I told you I can feel it," a woman said.

"The gates are open!" A man's voice.

"I thought reinforcements already came out here!"

"Mr. Emerson said it was covered! We'll have to report it on our way back."

Chains rattled and metal banged as the gate closed. Footsteps crunched in the snow. Warm hands prodded me, but I felt no pain.

"This one's alive!"

"Two more over here."

The man gasped.

"Beth, it's the queen!"

Footsteps ran. Hands brushed the hair from my face.

"Can you heal her?"

"The powers are quite new," the woman said. "But I'll try."

Words balanced on the tip of my tongue. *Too late.* Her magic poured into me, stitching wounds from the inside out. Pain exploded through new nerves as my body was welded back together. She didn't know how to dull the pain while she healed and months of procedures and strengthening were performed in seconds.

My lungs expanded. I drew a breath and screamed.

The hands dropped me in the cold snow.

My skin burned like I had been raked over hot coals. Tears swelled in my eyes. The scratching of clothes on my flesh felt like jagged glass. Every breath hurt.

"Are you all right, Your Majesty?" The woman chewed on her bottom lip. She was a vampire, painted in Juno's symbols. Her lack of experience made sense. She hadn't had magic before.

I rolled onto my hands and knees and took shallow breaths to avoid puking.

"I—" Words caught in my throat. I coughed. "I'm okay now."

"I didn't realize it would hurt so much..." Her eyes were round, afraid. The male witch at her side palmed his sword nervously.

"It's all right." My voice came out a whisper. "You saved my life."

Beth settled on her heels.

"I need you to move these two vampires into the castle. Lock them in a room and guard it. Nobody goes in or out. You can heal them if they're injured."

I staggered to my feet. My body was whole, but tired. It didn't want to move.

The two stared at me with their mouths open. My bloodstained clothes were tattered under my scratched and dented armor. I'd depleted my magic and the remnants of Kadence's power. The two were probably trying to decide if they needed to carry me into the castle as well.

I rolled my shoulders and picked up my sword. I looked them in the eyes.

"Go," I said, soft but demanding.

They scrambled, lifting Renee and Cynthia into their arms and sloshing toward the castle.

I didn't want to see what remained of Reuben at my feet, but curiosity, or perhaps horror, called to me. What little the magic had left of him no longer looked human.

Natalie's magic jerked, pulling against my skin, sticky and thick. She needed me. I ran back into the city.

Chapter Thirty

BODIES LINED THE GRASSY FIELD, DEMONS WITH CRUSHED OR missing heads, witches and vampires still bleeding into the dirt. Dust peppered the air, blending into the dark shadows of the streets. Trees swayed in the brisk winter night. The moon was a spotlight in the sky, casting an eerie glow across the city. I circled the perimeter, searching for threats with my sword up.

Natalie crouched on her hands and knees in the center of her circle. Her chest rose and fell. There was no blood. Her power pulsed again, scratching at my skin.

Six people formed a defensive perimeter around her spell. Rayhan loomed at the front, staring down at her. His face was flat.

"What happened?" I asked. "What's wrong?"

"She's fighting the demon king and queen." He gestured at Natalie with an open palm. "They tapped into her spell before it was finished. She hasn't moved in several minutes."

"Where are the others? I didn't see anyone on my way back."

"The demons are rallying through the main gates. We're trying to hold them in."

The demons possessing my parents had realized the potential of Natalie's spell. They were trying to get their creatures far away from her.

"Is the gate closed?"

Rayhan nodded. The plan could still work. They were trapped inside our walls as long as the gate held.

"I think she's losing," Rayhan whispered.

Trails of sweat ran down the witch's face, pooling in the dirt. Her shoulders shook as though she had a fever, despite the frigid temperature.

I touched Rayhan's arm.

"I'll help her," I said. "I promise."

He nodded, his thoughts elsewhere.

I didn't know where the demons were.

Elis's memories, the body of the demon I had slain, surged into my mind. The demon had been able to read his thoughts, feel his trapped emotions. The two possessing my parents would do the same. They would know what places meant the most to my parents.

The highest point of the battlefield was a short hill pressed against the southern wall. It peered down at the city, the perfect place to see strategy and tactics work in real time. If my father, the greatest wartime strategist I knew, was observing a battlefield, that's where he would be.

I sprinted. Demons and witches clashed in the street. Vampires spewed magic across the cobblestone. Multiple times, I had to sputter to a halt to avoid being blasted by a novice magic-user. Mumbled apologies faded in the distance. I ran.

My lungs burned. I had no plan once I found them. I had my sword and my skills, but they weren't enough. I only needed to distract them until Natalie could finish her spell.

The base of the hill spilled in front of me. A cluster of three demons turned at my approach and hissed, clawed hands raised. These weren't the sporadic individuals barreling through the city. I recognized the choreographed stance of trained guards.

The king and queen demons were up there, and these three guarded the pathway.

I wiped a trail of sweat from my forehead.

"Come on, then." I gestured with one hand, letting the comforting taste of battle cleanse away my lingering exhaustion.

I raised my sword. They charged and cut at me, claws first, and I jumped back.

A black shape fell from the tree line stretching overhead, interrupting my swing. Kadence caught himself in a crouch, one hand balancing on the ground and his hammer in the other. He smiled at the demons, flames in his eyes.

"You're in my way," I said, but a smile crossed my lips.

"I always am."

Rising from his squat, his hammer swung up to catch the underside of one demon's chin. Her neck snapped and she staggered.

I plunged my sword into her chest and twisted. Blood poured from her mouth and she laughed. She scratched at the blade with both hands, trying to pull it from her chest.

"You are weak," she hissed.

I plucked out the sword and cut through her neck. "You are dead." Her black eyes blinked. I wrinkled my nose. "Or at least mostly dead."

Kadence swung at one demon, and the creature grabbed his hammer. Kadence staggered. The demon pulled the hammer and threw it down the street. The weapon sparked against the rocks, settling in the rubble of a ruined building.

The demon rushed Kadence. The king ducked the striking claws and grabbed the demon by the throat. His eyes turned to melted silver. He sunk his teeth into the demon's neck and the creature clawed at him. Black talons pierced his skin, but Kadence didn't flinch. He pulled back and twisted the demon's head, until it popped with a sickening crunch. The monster fell.

Face twisting, Kadence spit onto the ground. He wiped his mouth with the back of his hand.

"Disgusting," I said.

"It tasted that way too." Kadence stalked to retrieve his hammer, and a pause settled between us. Then, Kadence smiled a harsh line of teeth in the darkness. The look released some tension from my chest and I let a quiet laugh slip through my lips. Caught together in the midst of battle, all we had been through rattled across my mind. From fear and hatred to desire and the beautiful start of something more.

Kadence held out his bloodstained hand to me. I wrapped my fingers through his.

"They're up there, huh?" he asked, staring at the incline. The top of the slope disappeared from our viewpoint.

"Sure are," I said. I wanted to freeze time here, with his hand in mine. I wondered if Kadence's hesitation meant he shared the same thoughts.

"We can't both go," I said, after a moment. "One of us has to rule when this is over."

"Zavier and Madeline can handle it."

Probably better than we could.

"Come on, Sal. Come fight with me."

I took the first step and Kadence walked beside me. I took a deep breath, memorizing his smell of leather and smoke.

We trekked up the hill, one step at a time. My pulse raced with anticipation, but I never wanted to reach the top. Kadence was so warm and smelled so good. I wanted to wrap myself tight in his arms forever.

He brushed one hand across my fingers. Sparks trailed through my skin, setting my body on fire. Desire and dread weighed heavy in my stomach.

"When this is over, I'm invoking the terms of the surrender." His breath was short. "You're never allowed to be with anyone else."

"I'll fight you about it," I teased.

"Is that a promise?"

"I'll make your life a living hell."

"So it wouldn't be any different."

I smacked the back of his head gently. "Be careful, or I'll push you over the edge."

"Then you'd have to fight the demons all by yourself."

"I can take them."

"I love this plan. You fight, and I'll just watch."

"Great."

"I can't wait."

The incline flattened.

"If I don't make it, I know you'll take good care of my people," Kadence whispered, all playfulness gone.

Tears burned my eyes and I pushed them back. "I know you would too," I said.

I raised our connected hands to press a kiss against Kadence's knuckles and wished we were anywhere else.

A flicker illuminated the path. The forest opened into a field, a fire burning in the center. The city spanned behind us, specks of light in a black sea. It reminded me of the overlook at home that sat atop the highest hillside and peered across our entire valley. This view had a few more demons.

The demons wearing my parents' bodies stood beside the fire. The demon Tolen's eyes opened as we approached. The demon Estelle sat motionless on the ground.

I drew my sword and spun my wrist, warming it up. The cold had settled into my skin. My tired muscles complained, threatening to cramp. I let adrenaline drift the pain away.

"You're late." My father's eyes were bottomless pools of black ink. The demon Estelle didn't even twitch at the words. Pulses of power rubbed across my skin. She was the one fighting Natalie.

"We were busy destroying your creations." Kadence's teeth clenched.

The vampire had shed any hint of tenderness. He was reborn in anger, agony. The silver moonlight danced off ice in the air, cascading him in a celestial fog. He resembled a god, here for a reckoning.

The demon snickered. "Every head you cut off will heal." He smiled with pointed teeth. "I would be surprised if you killed a single one of my children tonight."

"What happens if I smash your head?" Kadence lifted his hammer.

"You can try."

Kadence leapt toward him, his hammer overhead. He arched the weapon, a graceful strike. His feet knew where they needed to land.

The demon moved, a blur.

Kadence struck empty air.

"You're nothing but a stupid child." Claws over a foot long sprouted from the demon Tolen's fingers. "It will be a pleasure to kill you."

He slashed at Kadence, cutting triple lines into his armor. The vampire danced away, and the demon gave chase. My heart ached to follow them, to help Kadence bring down the creature that stole my father.

Instead, I studied my mother's body. The snow had melted near the fire, leaving a circle of exposed dirt. She perched on the ground in a seated position, hands loose in her lap. There wasn't a hair out of place, not a single spot on her dress. She looked exactly how I remembered her—perfect.

I smashed the hilt of my sword at her head. Her pristine blue eyes snapped open and she rolled. My sword hit the ground. Flashes of pain dashed up my fingers.

She looked me up and down, then tilted her head. Disappointment lingered in her eyes. Anger and rage surged through me.

"Poor Sal." Her voice burned like acid in my ears. "Your mother is everything to you. She taught you how to be a princess, a queen. How to tie your shoes and be quiet like a good little girl. Well, your mother isn't very impressed by you. Tell me, how does that make you feel?"

She cut at me.

I stumbled, off balance. Her claws were layered with dried blood. How many of my people had she killed tonight? I ducked her blow and lifted my sword.

Her claws met the blade and I forced her hand down.

I punched at her face, but she was gone.

Natalie's magic thickened in the air. I'd broken the demon's concentration, and now I needed to survive long enough for Natalie to finish the spell.

"Look what you've done, Sal." Her face turned sharp. "I was working so hard, and you came and ruined it. I'll have to finish you quickly." She charged, claws first.

I backpedaled, stumbling over the ragged ground. My back pressed against a tree. Her lips curved in a half-smile. She thought I was trapped. Black claws came closer, closer.

She slashed. I ducked, and her claws split the tree trunk, gouging inches into the wood. She tugged, but the thick and solid wood held her fast.

I circled behind her, my sword raised. She turned her body to keep me in sight.

"Come closer," she whispered from my mother's lips. "I can't reach that far."

Fine. I stepped into her range. Her claws dashed lightning fast. Pinpricks of pain bubbled through my arm, ruining my aim. I missed her head and my sword cut across her back. I retreated and we both had blood on our blades.

The demon slashed at the tree, sending splinters into the air. The wood held.

She watched while I lunged toward her, arm raised, ready. She cut at me, and I fell, sliding under her. My sword tore across her ankles, sending blood and chunks of flesh flying. If I couldn't take her head, I would tear her apart piece by piece.

The demon growled, a feral sound. The hair on my arms stood up.

She raised her claws again. In one motion, she swiped at her own wrist, separating the limb in a clean strike. Blood flowed down the stump, but the wound healed in moments.

I staggered back, away from the freed creature. She turned to me with hellfire in her eyes.

"You will die very slowly." She promised, holding the bleeding stump up even as her power healed a layer of skin over it.

The demon slashed with her remaining hand. I sidestepped, but her claws were already there. One cut across my cheek, spilling hot fluid down my face. I scurried backwards.

"I will rip the skin from your body."

Slash. A cut appeared across my raised arm.

"I will pluck the eyes from your skull."

Slash. Another slice down my hand.

"Then, I will eat your organs one by one, starting from the least important so you can live long enough to watch."

Slash. A new wound cut my brow. Blood spilled into my eye.

She wasn't used to fighting one handed. It slowed her down, made her sloppy. I blocked her next blow with my sword. She punched me in the face with her raw stump. My breath paused and lights flickered beneath my eyelids. My back met the cold, hard ground.

My mother's demon laughed. She kicked the back of my head. The world spun. Nausea swirled in my stomach. If I could sleep for a moment, I would be all right. My eyes drifted closed.

The demon grabbed the leather strap between my chest plate and shoulder and dragged me up. The motion made me sick, snapping me from the verge of unconsciousness. I tried to grab her hand, but my fingers refused to move. My sword slipped to the ground.

She pulled me to the edge of the lookout. The ground loomed twenty or thirty strides below. She turned, forcing me to look over the city.

"What do you see, Sal?" she hissed in my ear. "The city is gone. Your people are dying over rubble in the streets. My children already escape the dirt prisons you tried to bury them in. You have lost."

Natalie's magic snapped taunt. It paused, like a bird on the verge of flight, as it persuaded the earth to let it go. Her magic balanced on a knifepoint, a held breath.

I licked my lips. Dirt and blood coated my tongue.

"Maybe." My throat was raw. "Or maybe we both have."

The magic imploded.

The explosion from the buildings had sent a cascade of debris and dust through the city. Natalie's spell was a black hole, life and energy pulled away, drawn into her. People below looked like ants, barely visible in the faded lanterns. For a heartbeat, bodies froze in the streets, suspended in the depths of her power. One by one, they dropped. Her magic consumed them, ate them, and asked for more.

A deep, male scream echoed through the forest. The demon Tolen's throat tore with pain for his losses.

The magic stopped, one second to the next, and it was gone. Yells floated up from the city. Terrified demons scattered between ruins. They looked for their leaders, but none could be found.

"You." The demon shook me. My head lulled. "Do you have any idea what you have done? How many of my children you killed?"

Not enough. The demons were still here. Thousands of monsters streamed from the city, but none abandoned their hosts. They hadn't gone back to the Fields of Death. The demons would march on my kingdom next, killing us and the refugee vampires. We had lost.

Hope fled my body like a thief in the night. The numbness returned and I welcomed it. Anything was better than the pain.

"You killed them for nothing." Demon Estelle clenched her jaw. "We will destroy you all."

I struggled to raise my arms. They dangled, limp, lifeless.

Trees rustled. Demon Tolen stepped from the darkness, dragging

Kadence behind him. The vampire's neck bent at an odd angle. My heart jumped. Vampires could heal a broken neck, but Kadence would be paralyzed as long as the nerves remained fractured. Blood spotted my father's face, and one eye was swollen shut.

"Let's kill them both and be done with this," demon Tolen said. One of his teeth was missing.

"I wanted it to be slow." Demon Estelle pouted.

"We can torture someone else. This needs to be over now."

"Fine." She dropped me to the ground and snapped her clawed fingers under the leather straps of my breastplate. The armor tumbled to the ground.

Her hand plunged into the tender flesh of my stomach, tearing beneath her claws. Pain like broken glass and lightning shock stole my breath. She smiled as she dug through my body.

I tried to scream, but my lungs froze in my chest. My throat filled with blood. I would choke before she ever found my heart. Maybe that was what she wanted.

Through our touch, a whisper spoke my name. A familiar spark called me.

My magic flared. It was weak, brittle, but it pulled me closer to the voice.

I felt a spark. Something bright drowning in depths of darkness.

I gathered the magic in my soul and pooled it into a careful handful. If one drop escaped, there wouldn't be enough. I pushed the power into the hand tearing my body apart.

Something caught the magic like a fish on a hook. It took all of it and demanded more. I had none left. It whispered again, tugging on my soul. I didn't fight it. Maybe this was death, my magic leading my soul away while a demon clawed a path to my heart.

Except the whisper dragged me into the creature. Darkness consumed me, forcing me to tread through the vile mud of the monster's existence. Memories of pain and death flashed around me. I turned away from them. There wasn't enough room left in my mind.

My body was fading. I gasped for air, trying to force blood to pump through a broken heart. But I couldn't feel it. I wasn't there anymore.

The blackness ended as suddenly as it had begun. The white spark pulling me through the depths erupted into life and vibrancy. My mother's voice whispered my name, her magic cradling me. She was the light. I didn't have hands to reach for her, but she wrapped her soul around me, a blanket on a cold night. Her love filled and comforted me. I would have given anything to feel her hand slap the back of my head one more time.

"Mother," I wept into the light. "I can't do it. I'm so sorry. I've failed our people."

"Shhh," she whispered into my soul. "You've done well, Salvatore."

"I'm going to die here. Kadence is going to die." Was he already dead? "It's over."

"Your father and I are the ones that need to apologize. In our haste to end the war, we lost ourselves. We lost our people. We lost you. That was our greatest failure."

I waited for the bitterness and anger to surface. There was only blissful numbness.

"But it's not over yet, Salvatore." Childhood memories surfaced at her words – my mother bending over my homework pages, her gentle reminders during council meetings, wrapping me in a new dress and a tight hug. "Here, let me help you."

She poured that white light into me. Every ounce of her energy, her magic tore through me. The bitter evil of the demon trapped us. There was nowhere for the power to go. It swirled and shook, screaming for escape. Her power found the only way out: me.

The magic detonated. The discharge launched me into my body, pain ripping through my skin. My mother's magic followed, diving into me like daggers, filling me with everything she had left.

I drew a gurgling breath. The magic was too much. My body couldn't hold both of us.

My mother looked at me and the demon saw the light in my eyes. She pulled her bloody hand from my chest, too late.

I smashed the power into her. There was no control, no practice or skill. I screamed as my mother's life hammered into the creature that stole her body. The forest lit up from the blinding glare. The demon inside my mother's body screamed. Her flesh started smoking, and I poured more and more magic into her. It was the only way to free her soul. There would be no saving her body.

The smoke widened, peeling back sections of her skin. Muscles flashed underneath, before they burned away too. Layer by layer, my mother fell apart until she was ash in my hands. I held her, the brittle remains of the woman that had raised me, her voice still ringing in my ears, then a winter breeze pulled them from my grasp and scattered her to the wind.

The second demon watched through my father's face. He suspended Kadence by the throat, one clawed-hand poised to cut through his neck. He searched my eyes and what he saw made him go pale.

The demon dropped Kadence. He lifted his face to the sky, and black mist rose from my father's body, a dark shadow. It twirled in the air, taking a humanoid shape, and streaked through the sky, a foul and malicious shooting star. My father's body fell to the ground. I didn't go to him. I could feel he was gone.

Movement below drew my attention. Squinting over the plateau, I made out black mist over the city, swirling like a plague of locust. Screams echoed across the walls as the demons left their host bodies. Some people would survive, but they would be broken. Some would be beyond help and would find mercy in death.

My head dropped into the snow. Blood spilled through the gaping wound in my stomach and chilled my skin. The pain was gone. Each breath became a fight.

I relaxed. The ground felt comfortable. I let my breathing halt. It was a relief to finally stop fighting.

Snow crunched under heavy footsteps. Kadence collapsed to his knees next to me.

I opened my mouth. I had so much to tell him, but only blood trailed from my lips.

"Shh," he said. "I can fix this."

My heartbeat slowed. The last shreds of air fled my body. I hoped Kadence knew what I wanted to say. He would be a great king for our people.

Blackness took my vision. The crackle of the demon's fire echoed around me.

Someone rubbed sweet honey onto my lips.

Chapter Thirty-One

WE CARRIED THE DEAD ON STRETCHERS TO THE CASTLE. WE covered them with whatever we could find—tattered blankets pulled from the rubble, tipped guidon flags, towels singed with fire. We laid them in the main hall until it was full and then filled the royal suites upstairs. Walking between the rows made my throat pinch with sorrow.

We had lost five thousand people, not including the possessed ones that died once the demons fled—almost one third of our combined forces. Healers walked the fields picking up anyone who was injured. The remaining soldiers combed the forest for firewood, constructing funeral pyres. The first one would be lit in the morning and they would burn for several days. Families would miss the funerals, but the dead would be anything but alone.

My parents lie near the front doors. Our people walked around them with every stretcher brought in. Some set their swords or helmets beside their bodies. Despite their betrayal, our people grieved.

Natalie had been asleep for hours. Rayhan tucked her into bed under the protection of the remaining six soldiers who had guarded her. He walked the city for the fallen.

"Queen Sal." He carried the top of a stretcher with a small body covered by a white sheet. He pulled the shroud away.

Grace. Her grey hair curled around her blue-tinted skin. Blood had spilled from a slit on her neck, but the edge of a smile clung to her lips. She held a short sword in one wrinkled hand.

"How? She left with the evacuees."

Rayhan shrugged.

"She was very ill. We can heal many things, but not when our own bodies turn against us. She would have died soon."

Instead of dying warm and safe in the medic ward, she had taken up arms and waded into battle. She had searched for redemption.

"Look." Rayhan lifted her sword. Blood lined the edges. "She took someone out with her."

Rayhan carried Grace's body away, disappearing upstairs.

Cynthia chatted with soldiers who had been recently healed, making sure they were fed and rested. Madder dye and blood from the cuts I had carved into her flesh stained her skin. She caught my arm when I walked by.

"That was a good fight, My Queen." She gave me a wink, but darkness curled behind the light words. "There might be hope for you yet."

I set my hand against hers and smiled.

She turned back to her troops.

Renee still rested in a room in one of the castle towers. She had refused to speak to anyone. Saffa sent Remi to comfort her, two people with the same wounds.

Outside, lanterns began to fade as the oil burned away. Rays of sun barely peeked over the horizon, casting an eerie glow on the ruins. Tents propped along the castle grounds made a makeshift infirmary. Inside, people rocked back and forth with hollow eyes, consumed by memories of sharing their bodies with evil. Some were unresponsive. Several were bound for their own protection.

Their pain called to me, whispers of desperation.

I walked to the first tent. Three women shared a cot, perched on the edge, spaced to avoid touching each other. My magic licked them and edged away. They tasted foul.

One looked up, but she didn't see me. A strand of brown hair caught in her eyelashes. I tucked it behind her ear. She didn't move. Her pain was a thorn from a perfect rose, a dagger in my side. So many of my people, suffering.

I wound magic around the three girls and pulsed it through all the tents, a gentle tide of power. The tendrils came together, building into something grand and complex, beautiful and intricate. Thin brushes of magic strengthened into hundreds of wire strings and bound into one, ivory, and wood—a piano.

I struck a key. A note sang out.

The three women looked at me.

I pressed another key, two together. The magic pulsed, grabbing their pain and fear and turning it to silent music. I played more, letting the notes blend with sharps and flats, taking their past and sending it away.

Their eyes closed and they fell backward onto the cots. Sleep wouldn't heal all, but it would be a start.

I walked through the other tents. My magic played a simple lullaby, stealing memories, regrets, and burdens. As I passed, people relaxed in my wake, turning to their cots or chairs and finally resting.

At the last tent, as the young men wrapped in bandages, some missing limbs, closed their eyes, I let the music fade.

"That was nice of you." Kadence stepped from the shadows. His uniform was torn, his armor and hammer gone.

"They needed to rest." I looked over their sleeping bodies, watching the rise and fall of their chests. This did not heal them. They had a life-long journey ahead.

"Some would say they don't deserve it."

"Would you?"

Kadence caught me in his arms. His breath brushed my hair. I held him tight against me, breathing him in, hellfire and honey.

"I don't deserve you," he whispered.

Two soldiers passed, lugging kegs of ale. Celebratory shouts echoed. Grief and victory stretched heavy through the air, and there was only one way to reconcile the two. Drinking, talking, and feasting. The ovens were already at work.

"Don't worry. I'll never let you forget that."

Epilogue

SIX MONTHS LATER

Even on the edge of the city, I couldn't escape the sounds of construction. Merging the two kingdoms required much more than a new barracks building. Teams of contractors worked day and night building houses, farms, silos, and everything else. The new buildings tried to mimic the lost vampire city, but the rainbow kingdom would never be replicated.

Lost amongst the more urgent construction, Kadence's orphanage had fallen behind schedule. Since the current orphanage was structurally sound and safe, there were other priorities. I'd made sure to revive the project at the earliest opportunity and it was finally complete. Almost.

Spring lingered in the air, but a warm summer breeze rustled green leaves on the trees. The river played a tumbling tune. I let the sun warm my face. Sometimes, when it was too dark or too cold, I could feel the demon's touch again. Kadence was always nearby to take it away.

"The councils are not pleased that you're late to your own party." Kadence stepped from the newly cobbled road. He wore a fine, blue silk tunic over black breeches with a thick wool coat. His shoulders were stiff, hands tense at his side. He walked as though he would rather be wearing armor.

My dress billowed around the swing as I pushed my feet off the ground. Golden fabric cascaded down, catching sticks and leaves in the grass. My mother's lace jacket nestled over the strapless dress. It fit perfectly.

"They survived a demon horde, I think they will survive my tardiness."

Kadence's gaze roamed my body. A hot blush settled on my cheeks. He sauntered toward me, slow and precise, as a predator stalks his prey in the night. Fire trickled down my spine, sending tingles through my fingertips. I wiggled in the seat.

He grabbed the ropes of the swing and lifted it. My feet left the ground. His coat threatened to rip under the bulge of his muscles. He raised me eye level, his hands on either side of my head, trapping me on the swing.

"How late do you want to be?"

I leaned close, letting my breath settle on his lips.

He leaned to kiss me and I darted back.

"Put me down." I laughed. "I have something to show you."

He growled, but dropped the swing and stepped back, letting me arch forward in a whirlwind of lace and jewels. The rush tore a laugh from my throat.

My feet found solid ground and I grabbed the vampire's hand. I led him to the front of the stone building. The orphanage towered over us, new and shiny, ready to be a foundation for the care and nurturing of our most precious resource.

"You know I've seen this building before. I designed the plans," he said.

"Shut up."

Beside the door, a white sheet covered a long, rectangular plaque. Kadence raised his eyebrow. I plucked the sheet from the stone structure, revealing the words underneath.

The Cameron Hendricks Home.

Kadence stilled. I couldn't tell if he even breathed. His eyes searched the words as though wondering if he had misread.

"You named it after my mother?" He ran a finger across the chiseled stone.

"You mother made a terrible mistake that hurt you." I put my hand on his arm. "But she did it because of how much she loved you. She can't repair the choices she made, but her legacy can be one of warmth and love. It can live on through you and the lives of the people we've vowed to protect."

A single tear escaped the king's eye. He didn't wipe it away. It trailed down his cheek and dripped onto the black fabric.

Kadence took me in his arms, wrapping me in a sweet embrace. He smelled like fire and honey. His body fit mine perfectly. He buried his face into my neck and breathed me in.

"Thank you. I love you."

"I love you, too," I said. "But we do need to go. I don't think the officiant will wait forever."

"They can't start the wedding without the bride and groom." He gave me a crooked smile and I knew he was mentally peeling the dress from my body. "I think we can spare a couple more minutes."

He grabbed me again and there was nothing sweet about it.

Thank you for reading! Did you enjoy? Please add your review because nothing helps an author more and encourages readers to take a chance on a book than a review.

And don't miss more of the *Eternal Alliances* series coming soon.

Until then, discover THE NIGHT'S CHOSEN, by City Owl Author, E. E. Hornburg. Turn the page for a sneak peek!

You can also sign up for the City Owl Press newsletter to receive notice of all book releases!

Sneak Peek of The Night's Chosen

BY E. E. HORNBURG

Eira never dreaded sunset. Or the Moon Festival. Or returning home. Or seeing the Oxarian royal family. She had always looked forward to those things. But not today. If only she could stop time.

No, not stop time, exactly. If she stopped time, Eira would never become queen.

She'd spent her life, all twenty-odd years of it, preparing to reign. She wanted to stop the *wedding*, something she should have been as prepared for as ruling Cresin.

Eira twirled the betrothal band around her wrist. The wedding was going to happen, regardless of what she wanted. With a deep exhale, she closed her eyes and sang, hoping to ease the storm brewing inside and instead focus on the peaceful magic bestowed on her by Luana's priestesses.

The song ignited the crescent moon tattoo on her chest, and as it glowed, stars formed and sparkled around her head. Swirls of darkness poured out of her fingers and mingled with the betrothal band. The tune and words were meant to sooth and calm the soul, make the singer become one with Luana and be as peaceful as the night sky. Yet it did little to ease the darkness, ice, and stars warring underneath Eira's skin.

Luana grant me peace...grant me grace...

The wedding was this week. Tonight, she and Alvis were going to perform the opening ceremony for the Moon Festival, ushering in Luana's season, where the nights became longer than the day. This year, it would also signify the start of the wedding celebrations. As the Chosens of Luana and Ray, it was believed pieces of the souls of the god and goddess resided inside both she and Alvis, making them the closest to the deities their people would ever have. The two had been betrothed her entire life. Yet now the week arrived and she still wasn't ready.

A knock came at the door, breaking Eira's trance. With a wave of her arms, the stars and darkness vanished, and her tattoo faded. Taking a deep breath, she closed her robe and moved to the door, where the knocking was becoming incessant.

"Eira! Will you quit all your praying and let me in?" Rose's voice drifted from the other side of the door.

Her younger sister almost clubbed Eira in the eye with the velvet box she held as Eira pulled the door open.

"I'd imagine after a year of visiting temples, you'd have had enough of praying by now." Rose barreled into the room, leaning on her crutch, and dropped the box on the vanity with a thud.

"It was more necessary than usual today." Eira shut the door behind them and exhaled, pressing her lips together before placing her hands on her hips. "And maybe if I hadn't received dozens of letters from you and Father begging me to come home from those temples, I wouldn't need to pray so long this morning."

Rose waved Eira off. "It wasn't as though you hadn't planned on being home in time for the Moon Festival. We were simply reminding you."

She dropped her crutch and it clattered to the ground as she flopped onto the plush, deep blue bed, pale freckled arms outstretched. Her copper hair splayed out on the quilt like fiery waves.

Eira had only been home for a few days since her yearlong pilgrimage, and had a curious new fascination with Rose. In so many ways she was the same, but in spite of sending letters all year and seeing one another for the holy days, there was still something different Eira couldn't put her finger on. Rose had always been as fiery as her red hair and ready to speak her mind at any given chance. She never sat still for more than a moment. Yet now there was an air of unease and distance about her Eira didn't recognize. This was one of the reasons she was glad to be home, in spite of everything. She wanted to get to know her sister again.

"And it wasn't *dozens* of letters," Rose replied. "It's been a difficult year."

Eira crossed the room and sat on the bed next to Rose.

"I'm aware. It's not as though I was only sitting in temples praying the whole time. I went and visited as many of the villages that needed help as I could. They're recovering from the fires, but it's going to take a long time."

"I'm not only talking about the fire recovery." Rose propped herself on her elbows. "People have been...talking."

Eira shifted in her seat. "People talk often Rose, whether I'm here or not."

"Last night after supper, Father and I overheard the Oxarian king and queen talking. It appears they have been concerned about your dedication to the betrothal."

"Oh?" Eira rubbed the band on her wrist again, as though it were squeezing her tighter with each moment.

"It's been five years since your original wedding date. While Father and Alvis have been more than happy to let you go off to university and travel the kingdoms, and your pilgrimage came at the perfect time after the forest fires so you could help the people while you traveled, King Rahim and Queen Shideh and other nobles from Oxare don't see it the same way."

They were smart. Of course they were. They'd raised Alvis, after all, and he was one of the most intelligent people she knew. Eira had been running for so long, and now there was nowhere else to go.

She straightened her shoulders and smiled. "Well, I'll have to prove them wrong, won't I? The whole opening ceremony for the Moon Festival is the commencement of the wedding celebrations. Once they see me there, they'll know I haven't changed my mind about the wedding."

Rose groaned and pushed into a sitting position. "It's not only them. There're other people, too. They're wondering why you haven't been around."

"That's ridiculous," Eira said, through a clenched jaw. "Royals travel through their kingdoms all the time. Father did before he became king, and still does. Besides, after I get married, I'm going to be in Oxare with Alvis for half the year anyway."

"I know."

Rose's touch on her arm sent a wave of warm comfort through her, and Eira felt her shoulders relax. A hint at the closeness they once had.

"But you know how people are. Normally I wouldn't worry about it, and I've been defending you, especially with the guard, and you have so many who are loyal to you..."

Of course Rose defended her. It's what she'd been doing for her their entire lives. What they both had done for each other. No matter how many months Eira was away, she knew she never had to doubt Rose. Even when Eira doubted herself, if Rose was there, she knew all would be fine.

"But?" Eira prodded.

The hesitation in Rose's voice was enough to make Eira's concerns heighten.

"But it's not only gossip. Some members of the council eventually listened, and talked too. So did Queen Amelia." Rose grimaced at the idea of their stepmother. "You know how she is, though. I don't suspect any of the priestesses have gossiped, but you know how close High Priestess Nyx is to some of the council members. I don't want to concern you, but I'd be lying if I said I wasn't relieved you were coming home. This ceremony could be the start of your gaining back their trust."

The new complication brought more to consider, and Eira rubbed her temples to ease the faint throbbing that had started, and slid off the bed. While she respected High Priestess Nyx as the leader of Luana's temple, the two of them often disagreed in matters of theology and politics.

With Nyx having the ears of many councilmen, planting seeds of doubt, Eira was sure all eyes would be on her even more so during the ceremony and wedding celebrations. Regardless, whatever doubts Eira had about herself or this marriage, she couldn't—and shouldn't—let it interfere with ascending the throne someday. Her people needed to have complete confidence in her.

She may not have been ready to be married to Alvis, but her desire to be queen never faltered.

The remnants of an afternoon snack sat on the vanity next to the velvet box, and Eira took a piece of apple, popped it into her mouth, and gobbled it. When she opened the box to reveal a silver and blue diadem, the stardust sprinkled on the metal twisting around diamonds made it sparkle on its own without needing any light from the room. Eira lifted it out and perched it onto her long dark hair.

It was one of Cresin's oldest antiques and had been worn by Luana's

Chosen for hundreds of years. Eira didn't wear it often, but when she did, she found herself sitting straighter, with her shoulders back and head held high. When she wore it, she could imagine herself being a woman worthy to have it on her head and to live up to the legacy she'd been born into.

She could do this.

She had to do this.

People always said she looked like Queen Isadore—the first Chosen of Luana—and Luana herself. Not as though she ever had anything to compare herself to, other than paintings that followers of Goddess Efare created of what they supposed Luana and Isadore looked like. Legend said all of Luana's Chosen through the generations looked like Luana, and all Eira's life people claimed she had the closest likeness since Isadore, with pale—almost translucent—skin, blood-red lips, dark hair, and sky-blue eyes.

Each of the firstborn heiresses of the Cresin throne were the daughters and Chosen of Luana, as the firstborn heirs of Oxare are the sons and Chosen of Ray.

Rose grabbed her crutch and limped over to Eira. They stood side by side in front of the mirror, opposites at first glance, with Eira's gentleness and Rose's wild nature. On further inspection, the two sisters were perfect compliments to one another.

Rose groaned. "You're not even dressed yet and you already look perfect. It's not fair."

"Perhaps it would help if you changed out of your training leathers."

Rose had a unique and free beauty about her, but usually she was too busy beating the other members of the guard on the training grounds for many to notice.

Or at least, not for Rose to notice others noticing her.

Another knock came at the door. The familiar melodic voice of Priestess Cynth came from behind it.

"Your Highness? The opening ceremony is supposed to start soon. We need to prepare you."

Eira's heart sank. Once Priestess Cynth and the ladies-in-waiting came into her chamber, it would be nonstop preparations, celebrations, and being surrounded by people until she was at the altar and at Alvis's side for their wedding at the end of the week. She'd have no peace. No personal space. No chance of stopping the wedding.

Outside her window, past the white rose tree which bloomed and grew up the wall no matter what the season, the songs of Luana's priestesses floated in the air. Part of Eira wished to join them. They didn't know how lucky they were. Free to worship, to make friends, and even to take whoever they wanted to bed whenever they liked.

She could do it. Be one of the priestesses. She'd been bestowed with the same powers, and studied Luana's ways the way they had been—even more so as the Chosen. She'd trained and studied longer than most priestesses, and was given more power at her dedication ceremony as a young woman than the others. Traveling to all of Luana's temples over the past year had shown her this, especially when she'd been in the oldest temple in the Paravian Mountains and her magic awoke there.

Cynth's own mother, who was a priestess there, welcomed Eira with open arms, and when she'd left, promised there would always be a place for Eira.

The town was small, and the mountains dangerous, with strange winged creatures terrorizing them. But she'd still go back in a heartbeat.

And priestesses weren't required to marry.

Eira turned and glanced at herself in the vanity mirror, with the stardust circled around her hair, looking like the midnight sky. She was a queen. Or at least, was going to be.

Queen. This was what she should be focused on. Becoming queen was what was important here.

"Are you all right?"

Her sister's touch on her shoulder brought Eira back to reality.

She blinked and forced a bright smile. "Of course. Why wouldn't I be?"

Rose cocked her head, with a raised brow. "It's a big week, and we've barely talked for months. It's not an odd question."

Priestess Cynth knocked again. "I'm sorry to disturb, Your Highness, but we do need to prepare. Sunset will not wait for us."

No. It would not.

Luana bless it.

Eira took a couple deep breaths, touching her thumb to each of her fingertips to calm herself.

Her pulse slowed to normal, and her muscles relaxed.

"Yes, please come in."

A flurry of women entered the chamber with dresses and cosmetics overflowing in their arms and excited chatter pouring out of their mouths like a waterfall, drowning out the priestess's songs from outside. Lady Evony at the back of the group held glasses in one hand and a bottle of wine in the other. As the women went to work at removing Eira's robe, Evony, court's unofficial patron of festivities, passed out the glasses and poured the wine with extravagant flourishes and twirls, without spilling a single drop.

Whatever calmness had resided in Eira vanished. Her nerves fired off, her senses overloaded at the ruckus surrounding her. She barely registered the weight of the drink in her hand.

The ladies cheered when Evony raised a glass over her curly head of hair, and they all followed suit.

"To our royal highness, Princess Eira," Evony said, "her betrothed Prince Alvis, and the coming of Luana's season. Gods know all the fun happens in the night, after all."

The stardust in the ceremony gown Priestess Cynth held glimmered in her eyes as she looked over her shoulder at Evony.

"I wasn't aware you had the patience to wait for night for your type of fun," Cynth said.

Rose chuckled when Evony placed a hand over her heart and dropped her jaw.

"It's not my fault people beg for my company, no matter the time of day," Evony said.

Rose cleared her throat. "Less drinking, more helping." She stretched her permanently twisted ankle in front of Evony, and wiggled it in a circle. "I can never get my straps tight enough."

Evony sighed before she finished off her wine, then set the glass on the table with a thud, and cocked her voluptuous hip.

"Out of all my talents," she said, "this is the one I'm asked to do. Whoever said coming to Farren Castle was going to be glamorous, never mentioned this."

"Yes, I'm sure the fish in Slania are much more glamorous," Rose said.

"It took months to get the smell out of my clothes." Evony took the straps from the pile of Rose's ceremony clothes, and winked.

Within minutes, the white leather-like straps were wrapped around Rose's ankle, straightening and smoothing the limb. It had been a gift from their grandmother, who served Kutlaous, the god of nature, in Eral Forest. The straps were enchanted with fae magic to give Rose the strength she needed to walk without a crutch for short periods. Such as evening ceremonies and balls.

Or as Rose preferred, on the training grounds and while patrolling the castle.

The white of the straps faded until they were invisible, showing off Rose's tattoo, dedicated to Aros, the god of war and hunting. When unbound by the straps, the tattoo appeared to be thorny rose vines etched into Rose's warped and twisted skin. When straightened by the straps, it was the sword of Aros, with white and red roses wrapped around the blade, like the roses outside each of their bedchamber windows, planted after their mother died. A symbol of Rose's dedication not only to her god, but to their bond as sisters and princesses.

Something stirred inside Eira each time she saw it.

The time spent preparing went by in a blur of cloth and perfumes and stardust. The sparkling gown clung to Eira like a second skin once it was pulled over her head and down her body. The skirt swirled around her legs and ankles in a silver river. The neckline, like all of her ceremonial gowns, dipped low and wide to expose her tattoo. A symbol to be showed off and admired, proving she belonged to Luana. It was a fashion Eira had grown used to after she'd received her tattoo.

When she was younger and first growing into her body, she'd felt exposed and shy. Now she was proud to show her dedication to Luana and kingdom. She enjoyed the power mixed with sensuality in her costumes.

Where there wasn't fabric, there were crystals and stardust stuck and painted to her arms, legs, and bosom. This day, it was a gown she could hide in. In this gown, she not only belonged to Luana, but *was* Luana. Goddess of the night, darkness, and winter. In this gown, she was supposed to welcome the changing of the seasons, where the daytime was shortened to make way for longer nights.

She was also supposed to greet her lover, Ray, god of the sun.

Eira could only imagine what Alvis's ceremony attire would look like.

Perhaps Eira could at least pretend to be Luana if she was dressed for the part, and be separate from herself.

Time moved too quickly, and before she knew it she was being escorted by Priestess Cynth out of her bedchamber and toward the great hall. All the attendees were waiting for them there. Her father, stepmother, Alvis and his family, and all of the lords and ladies of the kingdom. Her kingdom. The one she'd spent months helping to regain their bearings after flash forest fires burned through the villages, leaving only ashes in their wake. The one she'd been born in, and who believed in her through every step of her life.

Until she'd started running away five years ago.

Now she returned, and people were talking. Eira's cheeks burned as shame washed over her. She'd been foolish and immature all this time. So many others had it far worse than she did, and Alvis was a good man. One of the best she'd ever known. He was the perfect person to bring the kingdoms of Cresin and Oxare together the way Isadore and Sanson did all those centuries ago, when they were at war with one another.

Rose was at her side when they approached the great hall's door, and squeezed Eira's hand. She was out of her training leathers and wore a simple silver gown which resembled a long jacket with short sleeves. It was shorter in the front, revealing tight leggings, and billowed out in the back like a cloak. If it weren't for Rose's usual playful smile, she'd look regal.

"You'll be wonderful," Rose said.

She gave her sister a warm hug, then walked away and into the great hall, leaving Eira and Priestess Cynth alone. Eira pushed her shoulders back and straightened her diadem, despite that her heart sank as it begged her to turn and run.

No, it was time she behaved like the future queen and Chosen they all pictured her to be.

Don't stop now. Keep reading with your copy of THE NIGHT'S CHOSEN, by City Owl Author, E. E. Hornburg

Don't miss book two of the *Eternal Alliances* series coming soon, and find more from A.N. Payton at www.anpayton.com

Until then, discover THE NIGHT'S CHOSEN, by City Owl Author, E. E. Hornburg!

Chosen of the Moon Goddess. Destined to rule. Fated to marry.

A quest to save her family, kingdom, and heart.

For the past five years Princess Eira has run from her impending wedding. As much as she loves her goddess and kingdom, she's searched the kingdoms for another way to rule as queen someday while also choosing her own husband.

Yet, Eira's claim to the crown falls into jeopardy when her father, King Brennus, is poisoned and fated to a sleep of living death and Eira is next on the assassin's hit list – who happens to be her stepmother, Queen Amelia.

After Eira escapes Queen Amelia's clutches she journeys to the northern Paravian mountains in search of an enchanted cup to save her father.

Her quest is more than she anticipated with evading Queen Amelia's guards, traveling with the one man she shouldn't be with, and having to bargain with the ancient dragon guarding the enchanted cup.

She'll have to decide how to save her family and kingdom, even if it means sacrificing her heart and all she's wanted her whole life.

Please sign up for the City Owl Press newsletter for chances to win special subscriber-only contests and giveaways as well as receiving information on upcoming releases and special excerpts.

All reviews are **welcome** and **appreciated**. Please consider leaving one on your favorite social media and book buying sites.

Escape Your World. Get Lost in Ours! City Owl Press at www.cityowlpress.com.

Acknowledgments

First, I'd like to acknowledge my husband, Jacob, and my sister, Kristina. Without either of them, this book would have never been finished. Of course, also to my parents, who fostered my love of reading and writing, and had to endure random laughter when I read a particularly funny scene. Sorry, I'm not sorry. A special thank you to my grandmother, who was my first beta reader and my first real fan, even if she didn't really have a choice. Finally, to my daughter, who taught me there is something more terrifying than putting my writing into the world: parenting.

Next, I'd like to acknowledge City Owl Press for the opportunity to see my book in print. It's a huge achievement that I'd always dreamed about. Particularly, thank you to my editor, Heather, who saw the manuscript in its early forms and didn't run away. *Hellfire and Honey* would not be what it is without you.

Finally, a huge thank you to all my readers. I hope you enjoyed these words and that, for a few moments, they helped you escape the real world. I hope to see you all in the future.

About the Author

A.N. PAYTON is a fantasy romance author who is also navigating the tides of motherhood. She has a degree in biology and is passionate about the intersection of fantasy and science. When not writing or chasing a toddler, she can be found working on one of her many side projects, playing video games with her husband, or sleeping.

www.anpayton.com

 twitter.com/anpayton2

instagram.com/anpayton.author

About the Publisher

City Owl Press is a cutting edge indie publishing company, bringing the world of romance and speculative fiction to discerning readers.

Escape Your World. Get Lost in Ours!

www.cityowlpress.com

 facebook.com/CityOwlPress

 twitter.com/cityowlpress

 instagram.com/cityowlbooks

 pinterest.com/cityowlpress

 tiktok.com/@cityowlpress